JOURNEY
INTO THE
FLAME

JOURNEY
INTO THE
FLAME

BOOK ONE OF THE
RISING WORLD TRILOGY

T. R. WILLIAMS

ATRIA PAPERBACK

NEW YORK   LONDON   TORONTO   SYDNEY   NEW DELHI

ATRIA PAPERBACK
A Division of Simon & Schuster, Inc.
1230 Avenue of the Americas
New York, NY 10020

First Atria Paperback edition January 2014

ATRIA PAPERBACK and colophon are trademarks of Simon & Schuster, Inc.

For information about special discounts for bulk purchases, please contact Simon & Schuster Special Sales at 1-866-506-1949 or business@simonandschuster.com.

The Simon & Schuster Speakers Bureau can bring authors to your live event. For more information or to book an event, contact the Simon & Schuster Speakers Bureau at 1-866-248-3049 or visit our website at www.simonspeakers.com.

Designed by Jill Putorti

Manufactured in the United States of America

10 9 8 7 6 5 4 3 2 1

Library of Congress Cataloging-in-Publication Data

Williams, T. R. (Tyler Ronald)
  Journey into the Flame : Book One of the Rising World Trilogy / by T. R. Williams. — First Atria Paperback edition.
     p. cm. — (Rising World Trilogy ; Book One)
1. End of the world—Fiction. 2. Survival—Fiction. 3. Rare books—Fiction.
4. Conspiracies—Fiction. 5. Quests (Expeditions)—Fiction. 6. Magic—Fiction.
7. Science fiction. I. Title.
 PS3623.I5646J68 2014
 813'.6—dc23
                                          2013023972

ISBN 978-1-4767-1336-6
ISBN 978-1-4767-1340-3 (ebook)

To the flame of truth within us all.

JOURNEY
INTO THE
FLAME

PROLOGUE

JULY 21, 2030

Every mile Camden Ford drove east from Oklahoma City along old Route 40 provided a fresh reminder of how little remained in the wake of the Great Disruption. The long drive home to what was left of Washington, D.C., gave him more than enough time to contemplate his mortality and the dangers he faced for the next thousand miles. He wished he could let his mind wander to football, kayaking, girls—all those things nineteen-year-old boys used to be able to enjoy. But he had to stay alert. You never knew what you might encounter on these near-deserted highways, and he had to make sure he arrived at the safe house in Clarksville before sundown.

He removed his cap and rustled his dark brown hair, allowing the wind blowing through the open window to provide a bit of cool relief on this hot July day. Weary from a long day of driving, he took off his sunglasses and surveyed the landscape around him. The world he'd grown up in was gone; the Great Disruption of 2027 had seen to that. Very little had changed since those catastrophic days three years ago.

Vehicles of all sorts lay abandoned along the road. Once-thriving farms were deserted, their fields untended. Roadside restaurants now served only dust to a stray passing wind. Camden slowed the car and grabbed his camera from the backseat, which was cluttered with survival gear: a cobbled-together water purifier, a gas mask, and a few vials of Androstenediol, an experimental anti-radiation medication. He took a few pictures of the abandoned farm and the forsaken town he was driving through. Pictures for posterity, he told himself. If there even would be a posterity. He sped back up as he glanced one last time at the town in his rearview mirror.

Camden had been sixteen when the Great Disruption occurred. He remembered that it had started with social and political unrest. Bombings were commonplace, as were assassinations of corporate and political leaders. The chaos escalated when an unexplained Carrington-class solar storm struck the earth, knocking satellites out of their orbits and taking down communications systems and electrical power grids. The world went dark.

Like other leaders in the U.S. government, Camden's father, a high-level administrator and engineer in the Department of Energy, rounded up his family and fled the devastation and mayhem in the nation's capital. They took refuge at their cabin in rural Virginia. Then, on December 21, 2027, also without explanation, an even more devastating natural disaster occurred: the earth began to shift four degrees south on its axis. Over the next three months, weather patterns changed, bringing rain to the deserts and drought to the rain forests. Earthquakes shook all seven continents as oceans unleashed tsunamis. In one short year, humanity returned to the Dark Ages.

Camden slowed again as he approached exit I-85. He saw a man sitting beneath a road sign, his head leaning back against the signpost. The gun in the man's right hand and the bloody wound in what was left of the right side of his head told Camden all he needed to know. Another suicide.

"People are just giving up," his father had said a few months ago, sounding sad and frustrated. "The conveniences of everyday life are gone. There's no electricity, no gas for their cars or fuel for their heaters, no food to buy. Most people don't know how to fend for themselves; they never needed to. And now there's no real government to speak of that can help them. These people choose death over life because life is hard. But we cannot judge these people. Only God can judge them, son."

God, Camden wondered as he pressed on the accelerator and sped up once more. *Where is God in all this?*

Camden's family had returned to Washington in the spring of 2028. A small group of dedicated government officials, business leaders, and social activists had congregated there in a "peace zone" surrounded by barbed-wire fences, U.S. Army tanks, and other heavy weapons. They'd come in an effort to restore order and rebuild the country, which, according to estimates, had lost half of its population. Camden's parents had helped to establish the World Federation of Reconstruction, and for the past two years, Camden had worked alongside them. Last year, having become trained in water purification, he'd started traveling to reconstruction zones all over the United States, assisting local leaders in restoring water systems. He had just completed a ten-week reconstruction assignment in the secured area of what had once been the city of Dallas, and he couldn't wait to get home. He would spend at most a week with his parents, and then he'd go off to help with the reconstruction effort in another city. Although the WFR had accomplished a great deal in two years, focusing its efforts on the nation's cities and metropolitan areas, wide swaths of small-town and rural America still lay in ruins, and the people who lived there believed the government had forgotten them.

As Camden passed a weathered road sign informing him that he was entering the state of Arkansas, he saw some activity in the distance. A crew of workers was at the side of the road near a WFR transport truck, while a white pickup was idling nearby. When Camden saw a wing and parts of a crashed airliner scattered in the field behind the workers, he realized a cleanup crew was collecting human remains.

The sudden series of solar storms that had hit the earth in 2027 had brought down more than seven thousand aircraft. Some of the planes had crashed into the seas and high mountains, never to be recovered, while others had plunged into populated areas, killing thousands of people. As Camden slowed down, he grabbed his camera and took a few pictures of the piles of bags at the roadside awaiting pickup. There was a part of Camden that was numb to these grim sights, but he was still glad he hadn't been assigned to a cleanup crew.

A worker a good distance away from the rest of the crew waved at Camden before he placed a skull in a bag. As Camden waved back at the man, a loud shot rang out. Then another, and another. Camden saw the workers up ahead falling to the ground. More shots followed. The road crew was under attack, and he was driving right into it.

Four bearded men in ragged clothes were crouched behind the hood of the idling white pickup truck, firing rifles at the workers. Two federation security officers lay prone in the field, returning fire. But the crossfire was short-lived; the exposed security officers went down, spraying their last shots into the sky. The entire WFR crew was being slaughtered.

Camden slowed the car and reached for the gun he kept in his backpack. Suddenly, the car shook, and glass was shattering. A bullet had hit the edge of his windshield. Camden slammed down on the accelerator. The engine roared, and the car screeched forward, bearing down on the gunmen as two of them reloaded their rifles. He ducked right and then left, struggling to control the car as bullets shattered the back window and ripped into the side of the car.

This is it, Camden thought, as he sped past the white pickup. His old car couldn't outrun the truck. But just as he took in the deep breath he thought might be his last, the shooting stopped. In the rearview mirror, Camden saw the four gunmen pulling boxes out of the cleanup crew's transport truck. Of course. They wanted the supplies more than they wanted him. Still, Camden kept his foot pressed hard on the accelerator for what seemed like a hundred miles.

I'm such a coward! Camden pounded his fist on the steering wheel, wishing he could have helped the workers. But it had all happened so fast. He was no hero.

After about twenty minutes, Camden stopped shaking. He leaned back in his seat and eased up on the accelerator. The car slowed to a safer speed. Camden wiped away the tears that were running down his cheeks. "No more," he said aloud. "No more. When I get home, I am done. My parents can do this without me. I'm finished."

Two hours later, as the sun was setting, Camden pulled out his Federation map. He was relieved to see that he was just a few miles away from the safe house in Clarksville, near the Ozark National Forest. The Federation manual warned workers not to drive after dark. More Forgotten Ones, as they were called, would soon be scavenging the countryside for anything that would sustain them. Some believed they were remnants of the Crowd Twelve movement, which had instigated the boycotts and protests against rapacious multi-national corporations and financial institutions before the Great Disruption. Others believed they were survivors of the nation's rural areas whose desperation had transformed them into cold-blooded killers. Whoever they were, the Federation manual was very clear: they were to be avoided. Camden laughed grimly to himself and thought, *If you can avoid them . . .*

The Federation had built shelters around the country, safe houses for workers who traveled from one reconstruction site to another. In the distance, Camden saw the Federation flag flying on a tall pole, a welcome sight after his encounter with the Forgotten Ones. Camden pulled his car into a spot close to the entrance and grabbed his backpack as he stepped out. He ran his fingers over some of the bullet holes in the side of the car. There had to be more than twenty of them.

The shelter seemed a bit quiet. Camden could see lights on inside the building, but that was all. He wondered where the security was. The shelters always had a couple of guards on patrol.

Camden entered the safe house. "Hello," he called. "I work for the

Federation. Is anyone here?" He rang the old-fashioned registration bell on the counter, but still no one appeared. "Hello?" he called again. He needed to gain access to the communications equipment to report the attack on the work crew.

He heard a sound from inside the small office behind the counter; he circled around and entered it. Camden gasped. The room had been ransacked. Tables and chairs were overturned, blood was everywhere, and the slaughtered bodies of four people and two uniformed guards lay in a pile in the corner.

Camden looked around the room. The radios must have been ripped out and stolen, because only frayed wires were still attached to the wall. Camden walked over to the broken supply cabinet and saw that almost all of the food and water rations had been plundered. Forgotten Ones again, he thought, as he rummaged through the remaining items, looking for anything that might be useful. Suddenly, Camden jerked back and almost fell over a chair; he'd felt something grab his right leg. Instinctively, he picked up the leg of the broken chair to defend himself. He spun around but saw no one, only the pile of bodies. Then he realized someone was moving underneath it.

Camden threw down the chair leg and his backpack and tried pulling the person from the pile. It was a young man not much older than he was. "What happened here?" Camden asked. "Who are you?"

The young man struggled for breath. "Robert," was all he could say.

Camden took a small towel from his backpack and wiped some of the blood off Robert's neck. Someone had stabbed him near the collarbone and left him for dead.

"Can you walk?" Camden asked, as he helped the young man to his feet. "We need to get out of here." Just then, Camden heard a door slam and voices coming from the rear of the building. He knew they didn't have much time. He grabbed his backpack and supported Robert as best he could as he hurried back to his car. He tossed some of his supplies into the passenger seat, laid Robert down in the back, and jumped behind the wheel. He left the parking lot so fast the car fishtailed, sending up a spray of gravel. Shots rang out behind him, and once again, Camden was speeding down Route 40, racing for his life.

Camden looked in his rearview mirror and saw the silhouettes of a group of men holding rifles shrinking in the distance. His heart pounding, he struggled to keep one eye on the road and the other on the men in the mirror. A flare shot into the sky. His heart sank, and his hands started to shake. This was a trademark of the Forgotten Ones. They used flares to alert others in their clan that a target had been spotted. More flares rose into the twilight sky. Camden was being tracked. *What the hell do I do? Where is the next shelter? And what about this guy in the backseat?*

Two more red flares pierced the darkening sky, but this time, they illuminated the sky ahead of him. The Forgotten Ones were waiting for him up there. A voice inside Camden's head screamed, *Turn off your lights, turn left here, do it now!* Camden spotted the turnoff, quickly shut off his headlights, and turned onto the dirt road.

The glow from the flares was dimming as Camden slowly drove down the tree-lined path, which narrowed as it wound back and forth. Camden's adrenaline was still coursing through his veins; his only allies were the rising moon and an unconscious stranger lying in the backseat. Suddenly, he slammed on the brakes; the road was too narrow now for him to continue by car. He sat there for a moment, deciding on his next move. If he returned to the main road, he would have to face the Forgotten Ones. And if he continued down the dirt road on foot, who knew what he would find? Camden turned off the engine and leaned back in the seat. His father's voice came to him: "The keys to survival are water and a dry place to hide."

Quietly, Camden got out of the car. With the Forgotten Ones prowling around, it wasn't safe to spend the night in the vehicle. He took his flashlight from his pack and moved toward the back of the car, where the young man with the bleeding neck lay unconscious. Camden leaned forward, taking him by the shoulder and whispering, "Robert, Robert . . ."

The young man moaned in pain, but with Camden's help, he managed to get to his feet. They set off down the trail. The only sounds were the cracking of twigs and the crushing of dried leaves under their feet. From time to time, Camden heard the howling of a distant coyote—at least, he hoped it was distant.

The moon was now in its full glory, and Camden could see a multitude of trails that led deeper into the forest. A well-cleared walking path to his right caught Camden's attention; it seemed to lead to a campsite. Camden paused, Robert clinging to his shoulder. He knew a campsite was the last place he should hide. *Whoever set up this campsite has to be coming back*, he thought. But he had to stop somewhere for a moment or two. He couldn't carry Robert, who was losing consciousness again, much farther. Slowly, without a choice, he led him down the twenty-foot path. Near the end, Camden saw a circle of carefully stacked stones forming a fire pit. It was filled with logs, twigs, and dry grass, ready to be set ablaze. On one of the stones was a book of matches, a valuable item these days. A few feet from the pit was a second stack of logs, large enough to keep the fire fueled for days.

Unable to support Robert's weight any longer, Camden laid him gently on the ground and gave him a drink of water from his canteen.

"Hello," he called softly. "Is anyone here?"

There was no answer. Camden felt dead tired and needed to get some rest. He wanted to strike a match and ignite the fire, but the risk was too great. The Forgotten Ones were surely nearby, even though he hadn't seen a flare since he'd turned off the highway. Gripping his flashlight, he inspected the campsite, walking around the perimeter.

As he was about to dim his light, Camden spotted a small brown leather bag with a single brass buckle lying on a tree stump. Camden picked it up and sat by the fire pit next to Robert. *Maybe it belongs to the person who built the campsite*, he thought.

Carefully, Camden opened the bag and found three leather-bound books inside. Using his flashlight, he examined the books' covers. Only a title, *The Chronicles of Satraya,* and a strange symbol embossed in gold leaf were printed on them.

(•)

Suddenly, there was a rustling in the trees. Camden dropped the books and removed the gun from his pack. Now on one knee, his finger on the trigger, Camden held perfectly still as he surveyed the dark woods beyond the campsite. He didn't see anyone. He looked up at the sky for red flares or any sign that he'd been spotted again. After a few silent moments, he lowered his gun back down and set it beside him.

Still tense, he turned his attention back to the books. He took the first one and opened the leather cover. As soon as he did so, a brilliant blue orb the size of an apple emerged from the pages. It hovered silently in front of him, its blue light casting an eerie glow over the entire campsite. He could not believe what he was seeing. As much as he wanted to get up and run, he couldn't move. His eyes were fixed on the radiant blue orb. As Camden stared at it, he began to hear a slight hum, like the sound of a soft flute. There was something soothing about the blue light and the humming sound. He blew gently on the orb, and it turned an even deeper shade of blue; then the hum grew louder. *What is going on?* he wondered. *I need to get out of here . . .*

But something kept Camden rooted to the spot. He raised his right hand and gently placed his palm under the orb, cradling it as he had done with falling snowflakes when he was little. The moment he did, he felt an electrical charge run through his body, a lightness of being overcame him, and then, miraculously, his body floated off the ground. A gentle wind blew, nudging him around the campsite, as if he were a feather floating on a stray current of air. Camden's gaze remained focused on the blue orb, and his mind went blank except for a single phrase: *In a time of great need, we are with you.* The phrase was repeated again and again by an unfamiliar, distant-sounding voice: *In a time of great need, we are with you. . . .*

After a lost period of time, Camden and the orb floated back to the fire pit, next to Robert, who was still unconscious. Somehow Camden knew it was time to release the blue orb. And when he did so, he was gracefully set back down on the ground. The flutelike hum faded, and the blue orb sank like the setting sun, back into the pages of the book. The bright blue light disappeared, and once again, only the moon illuminated the campsite. Camden looked down at the first page of the book and saw the words that had been running through his mind:

In a time of great need, we are with you.
As it has always been.

Suddenly, Camden heard the sound of rustling leaves again. Closer this time. His heart raced as he scrambled to reach for his gun. Standing now, he felt his right hand trembling as he pointed his small .38 at the edge of the woods, first to the left and then to the right. Red flares shot into the night sky.

The Forgotten Ones had arrived. And more were coming.

Like spirits from the forest, they started to emerge at the edges of the campsite, their clothes grubby, their faces haggard. Some held crossbows, others carried rifles, and most brandished clubs and sticks. More frightened than he'd ever been in his life, Camden continued to point his gun at the growing crowd. "Go away!" he shouted. "I don't have anything you want!"

At that moment, a young woman broke from the crowd. She appeared to be only a few years older than Camden. A rifle was slung over her shoulder. "Nice campsite," she said, as she struck a match and tossed it into the fire pit. "I'm surprised we didn't come across it before." The campfire roared to life, its flames filling the clearing with a warming orange light. The young woman had long blond hair, which was tied back with a piece of frayed rope. She had piercing blue eyes and a confident bearing.

"This isn't my campsite," Camden responded. "I thought it was yours. I don't have anything you want."

"I heard you the first time," the young woman said. She circled around him, unconcerned about Camden's nervously holding his gun. "Are you a magician?" she asked, as she took the book from Camden's hand.

"Me? No," Camden replied, realizing she must have seen the blue light and what had happened to him. "I don't know what that blue orb was. I just opened this book, and all of a sudden, I was floating around." By the light of the campfire, Camden could see her eyes moving down the page. "You can read?" he said, surprised.

The young woman gave him an annoyed look.

"Sorry. I've just heard some things about you people."

"Us people?" the young woman replied, still skimming the page. "Not all of us are what you think we are. If we were, you and your friend wouldn't be alive." Her reading was interrupted by a commotion coming from the crowd of Forgotten Ones.

"Don't move," said a voice behind Camden. "Drop your gun." Camden did as he was told. He could feel something cool pressed against the back of his neck. "Now, turn around." As Camden did so, he found himself face-to-face with a six-foot-four, muscular, and fearsome-looking man wearing ragged blue jeans and a ripped T-shirt, with a red bandana on his head. He was pointing the barrel of a shotgun at Camden's head. "Come on, Cassie," he said, giving the young woman an irritated look. "We got better things to do than mess around with these *cared-for* folks. Let's empty their pockets, grab their food, and go home." The man turned to Camden and cocked his shotgun, his lips twisting into a nasty grin. "I hope your sins don't keep you from heaven's gates."

This is it, Camden thought again. He took a deep, shuddering breath and closed his eyes. After surviving all the events of the Great Disruption, he was going to die at the hands of a shotgun-toting Forgotten One.

"Put the gun down," the young woman said. "Put it down right now, or I'll shoot you instead of him."

Camden opened his eyes and saw that the young woman had walked over and forcefully pushed the barrel of the man's gun to the ground. The man ripped off his bandana in frustration and stepped back. Camden could hear a murmur of voices.

The young woman turned to the crowd that was encircling them, pressing closer as more people came out of the forest. Red flares continued to shoot into the night sky. "We have wanted a miracle for a long time. Some sign that we will be all right. Something, anything, to let us know that we have not been forgotten . . ." She paused a moment, looking into the faces of those gathered around her. "You all saw the blue orb and the light," she continued. "You all saw him lifted off the ground. Maybe that is the miracle we have been waiting for. Not him"— she pointed to Camden—"but this." She held up the book in her hand.

The rumbling from the crowd ceased, and Camden could hear only the crackling of the fire. Whoever this woman was, she had the Forgotten Ones' attention. Camden watched as she opened the book again and began reading aloud.

In a time of great need, we are with you.
As it has always been.

Contained in the pages of these books are the answers to your deepest questions. They are questions that have been asked by many who have come before you. Now, in this time of great despair, these words will provide you with resolution. Within each of you is a secret. If it is uncovered, something will be triggered in you, something that has not been activated in a long while. You have been asleep. Now it is time for you to wake up and claim your freedom. The rising of mankind is upon the land.

In a time of great need, we are with you.
As it has always been.

The young woman stopped reading. Camden looked at her and then at the faces of the Forgotten Ones. He realized they were no different from him or any of the other survivors of the Great Disruption he had met in Washington and on his trips around the country. Everyone wanted a better life and a better world; everyone wanted to know that there was a greater reason why they had survived and now had to deal with the ravages of the disruption.

"Read on!" someone shouted.

The young woman walked over and stood next to Camden.

"Yes, read on!" yelled another, and soon there was a chorus of voices urging her to continue.

"See?" the young woman said to Camden with a gentle, sweet smile. "You do have something we need. *Hope.*"

1

What does one crave when money and material wealth are all but
gathered, when recognition and acclaim are won?
Power and control will be sought, the great temptations and
corrupters of mankind.
—THE CHRONICLES OF SATRAYA

CHÂTEAU DUGAN, SWISS ALPS, 7:00 P.M., LOCAL TIME, JULY 15, 2069

A great iron bell rang, its sound reverberating through the meeting hall
of Château Dugan for the first time in over forty years. High above the
stone mosaic floor, a chandelier hung on a heavy chain from the barrel-
vaulted ceiling, casting a dim, unsettling light. Flaming torches mounted
on the walls offered additional illumination. There were no windows in
the chamber, and only a solitary door provided access. Eleven people
sat at a large rectangular table made of dark polished granite, their faces
hidden by burnished gold masks that reflected the dancing light from
the torches. A twelfth chair at one end of the table was unoccupied; a
black rose lay on the table in front of it.

"Welcome, my friends," said the man who was seated in the most ornate chair at the head of the table. In front of him lay an original copy
of *The Chronicles of Satraya*. "Some time has passed since we all gathered
here. Please, let us reveal ourselves to one another and be assured that
we are among friends."

As if orchestrated, all eleven simultaneously removed their masks and set them down on the table. In silence, they looked at one another. The *salutis personatus*, or masked greeting, was a centuries-old tradition used by secret societies to signify anonymity. Some of the people at the table who were already acquainted acknowledged one another with a slight nod or knowing glance.

The oldest of those gathered, a slight, frail man wearing a forest-green ascot and grasping a black cane even while seated in a wheelchair, spoke with a raspy voice. "Why have you summoned us here, Simon? For what reason would you bring a group such as this together, and under the traditions of the old guard?"

"Because it is time, Dario." Simon leaned forward in his chair and pushed his mask aside. "After forty-two years, my friend, it is time. The Rising is over."

"Are you certain?" the old man asked.

"Yes. It is time to finish the work my father was unable to accomplish in his lifetime. The moment has come for us to reclaim what the Great Disruption and the rebellion of men took from us!"

A sharp-chinned blond woman interrupted. "Those days are over, Simon. They ended with the arrival of those books you now display in front of us. Put them away! Even after all these years, they still make me sick."

Before Simon could respond, a woman with dark, expressive eyes added, "I agree with Catherine. We all know the damage those books wreaked upon our stature in the world. People no longer need us. Camden and Cassandra Ford, along with the Council of Satraya, saw to that. But I do not have to tell you that, Simon. You know that story better than any of us."

Catherine acknowledged her with a nod. "Thank you, Ilia."

Simon watched with displeasure as some in the group nodded in agreement. Others, such as Dario, remained silent, waiting for Simon to prove Catherine and Ilia wrong. Simon did not make them wait long. "No, Catherine! No, Ilia!" he began. "The people need us again. I have found the way to bring back the old order."

The old order Simon referred to was that of a group who called themselves Reges Hominum, the Kings of Men. They were twelve immensely wealthy shadow families who, in league with one another, had discreetly controlled the fate of men for centuries, moving them like pieces on a chessboard. While the Great Disruption had loosened their tight grip on humanity by diminishing their wealth and mechanisms of power, *The Chronicles of Satraya* had forced them to let go entirely.

"What *way* can there be, Simon?" Catherine replied in an agitated voice. "Your father was a founding member of the Council of Satraya, working alongside Camden and Cassandra Ford, distributing throughout the world those insurrectionist books that did so much damage. I never understood how the great Fendral Hitchlords could commit such a foul deed and betray our trust. Perhaps you should start by explaining that, and then move on to how we can restore the old order."

"We all know that my father joined Camden and the others after finding his own set of the books," Simon replied, glaring at Catherine. "I assure you he did so only in order to channel the Satraya movement in a constructive direction, a direction that would have benefited us all. But when it became evident that this was not possible, he left the Council. Be assured, my father did not betray any of you."

Simon, now forty-three years old and the only son of Fendral Hitchlords, moved forward in his chair and placed his hands on the books, his glossy black hair reflecting the light from the chandelier high above. His dark brown eyes contrasted starkly with his alabaster complexion, physical traits that had been passed down to him from his forefathers, whose portraits hung on the chamber's walls. Simon could trace his lineage back to the fourth century, the time of Constantine and the first popes. The ten other people seated at the table were from similar dynasties, many of which had once been equal in worldly power, wealth, and influence to the Hitchlords family, although none was as old. Nor had any of them found an original set of *The Chronicles of Satraya.* Like his father, Simon was a student of the

Chronicles, but he studied the books for a different purpose from that of the rest of the world.

In an effort to defuse the tension between Simon and Catherine, Dario said, "We have all been through a great deal over the last many years. Catherine, please, let us listen to what young Hitchlords has to say. We owe his father that much. We can see that Simon possesses his father's passion. Now let us also see if he possesses his father's vision."

Simon nodded in thanks, letting his dark gaze leave Catherine to roam over the group seated before him. "The time has come for us to emerge from the shadows. As my father predicted, the world is beginning to forget the lessons of the past. He told me long ago that the *Chronicles* would share the same fate as other influential books throughout history such as the Bible, the Vedas, and the Kabbalah: they would lose their allure, and their lessons would be forgotten. My father was right. Look at the world now. People take their freedom for granted. They are giving up on self-reliance and are opting for the conveniences provided by governments and corporations." Simon pressed down on a hidden compartment in the table, revealing a control pad. With the swipe of his hand, a three-dimensional image of the world was displayed over the center of the table, surrounded by various graphs and charts. "See for yourself how people's consumption of food, energy, and drugs has increased exponentially in just the last three years. Thanks to some special work that I commissioned, we now have access to some secured government data. In particular, the financial and medical records of most of the people on the planet." Simon continued to navigate the controls until he isolated a particular piece of information. An image of Catherine appeared on the display. "Oh, Catherine, I'm sorry to see that you have a thyroid condition."

"That is quite enough, Simon," Dario said. "Shut that thing down."

Simon did as Dario requested, and the image disappeared.

"Simon, please understand that I want to support you," Catherine said, her tone noticeably more conciliatory now. "We all do. But my question still stands. What of those books there in front of you? What of the *Chronicles?* How do you plan to reverse the damage they and that Council have done?"

"The original Council of Satraya disbanded years ago," Simon answered, "and the current one has been castrated to nothing more than a quaint political organization."

"I also see that people are growing lazy again," a German man wearing wire-rimmed glasses interjected. "Yet the books still have a following, however small. They have empowered individuals, encouraged people to resist control and not rely on others. There are still people today who follow those precepts. Remember the Financial Reset of 2025 that was caused by Crowd Twelve? Remember how people banded together and launched the boycotts that were adopted worldwide, shriveling the bottom lines of several multi-national corporations? Remember how people protested en masse against the financial institutions, refusing to repay their loans or pay their credit-card bills? Many of our colleagues lost everything. Even your father suffered losses, Simon. I dare say CI2 would have succeeded in bringing down the world's economy had the Great Disruption not done it for them. How can we be assured that something like that will not happen again? Those who still follow the philosophies of the *Chronicles* are as recalcitrant as the members of Crowd Twelve."

"I will answer your question, Klaus, but before I continue, I must be certain of everyone's support." Simon leaned forward and placed his right palm on the table. "If anyone here does not wish to be a part of this vision, please leave now. You will not be judged for your choice." Simon's tone was steady, the expression in his eyes serious. He exchanged a cool glance with the woman to his right, who was cloaked in a crimson hood. There was silence in the hall as a few people looked at one another and at the black rose in front of the empty twelfth chair. No one took up Simon's offer to leave.

"Very good," Simon said. "We have found a way to rid the world of rebellion once and for all. The next Freedom Day celebration will mark the end times of the *Chronicles* and the beginning of a new era for humanity. We will once again be able to provide the world with stability and a sound financial system that restores our wealth and influence." Simon paused to look around the table. Catherine, his most vocal critic, now sat silent. "And yes, some will die. But unlike the plagues of the Dark Ages or the many wars that have engulfed the world or even the chaos caused by the Great Disruption, our method will be more merciful; those who perish will suffer no pain, and their passing will be instantaneous."

"The promise of having our rightful place in the world restored is attractive, indeed," said Dario. "But you still speak vaguely, my friend. And who is *we?*"

Andrea Montavon, who was seated to Simon's right, pulled back her crimson hood, revealing ash-blond hair and an exquisite face that showed few signs of her sixty-eight years of age. She turned her topaz-brown gaze from Simon to Dario. "I and my late husband have been assisting Simon in this quest," she stated. "I know that Simon's plans sound vague, but I assure you that the details have all been worked out meticulously. Over the last eight years, while some of you may have resigned yourselves to your fate, we have been proactive. Just as the *Chronicles* would advise us to do." She said this with a sly smile. Derisive laughter could be heard around the table.

"I was sorry to hear about your husband, Andrea," a bald man with a Japanese accent said. "I was told that Lord Benson's death was sudden and most unexpected."

"Thank you, Yinsir," Andrea said. "The black rose on the table honors him. He died in support of our efforts. He is terribly missed."

The German man cleared his throat and shifted in his chair impatiently. "Simon, if this plan of yours is some kind of population control, it has been tried before, and it didn't work. Why should we think it will work now?"

"No, this is not population control, Klaus," Simon retorted. "That has never worked. My great-grandfather learned long ago that humans have an unquenchable desire to live. Kill several million of them, and others will just propagate more rapidly. We are taking an alternative approach—let us call it population grooming."

"I prefer to refer to our plan as the Purging," Andrea added with a smile. "Simon, I think it is time for you to provide a few specifics."

Simon once again activated his holographic projector and set about presenting the details of his vision.

He spoke for a long while, and afterward there was silence in the hall. But the people seated at the table were not startled by the ruthlessness of his proposed solution. For centuries, their families had secretly manipulated world affairs in ways that would have appalled humanity.

"Brilliant," said a classically handsome middle-aged man with dark hair who was seated to Andrea's right. He clapped his hands together three times, the large black diamond of his gold ring catching the light of the torches behind him. "Absolutely brilliant! The two of you have been busy, indeed . . ."

"Thank you, Victor," Andrea said, acknowledging the praise. "Your family always did appreciate innovative solutions to problems . . ."

"In order to enact this vision, we will need to rely on the expertise several of you possess," Simon said. "Do I have your support?"

Dario pounded his cane on the floor three times. "Young Hitchlords, you have my support. I long for the day when we might rule again. It has been a long time since I have tasted that wine. Come now, and graciously tell us what name you have chosen for us."

Simon paused a moment. One by one, the eleven people in the hall tapped the table three times with their hands, an ancient code symbolizing their support. According to tradition, once named, the group would be forever bound to secrecy. "Era," Simon announced with great pleasure. "We shall be called Era." He picked up a golden incense burner resting on the floor next to his chair. "Let the lighting of this urn bind us," he said, as he struck a piece of flint to ignite the contents. "Let its smoke be the cloud that blinds our enemies and cloaks our passions. Inhale, my friends. We are now one." Simon took a great whiff of the smoke and passed the urn to Andrea, who inhaled deeply before passing it to the man seated to her right. One by one, each of the other nine people did the same. A slight smile came to Simon's face as the urn was passed back to him.

"In front of each of you," Simon said, "you will find a small tin container. Heed well the instructions you find inside."

The great bell sounded again. The eleven people grabbed the small wooden mallets resting on the table in front of them and with a single stroke smashed their golden masks. The shards slid across the polished tabletop, some falling to the stone floor. Their masks were no longer needed. As Era, they would act as one. "It is done," Simon announced. "We are united! Long live Reges Hominum, the Kings of Men!"

"Long live the kings of men!" the others repeated in unison.

2

Everything that we are looking for is right in front of us.
The sages of old put their messages in plain sight. Just stop and
look; life will have no choice but to reveal itself to you.
——THE CHRONICLES OF SATRAYA

NEW CHICAGO, ILLINOIS, 3:00 P.M. LOCAL TIME,
JULY 15, 2069, 6 DAYS UNTIL FREEDOM DAY

Logan Cutler had been restoring the same painting at the Art Institute
of Chicago for six months. The last few details were the most difficult, and the fast-approaching deadline was making the work stressful.
Logan loved to paint and enjoyed working on his own creations far
more than he enjoyed restoring other people's work. He had always
dreamed of having his own studio, where he could dedicate himself to
his own work and teach others how to express themselves through art.
But in order to do that, an artist had to gain recognition and the support of gallery owners who could sell his work for fantastic amounts
of money. Logan hadn't yet produced a masterpiece or even a painting
that had attracted the attention of the critics and the gallery owners.
He hadn't had the time. He needed to earn a living. The best he could
do was stay close to his passion by restoring other people's paintings.

It was 3:00 P.M., almost time to stop for the day. Logan looked at the
last section of the painting that needed restoring. It was the area that
was giving him the most trouble; he just couldn't seem to get the right

color mix. Everything he'd tried had resulted in the wrong shade or tone. Logan stood staring at the painting while mixing a small cup of paint, debating whether to try one last experiment. The strange ringing sound had returned to his ears. It always seemed to come at the end of the work day and interfered with his concentration. None of the doctors he'd visited over the last few years had been able to explain or treat it. All he could do was wait for it to stop.

"Logan!" a voice called out.

Startled, he spilled the cup of paint on his hand and his already-stained apron.

"Some mad woman is on the main line for you; she says your PCD is not answering."

Annoyed, Logan snagged a rag and wiped the paint off his hand, then walked over to the supply table and grabbed his personal communication device, where a holographic image of his ex-wife was projected.

"I still haven't received the child-support check," she said angrily.

Of course, mad woman, Logan thought. That should have clued him in to who was calling. "Yes, Susan, I know. I'll have the money tonight, I told you that last week."

"You've been saying that for months." Susan's voice was getting louder. "I'm going to call the attorneys!"

After fourteen years of marriage, Logan knew that tone all too well. He had married Susan when they were both only eighteen. He'd enjoyed their first couple years together, when they'd had few responsibilities except for their careers and had talked and dreamed of all the adventures they would have one day. They had plotted and planned the art empire that Logan was going to create and how they would deal with all the fame and money that would come his way. The arrival of children, however, delayed those plans. Their son, Jordan, and their younger daughter, Jamie, had consumed so much of their energy and time, and Logan had been forced to find a job that paid enough to support them. Before long, Susan had lost hope in Logan's ability to attain the fame and fortune they'd once dreamed about. As it turned out, Susan had been more interested in the wealth than in the art and four years ago, they'd divorced.

"Listen, I'll have the money tonight," Logan reassured her, starting to feel quite agitated himself. "You know what I'm about to do, and you know how hard it is for me to do it."

"I don't care how—just do it, and get me that money!"

Logan's thirteen-year-old son, Jordan, jumped into the projected image, interrupting his mother. "Hey, Dad, check it out! I'm building a model of an old SR-71 Blackbird airplane for my history class."

Not wanting to be left out, Jordan's eleven-year-old sister, Jamie, also entered the image. She was sporting a new dress and holding a violin. "Look what I learned to play!" she said, as she put the violin under her chin and played a piece Logan didn't recognize.

"When are you coming to visit, Dad?" Jordan interrupted, speaking over his sister's classical melody.

"The model airplane and the music are beautiful," Logan said, wishing he lived close enough to celebrate their accomplishments. "I'll see you really soon, and we'll all go out for pizza and ice cream."

Susan nudged the children away from the PCD. "If you want to spend time with them, get me that money," she said in a threatening tone.

"I will. I will, and tell the kids I love—" The call ended before Logan could finish his sentence. The projection was replaced by a list of unanswered messages. Logan's ex-wife was not the only one attempting to collect money from him. He still had outstanding lawyers' fees from the divorce, along with late credit-card and car payments.

Logan tossed his PCD onto the table, and the device went dark. He ran both hands through his long hair. Logan missed his children. His wife had received custody of them and moved more than a thousand miles away to the ocean beaches of Nevada. The western part of the state had become beachfront property after the earthquakes and tsunamis of the Great Disruption turned California into a chain of islands. The desert landscape of the gambling state had quickly been transformed into a lush and highly sought-after coastline. *Maybe I should move there and be with the kids,* Logan thought. Life had become pretty lonely, and every day seemed to be a repeat of the day before. *Maybe I could start my studio on the beach,* he fantasized, as he rubbed his ear and tried to get rid of the annoying ringing noise.

He walked over to the small break room that adjoined the restoration hall. His coworker Melissa was enjoying a cup of coffee and watching a news broadcast on the 3-D HoloTV. Logan went over to the sink to wash the remaining paint from his hands.

"Have you listened to this woman?" Melissa asked.

"Who?" Logan responded, not paying much attention to the broadcast.

"This woman, Cynthia Brown." Melissa pointed to the projection. "She and the Council of Satraya are planning their annual Freedom Day rally—if you can call it that anymore."

"Yeah, Freedom Day. I can't believe the twenty-first of July is almost here." Logan continued to scrub his hands. "My parents thought a lot of Cynthia. They used to listen to her all the time and go to all the local rallies. People needed to be reminded of the past, they would say. And we should never forget what happened after the Great Disruption and what the *Chronicles* did for us."

"Well, she's a bit out of touch, if you ask me. That whole Satraya thing is past tense. The Rising is over. Some people just don't know when to move on." Melissa added some sugar to her coffee as she continued to watch the broadcast. "I guess we still get Freedom Day out of it. Another day off is always good!"

Logan didn't pay much attention to the rally; he was still thinking about his family and his mounting debts. He dried his hands and gave Melissa a smile as he left the break room.

He walked back over to the large fresco he was restoring. It was a massive replica, five meters by three meters, of Michelangelo's *The Creation of Adam.* The original masterpiece, which had once graced the ceiling of the Sistine Chapel, had been destroyed in an earthquake in

Rome during the Great Disruption. The painting depicted God surging forth from heaven, vigorously extending his forefinger to the languid forefinger of Adam, the first man on earth, as he imparts to him the divine spark of life. The fresco reproduction belonged to a private collection; it had sustained extensive damage during the chaos of the Great Disruption but was still considered one of the finest remaining reproductions of Michelangelo's work. Logan gazed at it now, focusing on the gap between the finger of God and the finger of Adam. This was the problem area, because Logan couldn't quite match the color in the original masterpiece as depicted in the images from some digital archives he had studied. The various pigments he'd mixed weren't blending well with the lime-based plaster he was using.

"Logan, my boy!"

Another interruption, Logan thought as he turned to see Mr. Rampart, the museum's director, and another man Logan didn't recognize walking over to him.

"Logan, I would like to introduce Mr. Sebastian Quinn, the owner of this wonderful painting that you have been working on so diligently."

Logan greeted him with a firm handshake. "Hello, Mr. Quinn. It's nice to meet you."

"Likewise, Logan, and please call me Sebastian."

If first impressions mattered, then Logan was at a loss. It felt as if his mind went blank when he looked into Sebastian Quinn's coal-black eyes. As hard as Logan tried, he couldn't guess his age or what part of the world he came from. While he had never met the man before, Logan thought there was something familiar and comforting about him, something in his calm air and knowing expression. But Logan couldn't quite figure out what it was.

"Logan's parents, Henry and Alexandra Cutler, also loved the arts," Mr. Rampart said. "They used to volunteer many hours during the height of the Rising to get the museum back up and running. Logan comes from good stock."

"How is your work coming?" Sebastian asked.

"Good. Almost done." Logan shifted his gaze away from Sebastian to the painting. "I just have to finish this section here, where the two fingers almost meet." Logan pointed to the problem area. "But I'm having trouble matching the color," he admitted.

"I am not surprised. That is the most important part of the painting," Sebastian said, as he leaned closer to where Logan was pointing. "This painting has many secrets, you know. Michelangelo was a master at hiding messages in his work. He placed this one right under the nose of Pope Julius II, who commissioned it in the early sixteenth century." Sebastian continued to examine the painting, evaluating other places where Logan had performed some restoration work.

"Secrets?" Logan repeated with interest.

Sebastian smiled. "Come, step back and look at this masterpiece again. You, too, Mr. Rampart." Sebastian took Logan by the shoulder and moved him back a few steps. "Now, what do you see?"

Logan and Mr. Rampart stood silently a moment. Then Mr. Rampart took a stab at it. "The painting depicts God on the right and Adam on the left, and they are reaching out to each other with their fingers."

Sebastian waited a few moments for Logan to answer, but Logan remained silent, so he went on, "Can you see that Michelangelo has depicted God within the outline of the human brain?" Sebastian stepped forward and drew his finger around the outline. "This dark shape from which God emanates resembles a cross-section of the human brain. God's forearm and finger are emerging from what one could infer is a human being's forehead or, as the ancients referred to it, the third eye." Both Logan and Mr. Rampart stepped back a bit farther.

The third eye? Logan glanced over at Sebastian. *Who is this man?*

"It's so obvious now that you've pointed it out," Mr. Rampart said.

"It must not have been so obvious to the pope who hired Michelangelo," Logan countered, winning a smile from Sebastian. "With its veiled imagery, this painting seems to challenge the very belief that God is a being that exists outside of us. To the contrary, it seems to suggest that the heavenly spirit emanates . . . from the forefront of the human brain."

Sebastian continued to smile and nodded at the look of amazement on Logan's face. "Many assumptions were being challenged at that time. You've heard of Copernicus, haven't you? He was an astronomer who challenged the belief that the sun revolved around the earth. He had the audacity to propose that it was the other way around. This controversial idea paved the way for Johannes Kepler, Galileo, and other men to ponder the true relationships among the sun, the planets, and the stars when they looked up at the night sky. This, in turn, led to the Scientific Revolution and an open challenge to the way the physical world was viewed. Michelangelo did something similar in the spiritual realm, albeit more discreetly. To make even a few people ponder something they have never considered before is a great and valuable achievement. Do you ever wonder why people gaze at length at a piece of art that at first glance seems trite? Subconsciously, they know there is something more to see, and they can't stop looking at it. This is one of those pieces." Sebastian paused, allowing Logan and Mr. Rampart to take in his words.

Logan could think of only a few other people he'd met who spoke on such an abstract level. His mother and father were two of them. They both had read and studied *The Chronicles of Satraya* and had had these types of discussions. They'd spent long hours debating the esoteric nature of God, the Spirit, and the science of reality.

"And look there," Sebastian continued. "Look at how Adam has been depicted as lazy, only half attempting to reach out and accept God's blessing. Michelangelo is warning us that we should be watchful of our indolence, our laziness, that if we become complacent, we will lose sight of God and where his throne truly resides." Sebastian tapped his forehead.

Logan felt a new appreciation for the painting he had been working on for the last six months. He was anxious now to learn all of its secrets. "And what do all those faces around God represent?" he asked. "Those of the angels there, surrounding God inside the brain? And the space between the fingers—you said that was the most important part of the painting?"

Sebastian smiled. "Those are yet more secrets. I leave them to you to ponder. But I assure you, you will not be disappointed by the answers. Just be patient. They will come to you out of the blue."

Mr. Rampart, who didn't seem as intrigued by Michelangelo's hidden messages, looked at his watch. "Well, Logan, we will leave you to it. Mr. Quinn is passing through before he heads back home tomorrow. He wanted to make sure that you would be finished with the restoration a few days before the Freedom Day celebration."

"Yes, I'll be done by then," Logan said, disappointed that this intriguing man was leaving.

"That is good news," Sebastian replied. "I plan to donate it to a friend's art gallery." He shook Logan's hand, and then Mr. Rampart escorted him from the restoration room.

Logan turned back to the painting, viewing it differently now. He looked again at the last place that needed to be restored, the space between the fingers. *Secrets*, he thought. Sebastian's last words echoed in Logan's mind: *Be patient. The answers will come to you out of the blue . . . out of the . . . Wait, blue!* Logan thought. Of course—blue was the missing color. The paint he was mixing needed a subtle amount to achieve the right hue. Logan turned, hoping to catch Sebastian before he left the restoration room, but he and Mr. Rampart were already gone.

The mixing of the paint would have to wait until tomorrow. It was getting late, and Logan needed to take care of an important personal matter. As he cleaned his paintbrushes and put away his tools, he thought about all the great plans he'd had for his life and how most of them had gone awry. He recalled his father once telling him when he was a teenager, "If your life is not going according to your plan, there is only one thing you can do: Get a new plan!" Tonight Logan was going to do just that. A small smile came to his face. But the relief didn't last long. He wished his parents were still alive. Perhaps they could have suggested a better plan than the one he was about to enact.

3

The words we speak to you will one day be more valuable than
gold. For these words honor the great potential within you.
Guard these books, and spread their knowledge. For one day, they
may be the key to your survival and ultimate freedom.
—THE CHRONICLES OF SATRAYA

CAIRO, EGYPT, MIDNIGHT LOCAL TIME, 6 DAYS UNTIL FREEDOM DAY

Lightning cracked in the night sky. It was monsoon season in Egypt,
and the relentless rain flooded the streets of Cairo. Ever since the
Great Disruption and the shifting of the earth's axis, radical changes in
weather patterns around the globe were common. Torrential rains now
drenched the Middle East's deserts. The Mediterranean Sea overran
the northern part of Egypt as far south as Banha, a town fifty-three
kilometers north of Cairo. Water rushed down the Nile River, flood-
ing everything and anything along its shores. Lake Nasser, more than
a thousand kilometers to the south of Cairo, doubled in size as the
waters of the breached river drained into it. And when the waters finally
receded in the spring of 2028, the people returned to their homes, only
to find toppled structures covered with mud and the bodies of those
who hadn't escaped the deluge. During that period, a tyrannical group
known as the Khufus declared dominion over Egypt and its remaining
inhabitants, instituting a murderous reign that ended only when the
Chronicles were found. It took more than ten years and thousands of

workers to rebuild the thirteen kilometers around Tahrir Square, an area including the Giza Plateau and the pyramids, which had miraculously survived mostly undamaged.

A hooded figure carrying a slender briefcase emerged from the Fountain of the Pharaohs and ran across Wasim Hasan Road. He went quickly down the main street to the Cairo Museum. Under the cover of darkness, he splashed through the puddles and ducked under the canopy of the large trees that stood approximately a hundred meters from the entrance to the museum.

He surveyed the massive edifice before him. The Cairo Museum was currently closed for renovations. Temporary guardrails and a chain-link fence surrounded the main entrance. A single guard sat protected from the rain by a canvas canopy. The hooded man watched intently as the guard struggled against the wind and rain to light a cigarette.

The hooded man pulled a small tarp from his raincoat, laid it on the ground, and put the briefcase on it. Kneeling on the tarp, he placed his right index finger on a metal pad near the case's main latch. A soft beep sounded, and the three latches of the case sprang open. A lightning strike illuminated the courtyard as he removed a high-powered rifle from the case. He also took out a set of goggles and connected its one-meter-long cord to the butt of the weapon. He put the goggles on, and his view of the courtyard and the museum entrance became crystal-clear. Numeric distance indicators and a targeting support grid appeared in the lower right corner of his field of vision, indicating exactly where the bullet would strike.

Lucius Montavon Benson was an expert marksman. His father had taught him to shoot when he was a teenager on numerous hunting expeditions in the forests of Europe and on safaris in Africa. More recently, he'd honed his skills on human prey. This was the first time he was using this technologically advanced rifle. He was pleased that it was working as advertised.

As the rain poured down, Lucius lowered himself to the ground, lying prone on the tarp. He crawled out from beneath the tree's canopy and pointed the rifle barrel at the museum's entrance. As he scanned the area, the targeting grid found its object. Everything he viewed through the goggles had a pale green hue to it except for live targets, which were colored red. With the guard squarely in his viewfinder, the one red form in his field of vision, he waited patiently, watching every move the guard made.

Lightning struck. "One, two, three," Lucius counted in a whisper. Then came the sound of thunder. Again, more lightning, and as before, on the count of three, the thunderclap arrived. The guard leaned back in his chair. Another lightning strike, "One, two," and on the count of three, Lucius pulled the weapon's trigger. A pellet of red light exited the barrel of the weapon, but the sound of the discharge was lost in the boom of thunder. *Cool*, Lucius thought, as the goggles tracked the path of the bullet. He saw a trail of steam following the projectile as the rain in its path was instantly vaporized. The red bullet struck the guard at the exact spot the targeting grid intended: straight through the heart. The guard slumped in his chair, the cigarette still smoldering in his left hand. The red hue of the guard's body faded to green, like the rest of the surroundings.

Lucius moved back under the tree and scanned the area around him, checking for any unlucky souls who might have witnessed the killing. Fortunately, the area was deserted. Lucius put the rifle and the goggles back into his briefcase and quickly walked to the three-meter-high chain-link fence in the courtyard. After sliding his case under it, he climbed over the fence with little difficulty. The guard's body was still slumped in the chair beneath the canopy. Lucius checked the body for a pulse and found none. He knocked the still-burning cigarette out of the guard's hand and detached the security badge that was clipped to the guard's jacket.

To the right of the museum's impressive six-meter-high main entrance was a smaller service door. With a quick swipe of the security badge, the door opened, allowing Lucius to slip in and quickly make his way through the darkened hallways where scaffolding hugged the walls. Lucius pulled a small hand-drawn map from his pocket and, with only the light of his PCD, used it to navigate through the maze of rooms. The polished marble floors reflected the lightning that flashed through the tall windows. At the end of the south hallway, he came to the newly constructed Literature Antiquities Hall, which housed some of the oldest and most influential written works in human history.

Entering the hall, Lucius looked left and right. He'd been told the display cases were arranged chronologically according to their contents. He moved quickly through the large room, looking at the cases: 1200s, 1300s . . . He passed the 2000s and finally came to the 2030s.

He set his briefcase on the floor and pulled a small pen-sized laser out of his coat pocket. He carefully cut a hole through the protective glass case and placed the oval of glass on the floor. Then he reached into the case and grabbed its contents, a leather-bound book and an old leather pouch containing two more books. On the book's cover were the title, *The Chronicles of Satraya*, and a strange symbol embossed in gold leaf. Lucius was stealing one of the four original copies of the *Chronicles*. This set, known as the Pyramid Set, had been discovered by Madu Shata at the top of the Menkaure Pyramid in 2030, on the same day Camden Ford had discovered his set in the Ozark Forest in the former United States of America.

Why does Simon want these books? Lucius wondered. *He already possesses his own copy. Why take this risk?* It didn't make sense, but, like many times before, Lucius simply did what he was told. One did not question Simon Hitchlords.

Lucius put his PCD near his ear and spoke in a steady voice. "Simon."

Seconds later, Simon responded. "Hello, Lucius. Do you have them?"

"Yes, three books and a leather bag."

"Activate the projection system," Simon ordered. "Let me look at them."

Lucius placed his PCD on the floor and activated the holographic projection. The image of Simon was now fully displayed, large and looming.

"Open the cover of the first book," he said. "I need to see what is written there."

Lucius did as Simon commanded. There was handwriting on the inside cover:

نـــادين هيـامي أعلـن

"What does it say?" Lucius asked.

"Madu wrote it when he found this set. It says, 'I declare my love for Nadine.' Open the leather bag, and show me the other two books." Lucius did so. "Good," Simon remarked with a satisfied smile. "The set is authentic. Take the books to the airport. Your mother is waiting. And Lucius," Simon added, "be careful with the weapon. It is the only prototype we have."

Lucius heard footsteps and voices in the hallway. He turned off the PCD, cutting Simon off. He grabbed his briefcase and the leather pouch and ducked behind a display case. The voices were getting louder, and Lucius could see the beams of flashlights in the corridor leading to the Literature Antiquities Hall. To his right, on the floor against the wall, Lucius saw an open stone sarcophagus, its heavy lid resting next to it. A split second before the two guards walked in, Lucius ran to the coffin and lay down inside it. He could see the beams of the guards' flashlights bouncing off the ceiling and the walls of the room. They were speaking Arabic. Lucius slowly reached into his coat pocket, placed his hand on his pistol, and waited. From the tone of their voices, he didn't think the guards had noticed the hole in the display case. Just a few more seconds, and they would be gone.

Suddenly, Lucius's PCD activated. He'd turned off the ringer, but the device's light flashed. *Dammit*, Lucius thought. *Not good timing, Simon.*

The guards stopped talking. Lucius could hear footsteps approaching the sarcophagus. He drew the gun from his coat pocket, sat up quickly, and fired three rounds at the guards, who were less than six meters away. One fell to the floor. The other drew his weapon, firing back before taking cover behind a display case. Lucius leaped out of the sarcophagus, leaving the books and the briefcase behind, and also took cover. Shattered glass lay everywhere.

Lucius could hear the guard placing a call on his radio. Backup would arrive soon. Thinking quickly, Lucius took out his PCD. He quickly pressed a few buttons, and the imager projected a high-resolution 3-D image of a man standing a meter from where Lucius was hiding. The security guard leaned out from behind the display case and started firing, but his bullets only shattered more glass cases. Lucius jumped into position and, with a single shot to the head, took down the guard.

He retrieved the books and the briefcase from the sarcophagus and, with his gun still drawn, walked quickly through the hallways to the museum's service entrance. As he passed the corpse of the dead guard in the chair, he clipped the security card back onto the guard's jacket. He heard a siren in the distance as he climbed back over the fence. The rain was still falling, and the wind picked up. He ran through the courtyard and disappeared into the shadows of the empty streets of Cairo.

4

It has always been said that everything happens for a great
purpose. But ask yourself if that can also be said for prayers that
go unanswered.

—THE CHRONICLES OF SATRAYA

WASHINGTON, D.C., 7:00 P.M. LOCAL TIME,
6 DAYS UNTIL FREEDOM DAY

It was Cynthia Brown's last speech of the day, and it was also the
most important. The banquet room was filled with political leaders
gathered from around the world to celebrate the end of the rebuilding process that had begun forty years ago after the Great Disruption.
Reporters and journalists were stationed throughout the room. Security was heavy. No doubt, Cynthia noted, because the newly elected
president of the North American Federation would be arriving soon.
Enrique Salize was the first citizen of a Mexican state to head the
NAF since its formation forty years ago, when the United States,
Canada, and Mexico had to pool their remaining resources in order to
survive. The handsome fifty-year-old Salize was a skillful, charismatic
orator, and his promise of a smaller central government had won
favor with many voters, giving him the razor-thin margin he needed
to beat the incumbent president on election day. During the nearly
forty years of reconstruction, the government had accumulated a tremendous amount of power, and many people believed it was time to

return some of that power to the sixty-seven states that made up the Federation.

As the current leader of the Council of Satraya, Cynthia Brown had been invited to address the world's leaders on this historic occasion. Founded by Camden Ford two years after the discovery of the *Chronicles*, the Council's primary mission was to keep the Satraya philosophy relevant to the lives of people all over the world. After the Great Disruption, the *Chronicles* became a source of unity, a banner around which men and women rallied to rebuild the world into a better place. During that time, known as the Rising, people worked together to ensure the survival of mankind. Self-reliance was the new norm, and local and federal government powers were limited to carrying out only vital public health and safety services. It was a moment in history when government was truly by and for the people.

For the last thirty-seven years, the Council had been the organizing force behind the annual celebration of Freedom Day, the day on which the four copies of the *Chronicles* had first been discovered in 2030. It was a holiday for people to acknowledge their personal liberties and world-wide unity. The global event included spectacular fireworks displays, concerts, and a synchronized moment of silence called the Liberty Moment, which took place every year at 11:00 P.M. Greenwich Mean Time. At that moment, people would light candles and join their fellow citizens in a meditation on love, compassion, and freedom. While the *Chronicles* encouraged people to commune regularly in this way, once a year was all that most people could manage.

As time passed and the Great Disruption became a more distant memory, the importance of the Satraya message faded. Freedom Day had become more of a social holiday than a day of profound spiritual communion. People had become more reliant on governments and corporations. The result was that the Council had become more politically active.

"Are you ready, Ms. Brown?" asked Monique, Cynthia's assistant. The president had just arrived and was about to take his seat at the executive table.

"I certainly hope so," Cynthia answered. She took a deep breath. "Everyone out there looks so young. I hope they will listen."

"I'm sure they will," Monique reassured her. "I'm young, but I understand that people need to be reminded of the lessons of the past."

An eruption of applause interrupted their conversation as the president was announced to the audience. The lights on the stage brightened, and music began to play.

Cynthia followed the other speakers onto the stage, taking a seat behind the podium. She was going to be the third and final speaker tonight, following the president of the African Union and the head of the World Federation of Reconstruction, who was going to announce the organization's dissolution. Even though polluted waterways, ruptured bridges, and mangled roads still existed in many parts of the world, people had grown weary of continuing to fund the WFR, and leaders viewed it as a political liability. The remaining restoration work would become the responsibilities of individual countries.

As Cynthia scanned the audience, she saw other members of the Council of Satraya. She acknowledged them with a smile. The first speaker was introduced and greeted with a cordial round of applause. That was about all Cynthia heard before her thoughts turned back to her own speech. She looked down at her notes, determined to make her case persuasively.

Sometime later, she felt a tap on her shoulder. The older gentleman sitting behind her was indicating that it was her turn to speak. As the audience applauded her introduction, Cynthia patted her short red hair into place, buttoned the blazer of her dark blue suit, and quickly walked to the podium.

"I'm Cynthia Brown," she began in a sure voice, "and I have the great honor of being the leader of the Council of Satraya. As we celebrate the completion of the reconstruction efforts tonight, we should ask ourselves some important questions. Have we created freer and more equitable societies, or have we simply rebuilt the same old roads leading to the same old destinations? Humanity is once again at a crossroads, and we, the people of the world, have a choice to make. Do we revert back to the oppressive and elitist constructs of the past, the old ways of thinking that prevailed prior to the Rising, or do we stay brave, remain observant and self-reliant, and carefully guard individuals' rights and freedoms as we have done for most of the last thirty-seven years?"

Cynthia paused. The people in the audience looked bored. "I ask you to ponder these questions tonight," she continued valiantly, "because I am concerned. Now that electricity has been restored in seventy-five percent of the world, people seem more interested in the drama unfolding on their HoloTVs than in the government's amassing more and more power over people's lives. I realize this indifference makes life easier for you"—she heard a ripple of laughter in the room—"but is it wise to pass laws and regulations without first giving the people an opportunity to debate the merits of those laws? Do you see that people are once again falling into debt? Do you see that the financial institutions that have arisen in the last ten years bear an alarming resemblance to those that existed prior to the Great Disruption and conduct business in the same rapacious manner? Will we soon see countries follow our people into indentured servitude to these financial institutions?"

Cynthia heard gasps and a few angry cries from the audience. *Good,* she thought. *At least I've caught their attention.* "As is the case with every citizen of the NAF, all of my personal and professional information is now stored on a piece of glass that I am required to carry at all times, while the government stores this information in its data centers." She held up an identification glass, a thin piece of fiberglass the size of a credit card. "Why?" she asked rhetorically.

"And look at our pharmaceutical companies. They have come back stronger than ever. They have persuaded you and the other branches of governments to pass laws that require every man, woman, and child to make monthly visits to MedicalPods. A citizen's access to his or her personal bank accounts, place of employment, and other necessities of life is blocked if he or she does not comply. Mandatory vaccinations were good public health policy in the decade after the Great Disruption, when diseases ran rampant over large regions of the world, but these new policies requiring blood screening and precondition assessments every year are clear infringements on an individual's freedom!"

Cynthia saw many people turning to look at Ted Wilson, the CEO of Allegiance Pharmaceuticals, who had invented the MedicalPod System. He was seated at President Salize's table. Cynthia gave him a direct look that confirmed what was already well known: there was no love lost between the two of them.

"Can you not see," Cynthia continued, "that governments are beginning to attempt to control people as they did prior to the Great Disruption? Do we want to see the return of Crowd Twelve? Do we want to experience another rebellion, another financial reset? Crowd Twelve is not an accident of the past—it is a *product* of the past. It can and will happen again!"

Cynthia heard an uneasy murmur ripple through the audience as she paused and took a sip of water. "Fearmonger!" someone yelled. She looked over at the table where a man with long stringy brown hair and a fanatical gleam in his eyes was sitting. It was Randolph Fenquist, the leader of a political-action group called the Sentinel Coterie. He had a grim smile on his face. "Fearmonger!" the burly man seated next to him who had a hideous scar on his face shouted again. Fenquist coolly took the knife from his place setting and dug its pointy tip into the table. He slowly rotated it in a clockwise direction.

Cynthia was not deterred by the interruption. She had dealt with the Coterie before. "You would be foolish to think otherwise," Cynthia said, looking directly at Randolph Fenquist. "If you back people into a corner, they will band together and fight anything and anyone they feel is threatening their lives."

As she continued, she noticed two Council members leaving their table and walking to the back of the banquet room. She remained focused on her speech, even though more Council members were following them.

"My dear friends, now is not the time to take a step backward. The

Chronicles have given us a road map to a bright future. We only have to seize the opportunity and move intently to realize it. Thank you for affording me the opportunity to speak to you tonight," she said in conclusion. "Love and blessings to you all."

The audience applauded politely. As Cynthia and the other speakers left the stage, the anthem of the North American Federation began to play, and people in the audience rose from their seats to mingle before dinner was served.

Monique gave Cynthia a big hug when she arrived backstage. "That was wonderful. So inspiring!"

Cynthia shook her head. "Thank you, but I don't know how much of an impression I made. Their faces looked pretty blank. My hope is fading."

"Well, maybe this will boost your hope," John Davis said as he and another Council member, Jacob Summers, walked over to her. "We have some interesting news, something that may shift the tide in our favor."

He motioned for them to discuss it in the hallway, and they stepped out of the banquet room via a side door. John looked around to make sure they were alone. "The Forest Set has been located."

"The Forest Set!" Cynthia said, shocked.

"Yes, I just received a phone call from a reporter friend asking if we were going to participate in the auction at Mason One in New Chicago tonight. He told me that Camden Ford's set of the *Chronicles* is going to be auctioned, in about an hour and a half."

Cynthia was stunned. She was well aware that the Forest Set had disappeared thirty-two years ago, along with Camden and his wife, Cassandra. "I wonder if Camden and Cassandra are alive," she said. "And why didn't the auction house contact us sooner? They should have known that we would be interested in those books."

"All good questions," John responded, but he shook his head to say he did not have the answers.

"We need to get back to the office and see if we can secure the money to purchase the books," Cynthia said excitedly. "This is the opportunity of a lifetime, and we're going to seize it."

5

Every choice is yours. You and you alone bear the responsibility of
your decisions.
No matter how great or small they may be.
—THE CHRONICLES OF SATRAYA

CAIRO, EGYPT, 2:00 A.M. LOCAL TIME,
6 DAYS UNTIL FREEDOM DAY

A taxi pulled up in front of the private jet hangar at the Cairo airport. Lucius paid the driver with paper money, which was rarely used
since the establishment of the new electronic monetary system. It
was useful, though, for carrying out untraceable financial transac-
tions.

"Sorry, sir, I don't carry any paper money, so I can't give you change."
The driver gave Lucius a perplexed look. "Most everyone pays with
their PCDs these days. Do you have one of those, sir?"

"Keep the change," Lucius said impatiently, as he pulled up his hood
and stepped out of the taxi into the rain.

A Gulfstream ES2300 was waiting on the tarmac. A set of stairs led
to the open entry door, where a female flight attendant stood, waiting to
welcome passengers onboard. The plane was equipped with three Haz-
zly Electro Static engines, the latest in flight technology. The engines
could produce incredible thrust and were very efficient. A large electric

energizing truck sat behind the plane, charging the high-capacity fuel cells for the long-distance trip.

Carrying the briefcase in one hand and the leather pouch in the other, Lucius jogged up the stairs. The flight attendant shut the doors behind him, and Lucius inhaled the scent of leather as he entered the main cabin of the state-of-the-art aircraft. There were sixteen large seats, grouped in four sections, with a center table and a 3-D digital communication pad with universal PCD docking ports. Lucius saw his mother sitting in the right front section, talking to a projected image of Simon.

"What a relief!" Andrea said, as she looked up and saw Lucius. "Simon said he lost contact with you in the museum."

"Nothing I couldn't handle," Lucius said calmly. "Just a few extra details I had to deal with."

"Do you have them?" Simon asked anxiously.

"Yes, of course," Lucius responded.

"Let's see them, dear," Andrea said. "Put them here so Simon can see the result of your efforts tonight."

Lucius took the three books from the leather pouch and set them on the table. Simon's image stared at the books, his hand trying to reach out and touch them, but the image simply passed through them like a ghost passing through a wall.

"Excellent work, Lucius! I trust that you didn't meet with too much resistance. Although I do see that you did not escape the rain."

Lucius was surprised to see the flight attendant opening the door again and deploying the stairs. He looked out the window and noticed a man waiting to enter the aircraft. Not knowing who he was or what his intentions were, Lucius took his gun out of his jacket pocket. "Do you know who that is?" he asked his mother.

"No," Andrea said, as she looked out the window. "I have never seen him before."

"Relax, Lucius," Simon said, as the man boarded the plane. "Put your gun away. Macliv has come for the books."

The man called Macliv entered the cabin and walked over to Lucius and Andrea. He was a husky man with a blank face and a red and black tribal tattoo that circled his neck above the collar of his fitted white shirt. Lucius put the books back in the leather pouch along with a folded sheet of paper Andrea gave him and then handed the pouch to Macliv. The man nodded, and then, as quickly as he had arrived, he left the aircraft. "Talkative guy," Lucius said, taking a seat across from his mother. "Where'd you find him?"

"Andrea," Simon said, ignoring Lucius, "I have one other task for you before you land in the NAF."

"I do hope it will not take too long," Andrea replied. "We have much to do for our project, and time is short."

"No, it will not take much time at all," Simon assured her. "You will be able to accomplish it during your flight. There is a special event tonight in New Chicago. The Forest Set will be put up for auction."

"The Forest Set!" Andrea was shocked and sat up straighter in her chair. "How can that be? Are you saying that Camden and Cassandra have resurfaced?" Worry showed on her face. She had served on the original Council of Satraya with Simon's father, Fendral, and knew firsthand the events that had led to the splintering of the first Council.

"I must attend to other matters at the moment," Simon said, not bothering to address Andrea's concern. "I want you to secure that set. The price is of little importance. The auction house is expecting you to bid remotely, and an anonymous payment account has already been set up, so my name does not have to be mentioned. I'm forwarding specific instructions to your PCD."

The image of Simon disappeared abruptly. The 3-D communication pad went dark, and Andrea yanked her PCD from the docking station. Her face was still tense from the revelation that Camden's set of the *Chronicles*—and possibly Camden himself—had turned up.

"Mother, were you referring to Camden Ford?" Lucius asked, as he stood and took off his wet coat.

Andrea did not answer; she was thinking about her time on the Council, years that she would just as soon forget.

"Mother, what's wrong? Why does Simon want another copy of the books?"

"Lucius!" Andrea replied in a stern tone. "I have a headache and need to rest. Just sit down over there." She gestured to another section of seats. "We are about to take off."

"But this doesn't make sense," Lucius insisted. "We're supposed to be doing the work of Era. Instead, we're flying all over the world collecting these books we're all supposed to hate. And then some guy we've never seen before comes and takes the books that I risked my life to steal! We need to get clear on who we work for."

"Lucius, just go sit down!" Andrea ordered. She was annoyed with her son, not because his questions were not valid but because they *were*. Why *did* Simon want those books? And more important, why wasn't he concerned about Camden, Fendral's most hated rival? Andrea fastened her seatbelt as the engines of the plane revved. She could not deny that it appeared Simon was keeping significant information from her.

A member of the flight crew poured Andrea a glass of wine. Lucius had made himself comfortable across the aisle and had fallen asleep. Andrea took a sip of her drink and leaned back in her seat, closing her eyes.

Forty-two years ago, Andrea had been living in the spotlight of a very successful modeling and fashion design career when she met the international playboy Alfred Benson at one of the many high-society balls Fendral Hitchlords hosted at Château Dugan. Reports had it that Alfred instantly fell under her spell but that Andrea played hard-to-get. She was twenty-six, gaining renown as a women's rights advocate, and presumably wanted more out of life than to be the escort of a powerful, wealthy man. So, in order to secure Andrea's long-term affections, Alfred did the only thing a man in his position could do: he purchased a world-famous fashion house and turned the reins over to her. Three months later, Andrea and Alfred were married.

Andrea now had a platform from which she could further her ambitions for both her fashion career and her advocacy for women's rights

JOURNEY INTO THE FLAME

around the world. "Women need to be heard," she would say to Alfred. "Why should we sit back and allow so many short-sighted men to run our countries and corporations?" Alfred would smile and listen with only one ear as he planned his next safari in Kenya or scuba-diving adventure in Bali.

Andrea, meanwhile, continued to build her empire. To promote her women's advocacy group, Women of the Veil, she created a popular line of fashion accessories, scarves and hoods, which quickly came to signify that a woman was more than a pretty face or smile. As she traveled around the world, speaking to ever-growing enthusiastic groups of women, attracting the attention of the media and political leaders, she got a taste of power. And she wanted more.

But in 2027, the world came to a halt, and so did Andrea's dreams and ambitions. Within moments, her beauty, glamour, and, indeed, her movement, which had captivated a generation, suddenly became irrelevant.

The years that followed the Great Disruption were difficult for all the survivors. The value of paper money and stock certificates was defined by how long they could fuel a fire. The value of a house was judged by how good the locks were. What good were fancy cars if their electronics had been destroyed by the solar flare? What good were diamonds, precious gems, and gold when most people didn't have food to eat?

The Bensons, most of whose wealth had been wiped out by the financial convulsions that preceded the Great Disruption, retreated to farmland that Alfred had inherited in Switzerland. The land was replete with lakes and streams, food and water, and they would spend the next five years there until their close friend, Fendral Hitchlords, asked them to join him on a trip to Washington, D.C. While Alfred chose to keep his focus on the recovery of his family's fortune and prominence, Andrea went with Fendral and his young son, Simon, on the adventure. It was then that Andrea reemerged on the world stage, this time as a founding member of the Council of Satraya.

Andrea pulled her thoughts back to the present, opened her eyes, and adjusted her crimson hood. She was still worried about Simon's nonchalant attitude regarding Camden and the emergence of the Forest Set. But confronting Simon was not advisable. She'd been reminded of that when she'd seen the black rose he'd laid at the place her late husband used to occupy at the meeting table at Château Dugan. She looked through the window and out at the darkness, wondering if yet another man was going to disappoint her.

It was almost time for the auction.

6

Every step taken and not taken, every choice made and not made,
unfolds your life. Just be sincere in all you do or do not do.
—THE CHRONICLES OF SATRAYA

NEW CHICAGO, ILLINOIS, 8:00 P.M. LOCAL TIME,
6 DAYS UNTIL FREEDOM DAY

New Chicago had suffered greatly at the hands of the Great Disruption. More than half of the buildings along Michigan Avenue, once
known as the Magnificent Mile, had crumbled into heaps of concrete
and steel, taking all of their inhabitants with them. As a major population area, New Chicago had since received a great deal of government
support. Rebuilding occurred rapidly, and the city thrived during the
Rising. Survivors in the surrounding suburbs and exurbs made their
way to the city to start new lives, and soon it became a model for
how reconstruction efforts should be carried out around the world.
The world-renowned Mason One Auction House was located on the
corner of Michigan Avenue and East Huron Street, one of the busiest
intersections in the city. It was where the abandoned Allerton Hotel
had been, until John Mason bought and converted it in 2055.

In the car on the way there, Logan heard an unruly crowd chanting,
"Burn the books! Burn the books!" It gave him chills.

Soon the car pulled up in front of the arched entrance of the renovated building. The auction house had not only provided Logan's transportation for the evening, but it had also provided his attire. He adjusted the uncomfortable tie and brushed his long brown hair out of his eyes. The driver opened the door for him, and a team of policemen ensured that the protesters didn't harass any of Mason One's patrons.

A woman in a pink tweed suit walked out from the main entrance toward Logan. "Good evening, dear," she greeted him. "Let's go inside, away from the madness out here. Why these Coterie people are so determined to disrupt things is beyond me." She shot an unfriendly look at one of the protesters as she grabbed Logan by the arm and escorted him inside.

Ms. Crawley, the auction house coordinator, was in her late sixties but looked much younger. She always had a set of reading glasses around her neck, and she was as sharp as a tack. No one really understood the relationship between her and John Mason, but it was evident that Ms. Crawley usually got what she wanted. She reminded Logan of a mother hen.

"You'll be happy to know that some very prominent people have arrived at the last minute. It's not every day that we get to auction off an original set of *The Chronicles of Satraya*."

"Doesn't look like the people out there are too happy about it," said Logan. "I apologize for causing such a stir and waiting till the last minute to decide whether to sell the books. They meant a great deal to my parents, and I wasn't sure if I could part with them. But it turns out I need to."

"Everything is working out," Ms. Crawley reassured him. Whispering in Logan's ear, she added, "These collectors enjoy a bit of unexpected drama in their lives, and it makes the auction more high-spirited."

Logan nodded. "Thanks for keeping my identity quiet," he said. "I don't want any attention."

"I understand, dear," Ms. Crawley said, as she escorted Logan into the great auction hall.

Logan had inherited an original copy of *The Chronicles of Satraya* that was known as the Forest Set when his mother and father died two years ago. He remembered watching them page through the books as they sat together discussing its many short stories and philosophies. Some nights they went on for hours debating the meaning of what they had just read. Logan would fall asleep in a chair, waking up the next morning alone in the study with a blanket over him.

He still didn't fully understand how his parents had come to possess the books. Whenever he'd asked, he'd received only vague answers:

"A very good friend of ours gave them to us for safekeeping," his father had told him when he was around ten years old. "Your mother and I knew him when we lived in Washington, D.C., before you were born. He had to go on an extended trip on behalf of the Council and didn't want to take them along."

"You mean Camden Ford?" Logan asked. "My teacher, Mr. D, says the Rising would not have happened without Camden and the Council of Satraya. He says that without them, we might not be here, at least not like we are today."

"I suppose that is true in some ways." His father smiled. "But I think the books deserve most of the credit. The books are what really inspired people."

"Mr. D said that Camden disappeared after the first Council of Satraya broke up, and nobody knows why he left or where he went."

"Yes, that is true. It's one of the great mysteries of the post–Great Disruption period. But before he left, he gave your mother and me these books. Camden wanted us to keep them safe and never tell anyone we had them. He said he would return one day and reclaim them."

"You mean he wanted you to keep them a secret? Why?"

"He didn't say; he just made us promise. And you have to promise, too."

"I promise."

As the years passed, Logan lost interest in the hows and whys of the books. He remembered seeing the books all over the house, sometimes on his father's desk or on the bookshelf, sometimes in his parents' bedroom or on the kitchen table. But whenever guests came over, the books were put away and out of sight. Logan witnessed his father's diligence about keeping his word to Camden. As time went on, Logan saw the books less frequently. By the time Logan entered his adult years, he hardly saw the books at all, and soon forgot about them entirely. That is, until his parents' death two years ago.

Logan had inherited all of his parents' worldly goods, along with a Destiny Box, a high-tech lockbox that was invented after the Great Disruption, when looting and identity theft had been rampant. A Destiny Box could be programmed to open at a certain time but only if the proper piece of DNA was placed on a sensory pad connected to the lock. When Logan's box had opened last year, it contained the forgotten books. They were the only things of value he possessed. That was why he had no choice but to do what he was about to do. He needed the money. Surely his parents would have understood that.

"All right, first things first." Ms. Crawley broke into Logan's thoughts. "Let's get you something to drink." She led Logan over to the bar. Glasses of wine and champagne stood ready on the counter, and waiters were circulating through the crowd serving hors d'oeuvres.

"You're right, there are a lot of people here," Logan observed.

"Yes, it's a very good turnout." Ms. Crawley seemed to know everyone, acknowledging people with a wave or a wink as they walked by. "What would you like to drink? Champagne? Or maybe some of our very own wine from one of John's wineries?"

"No, thank you," Logan said. "I don't really drink." Ms. Crawley handed him a glass of champagne anyway. "Are all these people here to bid on the *Chronicles*?" Logan asked, surveying the crowd.

"Heavens, no, dear," Ms. Crawley said. "The *Chronicles* are certainly the jewel of tonight's auction, but we have many other interesting items for sale this evening. Speaking of which . . ." She put on her reading glasses, took out her PCD, and displayed an image of the night's auction program. "See, the *Chronicles* are sixteenth on the list, the final item of the evening."

Logan pointed to the display. "What's that number next to it?"

"That is the starting bid, dear." Ms. Crawley looked at Logan and squeezed his arm. "We have had a few preauction bids from people who are unable to attend."

Logan could only raise his eyebrows in disbelief. Just that starting bid would solve all of his financial problems.

Ms. Crawley smiled. "This is the art world. All logic is thrown out the window."

Logan remained speechless as Ms. Crawley turned off the display and put her PCD away. "The auction is going to start in about fifteen minutes. When you hear the bell, that will be your signal to take a seat to watch the night's events unfold."

"Yeah, that sounds great," Logan responded, still thinking about the large number he had seen.

Ms. Crawley gave him a pinch on the cheek and walked into the growing crowd, greeting the attendees.

Logan was glad he didn't know anyone there. Being an anonymous seller seemed to ease his guilt. *Just a few more hours, and everything will be better,* he thought, as he took his champagne flute and walked over to the large windows overlooking the busy streets of New Chicago. It was twilight. He could see the protesters marching up and down the sidewalk in front of the auction house and the police working to contain the crowd. Away from the ruckus, people were out walking, some with their pets, some with their children, and yet others by themselves. An open-air tour bus drove down Michigan Avenue, showing visitors the landmarks of New Chicago. In the distance, Logan saw the old Willis Tower, now nicknamed Stump Tower. During the Great Disruption, the top thirty-three floors had toppled over and crushed a whole city block. The top of the building hadn't been rebuilt. It had just been capped with a platform that was used as a broadcasting facility.

"Everyone has someplace to go, something to see, and something to do, don't they?" a familiar voice commented. "Most, though, look straight ahead as they walk, missing the chance to greet all the interesting people walking by."

Logan turned around. It was Sebastian Quinn, the gentleman he had met earlier that day at the museum. "Mr. Quinn," Logan began, then caught himself. "I mean, Sebastian." He reached out and heartily shook his hand. "I didn't expect to see anyone I knew tonight. Are you here to buy more artwork?"

"No, not tonight," Sebastian responded. "I am more intrigued by the Satraya books. I recently learned they were going to be auctioned off."

"Yes, the books," Logan said awkwardly. "Their coming up for sale surprised many people." He paused, experiencing another pang of guilt. "I bet you have a wonderful collection of books. They would be a great addition to your library."

"No, I am not here to purchase them," Sebastian said, taking a sip of his red wine. "I came tonight to see where the books will choose to go."

"That's an interesting choice of words," Logan commented.

"I suppose that after our meeting at the museum, you think I am a bit eccentric," Sebastian said. "But there's something special about the original sets of the *Chronicles*. Books such as these are not possessed randomly. There is a great purpose to their journey. They helped save the world, you know. They picked the exact four people who would best serve humanity. Do you think those four individuals found them by chance?"

Logan didn't answer. All he knew was that Sebastian was the most intriguing person he had ever met. He had an indescribable presence, a gentleness in his eyes and in his voice.

"Yes, I must sound a bit eccentric to you. It is just that I am an admirer of Satraya lore."

"No, no, I understand," Logan said. "My parents were also part of that generation. You remind me of them, actually, especially my father." He was sure his parents would have enjoyed meeting Sebastian. He was about to tell him that he'd figured out the proper paint color for the last bit of restoration work on *The Creation of Adam* when the bell rang.

"Ah, the night is about to begin," Sebastian exclaimed. "Hurry, you should get to your seat. You don't want to miss the sale of your wonderful books." Sebastian urged Logan along with a smile before he turned and took a seat near the back of the room.

My books? Logan thought. *How does he know they are my books?*

Logan looked around and found Ms. Crawley heading to her place near the auctioneer's podium. "Ms. Crawley?" he said. "Did you tell anyone that I'm the current owner of the books?"

"Of course not, dear. We keep that information strictly confidential when a seller requests anonymity. Now, go and find a seat, we are about to start."

Logan took a seat along the aisle, close to the center of the room. He looked for Sebastian but was unable to spot him. *There's more to this man than meets the eye,* he thought. He wanted to talk to him again when the auction was over.

The bell rang for the second time, and the background music stopped. The lights in the hall dimmed, and a spotlight shone over the auctioneer's podium and the area where the items on the night's program would be displayed for sale. Along the right and left sides of the hall, large HoloPads stood upright on the floor, projecting the images of six people.

"Welcome, everyone, to Mason One and what we hope will be a very exciting and satisfying evening," Ms. Crawley said from the podium. "We also welcome our guests who will be participating remotely. I am proud to say that we are the first auction house to utilize HoloPads. With the support of modern technology, these six bidders can see and interact with everything that goes on tonight, as if they were here."

Logan looked at the projected images, which were crystal-clear and three-dimensional, as if the remote bidders were right there in the room. Each pad had a camera, a speaker, and a microphone that would allow the person using it to engage seamlessly with the people in the hall. Ms. Crawley made a few more procedural announcements and then signaled to the auctioneer to begin. With the pounding of his gavel, the auction was under way.

"The first item up for sale," the auctioneer began, "is a gold dagger from the collection of Freeman Dawns. It dates from the era of the Roman Republic . . ."

Logan's thoughts drifted to the conversation he'd just had with Sebastian. Did the books really choose their owner? Did they somehow choose his father, as they'd chosen Camden Ford all those years ago? His next question was both obvious and disturbing: *Did they choose . . . me?*

After lot number ten was auctioned off, a short intermission was called, and people rose to refresh themselves. Logan joined them, taking a glance around the auction hall. He saw Sebastian, speaking to an unusual-looking man wearing a knee-length black fitted jacket with a row of ornate gold buttons down the front. In his right hand, he carried a walking cane with a silver handle. In his left, he held an antique clock whose alarm sounded like a woodpecker, an item he had just purchased at the auction. The man's face was obscured by his long gray hair, which fell to his shoulders.

Logan's attention was drawn next to two of the HoloPads and the projected images of two older women who seemed to be staring at each other. They hadn't yet participated in any of the bidding. The lady on the right was dressed very stylishly and was wearing a crimson hood which cast a shadow over her face. The lady on the left was dressed in a dark blue suit. Logan recognized her as Cynthia Brown, whom he had seen on the HoloTV, speaking at the Freedom Day rally.

"It looks as if the Council of Satraya is interested in the books after all," Ms. Crawley said, handing Logan another glass of champagne. "A bit strange. I kept calling them and leaving messages about the auction, but no one ever responded. Oh, well, those Satrayians were always an odd bunch."

"Who's the woman wearing the crimson hood?" Logan asked.

"You are probably too young to remember her. That is Andrea Montavon."

Logan considered her a moment. "She was a member of the original Council of Satraya," he remarked, recalling a history lesson from his youth.

"One and the same," Ms. Crawley confirmed. "Years ago, before you were born, Andrea was a very successful model and fashion designer. She was also gaining renown as an advocate for women's rights. You see that head scarf she's wearing?" Logan nodded. "It was part of her collection and a signature accessory of the women's solidarity and empowerment movement she fostered. The movement was called Women of the Veil. I had a forest-green one myself." Ms. Crawley giggled girlishly. "She was an inspiring woman in those days."

"What happened to the movement?" Logan asked. "You don't hear about the Women of the Veil anymore."

"The Great Disruption happened," Ms. Crawley replied, shaking her head. "That stopped the movement dead in its tracks. Andrea wasn't in the public eye for some time after that, and when she returned, it was with the Council of Satraya. Women were hopeful that she'd revive the movement then. But for some reason, it didn't happen. I think her marriage to Lord Alfred Benson had something to do with that."

Logan nodded, still looking at the figure in the red hood. "They said she became a recluse after the first Council disbanded," he said.

"No one really understood why she withdrew from public life," Ms. Crawley said with some disappointment. "She's still as beautiful as ever."

Ms. Crawley checked her watch and then waved to the back of the room, where the bell rang immediately, signaling that the auction was going to start again. The lights dimmed, and the spotlight beamed down on the podium. Logan continued to watch the images of the two women, who had not stopped staring at each other. The auctioneer pounded the gavel, and the auction was under way once more. *Six more items,* Logan thought. And before he knew it, as the auctioneer pounded his gavel for the fifteenth time, it was just one.

"Lot number fifteen sold for one million four hundred thousand credits to bidder 102," the auctioneer announced. "Thank you, sir. I am certain your lovely wife will be very happy with her gift."

The crowd applauded. The auctioneer had been putting on quite a show all night.

"Next is lot number sixteen," the auctioneer said in his most dramatic tone of voice, looking to his left as the last and final lot of the evening was carried out. A murmur started in the crowd, and Logan moved forward in his chair. People who had spent much of the evening milling around and socializing at the back of the room ceased their conversations and moved closer to the podium.

"Lot number sixteen," the auctioneer continued, "a rare, original copy of *The Chronicles of Satraya*. It is one of only four sets in the world, and it is offered tonight for sale." Even though he hadn't been named, Logan felt as if a spotlight had been turned on him. He felt sweat break out on his forehead, as a wave of guilt flushed through him.

Meanwhile, the auctioneer's assistant held each book up, one at a time. The volumes of the *Chronicles* were in good condition, with the Satraya symbol shining on the cover of each book and the gold-embossed titles still unblemished. "One of the other sets of the *Chronicles* is on display in the Cairo Museum, and the other two are believed to belong to private collections in Switzerland and India," the auctioneer explained. "The books in this set have been authenticated by the unique watermarks located on the first page of each volume. There can be no doubt—this is the Forest Set found by Camden Ford himself."

The murmuring in the room increased. People craned their necks, trying to get a glimpse of the books, the most influential work of literature since the Great Disruption.

While the assistant was holding up the third volume, a folded piece of paper fell from the book and floated to the floor. The auctioneer quickly picked it up, reassuring the crowd. "Don't worry, it is not one of the book's pages; it's just a stray piece of notepaper." The crowd laughed as he showed it to them, proving his point. The auctioneer handed the note to Ms. Crawley. Logan wondered what it said and who had written it. Probably his father.

"The starting bid for this item has already been set," the auctioneer announced. "Bidder 901, who could not attend tonight, has set the price at six hundred fifty thousand credits. Do I hear seven?"

"Seven," shouted bidder 204 in the back row.

"Eight," from bidder 4, a young man in the front row.

"One million," called out an elderly man attending via HoloPad.

The bidding continued at a fast pace. "One point one, one point three, one point five, one point seven!" the auctioneer shouted in rapid succession. The bids moved into the twos and then continued into the threes. The pace was fast and furious. As each bid was called, Logan looked from right to left, up and down the auction hall, trying to spot the latest bidder. The auctioneer worked the audience masterfully, pitting bidder against bidder.

"The current bid stands at three point two million credits. Do I hear three point three?"

Logan scanned the audience. The bidding had come to a halt. "That might do it," Logan whispered out loud.

"Oh, no, I don't think so," said the man sitting next to him. "Look at those two ladies. They have been lying in wait for the right moment." He gestured to the images of Cynthia Brown, who Logan could see was seated at a large table of some kind, and Andrea Montavon, who was sitting with her legs crossed in a high-backed leather chair, her elbows perched on the arm rests. Neither woman had bid on anything all night, and now they were looking directly at each other. The man whispered, "I think the auction is about to get very interesting . . ."

"Hello, Cynthia," Logan heard Andrea say in a cold, level voice as she adjusted her hood, allowing her face to emerge from the shadowy light.

"Hello, Andrea," Cynthia replied in a similar tone. "It's been a very long time."

The auctioneer turned to Ms. Crawley, who responded with a slight hand wave, indicating that he should proceed. Bidders didn't typically engage in conversations. The atmosphere in the room grew tense.

Andrea raised her hand, still looking directly at Cynthia. "Three point five," she said calmly. The room was quiet. Logan could almost hear his heart beating.

Cynthia was next. "Three point seven." Back and forth they went, every subsequent bid coming quicker and quicker. All the auctioneer needed to do was confirm the bids. No other bidders appeared interested in entering the showdown.

The bid was at four point three, and the auctioneer was now waiting for Andrea. "I didn't know the Council had money like this to waste on an old and faded piece of history. Four point five," Andrea added, raising the bid.

Cynthia smiled. "Old and faded, perhaps, but still valuable—or you wouldn't be here. Four point seven."

It was apparent that the two women were engaged in more than just a bidding war. This was personal, Logan realized. He was dumbfounded by the whole thing. *How can these books be worth this much money?* Into the fives they went. Andrea owned the current bid, five point two million credits. It was Cynthia's turn to respond.

Suddenly, the image of Cynthia turned neon green, filling the room with a blinding light. People in the audience gasped, instinctively covering their eyes. Then there was an ear-splitting pop as the projection vanished in a flash. People were screaming, and Logan watched as those seated close to the exits ran out of the room.

Ms. Crawley jumped from her seat. "George! We have an issue here! Please check the HoloPad. Ms. Brown has disappeared. Quickly, please!"

The technician ran over to the HoloPad and began checking the wires and testing the device's buttons.

"Please, everyone, it seems we have experienced some kind of technical problem," Ms. Crawley announced. "Please be patient while we attend to the matter."

The people in the audience slowly regained their composure, speaking to one another and laughing nervously. Those who had panicked and fled returned to the auction hall with sheepish grins on their faces. But the image of Cynthia Brown could not be restored.

Ms. Crawley took out her PCD. Logan assumed she was calling Cynthia on the device, but she didn't seem to be able to reach her that way, either. Logan turned next to the image of Andrea, waiting patiently. He marveled at her imperturbable demeanor. George, the technician, insisted that everything was in working order. He didn't know why he couldn't reconnect with Cynthia via the HoloPad. The other HoloPads were working and displaying their images, he said. After another unsuccessful attempt to contact Cynthia, Ms. Crawley signaled to the auctioneer to continue.

"The current bid stands at five point two million credits," he said. "Do I hear five point three?"

It was as if the air had been let out of a balloon. The excitement and the suspense of the last few minutes of the auction had disappeared along with the image of Cynthia Brown. "Do I hear five point three?" he asked again.

Still only silence. The entertainment was over. Everyone knew who would be the winning bidder.

"Going once!" the auctioneer shouted. "Going twice! This is your final opportunity," he warned, trying to coax one final bid, to no avail. "Sold to the beautiful lady joining us from afar for five point two million credits!" The auctioneer pounded his gavel for the last time that evening, and the room filled with the sound of applause.

At a signal from Ms. Crawley, the side doors of the auction hall opened, and most of the audience began to exit. Some stayed behind to socialize and enjoy one more drink. Waiters started making their rounds again, and the single remaining HoloPad image, that of an elderly man, was laughing and talking animatedly to a group who had gathered around it.

Logan walked over to the large windows overlooking the city. A moment later, Ms. Crawley joined him. "Well, dear, you have become a wealthy man tonight."

"It is a lot of money," Logan affirmed, still trying to process everything that had happened. "More than I ever dreamed of."

"I need to wrap up a few details for the night. Grab some more champagne, celebrate, and I will return shortly." Ms. Crawley walked away with the auctioneer.

Logan did as she suggested and grabbed a champagne flute from a passing waiter. He searched for Sebastian to ask him if he thought the books had made the right choice, but he could not find him. He walked over to the technician, who was still fiddling with the broken HoloPad. "See anything wrong?" Logan asked.

"Not one damn thing," the technician answered. "This stupid device should be working. Hey, you got your PCD handy?"

Logan nodded, taking his PCD out of his pocket.

"Dial this number," the technician said, and then rattled off some numbers. Logan did so, and within moments, his PCD was connected with the HoloPad, and the image of Logan's face was being projected. "See, the damn thing works," the technician said in disgust. "This isn't our issue."

"I see you have it working now," Ms. Crawley said in a vaguely accusing manner as she walked over. "What was the problem with our equipment?"

"It wasn't our problem."

Ms. Crawley rolled her eyes and turned to Logan. "As far as you're concerned, dear, everything is in order." Ms. Crawley handed Logan an envelope. "Your receipt of sale and the note that fell from the book. You should see a deposit in your account in the morning."

"Thanks, Ms. Crawley," Logan said, stuffing the envelope into his pocket. "Thanks for all your help."

"When you're ready to leave, just let them know at the door, and they will fetch the car to take you home. Oh, and you can keep the suit. Consider it a gift from Mason One." With that, Ms. Crawley gave Logan a hug and a kiss on the cheek and returned to the remaining guests. Logan watched as one of the auctioneer's assistants carefully packed the books for delivery. His guilt returned in full force; he had just severed one of the few remaining connections to his parents. He walked back over to the large windows, drinking his champagne. It was almost ten o'clock, and the streets were still busy. Yes, Logan thought, feeling drained and lonelier than ever. Sebastian was right. Everyone did have something to do; everyone had someplace he or she needed to go. Except him. Logan drained his drink and decided to stay for another.

Many flutes of champagne and hors d'oeuvres later, Logan half-stumbled out of the auction house and into the car that Ms. Crawley had arranged to take him home. He leaned his head back, tired and a little drunk. After the auction, Logan had tried to celebrate the fact that all his debt had been cleared, and that his ex-wife Susan wouldn't be hounding him for child support any longer. It had been a long time since he had been free from financial burdens. Logan closed his eyes. He could hear the faint murmur of a news report that the driver was listening to on his PCD.

"No surprise given that fear-mongering speech of hers," the driver said in a raised voice.

Logan reopened his eyes. "Who are you talking about?" he asked.

"You didn't hear?" the driver said, looking at him in the rearview mirror. "Cynthia Brown, the head of that Council of Satraya, was killed tonight."

7

Silence will ally you to spirit in ways that words cannot.
—THE CHRONICLES OF SATRAYA

NEW CHICAGO, ILLINOIS, 6:00 A.M., 5 DAYS UNTIL FREEDOM DAY

Logan was dropped off in front of his home on Barry Street, a few miles north of downtown New Chicago. He opened the black iron gate and walked up the four concrete steps to the front door, as he had done so many times before. But then he paused. Something was not right. The front door lock was broken, and the door had been forced open. He looked through a side window and saw a light on inside the house. *Run, run and call the police!* Logan turned around. The street was empty, and there wasn't anyone else in sight. The car that had dropped him off was now far down the street and about to turn onto Racine Avenue.

Logan slowly pushed the door open, trying not to make any noise. The living room had been ransacked; the furniture was tossed about, drawers opened, their contents emptied on the floor. Logan walked down the hallway to the kitchen, which had also been ransacked. The table and chairs had been overturned, and the contents of the cabinets and drawers were scattered about. Even the refrigerator had been emptied. *Who did this?* Logan's foot slipped. When he looked down, he saw that he was standing in a small pool of blood. He lurched backward and noticed a red trail leading from the kitchen to the staircase.

He followed the trail of blood up the stairs. The hallway light was on, and he could see the trail leading to the master bedroom. As he passed the two smaller bedrooms, he saw scattered clothes and mattresses flipped onto their sides. As Logan approached the master bedroom, he saw bloody handprints smeared on the white double doors. As he entered the bedroom, Logan's fear turned to shock. On the bed were two bodies lying facedown. Two large knives were protruding from their backs. The sheets were soaked in blood. He screamed.

BANG! BANG! BANG!

Logan awoke, startled, his heart racing. Someone was knocking at the front door. He took a deep breath and tried to collect himself. He'd had this nightmare before—if only it were just a nightmare. But it was more than that; it was memory, too. This was how he'd discovered his parents on that warm July night two years ago, less than a year after he'd moved back in with them after his divorce. Logan had returned from a long night of work at the museum and had found his parents brutally murdered in their bed. The police found no clues to the killer's identity and eventually declared the case unsolved.

Logan's parents had bequeathed him the *Chronicles* along with the house. He had put the house on the market several times, but the gruesome story of the murders had deterred any interested buyers.

The knocking on the door continued. Logan was still wearing the black suit he'd worn to the auction. He had fallen asleep in the study while thinking about his parents and trying to convince himself that he'd done the right thing in selling the books. An idea that was hard to justify after being told the fate of Cynthia Brown.

"Coming!" Logan shouted, as he rose from his father's favorite chair. He ran his hand through his hair and rubbed his eyes.

When Logan opened the door, he was taken aback. An older man in a floppy wide-brimmed hat and carrying a clumsy tote bag smiled back at him. "Mr. Perrot!" Logan exclaimed, greeting the older man with a heartfelt hug. "It's been a while. Come in. Come in."

"Hello, my boy," said Mr. Perrot as he took off his trademark hat. "It looks as though you had a rather festive evening last night."

"Yes, I think I might have had a bit too much to drink." Logan ran his hand through his hair again and looked at the clock hanging on the wall; it was 6:22 A.M. "Early to be on a stroll, isn't it?"

Mr. Perrot shrugged pleasantly. "Old men are early to rise. And besides, sleep has not been a comforting friend these last years."

Logan nodded. He knew that Mr. Perrot had taken the death of Logan's parents hard. "I see you're still wearing your favorite hat," he said affectionately.

"The habits of young men follow them into old age, I fear," Mr. Perrot said. "I bought your father a hat like this once, but he said your mother wouldn't let him wear it. I always suspected that he was really the one who didn't like it," he added with a laugh.

Alain Perrot had been Logan's father's closest friend, a part of Logan's life for as long as he could remember. He and his daughter, Valerie, who was Logan's age, had often joined Logan's family for weeknight dinners, weekend picnics and barbecues, and all kinds of holiday celebrations. Although Mr. Perrot lived just a few blocks away, Logan hadn't seen him in months. He felt bad that he'd been so wrapped up in his own problems that he hadn't made an effort to visit this old family friend.

"It's really nice to see you. It's been too long," Logan said as they walked into the study and sat down. "How are you, Mr. Perrot?" Logan noticed that he looked thinner, and his hair was a bit grayer. His dark eyes lacked their usual sparkle. Something seemed to be bothering him. "Is everything OK? You seem a bit preoccupied."

"You are as observant as your father was," Mr. Perrot said. Then he paused a moment. "I went to sleep last night without a care in the world, and when I woke up this morning and heard the news, well, I felt a great weight had been placed upon my shoulders, one that I haven't felt for many years now."

"The news," Logan repeated in a solemn voice, remembering his drive home last night. "You mean Cynthia Brown."

"The authorities and the Council are not saying very much at the moment, only that her death is being investigated as a homicide. Cynthia and two other Council members, John Davis and Jacob Summers, were found dead at the Council's headquarters in Washington, D.C., along with a fourth victim. A young lady by the name of Claire Williams, who is reported to be Jacob's niece."

Logan sank back into his chair, feeling deeply disturbed.

"You look even more perturbed by this tragedy than I am. I was hoping you would be able to cheer me up, not the other way around."

"This is all very strange," Logan said, gravely shaking his head. "I think I might have been a part of this." He grabbed his PCD and checked his bank account, wondering if perhaps last night had been another bad dream. But it wasn't; more than four million credits were now in his account. All of the debt collectors had been automatically paid off by the central banking authorities, and all of the overdue child-support payments had been sent to his ex-wife. "I think I might have made a big mistake," Logan said, as if confessing to the crime.

"My dear boy, how could you possibly be involved in this?"

Logan set his PCD down on the table next to him. "Last night, I auctioned off my father's copy of the *Chronicles*," he admitted. "And Cynthia Brown was one of the bidders."

The color drained from Mr. Perrot's face.

"At the start of the auction, there were many bidders," Logan continued. "But at the end, it was only Cynthia and one other person."

"How could Cynthia be in New Chicago?" Perrot interrupted.

"She participated remotely via HoloPad. So did the other woman." Logan was growing more anxious as he recalled the final moments of the auction. "They kept outbidding each other, like they were fighting each other for my copy of the books. Cynthia and Andrea kept—"

"Andrea, you say?" Mr. Perrot interrupted. "Was she wearing a hood? This other woman, was she wearing a crimson hood?" Mr. Perrot asked with great intensity.

"Yes, Andrea Montavon." Logan nodded gravely. "You could barely see her face."

Now it was Mr. Perrot's turn to sink back into the sofa. The weight on his shoulders seemed to become even more burdensome. "They're back," Mr. Perrot whispered. "And I fear I know what they're after."

Logan asked, "Who are *they*?"

"First, Logan, you have to tell me everything that happened last night. From the beginning. Don't leave anything out. Tell me everything."

Logan told him. From the car picking him up, to the conversation with Ms. Crawley, to the bidding war, to the disappearance of Cynthia's image on the HoloPad and his arrival home, Logan told him everything.

"In twenty-four hours," Mr. Perrot summarized when Logan was done, "one copy of the *Chronicles* was stolen, another was bought at auction, and three members of the Council of Satraya were murdered."

"Another copy was stolen?" This was news to Logan. "Which copy?"

"The Pyramid Set," Mr. Perrot answered. "It was stolen last night from the Cairo Museum. Three guards were found dead."

"Sir, you said that they're back. Who are *they*? And why are you so alarmed that this woman Andrea bought my father's copy of the *Chronicles*?"

"There is something I want to show you." Mr. Perrot waited a moment before speaking. "How much did your mother and father tell you about our lives before we came to live in New Chicago? About our volunteer work with the Council of Satraya and the rebuilding efforts?"

"Not much, really, just that soon after I was born, we moved to New Chicago, along with you and your daughter. Their work didn't sound as important as they made it out, if you ask me." Logan waited a moment for Mr. Perrot to continue. "But why are *you* asking *me* about my parents? You were their best friend."

"There is something I want to show you." Mr. Perrot pulled a photo album out of his tote bag and put it on his lap. "Come, sit next to me. I have a story of sorts to share."

Logan got up and took a seat next to Mr. Perrot.

"Your parents and I, along with Cynthia Brown and a slew of others, worked tirelessly with the original Council of Satraya to disseminate the knowledge in the books around the world." Mr. Perrot opened the photo album to a photograph that took up an entire page. Logan leaned in closer to get a better look at the wide-angle shot, which was blurry at best.

"There certainly were a lot of volunteers," Logan said, as he scanned the rows of smiling people.

"There must have been at least a hundred of us back then," Mr. Perrot confirmed.

"And look, they're all wearing the Fundamental Four on their shirts," Logan observed. "You don't see them very often these days."

"No, you don't. Those are the symbols described in the *Chronicles*," Mr. Perrot said. "Peace, Joy, Love, Freedom. In those days, everyone wore them as a sign of unity."

Logan turned the page of the album to another blurry picture, this one of a wedding. "Who's getting married?" he asked.

"That was the wedding of Camden Ford and Cassandra Toliver," Mr. Perrot answered. "Camden found the *Chronicles* and his wife at the same place and at the same time." Mr. Perrot smiled and paused for a moment. "It was known as the wedding of the Magician and the Scholar."

"Strange nicknames," Logan said. "Should I ask?"

"A story for another day, perhaps," Mr. Perrot responded.

Logan turned the page again, now to a picture of a park with many chessboards set up on either side of a long path.

"We had very good chess players in that group," Mr. Perrot explained with a smile. "The best was Madu, the one who found the Pyramid Set. Camden and Cassandra were very close seconds."

"Is that why they were called the Magician and the Scholar?" Logan asked jokingly.

Mr. Perrot laughed. "That was part of it."

Logan kept turning the pages, noticing some empty places in the album. "Some of the photos seem to be missing," he said.

Mr. Perrot just shrugged his shoulders. "Lost over time," he said.

Logan came to a picture of a rosy-cheeked, red-haired teenager with a big smile. "This is a young Cynthia Brown, isn't it?" Logan stared, comparing the image with his recollection of Cynthia from the night before. "Was she a member of the Council back then?"

"Not then," Mr. Perrot answered. "At the time, Cynthia was a young volunteer who believed wholeheartedly in the power of the books and helped in every way possible. She was as dedicated as any of us." Mr. Perrot paused, staring for a long time at the picture himself. "Now she's dead."

"Sir, you said, 'They're back,'" Logan said. "Who are *they*, and why do you seem so concerned by them?"

"They," Mr. Perrot began, turning a few pages to a picture of three people sitting at a picnic table, "are Fendral Hitchlords; his son, Simon; and Andrea Montavon." Mr. Perrot tapped his finger a few times on the crimson hood shown in the photo.

"That's the woman I saw last night," Logan confirmed. "At the auction house, Ms. Crawley told me Andrea always wears one of those head scarves."

Mr. Perrot nodded. "As history recounts, Fendral found his copy of the *Chronicles*, known as the Train Set, at a rail station in Switzerland. He served on the Council along with his young son, Simon, and his close confidante, Andrea Montavon."

Logan continued to stare at the woman in the picture. "She was beautiful," he could not help but murmur. "Ms. Crawley said she was quite a prominent person in her day."

"In her day, yes," Mr. Perrot said as he gazed out the window. "She was a very complex woman. On the one hand, she had a great compassion for the plight of people, particularly women. She would go on and on about how women needed to be heard and how they needed to rise up and take some of the male leaders of the world to task." Mr. Perrot smiled, turning back to the album. "I found her passion and her commitment to the women's rights movement admirable for a time."

"She sounds inspiring," Logan said.

"She was. But then another side of her would emerge," Mr. Perrot continued, "a much darker, more malcontent side. She was willing to do whatever was necessary to regain the lifestyle she'd enjoyed prior to the Great Disruption." Mr. Perrot shook his head. "Over time, Fendral and Andrea became less supportive of the Council's mission and more concerned with interpreting and controlling the message of the *Chronicles*. They came to believe that the doctrines put forth by the *Chronicles* needed to be revealed to people gradually and that *they* needed to be the ones to reveal them."

Logan looked again at the picture of Fendral, Simon, and Andrea.

"A rift formed within the Council," Mr. Perrot continued. "Once-civil discussions turned into heated arguments. Almost every meeting became contentious. I spoke to Andrea privately, pleading with her not to let Fendral's obsession with control overshadow the good that everyone was doing. But Andrea sided with Fendral."

"What about the other Council members?" Logan asked. "Camden, Cassandra, Madu—couldn't they all band together and outvote Fendral and Andrea?"

"At first, that is exactly what took place," Mr. Perrot answered. "But then strange things started happening to the members who sided against Fendral. Deya Sarin, who found the River Set, returned to India after her husband crashed his automobile because of supposedly faulty brakes. During the inspection of the car, they found a black rose on the floor of the backseat. And Madu, the finder of the Pyramid Set, was mugged and almost killed, but nothing was stolen from him. He woke up in the hospital the next day and found a black rose placed at his bed-side. He returned to Egypt, where he donated his copy of the *Chronicles* to the Cairo Museum. Your parents and I came to believe that there was more to Fendral and Andrea than met the eye, something sinister."

"So did Fendral and Andrea gain control of the Council?" Logan asked.

"By all accounts, they should have, but for some reason, they didn't." Mr. Perrot was pensive for a moment. "To this day, I don't know why Fendral and Andrea abruptly returned to Switzerland. I suspect Camden Ford knew, but he was very evasive whenever anyone questioned him about it."

"So that's why the Council had to start over," Logan said. "They skipped this part in history class."

Mr. Perrot gave a weak smile and nodded. "After Fendral, Simon, and Andrea departed, Camden turned the reins over to Cynthia. His confidence in her proved to be correct. She recruited a new group of members, and they restored the Council to its original strength and purpose. In fact, it was Cynthia who completed the Freedom Day and Liberty Moment project. It was she who led the Council through much of the Rising."

Logan nodded, taking it all in. "And now you think that Fendral and Andrea had something to do with her death?"

"No, not Fendral," Mr. Perrot corrected. "Fendral died six years ago. As far as I know, he left everything to his son, Simon. But news has been scarce; ever since they left the Council, they've stayed hidden. Not even Andrea made any public appearances—until now, that is. I have a feeling she is up to something, and Simon, too. I think Simon inherited more than his father's estate. Even though he was only thirteen back then." Mr. Perrot pointed to the grinning young boy in the picture. "He already exhibited his father's cunning. The events of the last twenty-four hours are related, I know it."

"It does sound like they have something to hide," Logan said. "But there was nothing illegal about the auction last night. And if they had

something to do with the murders of the Council members or the rob-
bery in Cairo, well, maybe we should just let the police handle it."

Mr. Perrot raised an eyebrow. "You mean the same way they handled
your parents' murder?"

"My parents?" Logan said, his tone more serious. "What do you
mean?"

Mr. Perrot paused, uncomfortable with Logan staring at him. "I
don't think your parents' killing was just a random act of violence as
the authorities concluded."

"What are you saying?" Logan demanded. He stood up. "Are you
saying their murders were premeditated?"

"The way your parents were killed has always bothered me. It was so
brutal, as if the assailant wanted something from them." Logan began
to pace, not knowing how to react to what Mr. Perrot was insinuating.
"Your parents had Camden and Cassandra's copy of the *Chronicles*. I believe that Simon and Andrea somehow found out and that they wanted
those books for themselves."

Logan ran his hand through his hair, as he always did when he was
ill at ease. He'd spent two years trying to remove the image of his slain
parents from his mind, and now it came to him all anew, as if the hor-
rific tragedy had occurred just the day before. "Are you saying that
the Hitchlords and Andrea killed my parents because they wanted the
books? The very books Andrea purchased last night?"

"I know this may be hard to hear, and I know I don't have any proof,"
Mr. Perrot began. "But just look at the basic facts. Soon after your
parents were killed, Deya Sarin died in a boating accident. Her copy of
the *Chronicles* has never been found. Last night, Andrea bought your set
of the *Chronicles* at the auction, and the Pyramid Set was stolen from the
museum in Cairo. Not to mention that three Satraya Council members
were murdered while the bidding for the books was taking place." Mr.
Perrot paused. "Coincidence?"

Logan stopped pacing and shook his head. "Why would they want
all of the sets? Simon already inherited his father's. Why would he need

the others? And how did he know that Camden had given his set of books to my parents?"

"All good questions for which I have no answers," Mr. Perrot said with a frustrated sigh. "Did your father ever mention anything else that Camden may have given to him, other than the *Chronicles?*" Mr. Perrot asked. "A blue journal, perhaps?"

"No," Logan responded after a moment's thought. "I never saw anything like that, nor did my father ever mention it. The only things in the Destiny Box my parents' left me were the books. Why, what was in the blue journal?"

"Camden Ford was known to carry one around from time to time. But what was in it, I cannot say." Mr. Perrot rose and walked to the window with a worried look. "I may not have all the answers at the moment, but the questions I have are troubling. Do you think all of these events are unrelated? Do you think the police were thorough in investigating your parents' murders? And do you still think this is all a coincidence?"

Logan gave no answer.

8

Do you really know who is standing before you?
Can you say for certain that they are this or that?
Perhaps the person you despise the most is the one who will teach
you the greatest lessons.
For if you can learn to love them, whom can you not love?

——THE CHRONICLES OF SATRAYA

ISLE OF MAN, 2:00 P.M. LOCAL TIME, 5 DAYS UNTIL FREEDOM DAY

A twenty-five-meter, tri-electric-drive hydrofoil yacht glided into the private harbor at Peel Castle. The craft, named *Everlasting*, was guided skillfully by the captain to the midpoint of the long landing dock. Boat hands secured the mooring lines and tied them down. The yacht's only passenger rose to his feet. "We have arrived, Master Sebastian," the captain said as she shut down the engines and then radioed to the castle that they had arrived.

"Thank you, Christina," Sebastian said. "A fine trip, as usual."

"Will you need the boat again tonight, sir?" she asked, taking off her white captain's hat and letting down her shoulder-length auburn hair.

"No," Sebastian Quinn replied. "But keep her ready for tomorrow. I wouldn't be surprised if we will need to go out again soon."

"Very good, sir," Christina said, putting her cap back on and tipping it in farewell.

Sebastian disembarked and stepped onto the dock. Carrying a small

travel bag, he walked toward the stone entryway to the castle's courtyard. He had been away from home for a few weeks, and it felt good to
walk on the dock, to smell the sea air and see the round overlook tower
again. It had been a gorgeous summer day, but now the winds were picking up, and dark clouds were rolling in. A storm was brewing. Sebastian
stopped and looked at the ominous sky, which mirrored the unsettled
feeling growing inside him. He was reminded of a phrase he had read
in a book long ago: "*As within, so it is without.*" A light rain started falling
as he turned and resumed his walk to the courtyard.

Sebastian's mother and father had purchased the castle in 2034 from
the Manx National Heritage Foundation. After the Great Disruption,
visitors stopped coming to the castle, and the grounds were left untended for many years. The Heritage Foundation had been more than
happy to sell it but would only do so on the condition that the site
remain largely untouched and the name remain the same. It was also
stipulated that any new structures on the site be built apart from existing buildings and ruins. Sebastian's parents had honored that agreement. The only major addition to the grounds had been the large house,
which Sebastian had helped his parents design and construct. Situated
at the northwest corner of the courtyard, its tall tower provided a pan-
oramic view of the ocean and the rest of the Isle of Man. The house
had been built in the same style as the other buildings, and apart from
its modern plumbing and electrical wiring, it blended into its surroundings. Sebastian knew every nook and cranny of it, every secret passage.
There were only two ways to enter and exit Peel Castle; one was by the
harborside dock, the other by gated West Quay Drive, which was now
mostly used as a service entrance. Peel Castle had very few guests these
days, and they usually arrived by boat or helicopter.

As Sebastian approached the house's dramatic stone staircase, which
led up to the front entrance, he was greeted by his most trusted assistant and longtime family butler, Lawrence. "Welcome home, Master
Sebastian," Lawrence said. It was a greeting Sebastian had heard many
times in his life.

"Hello, Lawrence. Those words bring me a sense of peace that has eluded me for these past forty-eight hours."

"I'm sorry, sir. I take it that things are not in order."

"No, much is unsettled. Foes from the past have come forward, and they are wasting little time in reasserting themselves. Their presence has already been felt."

"Yes, we were sorry to hear the sad news of Ms. Brown's passing," Lawrence said.

"Send the money we promised for the purchase of the *Chronicles*," Sebastian instructed. "Even though the Council did not secure the books, I'm sure they could use it at this difficult time."

"Very good, sir," Lawrence said. "And what about the young man? Has he finished the restoration work? Is he safe?"

"No, he hasn't yet completed his work on the painting. And no, I do not think he is safe," Sebastian answered. "Let us pray that he unravels the mystery of the Michelangelo and the mystery of his own life."

"Take to hope, Master Sebastian," Lawrence said. "I am not sure what your parents would have said to you in a moment like this, but I am sure they would have advised you not to lose hope." With a kind smile on his face, Lawrence took Sebastian's hat and travel bag.

"You're back!" a young woman cried, running down the curved marble staircase carrying an exquisitely crafted violin in her left hand and its bow in her right. "I've been devouring all those books you told me to read, and I have many questions," she said, getting right to her point.

Sebastian greeted her with a kiss on the cheek.

"Your questions will have to wait," Lawrence said, provoking a dissatisfied look from the girl, whose name was Anita. "Master Sebastian requires a respite after his long trip. Dinner will be served promptly at six-thirty. Sara is planning a wonderful meal."

"Fine, I'll wait until dinner, then," Anita said with a touch of disappointment in her voice. She turned and ran back up the stairs, calling over her shoulder, "It's nice to have you back, Mr. Quinn."

"I have prepared the Tapestry Room for you, sir," Lawrence went on. "A glass of wine awaits you there."

"Thank you, my friend. You know what comforts me. And after dinner I will make use of the Arcis Chamber."

"Very good, sir, I'll see that it is prepared."

Sebastian entered the Tapestry Room through a set of tall, hand-carved double doors. At the center of the room, a single high-backed leather chair and an old cherrywood table rested on an exquisite blue and gold Kashmir rug. The chair faced the picture windows on the north wall, which provided a view of the ocean and the eternal crashing of the incoming waves. The walls of the large room were adorned with artwork from the past, portraits of kings and queens, fragments of ancient wall paintings that depicted pharaohs and gods, religious icons, and paintings of battles and hard-fought victories. The west wall of the room was shelved with great books, both new and old. A grand fireplace sat idle in the southwest corner, a seasoned cord of wood neatly stacked next to it. The ceiling featured a great stained-glass dome, depicting six angels observing from the heavens and a seventh angel who seemed indifferent. It was called the Tapestry Room because it was said to contain the threads that linked a person to his past, not only to Sebastian's own family history but to the history of mankind.

Sebastian walked to the center of the room and slowly lowered himself into the high-backed armchair. On the side table was a silver goblet, its interior lined with leafed gold. He picked up the goblet and read the familiar words engraved on it: "Destiny is a choice."

Lawrence always seems to pick the right goblet for every occasion, Sebastian thought as he inhaled the wine's bouquet. He lifted the goblet to his lips and drank its contents in one swift motion. Then he set the empty goblet back on the table, leaned back in his chair, and took up his smoking pipe, which had already been prepared for him. Looking out the windows, he could see that the darkest clouds were almost upon the island. The recent events in Cairo, New Chicago, and Washington, D.C., did not surprise him. *Men have been battling men since the dawn of time*, he mused. His mother and father had been in the middle of many such battles.

How can I do this myself? Sebastian thought as he looked at the portraits of his mother and father hanging on the wall. Sebastian's mother, Maria, had passed away fourteen years ago, and his father, Felix, died three years after that. Sebastian was alone, the last of his clan.

He reached over and picked up an old manuscript that Lawrence had placed there for him. It was titled *Enuntiatio de Tutela*, "Manifesto of the Guardians." Passed down from generation to generation, its author and date of origin were unknown. Sebastian remembered his mother reading the sacred words to him in her gentle, calming voice. There was one particular passage he would always repeat after she'd finished reading it. Sebastian closed his eyes for a moment, remembering.

You who have chosen this path and promised to follow the
Enuntiatio de Tutela
will be taught great philosophies and precepts. Service to mankind must be done
without condition and without expectation. Love and sincerity will be your
only allies on this journey.
You must believe that those you teach will one day become your inspiration.
For when the initiate learns more as a teacher than he did as a student,
Then and only then
Can he be called
Master.

Sebastian's deep contemplation was interrupted by the opening of one of the doors. The quick tapping of feet on the marble floor was followed by the loving kiss of Bukya, the German shepherd who had been with Sebastian since he was a puppy and enjoyed the run of the house. "I wondered where you were hiding," Sebastian said as he set aside the ancient document and rubbed Bukya's ears. "We have work to do, my friend. The world is in trouble, and it doesn't realize it yet."

9

Your technology has made you unaware of what is inside you.
Beware of whatever stops you from understanding your natural
ability. Beware of the artificial, for it is only a temporal thing.
—THE CHRONICLES OF SATRAYA

CHÂTEAU DUGAN, SWISS ALPS, 3:30 P.M. LOCAL TIME,
5 DAYS UNTIL FREEDOM DAY

Château Dugan was a large residence for one man. It was the only home
Simon Hitchlords had ever known. Servants moved busily through the
eighty rooms and countless hallways each day, working to keep the Château looking as regal as it had for centuries. The servants took great care
to see that the Château was always ready for the next social or political
reception—and for the next woman in Simon's life.

Simon strived to maintain the high standards that his father had
maintained, for it had been Fendral who had overseen the business of
running Château Dugan. Simon's mother hadn't cared to involve herself
in the day-to-day matters of running a home or in any of her husband's
and her son's activities. Even after the Great Disruption, she had spent
most of her time traveling abroad, trying to recreate the glittering social
life that she and her privileged friends had once enjoyed. But the days
of the old socialites had come to an end. So many of their peers had
lost everything in the Great Disruption or to the governmental policies
that had been instituted to stem the chaos.

Simon had always been close to his more practical-minded father. Fendral knew that the great families' ascent back to the top would require a calculated strategy. He knew that a man could not just declare himself king; first, he had to create a common enemy and show the people that he had just conquered that enemy on their behalf. Even though Simon was young when he and his father served on the Council of Satraya, he'd learned a great deal about politics and how to fight a war without anyone knowing the battle had been joined. His father had referred to the strategy as the Peacemaker's Bluff. "Don't fight your battles directly," he would say. "Find someone who hates your enemy more than you and manipulate them into confrontation. When the carnage is over, become the peacemaker. During the peace process, the opposing sides will welcome your leadership and all will be yours. Remember this, Simon."

The loss of his father and mother in a car accident nine years ago had distressed Simon deeply. With no brothers or sisters, Simon had inherited everything—the Château and all of its priceless artwork and arcana, along with the entire Hitchlords fortune. Well, perhaps he hadn't been all that distressed.

Sitting in his reading room, Simon browsed through the pages of a tattered blue journal. Its cover had the remnants of two bloody handprints, one smaller than the other. As he turned the handwritten pages, his eyes were drawn to the strange mark in the upper right corner.

Simon paused at places where pages had obviously been torn out. That bothered him. *Why were they torn out? What am I missing?* He couldn't let it distract him. He kept turning the pages until he found the entry he was looking for, one he had read many times before.

December 24, 2033. It has been just over three years since I found the books in the forest. I am learning that they contain more veiled secrets than we'd thought.

In addition to the printed words on the pages, I am beginning to see strange Old English–styled writings and symbols on the pages I'd at first thought were blank at the end of the third book. Symbols beyond the Fundamental Four. I haven't told anyone, not the Council, not even Cassandra, although I suspect that she might also be seeing them. The Satraya Flame seems to be the key. If you truly begin to master the flame and then look at the pages, the hidden writings and symbols appear. These symbols are different as they seem to float on the page. They seem to hold the promise of something powerful and supernatural.

Simon paused for a moment and looked up at the crackling fire in the fireplace. He remembered watching Camden scribble in the journal during Council meetings. Simon's father, Fendral, had attempted to browse through it one day, but Camden caught him and thereafter guarded the journal more closely. Simon looked back down and continued to read.

There are three blank pages at the end of Book III. Two of the pages have hidden symbols and writings on them. Combinations that look like "Be" and "Te" on the first blank page, written in the same Old English style. On the second, I've seen the word "Solokan." It always appeared below a fragment of a solid line and an arc of some sort. The third page is still a mystery to me. It seems to have only a partial symbol and some scattered letters, among them clearly "m" and "o." I don't have the focus yet to see the complete symbol or decipher the words.

Tomorrow I am going to ask Deya and Madu if they are seeing hidden symbols in the final pages of the third volume in their sets. I am going to borrow their books for the night. I dare not ask Fendral.

When Simon had finished reading the entry, he closed the journal. He was not the first in his family to study the occult. Other Hitchlords men had studied many different doctrines, hoping to attain the powers they promised. After his parents died, at the urging of Andrea's husband, Lord Benson, Simon had spent a great deal of time studying the history of his lineage and the activities of his forefathers. He also studied the esoteric works his family had secretly acquired, sometimes by questionable means: books, papers, scrolls. Now Simon browsed through an old leather folder containing some of them. There was a handwritten letter dated March 18, 1882, which was purported to have come from the original collection of the Mahatma Letters, currently locked away in the British Museum. Of course, this letter had been appropriated before the six-volume collection reached the museum. The exquisite penmanship of the letter and the masterful strokes of the sage's blue pen impressed Simon. He was particularly interested in the part of the letter that dealt with the power of symbols.

Regarding your question about symbols. The most direct answer to your query is an emphatic yes. Symbols do hold great and immense power. We must tread lightly here upon the subjects of images, marks, and motifs. There exists information that cannot be communicated by any language that you possess. It is only through proper inward study and contemplation that the secrets of the symbols are revealed. But rare is the person who can cleanly wield the power which is bestowed upon them. Therefore, we who guard them do not cast them before man carelessly. For in the wrong hands the symbols could unleash great harm upon our world.

The cross motif, of the venerable Yeshua Ben Yosef, is regarded as such a symbol. In our ancient span, it was revered as the Intersection of Man, where his journey from left to right intersected with his journey from lower to higher (excuse our words, for we possess not tongue to properly impart this mark). It depicted a standing man or woman with their arms spread open, welcoming that which was before them into their heart. It represented unconditional love, which could not be spoken but only experienced. We are saddened to see that it has been used for such vile subjugation over the last two of your ages. In the old ways, this is a mark to be embraced by all men and women for it applies to each equally.

Second, the original Shield of David, the inverted triads. One representing man's journey from heaven to earth and the other representing his journey from earth to heaven. How has your world used this most powerful of symbols? This too is an old and ancient mark whose original meaning is lost to you, but not to us. This too is a mark to be understood and adopted by all men and women.

There will soon be one born into your world who will pursue a particular mark. It is yet another old symbol that will be misused for a terrible act. The mark of the sun and of the fourth seal will soon be bloodied for eons to come. Its original beauty will be lost, only held sacred by those who left long ago. Be wary of the one who chooses the Swastika, for his abuse of the mark will last for many ages.

Symbols are put away for great purpose. But we cannot permanently shield them from view. We have not that claim upon them. All symbols are for all the children of the spirit. When properly and adequately focused upon, they endow the observer with great powers. No symbol judges right from wrong, no symbol is the arbiter of good and evil. The symbol only transmits information and power from the moment it was fashioned.

Simon closed the folder and set it on top of Camden's journal. *Symbols,* he thought. *And secrets. As Camden wrote in his journal, the Satraya Flame is the key . . .*

One of the first techniques described in the *Chronicles,* the Satraya Flame involved sitting motionless in front of a lit candle. With diligent practice, an individual would be able to still his mind and reach a point of utter clarity. The mysteries a person would be able to realize in that moment of clarity were said to be indescribable and could only be experienced.

Like his father and Andrea, Simon had not been able to muster the discipline to accomplish the task fully. At least, not until he'd obtained Camden's journal, read its entries, and discovered what an irresistible prize such discipline would yield. Having worked diligently over the past two years to master the Satraya Flame, Simon had begun to apply the same technique to the blank pages of the books. His father's set of the *Chronicles* held secrets just as the other sets did. Odd shapes and lettering similar to what Camden had described. Simon's personal quest was to learn all of those secrets. No one in Era, not even Andrea, knew of his pursuit.

Just then, there was a knock on the door. One of Simon's servants entered, carrying a leather bag. "Good evening, sir. Macliv has just arrived, and he sent this forward. He brought a guest and is waiting for you in the lower chamber."

Simon nodded. "Set them down."

The servant put the leather bag on the desk and exited the room, closing the door behind him. Then Simon opened the bag. Along with the books he'd been waiting for, he found a note from Andrea.

Dearest Simon,

Here are the Chronicles *from Cairo. I will be visiting the doctor at G-LAB to ensure that everything there is proceeding as planned. We will take care of some business in Washington, D.C., and then travel to the activation site for the day of victory.*

Fondly,
Andrea

Simon tossed the note into the fire and pulled the Pyramid Set from the leather pouch. He put the books on the desk in front of him, next to his father's set of *The Chronicles of Satraya*, which was known as the Train Set. The Forest Set, which had been acquired at the auction the night before, was scheduled to arrive the next morning via armored courier. The only set missing was the one Deya Sarin had found, the River Set. And soon he would have that one, too.

"Your nightmare is coming to pass, Camden," Simon said, laughing.

He rose from his desk. He had a guest to greet in the dungeon.

10

Opportunities for adventure are all around you. Whether the
adventure is small or large, short or long, find the courage to go on
one. It does not matter where you think it will lead; just know it
will lead to where you have never been.

—THE CHRONICLES OF SATRAYA

NEW CHICAGO, ILLINOIS, 9:00 A.M. LOCAL TIME,
5 DAYS UNTIL FREEDOM DAY

"Even if I were convinced that Simon and Andrea were responsible for my parents' murders and all that happened last night, what
would you have me do?" Logan asked Mr. Perrot. "There's nothing I want more than to bring my parents' killers to justice. But if
they're as ruthless as you say, then nothing and nobody is off limits
to them. How do we guarantee our own safety? Or the safety of our
families?"

"We can't," Mr. Perrot stated matter-of-factly. "This will be a risky
undertaking. The authorities cannot help us until we manage to get
some evidence implicating Simon and Andrea. And in order for that to
happen, we have to take matters into our own hands."

"What are you saying?"

"The theft in Cairo is one thing, but the murder of Cynthia leads
me to believe that something worse is coming. Andrea does not do
things without having a grand purpose in mind. We must do what the

Council members and the volunteers didn't do all those years ago: we need to confront Andrea directly."

"Where do we find her?" Logan was pacing with his hands in his pockets. He turned to Mr. Perrot. "Do you think Ms. Crawley at the auction house might know where she lives?"

"No, Logan," Mr. Perrot answered. "These people are not so easily found. We have to do something that will draw them out."

Logan suddenly stopped his pacing. "I forgot about this," he said, as he pulled an envelope from his pocket. Logan removed the note and unfolded it. "It fell out of one of the books last night during the auction." Blue wax seemed to have melted and dripped all over it. "It's hard to make out," Logan said, as he went and grabbed a magnifying glass from his father's desk. Mr. Perrot put on his reading glasses. Together, they attempted to read the faded writing.

November 19, 2037

To My Dearest Friend Baté Sisán,

    I hope life finds you well and in good spirits.

    I am writing this letter because I suspect that my entire world is being watched. I cannot confirm it, but I feel it. The Council has splintered, the group has broken apart. Your warnings were not heeded. I wish they had been.

    Deya and Madu have returned home. We are leaving tomorrow. I fear for them and us. I have persuaded Robert to come with us. I know that it was not what we had planned. But I don't know how to help anymore; we have to protect our families. I suspect that I may never see you again. I will never forget your help.

    Maybe the answer will come in the flame to the person brave enough to look. Sadly, that person cannot be me. I will hide it under the old meeting place. 4B5W. The King's Gambit is our best and only option. They must accept it. I pray to the star above that everything will unfold properly. It is now in the hands of destiny to select the finder.

                              Your friend, Camden Ford

Logan and Mr. Perrot were silent for a few moments. Then Logan asked, "Who is Baté Sisán?"

"That is a name I have never heard before," Mr. Perrot answered.

"It's odd that the letter was never sent," Logan commented. "Why write a letter like this and not send it?"

Mr. Perrot shook his head and then repeated a part of the letter: "'I will hide it under the old meeting place . . .'"

"Do you know what it means?" Logan asked.

"I believe so," Mr. Perrot answered. "It must be the old meeting place in the basement of the current offices of the Council of Satraya in Washington, D.C. The harder question to answer is what we are going to find when we search there."

"What do you mean, when we search there?"

"Well, my boy, you said you wanted to see your parents' killers brought to justice. Here is your chance. And mine. It seems as though an old man has been granted a second chance. I am going to make the choice I failed to make all those years ago. I am going to enter the fight." He turned to Logan and waited. "Now the only question is, what are you going to do?"

Logan stayed silent and continued to look at Mr. Perrot.

"If fear endeavors to guide your choice, then to the wise one, the choice has already been made," Mr. Perrot recited.

"A line from the *Chronicles*?" Logan asked.

Mr. Perrot nodded.

Logan folded the note and put it back into his pocket. *I guess I have someplace to go and something to do now,* he thought. "How long do you think we'll be gone?"

Mr. Perrot smiled. Their adventure was on.

11

Find a place to go that is yours. It can be under a tree or atop a great mountain, it matters not. But wherever it might be, call it your own.

—THE CHRONICLES OF SATRAYA

ISLE OF MAN, 9:00 P.M. LOCAL TIME, 5 DAYS UNTIL FREEDOM DAY

The Arcis Chamber was the easternmost room in Sebastian Quinn's home. Twelve onyx pillars adorned the curved wall of the circular room, and between the pillars stood twelve statues carved from limestone. Twelve sages of old, six male and six female. The familiar embodiments of Yeshua Ben Yosef, Buddha, Saint Germain, and the ancient one named Ramachandra stood next to others, such as the Lady of Light, of whom history spoke little but whose contributions were profound. The black and white checkered floor was clean and polished, reflecting the dim light that emanated from behind the statues and from the great chandelier that hung from the center of the domed ceiling. Soft violin music filled the room, the sound of a bell and the strumming of a harp occasionally joining the calming melody. A soft drumbeat could also be heard in the background. A hint of roses scented the air. A circular mat with a cushion had been laid in the center of the floor, and directly to the right of it was a goblet of water. A meter in front of the goblet was a golden candlestick holding an unlit blue candle. A silver lighter rested on the floor next to the candlestick.

Sebastian entered the chamber, walked across the checkered floor to the center of the room, and stood with his feet together behind the mat. He closed his eyes and allowed the serenity of the room and the music to envelop him. He put his hands together as if to pray and slowly bowed. Then he straightened, inhaling deeply and exhaling slowly. In a focused state, he opened his eyes and walked over to the candlestick. He picked up the lighter and lit the blue candle. The struggling flame crackled at first, then settled into a still, brilliant light. With a single voice command, the lights in the Arcis Chamber slowly dimmed to darkness. The only illumination came from the solitary flame at the center of the chamber.

Sebastian sat on the cushion, crossing his legs and moving into a half-lotus position. He took a sip of water from the goblet, then placed his hands gently on his knees. He took in a deep breath and exhaled slowly. The flame, which stood at eye level a meter in front of him, quivered in response to his exhalation but within a moment returned to its steady burn. Sebastian fixed his eyes on the flame, and as if a switch had been engaged, he held perfectly still. The faces of the statues, which were dully illuminated by the candlelight, looked like ghosts and wayward spirits. Sebastian tightened his focus, and the ghostlike faces disappeared. The music played on, a flute now joining the violin and the harp. Sebastian deepened his focus again, and the sound of the music faded away. He had mastered his will, and with that mastery, he could push away the sensual world and make room for something else. His mind was matching the stillness of the flame.

As known by the adepts of old and as taught in the *Chronicles*, time was of little consequence; in the center of the flame, one lost all sense of it. The soft music continued to play in the Arcis Chamber, the candle continued to burn, and the fragrance of roses still hung in the air, but not for Sebastian. In his mind, he was reaching a deeper state of the Satraya Flame. He had blocked out any awareness of his body, his surroundings, and any stray thoughts. His only focus was the flame, and even now, that began to fade. He heard nothing, only perfect silence. Different hues of color began to cross in front of his open eyes, as if clouds were passing in the sky. If thoughts could take shape and form, they would most certainly appear as these moving mists of magnificent colors.

Sebastian's parents had been adepts at using the flame, too. They had taught him the technique at a very early age, a seemingly simple act of his mind but one that took practice to perfect. When he was young, his parents had him focus on the candle every day. Sometimes they would try to distract him by blowing in his ear or running a feather across his neck, but he'd known he had to remain focused on the flame. They would encourage him, saying in the gentlest, sweetest voices, "A bit more, Sebastian, a bit more. Every moment you become closer to the flame is a moment you become closer to all things. In the flame of Satraya, all that you wish to know will be revealed. The key is sincerity. A bit more, my love, a bit more."

Now, Sebastian deepened his already mindful focus and brought up the image of the mystical Satraya symbol of Future Sight named Solokan. It was one of the hidden symbols located on the blank pages in the *Chronicles*. When focused on properly, the symbol would provide the adept with a view into the future. Sebastian held the image in his mind. The floating clouds of color disappeared, and all that remained was blackness. Even the candle that had assisted in bringing him to this timeless moment vanished. A soft buzzing sound began, like the low-pitched hum of a passing bee. Sebastian held the focus a bit more. The sound grew louder and louder. The blackness unfolded, becoming darker and darker. Soon the sound became almost unbearable. *A bit more*, Sebastian told himself, *a bit more*. And in a split second, he heard a loud bang, like the firing of a great cannon. His mind shifted.

As if he were in a lucid dream, a scene unfolded in front of him. He was hovering over an Indian village. Below him, he could see many hovels and dirt roads, sink holes formed by the Great Disruption on the village's outskirts, and a fallen bridge, lying in ruin and half buried in a dried riverbed. Something was not right in this most real of visions. But Sebastian was too high up to see. Slowly, he descended and moved closer. A strange green light permeated the village. Where were the people? There were no men, women, or children walking about. He floated closer and moved in and out of the bamboo structures. Something was indeed wrong. All of the villagers seemed to have disappeared.

Sebastian now stood on one of the dirt roads and looked around. Suddenly, a body fell from the sky and smashed on the ground. Then another and another. One by one, human corpses came crashing down, their skulls cracking open like eggs. But the skulls were empty, their brains gone. *How can this be?* Sebastian's heart beat faster and faster. *What curse has befallen these people?* He was losing his breath. Another great blast from the cannon was heard, and Sebastian snapped out of his vision. He was back in his body, sitting at the center of the Arcis Chamber.

Slowly, he became aware of the candle. He became aware of his body and of his surroundings. He could hear the soft music and smell the scent of the roses again. He remained seated for a moment, gathering his thoughts and trying to process what he had just seen. The foreboding of the storm clouds paled in comparison with whatever this vision portended.

After centering himself, Sebastian slowly rose and bowed to the candle before blowing it out. A small trail of smoke floated from the smoldering wick. At a single spoken command, the lights in the chamber came back on, once again illuminating the pillars and the statues of the sages. Another command was given, and a 3-D image of Lawrence was projected in front of Sebastian.

"Greetings, sir," Lawrence said. "I hope that you enjoyed the flame."

"Lawrence, please ready the resources," Sebastian instructed. "I am off to India tomorrow, to a village outside of Banaras."

12

*The answers to the greatest mysteries in your life must be actively
sought, for in the adventure and the journey to reveal them, there
lies your greatest wisdom.*
—THE CHRONICLES OF SATRAYA

WASHINGTON, D.C., 5:00 P.M. LOCAL TIME,
5 DAYS UNTIL FREEDOM DAY

"There it is," said Mr. Perrot. "The old meeting place. That is where it
all started."

Logan and Mr. Perrot had taken a 1:00 P.M. flight from New
Chicago and arrived in Washington, D.C., the former nation's capital, late in the afternoon. They stood across the street from the
Council of Satraya offices, which were in a red brick building at
the corner of 18th Street and New York Avenue. Its signature red
façade and the tall brick wall that bordered the property stood in
stark contrast to the many modern post-Disruption office buildings
that surrounded it.

Logan and Mr. Perrot could hear the noise coming from the construction site one block north on F Street, where cranes were hoisting
steel beams for a sprawling new office complex that would cover four
square blocks and serve as the new home of the Allied Republics, an
international organization formerly known as the United Nations. The

IMF and other banks that had once occupied those blocks had little value during the Rising and were never rebuilt.

"I remember reading about this place," Logan said. "It used to be called the Octagon Museum."

"Do you know why it was given that name?" Mr. Perrot asked. "As you can see, the building is not shaped like an octagon."

"No, it isn't. Do you think I didn't pay attention in my architectural history classes?" Logan retorted with a smile. "In the eighteenth century, round rooms were usually built with eight angled walls inside. They were called octagon salons. My guess is there is a room like that in the building."

"You are correct," Mr. Perrot said. "The entrance hall is circular."

During the rebuilding efforts after the Great Disruption, the Council of Satraya started using the basement floor of the once-renowned Octagon Museum for its meetings and other activities. Over time, as the Council grew and its projects flourished and expanded, it was granted ownership of the building. But now the home of one of the most influential groups in the history of mankind was secured by local police and agents from the World Crime Federation. Yellow security tape stretched around the brick wall that surrounded the building, effectively blocking the gated entrance to the front door.

"How are we supposed to get in?" Logan asked as he adjusted the backpack of supplies he'd brought along for their journey.

"You didn't suppose that our little adventure was going to be easy, did you?" Mr. Perrot said. "Let us be patient and see what opportunities arise." He took Logan by the elbow, and they walked slowly north on 18th Street. They saw a policeman standing at the main entrance, while another officer walked around the perimeter of the property. Visitors lingered on the sidewalk after being turned away, apparently wondering what all the commotion was about.

"What are you looking for?" Logan asked Mr. Perrot. "Let's come back later when there aren't as many people around."

Ignoring Logan's suggestion, Mr. Perrot continued to watch the guard and assess the scene. "I have an idea," he whispered. "Look at the entrance to the building next door. The gate is open, and I don't see any security guards or police. Maybe it's still there."

"Maybe what's still there?"

Mr. Perrot didn't answer. His gaze was still on the patrolling officer, who had stopped to talk to two attractive women who were walking past. "And here it is," Mr. Perrot said then. "Our opportunity." He squeezed Logan's elbow and escorted him across the street. When they reached the open gate, Mr. Perrot pushed Logan into a small, confined area between a set of tall shrubs and the brick wall that surrounded the neighboring Octagon building. The policeman had finished talking and was once again making his rounds.

"What are we doing?" Logan asked in a low voice.

"Help me look," Mr. Perrot said. "Help me push away the dirt. Quickly, quickly!" In a rush, Logan did so. After clearing some debris, their fingers touched smooth metal. "Ah, you see," Mr. Perrot said, "old secrets afford new opportunities."

"What is this?" Logan said, shocked to see the submarine-like hatch door in the ground.

"As I said, it's an opportunity." Mr. Perrot began to turn the handle, and Logan helped him lift the door open, careful not to let the squeak of the old hinges give them away. Once it was open, the top of a metal ladder could be seen in the hatchway. "Could you get your little device to illuminate our situation here?" Mr. Perrot asked.

"Little device? Oh," Logan said, as he grabbed his PCD and pressed a few buttons to project an ample light.

"Follow me," Mr. Perrot said.

Logan followed Mr. Perrot down the ladder and carefully closed the lid behind him. He descended slowly, making sure of his footing, one rung at a time.

"Still can't believe that policeman didn't see us," Logan said, as he climbed down. "That seemed too easy."

"Many things have happened in our history because a man stopped to talk to a woman."

Logan chuckled.

After a surprisingly short climb, they found themselves in a dark tunnel. Mr. Perrot flashed the light around. The dusty tunnel was about three meters tall and four meters wide.

"What is this place?" Logan asked.

"It is an old escape tunnel that the first Council was required to build," Mr. Perrot answered. "During the Great Disruption, many buildings collapsed, and people were trapped in them. New safety laws were enacted. In order for us to use the building, the WFR required that secondary exits be installed. This particular tunnel was our emergency exit. I never expected to have to use it to break *into* our offices."

Mr. Perrot used the light from Logan's PCD to point the way down the extremely dusty and dingy corridor. Lining the walls of the tunnel were large plastic boxes with well-sealed lids. "Survival supplies?" Logan asked.

Mr. Perrot nodded. "In case things fell apart again. The boxes contain food, bottles of water, and other essential items." He shone the PCD on some of the boxes' labels. "It's been forty years now; I'm sure much of the food has passed its shelf life." Logan pried open one of the lids and was immediately repulsed by a foul odor.

The tunnel was not very long, only about fifteen meters. At the end, they found another fortified door. Mr. Perrot handed the PCD back to Logan and turned the handle. The hinges squeaked after years of disuse. Mr. Perrot pushed the door open.

Feeling along the wall, Mr. Perrot continued inside until he found the light switch. He and Logan found themselves standing in what appeared to be a storage room. "So it was a hidden door," Logan said, observing that from the inside, the door appeared to be part of an old bookshelf.

"It wasn't like that when we built the tunnel," Mr. Perrot said, gazing around the basement. Small windows lined the upper parts of the beige-painted concrete walls, and large wooden pillars around the perimeter of the room provided support for the coffered ceiling, which had a mural of an open night sky painted across it. "The shelves weren't here when I worked for the Council," Mr. Perrot continued. "Neither was this furniture."

"Look at this room," Logan said in wonder. He was more interested in the architecture and design than in the dusty rugs and boxes that were scattered around. "The ceiling is exquisite. And this floor, it's right out of the time of the Freemasons."

"Yes, it is still the same grand floor," Mr. Perrot said, looking at the very large black and white alternating tiles. "This used to be the meeting place of the Council of Satraya. There was a large table at the center. We would sit there for hours planning how to spread the words and philosophy of the *Chronicles.* I wonder what they did with it. We were such idealists then . . ." Mr. Perrot's voice grew softer.

"Sort of like King Arthur and his knights," Logan said with a laugh. He walked around, looking at the various items, opening boxes and rummaging through their contents.

"Yes, very much like those knights," Mr. Perrot said in a serious tone. He gazed around the room. "To think that now it's just a storage room, full of dust and things from a forgotten time."

"I still can't get over the ceiling," Logan said, looking up at the mural of the heavens at night. "They painted the Big Dipper perfectly. That is a beautiful piece of work." He gazed at it a bit longer and then turned back to the room. "How are we supposed to find anything in here?" he asked, looking around at a scene that could only be properly called a mess.

"I think the more pertinent question is, what are we looking for?" Mr. Perrot said. "Would you read the letter again?"

Logan reached into his pack and took out the piece of paper that had fallen from the volume of the *Chronicles.* He read it aloud again, as Mr. Perrot listened intently. Then, suddenly, Mr. Perrot stopped him and asked him to reread a section.

Maybe the answer will come in the flame to the person brave enough to look.
Sadly, that person cannot be me. I will hide it under the old meeting place.
4B5W. The King's Gambit is our best and only option. They must accept it. I
pray to the star above that everything will unfold properly. It is now in the hands
of destiny to select the finder.

Logan slipped the letter back into his pack.

"Well, one thing I do know is that this is the old meeting place," Mr. Perrot stated. "What we now have to figure out is what Camden wanted someone to find."

"What does 4B5W mean?" Logan asked. "Maybe it has to do with the boxes on these shelves." He began to examine some of their labels.

"Remember, none of these shelves or the furniture was here during our time," Mr. Perrot said. "So that clue must relate to something that was part of the original room. Camden was a strategist; he would not have made this obvious. In all the years we played chess, I only managed to beat him a few times. I think he let me win occasionally so I would continue to play with him. But even then, he was always a few moves ahead of me."

Logan smiled at the thought. Then his smile suddenly deepened. "Chess!" he exclaimed. "Look at the floor, all the black and white tiles. It looks like a chessboard, doesn't it? And 4B5W. That could be four black and five white tiles!"

Mr. Perrot looked down at his feet. Then he, too, broke into a smile, shaking his head. "Yes, of course! The King's Gambit—that is an opening move in chess. My old friend is still a few steps ahead of me."

"But we need a reference point," Logan pointed out. "Four and five from what square and in what direction?"

The two pondered for a moment, stumped.

"Maybe there is a mark on one of these tiles," Logan suggested, kneeling down to get a better look at them.

Meanwhile, Mr. Perrot walked over to a corner of the room and started to count the number of tiles from one corner to another and then did the same to the opposite corner. The room was indeed a perfect eight-by-eight chessboard. *The King's Gambit,* he mused. Camden had used that opening on him many times. *But I need to know the proper orientation.* Mr. Perrot continued quietly to recite the words in the letter. One line in particular intrigued him. "Why would Camden write that?" he asked aloud.

Logan, who was crawling on the floor inspecting the tiles, stopped and looked at him. "Write what?"

"'I pray to the star above.' Why would he write that? In the time that I knew him, Camden never prayed to anything, let alone a star in the sky. That line doesn't make sense."

Logan's eyes widened. "Sir, you may want to look above you," he said, pointing to the mural on the ceiling.

Mr. Perrot looked up. The two stars that formed the Big Dipper's outward edge pointed to another, the brightest star in the mural. "Ah! Look there, the star above, a depiction of the North Star! Well done again, Logan. I think you just found our reference point."

Logan helped Mr. Perrot move a table out of the way and roll up the carpet, so that he could position himself directly beneath the star. "So this is E2, the starting position of the first pawn in the King's Gambit. First we move to E4." Mr. Perrot moved forward two tiles, emulating the chess move. "My opponent then moves his pawn to E5, directly in front of me." He signaled to Logan to take that position. "Next, I move another pawn from F2 to F4." Mr. Perrot slid over one tile and dropped his hat on his previous position. And so now you have to make a choice," he explained, looking at Logan. "You can either take the gambit or not."

"The letter says, 'They must accept it,'" Logan recalled. "So that means I take your pawn." Logan joined Mr. Perrot on the black tile.

"I think we may have solved it," Mr. Perrot said calmly.

"Well done, sir."

"Let us see if we find what we are supposed to find before we congratulate ourselves." Mr. Perrot picked up his hat and looked around the room. "What are we going to use to pry up this tile?"

"I have something." Logan put his backpack on the floor and took out a small beveled-edge chisel. "This will do the trick."

"Do you always carry your restoration tools with you?" Mr. Perrot asked in an amused tone. "Or is that a magical bag?"

Logan grinned and started to pry up one of the corners of the tile. To their surprise, it moved rather easily. "Here, help me lift it."

"I believe we have found what we are looking for," said Mr. Perrot, as he looked down at the ground. In a hole dug under the tile was a tin container about the length of a shoebox.

"We found the treasure!" Logan exclaimed, only half-jokingly, as he pulled out the container.

Suddenly, Mr. Perrot put his index finger to his lips, indicating that they should be quiet. They heard the sound of footsteps outside the interior basement door, then the murmur of voices. "Quickly, Logan!" Mr. Perrot whispered. "Hide the box!" Logan immediately stuffed it into his backpack. Then he brushed the loose grout and mortar back into the hole and put the black tile back into place. Mr. Perrot helped move the carpet and the table back over it.

They stood up just as the door to the storage room opened. Two uniformed police officers entered and appeared as surprised to see Logan and Mr. Perrot as Logan and Mr. Perrot were surprised to see them.

"Arms up!" a policeman yelled as he drew his weapon. His partner readied his gun, too.

Mr. Perrot and Logan followed the officer's command.

"What are you two doing, and how in hell did you get down here?" the policeman demanded.

"We seem to have lost our way and ended up in this dreadful basement," Mr. Perrot replied naturally, playing the old eccentric card. Logan might have smiled if he weren't so stunned.

The second officer frowned, then put away his weapon and proceeded to confiscate Logan's backpack and PCD.

"I can show you a much more dreadful place," he said with a sneer as he snapped handcuffs on Logan and Mr. Perrot. The two officers led them forcefully from the storage room and up a set of stairs to the first floor. There they were met by a woman wearing a well-tailored pantsuit and a badge, whom Logan thought for a fleeting moment he recognized. The woman glared at Logan and Mr. Perrot as the officers explained where they had been apprehended. "Lock them in that room over there until I'm ready to deal with them," she ordered. The policeman handed her Logan's backpack.

13

Understand your enemy, and it will set you free. For when you see
yourself in him, you will break free from your own judgments and
self-inquisitions.
—THE CHRONICLES OF SATRAYA

The walls were coated with reflective white paint, and the lacquered
floors reflected the bright light of the overhead lamps. He had no idea
where he was or how long he had been there. He only knew that he was
being kept in this strange place against his will. Blood dripped from
the tips of his fingers. The crimson handprints on the walls tracked
his progress as he had tried frantically to find his way out of the maze.

Each long hallway resembled the previous one he'd run through.
Each locked door he came to was identical to the one he'd just passed.
Occasionally, he came across a door that was open a few inches. But
no matter how hard he pushed or tried to pry open the door, lacerat-
ing his hands on the door's sharp edges, it wouldn't budge. Wearing
the tattered remains of his dark blue business suit, he scurried around
barefoot—they'd taken his shoes—like a trapped rat. His frustration
mounted every time he entered what he thought was a new hallway, only
to be taunted by the sight of his own blood smeared on the white walls.

From time to time, the lights would go out, and he would find himself in complete darkness, having only his sense of touch to guide him.

Exhausted now, he fell to the floor, his confused mind racing, trying to rationalize his plight. *Who would do this to me? What is this madness about?* His thoughts turned to his family, his wife and children. He reached into his pocket and pulled out a bloodstained picture of them. *I can't give up. I have to keep going.* He mustered his remaining willpower and rose to his feet. He had to continue to search for a way out, even if it meant the death of him.

"Andrea, I'd like to tell you a little about our subjects before we conduct our final tests," Dr. Malikei said in his German-accented baritone voice. "Kindly join me, if you will."

Andrea stopped reading a message on her PCD and walked over to where the doctor was sitting.

"Our nine participants, like their predecessors, have joined us from various walks of life."

"I am not sure that 'participants' and 'joined' are the proper terms," Andrea said, as they gave each other a baleful smile.

"They were selected most methodically," the doctor continued. "We considered their careers, their lifestyles. We studied them from afar for many months before bringing them here. When they arrived, we told them that they had been selected for a social experiment. We assured them that they had no cause to worry, as the experiment was a joint project of the government and the local university concerning SIS, sudden isolation syndrome."

"SIS? Is that a real behavioral syndrome?"

"Of course not. But we described it as a type of depression that manifests when an individual is removed from his usual environment and placed in a new one where he has limited social contact. We even let them meet others in the test group so that they could see that other people were participating in the experiment. We assured them that their being brought here so abruptly was part of the exercise and that they would be well compensated for their trouble."

"The promise of monetary gain can be quite persuasive and reassuring," Andrea said.

The doctor pointed to a wall of monitors displaying the various experimentation rooms in the secret genetic research laboratory referred to as G-LAB. "We have a teacher, a housewife, a MedicalPod technician," Dr. Malikei explained, half distracted as he fiddled with the controls.

"Doctor," Andrea said, bringing his attention to the monitors, "I thought you said there were nine test subjects?"

"You are correct. We seem to have lost subject number six, our businessman." The doctor pressed a few buttons, and they both watched as the monitor began to switch between video feeds. "It looks like he left some time ago."

"Shouldn't you be a bit more concerned about finding him?" Andrea said sharply.

"He cannot go far—they never can." The doctor continued to manipulate the controls. "Ah, there he is. He is trapped in the Hall of Mazes. Now, why would he leave his room?"

"You seem surprised," Andrea said. "And do I detect a note of disappointment in your voice?"

"No, no. It is only that I seem to have lost a small wager. I was certain that subject number five would be the one attempting to escape." He pointed to a monitor that showed a young man writing in a notebook. "Let us make the most of this opportunity," the doctor said. "Like all of our other subjects, the businessman has been injected with the serum. But before I conduct the test, I would like you to observe a little trial. It will illustrate an intriguing point that is the basis of our efforts."

Andrea watched in silence as Dr. Malikei turned on the lights in the Hall of Mazes.

"See there! The businessman hastens to one of the partially opened doors, trying to escape. But alas, he cannot. I have not opened it adequately. He wants liberation; he wants desperately to leave his confinement and return to the life he once knew. In each of our prior test groups, there was always one subject who didn't trust the explanation we provided, who didn't believe anything we told him. We had one group in which there were two such subjects." The doctor and Andrea watched as the businessman used every ounce of his strength to try to force the door open. The bloody tips of his fingers were repeatedly cut by the door's sharp edges. "I will frustrate him further—watch as I close the door now."

"I would certainly hate to be the subject of one of your experiments, Doctor," Andrea observed, as Dr. Malikei pressed another button, dimming the lights in the maze. "You seem to take great pleasure from them."

"All in the name of science," he said with a laugh. "What is most noteworthy here is the inaction of the other subjects," he added, redirecting Andrea's attention back to the bank of monitors. "The other subjects can leave their rooms at any time. Like the businessman, they can walk out their doors and into their own areas of the maze and search for a way out. But they do not. They are satisfied with what we have told them, and as long as we provide them with food and drink and keep them focused on some type of busy work such as crossword puzzles or routine math problems, they are content. But no matter how hard we tried to reassure our businessman, he could not be convinced. He displays the characteristics that we want to purge from this world. He is a Satrayian through and through." The doctor received a message on his PCD. "Excuse me for a moment, Andrea. I shall return promptly."

As the doctor walked away, Andrea's eyes strayed back to the monitor that showed the man in the labyrinth, the Satrayian who was attempting to break out of the box he'd been confined to. She couldn't help but relate to him, his determination, his desire to break free.

She thought about her time on the Council of Satraya, which now seemed like a faded memory. It was filled with many unforeseen twists and turns. What plans she had then, for freedom, for power. But destiny, it seemed, had laughed in her face. She had fallen in love with a man, not with what a man's money could buy for her. She found herself forced to choose between a simpler, altruistic life and the life of glamour, wealth, and recognition that she'd once known and still craved. She had also made a mistake she wanted never to think about again.

She had returned to Switzerland without accomplishing Fendral's goals, and a few years later, her life had taken another unexpected turn: she'd become pregnant and given birth to Lucius. Her husband, Lord Alfred Benson, was an absentee father, and Andrea had been left to raise Lucius, a sickly child, alone. Her plans to rebuild her political movement had to be put on hold.

At least, until Fendral—and after his death, Simon—put into place another plan.

Andrea couldn't take her eyes off the businessman as he scurried through the maze, pounding his fists against the walls, searching for a way out. "I understand him," she whispered.

"What was that?" The doctor had returned, carrying two long thin boxes. Andrea shook her head, indicating that it was unimportant. "I apologize for that interruption, but I have some good news for you: we have found a way to enhance your neurotrophin-3 levels, specifically by enhancing the NTF-3 gene."

"Please speak English, Doctor," Andrea said. "What does that mean for Lucius and me?"

"Of course." He nodded. "We have found a cure for your nerve disorder. Relief will come shortly. We were able to use our work here to create something that will clear the abnormalities in your cellular biology. And your son's."

"A designer drug." Andrea smiled with relief. This was what she'd long been hoping for.

"Yes, something very much like that." Dr. Malikei handed Andrea the boxes. "Take these, please. They contain syringes. One is for you, and the other is for Lucius. Inject yourselves, and after seven days, return here, and we will perform the final step."

"Thank you, Doctor." Andrea gave him a kiss on the cheek. "May we return sooner for the final treatment?"

"No," he said emphatically. "We must allow sufficient time; otherwise, the consequences would be dire, to say the least."

"Then seven days it is." Andrea put the boxes in her bag. "Now, what were you saying before we were interrupted?"

"Ah, yes, let us continue." He brought up a display that presented a plethora of readings, from heart rate to blood pressure to tactual sensory measurements. "We have implanted a biofeedback chip in each test subject so we can track brain activity and body chemistry as they perform specific tasks. We are particularly interested in people like the businessman. We need to better understand the nature of his neuro-activities."

"Yes," Andrea said. "'Understand your enemy, and it will set you free.'"

The doctor turned to her. "I see that you haven't completely forgotten the *Chronicles*," he said with a smile. "We need to isolate the chemical and neurological nature of free will so that our purge performs as engineered."

"But doesn't everyone have free will?" Andrea remarked. "People make choices every day. Surely free will alone cannot be our selection criterion for the Purging."

"You are correct, but there is a subtle distinction that needs to be understood," the doctor explained, a mischievous smile sliding across his face. "It is true that most people are capable of exercising free will. They are free to choose what they will eat and what they will wear. They are able to choose their profession or where they wish to work. But here is the distinction: most of them make those decisions from a domain of choices. If we say to people, 'Choose one of these four pairs of shoes,' most will do so without issue. Most will analyze their options and pick the pair they like best, even if none of the pairs is actually appealing to

them. But there are those who will not pick one. They will desire another option and will walk around barefoot if need be. Some will even
endeavor to make their own shoes. We call them Freedom Seekers. They
are the true enemy of order. And *they* are our target. We just have a few
more tests to run before we conduct one outside the facility."

"Actually, we were forced to accelerate the schedule a bit," Andrea
said. "Outside tests have already begun."

"I was not aware of that," the doctor said, clearly displeased. "Why
wasn't I told?"

"Calm yourself, Doctor," Andrea said in a reassuring voice. "You'll
be happy to know that the tests have been successful."

The doctor paused as his displeasure turned to morbid curiosity.
"How successful?"

"Smashing," Andrea said. "Exactly as you predicted."

"Yes!" The doctor pumped his fist in the air. "Then we have done
it. We have isolated the composition of free will. We have found what
makes a Satrayian."

"Freedom Seeker," Andrea said, looking at the businessman, who
was still wandering through the maze. "And what do you call everyone
else, Doctor?"

Dr. Malikei grinned. "The others we call humans."

14

Whom do you trust with your life—your mother, father, wife, husband, friends?
Do you really trust that which you call God?
Perhaps a more profound question is, can you be trusted with someone else's life?

—THE CHRONICLES OF SATRAYA

WASHINGTON, D.C., 7:00 P.M. LOCAL TIME,
5 DAYS UNTIL FREEDOM DAY

Mr. Perrot and Logan sat in a pair of uncomfortable brown plastic chairs, awaiting their fate in a small room just off the entrance hall of the Council of Satraya building. Through a small window in the door, they could see the head of a uniformed policeman standing outside the room.

"You think they'll keep the box we found?" Logan asked, fidgeting in his chair. "And what do we say when they start asking questions?" He looked at Mr. Perrot, who sat serenely with his arms crossed over his chest. "You seem awfully calm about all of this."

"All we can do is answer their questions with the truth," Mr. Perrot said.

"The truth. Really?" Logan was certain they were going to need more than that in order to avoid spending the night in jail. "People don't usually associate the truth with conspiracy theories."

"We need to have a bit more faith," Mr. Perrot said. "Particular events have taken place for a particular reason."

Logan shook his head, little comforted by the cryptic words. Through the door's window, he saw people looking in at them. One in particular caught his eye. The woman who seemed to be in charge.

"Mr. Perrot, remember that woman who told the officers to put us in here? I have the feeling I've seen her before."

"Indeed, you have—many times, actually," Mr. Perrot said, sitting up straighter in his chair. "That is Valerie."

"Valerie?" It took Logan a moment to make the connection. Then his eyes widened. "Valerie? You mean, that's your *daughter*?" He rose to his feet and attempted to look out the window. The officer on the other side gave him a stern look and motioned for him to step away from the door.

"The one and the same," Mr. Perrot replied.

"What happened to her glasses? Her short hair? Her braces?" Logan rattled off a description of Valerie's appearance the last time he'd seen her, about fifteen years ago. Now Valerie stood a slender five-foot-eight, just a few inches shorter than Logan. Her long brown hair was tied back, and she looked very professional in her tan pants and matching jacket. "When did she start looking like—like—well, like that?"

"Yes, I suppose it has been many years since the two of you have seen each other," Mr. Perrot said. "Much has happened in that time, including her becoming a well-respected agent at the WCF."

Logan still could not believe it. He tried to sneak another peek at her as he spoke. "That's good news for us, right? She'll get all this cleared up, and we'll be on our way." He could see that Mr. Perrot didn't share his sense of relief. In fact, he seemed a bit uneasy. "You don't seem happy to see her."

"It is not that I am not happy to see her," Mr. Perrot said. "I am certain that she will clear all of this up for us."

"Then what's the problem?"

"Her work has taken her into some very dangerous situations before," Mr. Perrot explained. "However, I fear that she has never yet encountered the likes of Andrea and Simon. Evil and cunning to this degree are rare. I would have liked to keep her out of any criminal investigation involving them."

"You just told me we were all brought into this for a reason, didn't you?" Logan reminded him. "Maybe she should know what it is she's been brought into."

Mr. Perrot was about to reply, when the door opened and Valerie herself walked in. "Sit down," she said, with little patience in her voice. She took off her tan blazer, revealing a holstered Smith & Wesson M&P40 strapped around her chest. Then she tossed a yellow file marked "Confidential" onto the table. She placed both hands on the edge of the table and addressed Mr. Perrot first. "Dad, what are you doing here, and why is Logan with you?"

She remembers me, Logan thought, as his memory of her face now became clearer. "Hey—hi, Valerie," he said awkwardly.

She turned and stared at him. Her stoic expression did not change. Logan had seen that look in her light brown eyes before. A flood of memories came to him as he remembered the two of them growing up together, their families spending holidays and special occasions at each other's home. *She's not that awkward girl in glasses anymore.*

Mr. Perrot tried to speak, but Valerie wasn't in a listening mood. "Do you know how much trouble the two of you are in?" she said, taking a seat. "Four people died upstairs last night, and you two just might become the prime suspects."

"Suspects!" Logan said, shocked. "We didn't do anything. We were both in New Chicago until we got on that flight this afternoon. If you let me have my PCD, I'll show you the tickets."

"We're looking at your PCD right now," Valerie said.

"Good, then you'll see we aren't lying."

"What we're trying to say, dear," Mr. Perrot said, "is that we have information that we believe will be useful to you during this investigation."

There was a knock on the door, and a man's face appeared in the window.

"Dad, I don't have time right now for one of your stories. That's my boss out there, and I bet he wants to know if you and Logan represent the quick and easy resolution of this case."

"I assure you it wasn't us," Mr. Perrot calmly said. "You know that I am and always have been a great supporter of the Satraya movement. When I heard the shocking news of Cynthia's murder, I felt an obligation to provide some vital facts."

"So you and Logan hopped on a plane and flew a thousand miles? Why didn't you just call, Dad?"

"Well, our information is a bit complex," Mr. Perrot replied. "And I thought you were working in Spain on a case. So Logan was kind enough to accompany an old man on a journey. We thought that a face-to-face meeting with the authorities would best serve our purpose."

"I see. And what purpose would that be?"

"To assist with the case, of course," he replied. Valerie gave her father a look as if she couldn't believe it. And then another as if she could.

"I *was* working on a case in Spain," she said in frustration as she stood up. "But they pulled me to work on this one. I arrived just a few hours ago, and I'm still trying to understand what the hell happened here. And how—"

Before she could continue, a portly older man entered the room carrying Logan's backpack and his PCD. "They check out, Chief," he said. "The tickets on the PCD were bought today and match up with the airport security data. We have surveillance that shows both of them getting on a plane in New Chicago earlier this afternoon."

"Thanks, Charlie," Valerie said with a note of relief, as she took the backpack and PCD from him. "As for the two of you," she continued, her annoyed demeanor quickly returning as she addressed Logan and Mr. Perrot, "I am still trying to comprehend how you got into this building without anyone seeing you."

"We used the secret tunnel," Logan blurted out as Mr. Perrot placed his hand on his shoulder, trying to forestall his response.

"The secret tunnel?" Valerie looked at him incredulously.

"Yeah," Logan said. "We waltzed in here using the tunnel."

"Well, you see," Mr. Perrot interrupted, "that is part of the important information that Logan and I would like to share with you. If you would allow us to explain, we have quite an intriguing tale to relay."

"Well," Valerie said, as she slid Logan's backpack and PCD over to him. "Why don't you show me just how you waltzed in here, then?"

She escorted them out of the room, and they waited a moment while she spoke to her superior, who didn't look happy with what she was telling him. Once the brief conversation was over, Valerie was joined by the portly man wearing a rumpled gray suit and a white shirt with a poorly knotted blue tie. She introduced him to Logan and Mr. Perrot as her trusted partner, WCF agent Charlie Baker. The four of them walked downstairs to the basement storage room.

"All right, Dad," Valerie said matter-of-factly. "Where's the tunnel?"

Mr. Perrot walked over to the bookshelf and pulled it open as far as the rusty hinges would allow.

"Really? Just like that?" A dumbfounded Charlie walked over and examined the hidden door. "How did you know about this, sir?"

Mr. Perrot did not answer; he merely looked at his daughter.

"We'll get to the bottom of that shortly," Valerie said. "But first, let's get the crime-scene team down here to do their thing."

"Come on," Logan said enthusiastically, about to enter the tunnel. "I'll show you the ladder we climbed down."

"Not so fast." Valerie grabbed his arm. "We need to let the site investigators go in first so they can collect evidence. It's likely the two of you already contaminated the scene."

Two investigators dressed in loose-fitting white jumpsuits entered the room and started setting up their equipment. They carefully removed the door, opening a clear path to the tunnel, and set up two bright lamps by the doorway. Valerie and Charlie, along with Logan and Mr. Perrot, watched as the investigators entered the tunnel and began processing it for evidence.

"Looks like we have three sets of footprints in the dust here," one of the investigators called out. "Two large pairs of shoes, probably belonging to males, and another smaller pair. Looks like they were left by a pair of high heels."

"Who else was with you?" Valerie asked her father and Logan.

"No one," Logan answered.

"It was just the two of us," Mr. Perrot confirmed. "I assure you."

"Take off your shoes."

Logan and Mr. Perrot handed their shoes to Charlie, who took them to the investigators.

"Should we tell her about the box?" Logan whispered to Mr. Perrot.

"No, not at the moment," Mr. Perrot replied. "I would like to examine its contents before we do so."

"They're a match," the investigator called out from the tunnel, re-emerging with the shoes. "These two pairs match the two sets of larger prints—all the prints are fresh. The third set of prints appears to have been made by a female." He brought up an image on his PCD. "Central Lab has identified the shoes as Pierre Masu—women's size six and a half."

"Pierre Masu." Valerie recognized the name. "That's not a cheap brand."

"There wasn't anyone else with us when we came through the tunnel," Logan said again. "Just me and your father."

The investigator went back to work in the tunnel, and while Charlie took a call on his PCD, Valerie pulled her father and Logan aside. "Who else knew about this tunnel?" she asked.

Logan and Mr. Perrot remained awkwardly silent.

"Right—that's part of the story you need to tell me. Well, now would be a good time to start."

15

All desire to be free. The question you must ask is, what will you risk to ensure that freedom?
—THE CHRONICLES OF SATRAYA

CHÂTEAU DUGAN, SWISS ALPS, 4:00 A.M. LOCAL TIME,
5 DAYS UNTIL FREEDOM DAY

The old dungeon under Château Dugan had changed little since the Dark Ages. Its stone walls and iron doors were an intimidating sight for even the bravest souls. Eight rooms surrounded a large common area, where a reputedly bottomless well had emitted a foul odor for as long as anyone could remember. The only modern convenience in the dungeon was electricity. In keeping with the dungeon's original purpose, it had been installed to facilitate punishment.

Macliv had been plying his craft in one of the rooms for many hours now. "You really should tell Mr. Simon what he wants to know," he advised the badly bruised man who sat naked, chained to a metal chair. On the walls surrounding him were the futile etchings of past visitors.

As it was very hot in the dungeon, Macliv had removed his shirt, revealing a full tribal tattoo that ran from his upper neck all the way down the right side of his torso and his right arm, ending at his wrist.

Buckets of salt water sat ready to wash the blood off the prisoner's body.

The chamber door swung open. "Macliv, how is your interrogation progressing?" Simon asked as he entered.

Macliv shook his head and slapped the prisoner on the side of his face. Simon walked over and bent down so that he was face-to-face with him.

"You are Lokesh Sarin, the son of Deya Sarin, are you not? The woman who found a set of the *Chronicles* in the Ganges River?"

"Yes," Lokesh responded. "Deya was my mother."

"Excellent. See how easy this is, Macliv," Simon said, turning to the torturer. "You just have to ask the right questions." He looked back at the battered young man and smiled. "Before your mother died, she had in her possession a copy of *The Chronicles of Satraya*, is that right?"

"Yes," he said.

"Once again, excellent. I need to know where I can find those books."

"I don't know," the prisoner said, a response that quickly earned him another blow to the back of his head. "I am telling you the truth. No one knows what she did with the books before she drowned in the river eighteen months ago. She must have taken them with her—she took them everywhere. Her boat capsized, and the books must have been lost."

"I am told she didn't have them at the time," Simon said with certainty. "Macliv, did Deya have the books with her when she drowned?"

"Not that I saw," Macliv said matter-of-factly.

"See, she didn't have them," Simon repeated. "I tried for some time to buy the books from her. I proposed to pay her more money than she and your father could ever amass in their lifetimes. But she refused to consider any of my offers. Now, we need to know where those books are. So I ask again, where are the *Chronicles*?"

"You killed my mother!" Lokesh shouted, as he struggled to break free of his bindings. "Even if I knew where the books were, I would never tell you. She would never want you to have them!" He spit into the air, the chains making a loud clanking sound against the metal chair as he struggled to break free.

Simon looked at Macliv, who was now standing in the corner of the room, cutting an apple with a very sharp knife. Simon took a small box from his jacket pocket. "Macliv, I want to show you a special gift from Dr. Malikei. Did you know that your brain works harder when you lie than when you tell the truth? It's a fact. People lie because they fear telling the truth. They believe that they will get punished or that they will hurt someone else by their admission. Our doctor has created a serum that deadens the amygdala region of the brain, thus eliminating fear. When a person is no longer afraid, he no longer needs to lie."

"It's like a truth serum," Macliv said.

"It is more than that," Simon said. "Militaries around the world would love to get their hands on this serum. They could create the perfect soldier, one without fear. But the doctor still has some work to do on it." He took a syringe in the shape of a small handgun from the box and inserted a capsule containing a red liquid. "Currently, it is a one-way trip, and the patient doesn't last very long." He put the syringe to Deya's son's forehead. "This is only going to hurt for a second," he said, before pulling the trigger.

The young man let out a bloodcurdling scream and slumped forward in the chair.

Macliv stopped eating his apple. "How long will it take to work?"

"Only a few moments," Simon answered. "His body will not resist. He is in pain; he will welcome the relief from fear. The serum also contains a muscle relaxant that will eliminate any desire to struggle physically." Simon put the syringe back in the box and put the box back in his jacket pocket. "See, it is already beginning to work," he observed, as the prisoner sat up, his eyes fluttering open. "Go ahead, Macliv. Ask him his PCD access code. He will gladly tell you now."

"What is your PCD access code?"

"LS498," the prisoner instantly answered.

"This is a most wonderful drug—one of the doctor's finest, I have to say." Simon leaned down so that his face was level with the prisoner's. "Now, let's get on with this. What did your mother do with her copy of *The Chronicles of Satraya?*"

"No one knows," Lokesh answered.

"Someone must know," Simon insisted. "She must have told someone."

"Not even my father knows," Lokesh answered. "He thinks that she must have hidden them."

"Where would she hide them?"

"I don't know."

"Does your father know?"

Lokesh did not answer this question.

Simon paused and thought about how to proceed. He believed Deya's son was indeed stating the truth, but Deya had to have left a clue. Simon just had to ask the boy the right questions. He thought a moment longer, then said, "What was the last thing your mother said to you before she went on her trip?"

"She told me that she loved us," Lokesh answered.

"Did she give you anything?"

"She wrote us a letter."

"What did the letter say?"

Lokesh's eyes closed, and his head fell forward.

Simon slapped him across the face to revive him and repeated the question. "What did the letter say?"

"She told us to take care of the garden." Lokesh could barely remain conscious, and his head kept slumping forward. "She told us to make sure that the pond was always filled with water."

"What else did the letter say?"

"Nothing else." Lokesh's answer was barely audible.

"Where is the letter now?" Simon asked. Then, more loudly, "Where is it?"

"I threw it away," Lokesh mumbled.

"What was so special about the garden?" Simon pressed.

"Nothing anymore." Lokesh was fading in and out of consciousness. "Once it was beautiful, but my parents let it grow wild after my father got sick."

Simon paused again. *Why would Deya want her family to tend to a garden that she herself had ignored?* His interest was piqued. "And what about this pond—why is the pond so special?"

There was no answer. Simon hit Lokesh again and shook him, but it was too late. Lokesh had died, his one-way trip ended. Frustrated, Simon kicked over a bucket of water. He paced the room for a few moments. "Looks like I'll have to go to India and see this garden for myself."

Macliv nodded. "What should I do with the body?"

"Let him visit the bottom of the well," Simon said coldly. "And then join me upstairs. You will be going with me."

16

What we have written, what we present to you with our simple words, is philosophy. It is not yet Truth to you. It is not yet Wisdom to you. But if you embrace our words sincerely, an experience will unfold for you, and then our philosophy will become your Truth and your Wisdom.

—THE CHRONICLES OF SATRAYA

WASHINGTON D.C., 9:00 P.M. LOCAL TIME,
5 DAYS UNTIL FREEDOM DAY

Mr. Perrot and Logan entered Valerie's top-floor apartment in a newly constructed eight-story building in the Glover Park district, a short cab ride from the Council of Satraya offices.

"This apartment is immaculate," Logan said. "There's not one thing out of place."

It was true. From the living room to the kitchen and the small dining room, everything was sparkling clean. Off the living room was a set of French doors that led to a balcony overlooking a portion of Washington.

"Yes, my daughter is a rather organized and precise young lady," Mr. Perrot replied, escorting Logan into the den. "I suppose it is one of the reasons she is such a splendid agent."

"And I see she loves Asian design," Logan said. He walked over to a hand-painted Mandarin cabinet standing in the corner of the room.

"I knew she went into police work, but I didn't know she was so successful. Not that I'm surprised—she always ordered me around when we were kids."

"Probably practice for her current job. She's a lead investigator, you know." Mr. Perrot took a seat in a high-backed chair while Logan sat on the couch. Each took a deep breath of relief, acknowledging the events of the day with a smile and some giddy laughter born of fatigue. "Seems as if fate was on our side today, bringing in my daughter to salvage our adventure."

"Yes," Logan agreed. "But that was a bit too close."

They exchanged another deep sigh. Then Mr. Perrot leaned forward in his chair. "Now," he said, "let's have a closer look at that box."

Logan nodded. He took the box from his backpack and placed it on the coffee table between them. The unassuming tin box had a simple latch that secured the lid. Logan wiped the dirt off it.

"Go ahead, my boy. Open it."

Logan obliged, slowly unhooking the brass latch. Mr. Perrot watched intently, as Logan removed the items from the box and placed them gently on the table. A blue candle, a lock of hair in a plastic bag, and a roll of papers bound only with a piece of string lay before them. "That's it," Logan said, as he closed the lid and set the box aside. "What do you make of it?"

"Interesting—only three items." Mr. Perrot picked up the blue candle; it was about ten inches long and one inch in diameter. The wick was burnt, and there was melted wax along the side. "This candle has been lit," he said.

Logan was looking at the lock of black hair. "Why would someone seal a lock of hair into a small plastic bag?"

"Peculiar, indeed," Mr. Perrot agreed, as he set the candle down and picked up the roll of papers. "Camden didn't have black hair and neither did Cassandra."

Logan set the bag down and took the papers from Mr. Perrot. He loosened the string, and the papers unrolled. Logan set them on the table and pressed them flat with the palms of his hands. "It appears as if they were ripped out of a book. The edges are torn." He examined the papers more closely. "The writing looks similar to Camden Ford's in the note that fell out of the book at the auction. I wonder if the wax on it came from this blue candle."

Mr. Perrot looked at the pages as Logan handed them to him. "Yes, the wax of the candle does look similar. And the handwriting is familiar. I believe these are pages from Camden's journal."

"How can you be sure?"

"By the mark in the upper right corner." Mr. Perrot pointed to a little hand-drawn symbol.

"I often used to watch Camden write his entries. Every time he wrote on a new page, he drew that symbol on the upper right-hand corner. When I asked him what it meant, he refused to say, and I didn't push it. I wonder where his journal is now." Mr. Perrot glanced at all the pages, confirming that they bore the mark. "I always loved sitting back and having a good story read to me," he said, as he handed the pages back to Logan with a smile.

"This is interesting," Logan remarked, quickly flipping through them. "Most of the pages are dated 2035, but this one page is dated 2037."

"That's the year the Council split."

Logan nodded. "Something tells me to start with that one." He began reading aloud.

November 21, 2037. I fear that this will be my last entry for some time. I have written a letter to Baté, but the opportunity has not arisen for me to present it. It would be so much better if I could meet with him, but I don't have a choice in the matter. I never did. The Council has broken up, and we need to leave. Robert is coming with us. I said good-bye to Deya and Madu last night. They both have their own plans. I hope they will be safe.

Logan stopped his reading. "Who is Robert?" he asked.

"Robert Tilbo. He was the man Camden rescued from the Forgotten Ones at the safe house, the day he first discovered the *Chronicles*," Mr. Perrot answered. "He served with Camden and Cassandra on the first Council and also disappeared after the splintering."

Logan nodded. *Another disappearance*, he thought. Then he continued to read.

All my fears about Fendral and Andrea were confirmed last night. I overheard them talking in the hallway before the Council meeting. I heard Fendral say that he had figured out a way to restore his family's place in history. It had to do with securing control of the Council. He told Andrea that if his plan worked, the Hitchlords and Benson families would once again rule from the shadows. And he promised she would have a seat next to them.

I took my chance and barged in on their conversation. Then I confronted Fendral with a secret I'd uncovered which I dare not include here. The only move I had left to save the Council was to threaten Fendral with the release of the information. It seemed to work. For the first time ever, I saw fear in his eyes. We both agreed to depart from Washington and leave the Council to Cynthia. I told him directly that should he attempt to influence the Council in any way, I would publicly release his shame and bring an end to the Hitchlords dynasty.

"Sit where you may mind your enemy,
Remember forever their names as if etched into stone.
That which supports you in your vigilance
Will ultimately be your savior."

We are leaving tonight. We are not going to risk our safety by playing any part in Fendral's deadly games.

Logan finished reading the entry and looked up at Mr. Perrot in silence.

"So Camden blackmailed Fendral into leaving the Council," Mr. Perrot mused. "I suspected he knew something about him that the rest of us did not. I wonder if it has anything to do with what Simon and

Andrea are up to at present. If we can find out what it is, perhaps we can use it again."

Logan's mind was elsewhere. "There's that name Baté again," he said. "And what about that strange quote near the end?"

"The quote—I have no recollection of it. It does not come from the *Chronicles*."

Logan turned the page over and saw a short scribbled list on the other side. The name of Hitchlords was at the top, with what seemed to be some members of the Hitchlords lineage underneath it. The names of organizations were written in the margins next to them. Logan read them out loud.

"My knowledge of these organizations is limited," Mr. Perrot said. "I never heard of 'Thule' or 'MJ-12,' but I do remember the 'Federal Reserve.' It was at the center of the financial world prior to the Great Disruption. Everything it attempted to stave off the Financial Reset of 2025 was met with vehement resistance. I dare say if your father was correct, the Hitchlords family was involved with one of the most influential clandestine groups in history. However—" He broke off. "However, none of this ties Simon and Andrea to the murders of the Council members or your parents. Keep reading; perhaps those other pages, from 2035, will provide something for immediate use, maybe even the secret Camden used against Fendral."

July 16, 2035. Freedom Day is coming, and this morning, I took my walk through the park earlier than I usually do. The festival crews were going to arrive at 10:00 A.M. to begin decorating. I wanted to get there when all was still quiet.

"I wonder which park he's talking about," Logan stopped to ask.

"Before the Great Disruption, it was called the Ellipse," Mr. Perrot answered. "But afterward, the circle was completely rebuilt and renamed Compass Park. It was given that name in the hope that people would never lose their direction again. Camden went for walks there every chance he could get, usually in the mornings. I would join him from time to time."

Logan nodded and continued.

I sat on a bench and was looking up at the sky, in a daydream of sorts. I can't recall what I was thinking about. A man sat beside me and asked me a strange question. "If the universe wanted to tell you one thing, what do you think it would be?" I looked at him, not really knowing if or even how I should answer the question. Without waiting for me to answer, he introduced himself as Baté Sisán. He stood, tipped his hat at me, and wished me a good day. He walked away as suddenly as he had arrived. I don't know who this man is, but his question is still haunting me. Maybe I'll see him in the park tomorrow. I plan to go early again.

"There is nothing more from that day," Logan said, as he set the page down. "Here's the next entry."

July 17, 2035. I met him again this morning. Baté. We spoke longer today as we sat on that same park bench. I told him that I had thought about his question but didn't have the answer. He told me the answer would come in time and that it was only for me to know. He is an intriguing man. He knows things about The Chronicles of Satraya *that no one else knows. Insights that I myself have not even thought to ponder. The books have only been distributed for a few years now, yet he knows them and recites their words from memory. He asked me questions about my experience with the blue orb in the forest and then made comments that deepened my understanding of the answers. He is stranger than anyone I have ever met. I can't for the life of me read him. I couldn't even tell you how old he is or what part of the world he's from. His face and eyes are timeless. That is the only way I can describe him.*

I asked him if I would see him in the park tomorrow. He replied, "Only tomorrow can say." And once again, he tipped his hat, wished me a wonderful day, and walked off. I hope he's there tomorrow. As strange as I find him, I feel I need him in my life. Tomorrow can't come soon enough.

"Baté Sisán," Logan mused in a whisper. The name, which he had first read that morning, was beginning to carry more weight.

"Please continue," Mr. Perrot said.

July 18, 2035. After dropping Cassandra off at her violin lesson, I went back to the park. I was not disappointed. Baté was already sitting on the bench when I arrived. We spoke at length today. I had many questions about the Chronicles *and their teachings. Before he answered any of them, he challenged me. He asked if I knew the difference between philosophy and truth. He asked if I knew what wisdom was. He reminded me of the simple verity that was written in the* Chronicles: *Philosophy must be combined with Experience if we desire Wisdom. We must have spoken for hours on this simple subject. I realized very quickly that there was so much more I had to understand about these books.*

Before he left, he asked how I was doing with my work on the Satraya Flame. I asked how he knew about that. He just smiled and asked the question again. I told him that I had reached something of a block. I explained to Baté that each time I focused on the flame, I got this incredibly loud ringing in my ears. The sound is so loud that it distracts me from meditating on the flame, and so I stopped working on it.

Logan paused. There was a strange look on his face, something between understanding and fear. "I think I know that sound," Logan said, half thinking aloud. "It happens to me when I paint. I get this loud ringing noise in my ears, and I can't work anymore. None of the doctors I've gone to can explain it."

Mr. Perrot nodded solemnly. "Perhaps the pages can," he said. "Please. Read on."

Baté explained that the Satraya Flame has many levels and that each level has a secret. He said the flame is only a tool to understand focus and the stilling of the mind. He explained that the ringing I hear indicates that I am reaching a deeper level of mind. He advised me to continue the flame work and embrace the ringing, to allow it to consume me as if I were listening to a magnificent symphony. Embrace it as I would a piece of inspirational music, he said. On the other side,

I would find the next secret of the flame and the next door. Every experience with the flame has purpose. And with that, he stood, tipped his hat, and wished me a wonderful day.

"There is another entry from later that same day," Logan observed.

July 18, 2035. I did as Baté told me this morning. I focused on the flame, and as before, the ringing came, louder than ever. It took me several attempts, but I was finally able to break through. I forced myself to focus beyond the sound. As Baté suggested, I embraced it as music. I don't have words to describe what I saw in the flame. I actually can't even say that it was in the flame. I don't know what happened. I saw things, some good and others bad. It was as if I was actually there.

Without stopping, Logan read on.

July 19, 2035. No Baté this morning. I'll keep focusing on the Satraya Flame.
July 20, 2035. No Baté this morning.
July 21, 2035. No Baté this morning. But my work with the flame is getting easier and easier. Today is Freedom Day. I will be spending all day with Cassandra and the rest of the Council at Compass Park. The celebration this year is going to be large.
July 22, 2035. Yesterday's Freedom Day was wonderful. Cassandra looked stunning at the evening dance. When I returned to the park this morning, once again Baté was not there. As mysteriously as he arrived in my life, he has disappeared. But I owe him a great deal of thanks. The Satraya Flame has become wisdom to me and no longer a philosophy. I am beginning to experience it, as he promised I would.

"Strange." Logan flipped through the remaining sheets. "The next entry is months later."

November 10, 2035. He was there again after all these months. Baté. He was in the park feeding some pigeons. I was so excited to see him I gave him a hug. He asked me straightaway about my Satraya Flame work. I told him that

I had done as he said, and it worked. I described my experiences and what was happening to me in the deeper levels of the flame. He smiled and said, "Is not truth wonderful?" He then did something I did not expect. He invited me to come visit him at the home he is renting. I am to go on the night of the 12th. He told me that he wanted to show me something. A "deeper secret" of the flame, as he put it. I couldn't refuse.

Logan set the page on the table. "And here is the last one," he said.

November 13, 2035. I spent last night with Baté, and it changed my life. I am sworn to secrecy, but Baté told me that I could write about it in my journal. He said that one day, it might prove useful. How he knew about my journal I do not know, nor did I ask.

We both sat in the center of a small room he had prepared. He'd moved all the furniture off to the side and cleared the middle of the room. Between us, he placed a strange candle. Actually, it was two blue candles attached by a bit of melted wax. He told me I had progressed enough in flame work that it was time for me to experience a deeper truth. He said the technique was called the Manas Mantr, or Spirit Talk. He said this would be the last time I would physically see him, but if I desired, we could communicate through the flame. He didn't tell me why this would be our last physical meeting.

He told me that one day, when my mind was sufficiently developed, I would no longer need the support of the physical flame and would be able to rely strictly on the discipline of my mind, but until that time, the candle would be our link. He showed me a hand-drawn picture of a small room. It looked like an old study with a small desk at the center and books of all kinds on the shelves. He instructed me to bring up the image of the room and hold it in my mind when I had reached a certain place during my flame meditation. I asked what would happen, and he said not to worry about it. Just maintain the focus, and I would know what to do when it happened.

Baté explained that the physics of where I was about to go were very different from here. He handed me a blank piece of paper and a pen. He told me to write down any questions I had and to hold the paper in my hand as I focused on the flame. He further explained that what I had with me now was what I would have when I got there. None of it really made sense to me, but I did as he instructed and wrote down the only question I could ask.

Without further discussion, Baté struck a match and lit the wicks of both candles. He told me to focus on the flame to the right while he focused on the other. I don't know how long we sat there. As I had practiced, I went beyond the ringing sound that had stopped me before. I brought my mind to a quiet place. All I remember from that point is that when I started to focus on the picture of the room that Baté had drawn for me, the sketch in my mind suddenly became real. It was as if I was actually there. The desk became real; the books on the shelves became real. I could open the books and read them. Everything was tangible; it was much more than a dream. It was as if I had left this place and gone somewhere else.

The surface of the desk was empty, except for a single piece of paper with some writing on it. I bent over and read what it said. "What is the question that you hold in your hand?" I had almost forgotten why I was there. I looked on the desk for a pen but didn't find one. But then I remembered that I had already written my question, and when I looked at my hand, there was the piece of paper I'd written it on. Somehow the paper had come with me to this strange place. I laid the paper on the desk, and in a split second, I found myself back in Baté's house, sitting on the floor. One of the candles was still burning. The other was gone. So was Baté. I have so many questions.

Mr. Perrot picked up the blue candle and inspected it, turning it over in his hand. "This must be the candle he is describing." He pointed out some small pieces of melted wax stuck to it, the places where it was presumably attached to the other candle.

"But what are we supposed to do with all of this?" Logan asked. "There was nothing more about Fendral's secret."

"No, maybe not directly," Mr. Perrot said, "but we have to be pragmatic. There is a reason Camden tore these particular pages from his journal and hid them. There is also a reason for his leading us to find them. Perhaps he wants to take us further. After all, you just said you hear the same ringing sound he did. Maybe, Logan, maybe you must be the one to follow in his footsteps."

Logan stared at Mr. Perrot in silence. He knew what his old friend was suggesting. But could he do it? Could he put his doubts and his fears aside? Could he do this for his parents? He set down the last journal page and put the pages back in order. "We're going to need a match," he said.

17

May this be the last moment of your fears.
May this be the last moment of your doubts.
May this be the last moment of your uncertainties.
May this be the first moment of your future.

—THE CHRONICLES OF SATRAYA

WASHINGTON, D.C., 10:20 P.M. LOCAL TIME,
5 DAYS UNTIL FREEDOM DAY

Mr. Perrot and Logan rearranged the furniture in Valerie's den. They pushed the couch, the table, and the rest of the furniture off to the side. Logan took out a sheet of paper from his backpack and, after consulting with Mr. Perrot, wrote a question on it. Then Mr. Perrot dimmed the lights, and Logan sat on the floor in the center of the room. Mr. Perrot found a candleholder, placed the blue candle in it, and handed it to Logan.

"How do we know this is going to work?" Logan asked.

"I have no evidence to support it and none to discount it," Mr. Perrot answered. "But that is what faith is all about."

Logan nodded.

"To start, the *Chronicles* say to place the candle about an arm's length away from you, with the flame at about eye level."

Logan took the candle and did as Mr. Perrot instructed. "Sounds like you've done this before."

"Camden once instructed a group of us about the flame. I worked on it from time to time through the years," Mr. Perrot said. "I made some progress but not to the degree that Camden seemingly accomplished. You, on the other hand, may have progressed to a key point. Even though you never focused on a candle, perhaps focusing on all the artwork you have done sufficiently advanced your powers of concentration. It is written in the *Chronicles* that all of the techniques described are just tools. The most important thing is to learn how to silence our chattering minds. I wonder if you didn't just find a different tool."

"I never really embraced the fundamentals taught by the *Chronicles* like my parents wished," Logan admitted. "But as you said, maybe painting was my tool."

"Let us hope so," Mr. Perrot said. "Now, remember what Camden wrote. If the ringing sound starts, you have to keep focusing and keep going. Are you ready?"

"Wait," Logan said. "Let me look at the drawing of the study again. I want to make sure I can remember what the room looks like." Mr. Perrot handed him the sheet with the drawing. Logan opened and closed his eyes a few times, ensuring that the layout was etched in his mind. "OK. I think I've got it."

"Do you have the sheet of paper with our question?" Logan held up the folded sheet. Mr. Perrot lit the candle.

The only light in the apartment came from the candle. To Logan, Mr. Perrot soon appeared to be nothing more than a shadow. The candle flame crackled. Logan tried to relax, taking deep breaths and exhaling slowly. His mind was racing as he recalled the extraordinary events of the day: uncovering the secret tunnel, locating the hidden box, being apprehended by the police, seeing Valerie, and all he'd learned from reading the torn-out pages of Camden Ford's journal. He continued to stare at the flame, but the harder he concentrated on it, the louder his mind-chatter became. The flame was dancing like an anxious child as the minutes slowly passed. Logan could see the shadowed image of

Mr. Perrot on the couch, and he heard the ticking of a clock that was hanging on the wall.

"I don't think I'm getting it," Logan said out loud, adjusting his posture and flexing his shoulders.

"You have to hold still, fight any desire to move," Mr. Perrot whispered. "Camden said to start by focusing on something we enjoyed doing or some task we were good at performing. He told us it would help slow down our minds and help block out the chatter."

Logan readjusted until he found a more comfortable position. He scanned his memories for a pleasant moment and began to focus on a day when he was teaching his children how to paint. It was a scene of the ocean. He remembered how he'd taught them to draw the waves and sketch the sky with many floating clouds. He remembered his daughter, Jamie, coloring in her first whale and his son, Jordan, drawing a submarine. As Mr. Perrot predicted, Logan was feeling more relaxed, his mind clearing. The flame, which had been frantically moving to and fro, settled down before his eyes. His mind was finding a peaceful place, and the flame was matching it.

Mr. Perrot sat perfectly still, watching Logan as he stopped squirming, as his breathing slowed, with his chest expanding and contracting less often. Several long moments passed. Mr. Perrot also started to focus on the flame, trying to recreate his focus from long ago. But then, suddenly Logan began to shake his head. The calm was broken. Logan rubbed his ears fiercely.

"What's wrong?" Mr. Perrot asked as he jolted back from his own meditation.

"The ringing is back, worse than ever. It's almost unbearable."

Mr. Perrot sighed. "And for a moment there, it looked like you had achieved it."

"Things got better once I started focusing on my children. But . . ." Logan looked up and braced himself with determination. "Let's try again. I doubt even the great Camden Ford got it the first time."

"Maybe you can do as Baté instructed," Mr. Perrot suggested. "Allow yourself into the sound. Remember to embrace it as if it were a piece of music."

"Right—a piece of music."

Logan once again adjusted his body and began to refocus on the burning flame. It did not take very long for the ringing to start again. He remained steadfast this time, trying not to move. The more he attempted to dismiss the ringing, the louder it became. *Embrace it like music,* he thought. *Like music . . .* He brought to his mind the melody of a lullaby his mother used to sing to him. The ringing got louder, but so did the melody he was remembering. Soon the ringing sounded like a high-pitched whistle. He was fighting and struggling, caught up in a battle between the whistle and the song. It was becoming more and more unbearable, more and more impossible. But his eyes remained fixed on the flame, ever on the flame. He was about to give up, when the ringing suddenly stopped, the ghostly image of Mr. Perrot disappeared, and the slowly wavering flame faded into blackness.

18

Empty space exists because you believe it is real. What if the space
between your assumptions was filled with real and tangible things?
—THE CHRONICLES OF SATRAYA

WASHINGTON, D.C., 10:50 P.M. LOCAL TIME,
5 DAYS UNTIL FREEDOM DAY

"We are standing outside the Council of Satraya offices," a reporter
announced in a live broadcast. "Late last night, three Council members
and a young woman identified as the niece of one of the members
were found dead. Details are still limited at this time, but a source has
told us that the deaths are being investigated as homicides. The source,
who did not want to be identified, also confirmed that lead investigator
Valerie Perrot of the World Crime Federation has been assigned to this
high-profile case. Ms. Perrot began her meteoric rise in the WCF six
years ago, when she cracked the Double-R kidnapping case involving
six-year-old twin sisters in a suburb of New Chicago. Last year, in a
raid she coordinated and led, she took down a global prostitution cartel
based in Singapore. Ms. Perrot has been unavailable for comment, but
we expect to hear from her shortly.

"People are asking if the killings at the Council offices were politically motivated. One of the victims, Cynthia Brown, the head of the
Council, was no stranger to controversy. Some security professionals

are speculating about the involvement of the Sentinel Coterie, a radical organization that has been at odds with the Council of Satraya for many years. The Sentinel Coterie has accused the Council of slowing down progress and denying society its right to advancement. A Coterie spokesman told me today that while they disagreed with Ms. Brown on a variety of issues, the Coterie does not condone the use of force.

"Many are asking if this tragedy will mark the end of the Council of Satraya. Sadly and ironically, Freedom Day, a day on which we celebrate freedom and peace, is only five days away. Now, back to you in the studio and an update on the streak of mysterious disappearances in the southern region of the former U.S."

Valerie clicked off the 3-D image of the news broadcast being projected from her PCD.

"Hey, don't you want to keep watching?" Charlie teased with a smile. "You're a super sleuth!"

"No," Valerie grumbled. "Those reporters just make our jobs harder."

Valerie and Charlie were still in the basement of the Council of Satraya offices. More site investigators had arrived and joined the others who were still processing the newly discovered tunnel. "Anything from the Central Crime Lab on cause of death?" Valerie asked.

"Nothing yet," Charlie said. "They said there are no apparent wounds on the bodies."

"Let's go over the time line again."

Charlie brought his notes up on his PCD and relayed the victims' activities from the night before. Valerie was most interested in the HoloPad malfunction in New Chicago at 9:45 P.M. Central time, which ended Cynthia Brown's participation in the auction, and the cleaning crew's discovery of the victims' bodies in the second-floor meeting room of the Council building at approximately 12:10 the next morning.

"Do we have any video of the auction in New Chicago?" Valerie asked.

"We sure do." Valerie moved closer to Charlie as he brought up the video feed. "The auction was covered by the local press. I didn't see much when I looked at it earlier. The camera angle is from the back of the hall facing the auctioneer's podium." Charlie played with the video until he got to the part where the *Chronicles* was up for bidding.

"Stop—back it up," Valerie said. "Looks like this is where Cynthia starts to bid on the books. And is that who I think it is?"

"Yep," Charlie responded. "That's Andrea Montavon."

"I haven't heard her name in a long time," said Valerie. "She is certainly a beautiful woman." She stared at the image for a moment. "Any other bidders for the books?"

"We are getting a list from the auction house." Charlie resumed the video, and they watched the events unfold, intently looking for meaningful details. The camera panned the crowd as the bidding intensified. "I didn't notice that before," said Charlie, as he suddenly paused the video and backed it up a few frames. "Chief, isn't that your friend Logan?" Charlie zoomed in on the image.

Valerie groaned. "Looks like Logan and my father have a bit more to explain than just the tunnel."

Charlie resumed the video. A few seconds later, Valerie gasped at the flash of green light, the loud noise, and the sound of people screaming.

"We have our team in New Chicago checking out the data traces from the HoloPad to see what caused the malfunction and that flash," Charlie said.

Valerie stood pensively for a few moments. "Does this office building have any security cameras?"

"There are three," Charlie said. "One at the front door, one at the back entrance, and one outside the meeting room where we found the bodies. But I've looked at their files and didn't see anything interesting. Once the auction started, we didn't see anyone go in or out."

"Bring up the files from the camera outside the meeting room," Valerie said. "Can you put the two videos up side-by-side? Line them up so they start two minutes before Cynthia disappears. And roll slowly."

With a few strokes on his PCD, Charlie brought up the surveillance video outside the meeting room and projected it next to the video of the auction. "Looking for anything in particular?" he asked, as he started them rolling.

Valerie was silent for a minute, then said, "Pause it—right now! Let's move it frame by frame. Did you see that?"

"See what?"

"Back up a few frames, and look at the closed door of the meeting room. See there—at the exact moment that Cynthia's image disappears in a green flash in New Chicago, there is a simultaneous flash of green light coming from under the door." Valerie continued to advance and rewind the frame so that Charlie could see what she was describing. "So the question is what caused the green light. The door was closed the whole time, and no one came in or went out."

"Whatever caused the light was probably already in that room when they arrived," Charlie said.

"Or one of them brought it in with them," Valerie added. "Knowingly or unknowingly."

"Hey!" a voice called out. "We have something over here."

Charlie shut down his PCD, and he and Valerie walked over to an investigator standing by a desk a meter or so from the tunnel's entrance.

The investigator spoke quickly. "There's a strange burn mark on the top of this desk. Looks like something really hot was placed on it. It must have been recent—you can still smell the odor of scorched wood if you get real close."

"Whatever it was, it certainly left a strangely shaped mark," Valerie said, as Charlie took a picture of it with his PCD. The mark was three concentric circles with a cross in the middle.

"Any idea what caused the burn?" Charlie asked.

The investigator shook his head. "But check this out." He pointed to the ceiling. There was a hole in it, about one centimeter in diameter. "The hole goes up into the conference room where we found the victims."

"Let us know what you find," Valerie said, turning back to Charlie. "What about the Federation banquet—do we have any video of it?"

Charlie nodded and brought up a projection of the hall. "The press was all over the event. I'll start it with Cynthia's speech."

"Isn't that the head of the Sentinel Coterie sitting at that table?" Valerie asked as the video started.

"The one and only Mr. Randolph Fenquist," Charlie answered.

"The press may be right on this one," Valerie said. "We need to bring him in for questioning."

"We'll try," Charlie said. "Usually, when we try to speak to anyone in that group, they lawyer up. But I'll get someone to check them out."

The video continued to roll, now to Cynthia's speech. "Who's that girl at the side of the stage hugging Cynthia?"

"That is Monique Sato, Cynthia's personal assistant," Charlie answered. "She stayed at the banquet after the speeches. Witnesses said that Cynthia asked her to remain there to assist the other Council members as they met with the muckety-mucks." Charlie gave a short laugh. Then he switched to another camera feed. "Here is where Cynthia and the three others leave the hall. That's the last we see of her until the auction."

"Stay with Monique," Valerie ordered. They watched as she walked over to an older man with long, stringy brown hair and started talking to him. It was Randolph Fenquist.

"Why is Monique talking to the leader of the Sentinel Coterie?" Valerie asked. "What in the world could the assistant to the leader of the Council of Satraya possibly have to say to him?"

"Well, it's a political banquet. Everyone's your friend. Wait—what's he giving to her?"

"Pause the video," Valerie said. She and Charlie both tried to see what Fenquist had handed Monique, but she put it into her purse so quickly it was hard to tell. Charlie tried to adjust and pane the video but to no avail.

Something else had caught Valerie's eye, though. She zoomed in on the lower part of Monique's image, then angled her head a moment to examine it. Valerie smiled. "Look at her shoes. They're Pierre Masus." Charlie gave her a blank look. "The same brand of shoe that left the prints in the tunnel. Charlie, I think we've found our number one suspect."

Charlie gave an admiring nod. "And I bet you she's working for Randolph Fenquist."

19

What are you willing to do with what you know?
—THE CHRONICLES OF SATRAYA

WASHINGTON, D.C., 11:55 P.M. LOCAL TIME,
5 DAYS UNTIL FREEDOM DAY

Logan reached out and attempted to grab one of the many iridescent clouds that were floating by him. The ringing sound in his ears had stopped. He felt as if he were standing in the middle of a field in the frosty stillness of winter when a heavy snowfall hindered one's vision. No two clouds were the same, each boasting its own color, shape, and size. A soothing electrical current entered Logan's body as his hand passed through the clouds, as if he were a ghost walking through a wall. No matter how hard he tried to grasp a cloud, it would slip through his fingers and float away. A soft crackling sound came as the clouds, which were traveling in many directions, passed through one another. *Where am I?* Logan thought. *What is this place?* The clouds faded away, and the crackling sound diminished.

Logan found himself in the familiar restoration room of the museum where he worked. He was standing in front of the Michelangelo fresco that he was restoring. He looked closer at the space between the finger of God and the finger of Adam; there seemed to be some kind of static electrical discharge passing between them. It was like watching a lightning storm disturbing a once-peaceful prairie. Suddenly, the faces of the angels surrounding the image of God began to change. Thorny vines grew up around their heads. Thick old iron collars with broken chains materialized around their necks. The thorns continued to grow, piercing the angels' skin, causing them to bleed profusely. The largest and heaviest collar of all appeared around the neck of God. Eventually, the entire image of God himself began to blur into a pool of blood. Only the image of Adam remained untouched. But the bloodied finger of God could not reach him. As Logan stepped forward and reached out to touch the painting, to determine whether what he was seeing was actually blood, the painting disappeared, and the restoration room faded.

Logan's extended finger was now touching wallpaper that was peeling off a plaster wall. He retracted his finger and quickly spun around to view his surroundings. He was in an old Victorian-style room with a large four-poster bed. He was not familiar with this place. A hooked rug covered a good part of the wood floor, and a fireplace occupied a corner of the room, its ornate mantel barren. The antique chair in front of the fireplace was pockmarked from sparks and embers. A strong wind blew through the room, seemingly coming from nowhere.

Logan moved to a set of heavy drapes that were drawn. He pulled them open and saw two iron-barred windows that looked out only on darkness. Logan grabbed the bars and pulled on them, trying to remove them, but he couldn't. He felt trapped. Panic rose in him as he looked around the room, which seemed to be getting smaller and closing in on him. With one last effort, he pulled on the bars with all his strength.

He fell backward and landed heavily on a dirt path. Wherever he was now, it was sunny and extremely hot. He quickly rose to his feet and found that he was standing about thirty meters away from what appeared to be a Buddhist monastery. There was no one else in sight, so he walked down the dirt pathway leading to the entrance of the temple. Inside, two monks were working on a mandala, carefully pouring dark sand onto the ground. They didn't seem to notice Logan as he walked around them. They were completely focused on their task. Logan tried to speak to them, but they seemed deaf to the sound of his voice. He paused and moved closer to see the design they were creating. He had seen many mandalas before, but this one was different. He stepped back as the monks rose to their feet and bowed to it. A strong wind blew through the open windows. Logan watched as the monks faded from his sight and wind scattered the sand of the mandala. As the wind grew stronger and stronger, the sand swirled around the room faster and faster, until Logan was caught up in it like a piece of debris snatched up by a tornado.

When the spinning stopped, Logan found himself in the old study, which looked different from how he had imagined it. Camden's written description did not do it justice. The shelves that surrounded the desk seemed to rise into infinity, full of books and old, tattered scrolls. The study was illuminated by a dim light whose source Logan couldn't identify and was scented with susinum, an ancient Egyptian fragrance derived from lilies. Logan ran his hands along the shelves and attempted to read the titles imprinted on the books' spines, but the writing was in a language he could not comprehend. He turned and looked at the large, ornately carved desk. There were two neatly stacked piles of paper on the surface, which was inlaid with ivory and mother-of-pearl. He leaned over and tried to read what was written on them, but again, he encountered the language he didn't understand. All he could determine was that each pile contained eleven notes.

Logan felt something in his right hand. *Yes,* he thought. *This is why I came.* He was holding the note that he and Mr. Perrot had written for Baté. Uncertain about where to leave it, he gently placed it between the two piles of paper. Someone, or something, had meanwhile started to appear before Logan, the vapor of some shadowy figure. As he tried to make sense of it, the study faded, the shelves disappeared, and the desk vanished.

Logan found himself standing behind a minister performing a wedding ceremony. *I know where I am,* he thought. *This is the wedding of the Magician and the Scholar.* He recognized the setting from the photograph he had seen in Mr. Perrot's album. He stepped out from behind the minister and was shocked by the faces he saw.

Immediately, everything went black. Then fragments of images flashed before his eyes: a blue candle, Mr. Perrot's face, Valerie's apartment. He wondered where he would go next.

20

Are your dreams real? Are the visions of a child real?
When you are in your dreams, do they not feel real to you?
What is the difference between your real world and the world of
your dreams? Every dream, every vision you have, matters.
—THE CHRONICLES OF SATRAYA

WASHINGTON, D.C., 1:00 A.M. LOCAL TIME,
4 DAYS UNTIL FREEDOM DAY

Logan opened his eyes and inhaled sharply, feeling as if he'd been startled out of a nightmare. He looked around, trying to get his bearings. It took a moment or two before he recalled the candle and the flame. He remembered the box and the pages from Camden's journal. As he looked to his left, he saw the shadowy figure of Mr. Perrot seated on the couch and someone else seated next to him. Valerie had come home.

"Are you all right?" Mr. Perrot asked, as he stood and approached Logan. "You look a bit shaken."

Valerie reached over and turned on a lamp.

"I think so," Logan answered. He took the glass of water that Mr. Perrot handed him. "That was incredible—like a dream but much more real. How long was I gone?"

"You must have sat there for an hour or so," Mr. Perrot answered. "It was rather impressive to witness. You remained perfectly still and didn't move a muscle."

"Mr. Perrot, it was real. Everything we read about was real!" Logan blurted out, forgetting that Valerie was sitting there. "We have to put out the candle. We can't waste the flame." He quickly moved forward and blew out the wick. The candle had burnt down about three centimeters.

Logan awkwardly rose to his feet. His body seemed very heavy. He took a seat in a chair, feeling Valerie's eyes on him.

"Sorry about moving your furniture around," he said to her.

She had changed out of her work clothes into jeans and a pale pink T-shirt. Her silky brown hair touched her shoulders. She remained silent.

"I've told Valerie the full saga behind our little treasure-seeking episode today," Mr. Perrot said. "I believe she is a bit skeptical about our theories." He gave her a fatherly smile.

"That's putting it mildly," Valerie said. "Both of you are very fortunate that we have footage of Logan at the auction last night and airport footage of both of you leaving New Chicago for Washington this afternoon. It's the only reason the two of you are not behind bars at the moment."

"As I've explained, dear, it would seem that some past Council of Satraya members have unexpectedly resurfaced."

"Yes, I'm not sure how to take your theories about Andrea and Simon," Valerie said. "The whole Satraya thing has always eluded me; none of it seems based in reality."

"It's real to me," Logan said passionately. "My parents were killed because of this 'Satraya thing.'"

"I'm sorry about your parents, but there's no physical proof that Simon or Andrea or anyone else connected to them had anything to do with it. Or with the murders of the Council members or the theft in Cairo," Valerie said. "All we know is that Andrea succeeded in buying a set of old books at an auction."

"We know more than that," Logan said, determined to make his point. "You're just not willing to connect the dots. How do you explain that in twenty-four hours, two of the four original sets of the *Chronicles* changed hands, members of the Council of Satraya were murdered, and a woman who hasn't been publicly seen in more than twenty years has resurfaced? Further, if we hadn't pointed out the tunnel, you'd still be searching for your first clue regarding the murders."

Mr. Perrot could see that Logan's emotions were rising and that Valerie was about to match Logan's fervor. He put his hand on his daughter's knee. "Of course, dear, it is understandable that you feel that way. Logan was also taken aback by the fact that the woman who bought his family's most prized possession might have had a hand in his parents' killing. All I ask is that you remain open-minded."

Both Logan and Valerie sat quietly and allowed their emotions to settle a bit. Mr. Perrot gave them a few moments of silence. *These two haven't changed*, he thought.

Mr. Perrot gently coaxed the conversation along, as he'd done when they would argue as children. "Logan, why don't you tell us about your candle journey? I think you may have an interesting story to tell."

"I certainly do," Logan said. He paused for a moment and looked at the blue candle, wondering how to start. "The ringing in my ears was getting louder, and I tried my best to remain focused on the candle. I didn't think anything was happening, but then this strange feeling came over me, like electricity running up and down my spine. I couldn't feel my legs any longer, and I felt very light, almost as if I was about to levitate off the ground. Suddenly, the ringing sound stopped, and the flame began to dim. It was as if the candle was moving away from me down some long, dark tunnel. I felt as if I was getting really small and as if I wasn't in my body. It seemed I was just occupying a little point in my head." He pointed to the middle of his forehead. "I could feel a great pressure building there. And then everything went dark."

"The third eye," Mr. Perrot interrupted. "The *Chronicles* and other texts refer to that as the third eye. It is a place where we can purportedly see all things."

"We in the crime-fighting business refer to it as a drug trip," Valerie said sarcastically.

"Please, dear, you must keep an open mind," Mr. Perrot said. "I have always told you that the Satraya Flame brings forward interesting experiences. I remember a little girl once telling me about some exotic magical adventures she had in a kingdom made of clouds."

"You never told me about those when we were little," Logan said.

"That's because that place wasn't real," Valerie said defensively. "I didn't understand what any of that was about. I still don't."

"Please go on," Mr. Perrot urged Logan.

Logan gave Valerie an understanding look. Until an hour ago, he'd had his own doubts. "I get how you feel. All I can tell you is what I experienced."

"You're right. I'm sorry," Valerie said. "Keep going."

Logan began to recount his story, describing the painted clouds and how he suddenly appeared before the *Creation of Adam* painting. "It was like being in a dream; something was moving me from place to place," he said. Then he described how the painting had morphed.

"Blood, thorns, collars?" Valerie interrupted. "What is all that about?"

"I'm not really sure," Logan said. "As I said, it was like a dream where the pieces didn't add up."

"As Camden wrote, every experience in the flame has a purpose," Mr. Perrot said. "Let's hear the full story and see what we learn."

"The next place I went was an old Victorian-style room," Logan continued. He described it as best he could, certain he had forgotten many details. "When I tugged on the bars on the windows, I suddenly found myself outside on a dirt path."

Valerie sank back on the couch as Logan described his experiences with the monks. Her patience was clearly growing thin.

"I have seen many mandalas, but this one was different. It was very simple in design, and the monks only used black sand," Logan explained. "There were three circles, one within the other, and a great cross ran through them."

Valerie suddenly sat up on the edge of the couch. "What? What did you just say about the mandala?"

"The design was really simple," Logan said. "Three circles and a cross."

Valerie took out her PCD and projected the image she'd found earlier. Three circles and a cross. "We discovered this shape burned into the surface of a desk in the basement near the tunnel."

Logan nodded. "That's exactly the shape the monks were creating."

They all sat in silence, looking at one another, pondering the same question: How did Logan see the same image in his candle journey that Valerie had seen burned into the surface of the desk in the Council offices?

Just as Valerie was about to speak, her PCD rang. "OK. No one move. Talk about something else until I get back." She left the room to take the call.

Logan and Mr. Perrot watched her enter the kitchen, and then they looked back at each other.

"Well, Logan, I dare say you have my daughter's attention now," Mr. Perrot said.

"She's not very different from how I remember her," Logan said with a fond smile. "Still a whirlwind of energy and still ordering people around."

"Yes, those aspects of her character have never changed," Mr. Perrot acknowledged. "She certainly is passionate."

"Sir," Logan whispered. "There's more." Mr. Perrot moved closer to listen. "I somehow made it to the study." He described the room and the notes he had seen on the desk.

"Did you leave our note?" Mr. Perrot asked.

Logan nodded. "I think this candle is some kind of spiritual gateway, some kind of link, to that room . . ."

He went quiet as Valerie returned. She took a seat next to her father again. "So, dear, do you believe a bit more now?" Mr. Perrot asked.

"I certainly can't deny that Logan described the same image I saw on the top of the desk," Valerie conceded. "Maybe you saw it when the two of you were in the basement and your subconscious registered it. I'm not an expert in all this esoteric stuff. But yes, you certainly have my attention now."

"While you were gone, Logan relayed to me the last part of his adventure," Mr. Perrot said. "It had to do with the notes I told you about earlier. About the letters Camden Ford wrote to a man he called Baté Sisán."

Valerie was silent for a moment. Then she said, "Let's say that there's some validity to your story and that Andrea and Simon are somehow involved. There is still no evidence that links them to the murders. I'll consider bringing them in for questioning, but these are powerful people, and it's a safe bet that they are not going to cooperate. We also have to consider the possibility that the Sentinel Coterie may somehow be involved. We saw Randolph Fenquist speaking with Cynthia's assistant Monique Sato at the banquet. He slipped her something, but we couldn't make out what it was."

"The Sentinel Coterie! They are nothing more than a group of thugs." Mr. Perrot seemed uncustomarily upset. "Randolph is a man with an anarchist agenda and no one to listen to him. These events are far beyond his vision or execution. It is Simon and Andrea, I am certain of it! The murder of Logan's parents and the murder of the Council members are somehow linked to Simon and Andrea's desire to possess all four of the original copies of the *Chronicles*. Why, I cannot say. I only know that we need to draw them out."

"Draw them out with what?" Valerie said. "We don't have anything to use as bait."

There was a long silence. Mr. Perrot could only shake his head.

"Actually, I think I might have some bait," Logan said. Valerie and Mr. Perrot both looked at him curiously. "There's one last part of my candle journey that I haven't told you about. I found myself at a wedding." He stopped and looked directly at Mr. Perrot. "It was the wedding of the Magician and the Scholar."

"The magician and the what?" Valerie said. "What are you talking about?"

Logan continued to look at Mr. Perrot. "I think there's something your father needs to tell us," he said to Valerie.

21

Who are you when you believe that no one is watching you? Who are you when the eyes of the world look elsewhere? It is at that moment, your true inner character is on display.
—THE CHRONICLES OF SATRAYA

WASHINGTON, D.C., 1:00 P.M. LOCAL TIME,
4 DAYS UNTIL FREEDOM DAY

Adisa Kayin closed the door to the most revered room in the Council of Satraya building. The curtains at the large windows in the second-floor meeting room were half-drawn in an attempt to diffuse the sunlight that was streaming in. As the eldest member of the Council, he now assumed its leadership. Modest in stature and attired in the colorful garments of his homeland in Africa, Mr. Kayin took a seat at the famous Egalitarian Round Table, where the eight remaining Council members were already seated. As indicated by the name, the grand table's construction was inspired by the Arthurian legends of the past. Its circular shape conveyed that all who sat around it would be heard, and twelve of its thirteen pillar-shaped legs represented the twelve members of the Council. The thirteenth leg represented the benevolent beings that have assisted humanity throughout the ages.

Logan, Mr. Perrot, and Valerie occupied the chairs of the three slain Council members.

"At this table, all are equal," Mr. Kayin stated, making the solemn promise with which each Council meeting began. "We are here at the request of Ms. Perrot, the lead agent in charge of the investigation into the murders of our late colleagues. Late last night, she contacted me and relayed that there was urgent news that might give us a spark of hope. We do not know what you will say, Ms. Perrot, but we hope that your words will shift the direction of the ill wind that has blown upon us." He looked at each of his fellow members. "I thank you for attending on such short notice. So please—"

Mr. Kayin was abruptly interrupted by the sound of something hitting one of the windows. Valerie rose from her chair, placing her right hand on her holstered weapon, and cautiously walked over to the window to assess the situation. A few of the Council members sank to the ground. Recent events had put them on guard.

"Looks like the Coterie is causing trouble again," Valerie said as she placed a call on her PCD. "Please remain seated until we get the situation outside under control."

Logan could feel the lugubrious atmosphere in the room. He saw the fear and uncertainty in the eyes of the five women and four men who now made up the Council, and he watched as Mr. Kayin attempted to comfort them. It was hard to accept that this sad and frightened group of people was what was left of the once brilliant and robust Council that had helped the world rebuild after the Great Disruption. Logan walked over to Valerie, who was still talking on her PCD. Through the window, he could see the radical Sentinel Coterie members in front of the building, waving banners and placards and shouting obscenities. "If Randolph Fenquist is with them, arrest him," Logan heard Valerie say. He lingered at the window, trying to figure out what had been thrown at it. He saw no hints, however, and he eventually returned to his seat next to Mr. Perrot, who had remained calm during the fracas. Valerie finished her call, drew the curtains shut, and motioned to Mr. Kayin that it was fine to resume.

"As you can see, this is a very trying time for us," Mr. Kayin said. "Let us continue. Please relay to us your important news."

Mr. Perrot was the first to speak. *"Many have traveled before you, yet none has walked the exact same path as you. But there is a common aspiration that brings us together. We all have questions about the life we are living, about the choices we have made. We all have questions about why the world is the way it is. We all have questions about what we are supposed to do.'"*

The Council members seemed to perk up. Mr. Perrot was reciting verbatim from the opening pages of *The Chronicles of Satraya*.

He continued: *"'All things happen for a reason and a grand purpose. We have come to you during a time of great confusion and struggle in your world. We have done so in the past, and we are here again to help you through your troubled times. We are not here to make you believe in something different. We are not here to convince you that you are wrong. We are here to remind you of a great truth you have forgotten. We are here to provide you with a path. We are here strictly for you. We are here to set you free.'"*

The room was silent. The Council members weren't the only ones captivated by the words; Logan and Valerie were, too. Their parents had read passages from the *Chronicles* to them when they were growing up, but this was different. Perhaps it was the passage's relevance to the precarious situation they faced, or perhaps it was Mr. Perrot himself, his expressive voice and the noble spirit with which he spoke. Whatever the reason, Mr. Perrot now had complete command of the Egalitarian Round Table.

"These words are as true today as they were when my dear friends Camden and Cassandra Ford first read them to me from the books Camden found in the forest," he announced.

A murmur of voices rippled through the room. Until that moment, the Council members had only heard Cynthia Brown claim to have been a friend of Camden and Cassandra.

"You were friends with Camden and Cassandra?" a member asked incredulously.

"Where are they now?" another asked. "What happened to them? Are they still alive?"

Tension filled the room as they waited for an answer to the question people all over the world had been asking for the last thirty years.

Mr. Perrot shook his head. "Sadly, my dearest friends are no longer with us. Their fate is part of the story I am about to tell."

"Is this the news you wanted to bring us?" a member asked, clearly let down. "The spark of hope is that you can confirm that Camden and Cassandra are dead?" An air of disappointment filled the room, compounding the hopelessness reflected on the faces of the Council members.

"How can we be certain you were close to them?" another member asked. "According to Cynthia, Camden had very few trusted friends. Cynthia never mentioned anyone by your name."

"That is because Cynthia did not know the complete truth of that time," Mr. Perrot said.

"Are you calling her a liar?" someone else asked. The rest of the members started defending Cynthia; a few had started shouting.

"Silence, please," Mr. Kayin said in a loud voice. "Silence," he repeated as the members came back to order. "Let us allow Mr. Perrot to continue. Let us see if he is able to answer our questions satisfactorily."

Logan saw that Mr. Perrot, calm as ever, did not seem perturbed by the Council members' doubts.

"This table at which you all sit, the Egalitarian Round Table, possesses a secret," Mr. Perrot said. "A secret known only to those who helped construct it." He paused briefly, allowing anyone who wanted to refute him to speak up. No one did. "As we all can see, this table is supported by thirteen legs. But one of those legs has a flaw. It was made from a piece of uncured wood, and as it dried, it shrank ever so slightly, a single millimeter. A sheet of paper can be slipped beneath this particular leg."

Mr. Kayin wasted no time and tore a sheet of paper from his notebook. As the other Council members watched, he walked counterclockwise around the table and attempted to slide the sheet of paper under each leg. "That's the one," Mr. Perrot said when Mr. Kayin reached the eighth leg.

Mr. Kayin easily slid the paper beneath it just as Mr. Perrot had predicted. He looked at Mr. Perrot, dumbfounded. "How could you know this?"

The other members of the Council also looked shocked.

"Because, my friends," Mr. Perrot said as he stood, a solemn expression on his face, "I am Robert Tilbo. I was the young man Camden saved from the Forgotten Ones all those years ago and one of the original members of the Council of Satraya. And sitting next to me here is Camden and Cassandra's son, Logan Ford. This is the news we wished to bring you. This is the news that should bring you hope."

The silence in the room was almost deafening. Everyone stared at Logan. There were no murmurs, no side conversations. This was the information Logan had coaxed out of Mr. Perrot after returning from his candle vision. Logan had seen the faces of the Magician and the Scholar and also the face of the man handing them their rings at the wedding. They were faces Logan easily recognized. The Magician was Logan's father, the Scholar was his mother, and the ring bearer was Mr. Perrot himself.

"Why, that's me over there in that picture on the wall," Mr. Perrot said, pointing to a framed photograph and releasing some of the tension in the room. Everyone looked at the picture. "Much younger and a bit better-looking back then, I'm afraid." A smile came to his face.

"My fellow Council members," Mr. Kayin said as he retook his seat at the table. "I believe that this man is who he says he is. Let us give him our undivided attention."

22

*If all the world is a stage, are you satisfied with the supporting role
that you are playing? Or is it time, perhaps, to take the leading role?*
—THE CHRONICLES OF SATRAYA

WASHINGTON, D.C., 2:12 P.M. LOCAL TIME,
4 DAYS UNTIL FREEDOM DAY

"Esteemed Council members," Mr. Perrot began, "the events of the
last few days have certainly shaken our lives and the lives of people all
around the world who continue to understand the value of *The Chronicles
of Satraya* and their place in history. I know that some of you must be
wondering why Logan auctioned off his father's set of the *Chronicles* and
why I did not bring him forward sooner. The answers to these questions
and many more lie in the past and concern a secret power struggle that
occurred within the first Council of Satraya. Before I continue, I must
have your assurances that the information I am about to impart will not
go beyond this esteemed group. There may come a day when the world
can know the complete true history of the Council, but for now, it must
remain between us." Mr. Perrot paused for a moment as, one by one,
each member of the Council acknowledged his or her promise with the
traditional tapping of the right hand on the chest three times.

Satisfied, he continued. "The splintering of the original Council of
Satraya was said to have occurred because members had grown weary of

their work, and stress had taken its toll on them. At a Council meeting in late November 2037, the members decided it was time to return to their homes, and the Council's responsibilities were handed over to a capable young woman named Cynthia Brown. Her leadership and vision guided the Council for the next thirty years, and we most certainly honor her for that achievement. But I say to you now that the recorded history is in error. There was a more sinister reason behind the Council's splintering. At the center of that pivotal event were Camden Ford and Fendral Hitchlords."

Mr. Perrot took a sip of water and went on to explain what had really taken place all those years ago, including the recent details he had gleaned from the notes Camden had left behind. "Even though the Council did not operate under the authority of any government, Fendral and Andrea Montavon wanted the Council to wield a powerful political sword. Essentially, they wanted to turn it into an organization that enforced supranational laws. It would have allowed them to act with impunity as they amassed power over humanity. They masked their true motives with the reasoning that the sovereignty of the *Chronicles* should be guarded at all costs, that no one nation should ever claim authority over the books' philosophies. While Camden agreed that the *Chronicles* belonged to all people, he was not prepared to endow the Council with so much power over people's lives. He feared that Fendral and Andrea would twist the Council's ideals into a means of repression and control that would benefit a select few. Camden did not want the *Chronicles* to become the cornerstone of some new oppressive religion or one-world government. We only have to look at history to see the danger that Simon and Andrea posed."

Mr. Perrot recounted Fendral's threats and the mysterious agreement Camden had made with Fendral that had resulted in the Council being left in the hands of Cynthia Brown.

"But what happened to Camden and his family?" Mr. Kayin asked. "You all seemed to disappear into thin air."

"After Deya and Madu left the country with their families, Camden and I did not trust that Fendral and Andrea would honor their part of the agreement. With the help of Camden's father, who was a founder of the World Federation of Reconstruction, we were able to secure new identities. While the world puzzled over Camden's disappearance, we traveled to New Chicago and began new lives. Camden and Cassandra became Henry and Alexandra Cutler. I became Alain Perrot. And that is how we all lived for over thirty years."

"Did Cynthia know any of this?" a member asked.

"No, and we never spoke to her again once we left Washington. Camden did write to her as Henry Cutler from time to time over the years, though. Thanking her for her work on the Council and offering his support, occasionally a little advice." Mr. Perrot paused and bowed his head for a moment to look at Logan before addressing the Council once again. "Two years ago, Camden and Cassandra Ford were killed during a purported burglary. Six months later, Deya Sarin died in a tragic accident. And Madu Shata has not been heard from in a very long time."

"Are you saying that Fendral's heir is somehow responsible?" a member asked. "That Andrea is also involved?"

"Fendral's son is Simon Hitchlords," Mr. Perrot answered. "And yes, I do fear that he is attempting to pick up where his father left off."

"We know who Simon Hitchlords is. While he has not been seen in public in many years, he is considered one of the world's leading philanthropists," another member said. "He has donated a huge amount of money to medical research, and he sounds more interested in saving lives than in ending them."

Adisa Kayin spoke. "Mr. Perrot, in light of all that has happened, do you think that Simon and Andrea are responsible for the murders of our fellow Council members and friends? We know it was Andrea who was bidding against Cynthia at the auction the other night."

"We are not making that statement," Valerie jumped in, answering for her father. "We have no proof that Simon or Andrea is involved.

But we are not going to take any chances. I have assigned a security detail to this office and to each of you until this case is solved."

"My daughter, Valerie, assures me that the WCF is doing everything in its power to investigate the murders," Mr. Perrot added.

While Valerie brought the Council up to date on the investigation, Logan leaned back in his chair and thought about his parents. He was still coming to terms with being the son of Camden and Cassandra Ford. His candle vision the night before had unearthed a secret that had been concealed from him all his life. The marriage of the Magician and the Scholar, the marriage of Camden and Cassandra, was the marriage of his parents. Even now, Logan's heart raced as he absorbed that fact.

"It would seem that I am now released from the solemn oath I made to your parents when we fled Washington those many years ago," Mr. Perrot had said after Logan's revelation the night before. "I hope you understand why I didn't tell you. I swore to your parents. The world thought we'd perished, and for the safety of both our families, we needed to keep it that way."

"You should have told us," Valerie had said. "With all your suspicions and theories, you should have told us the whole story."

Mr. Perrot had had a tough time refuting his daughter. He'd only been able to drop his head in contrition as Valerie gave him a glowering look.

"No," Logan had said in a soft but confident voice, looking at Mr. Perrot. "You held true to your word. You did what you thought was right. My parents never doubted your commitment to our family or your friendship. And I'm not about to start." Mr. Perrot had raised his head, touched by Logan's magnanimity. "While I still need time to take in the fact of my parents' identities, I'd still like to hear the whole story. The story of Camden, Cassandra, and their dear friend Robert. Right from the start . . ."

Now Logan felt a tap on his shoulder. It ended his reveries and brought his attention back to the Council meeting. "Perhaps you would like to say something to the Council," Mr. Perrot whispered to him.

Logan gathered his thoughts, then stood and addressed the group. "In the last few days, my world has also been turned upside down," he said, as Mr. Perrot sat down. "I knew nothing of my parents' true identities before last night. But I did know that my father and mother loved everything about the *Chronicles* and lived their lives according to its philosophies. Until these past twelve hours, I didn't understand where their passion and dedication came from. I didn't understand the love they had for the books and why they cheered all the great strides the Council made over the years. Had I known who they really were, I never would have auctioned off the books. They would be in your possession today; I would have given them to you freely." He took a deep breath, still feeling overwhelmed. "While I may not be able to get the books back, I hope that my coming forward as the son of Camden and Cassandra Ford will inspire all of us to turn this sad moment into one that will galvanize all who value the *Chronicles'* philosophies and advance Satraya into the future."

At first, there was silence. Then Adisa Kayin started clapping his hands. Other Council members joined in, and soon the entire room was applauding Logan. Valerie and Mr. Perrot were also clearly moved. Mr. Perrot placed his hand on Logan's shoulder.

"It is no accident that you have come forward at this time," Mr. Kayin said to Logan. "While we still grieve the loss of our fellow Council members, you have given us hope that the mission your parents started long ago will continue. We have work to do."

Valerie had leaked the impromptu meeting of the Council of Satraya to the news media, and reporters and cameramen were gathered at the entrance of the building to hear what it was about. It was agreed that Mr. Kayin would address the reporters with Logan at his side and would declare him a standing member of the Council of Satraya. This announcement was the bait that they hoped would draw out Simon and Andrea.

"I do have one more question," said a member of the Council, looking at Mr. Perrot. "You stated that you, along with Camden and Cassandra, fled to New Chicago with new identities. If Simon truly was behind the murders of Camden and Cassandra, then I have to ask, how did he find them?"

Mr. Perrot, Logan, and Valerie could not answer that question. They had contemplated and discussed it the night before. But the only answer they could come up with was that someone else must have been involved, and that person must have betrayed them.

Unable to answer, Mr. Perrot suggested that they go down to meet the reporters.

23

Your science is just starting to touch on the great physical
mysteries of the universe. In the years ahead, you will find little
difference between scientific discoveries and what the old sages
have been telling you.
—THE CHRONICLES OF SATRAYA

WASHINGTON, D.C., 10:30 A.M. LOCAL TIME,
3 DAYS UNTIL FREEDOM DAY

"Good morning, Martha. There should be a TA Four badge ready for
Logan Cutler," Valerie said, as she and Logan stood at the security desk
in the lobby of the World Crime Federation building.

After the Great Disruption, various police agencies had been combined to coordinate security around the world, and the FBI merged
with Interpol and a few smaller agencies to form the WCF. All of the
primary FBI buildings, along with the legal attaché offices, had been
renovated to house this new force.

"Great, TA, a temporary agent. Sounds pretty official. Do I get a
gun?" Logan quipped.

"No," Valerie answered quickly. "But if I'm on the ground dead, feel
free to take mine."

Logan turned serious.

"Clip it on, and make sure it's always visible." Martha handed Logan the badge. "It will allow you to use the restrooms and the cafeteria. Your PCD has been linked to it, so we can track you wherever you go."

"Let's go," Valerie said, "and stay with me."

It had been decided that Mr. Perrot would fly back to New Chicago to look through Logan's father's old papers for anything more that would shed some light on Fendral's secret and what Simon and Andrea might be up to. They also hoped he would find Camden's journal.

As Logan followed Valerie through a maze of hallways, he tried to shrug off her sarcastic manner. He wanted to develop the same kind of rapport with her that he had with her father, but if their childhood was any indication, it was not going to be easy.

They took an elevator to the third floor, where the forensic laboratory was located. There Valerie opened the door of a supply closet, rifled through a stack of plastic-wrapped packages, took two, and closed the door.

"A few rules before we go into the lab," she said. "First, don't touch anything. Second, you have to put on one of these jumpsuits so you don't contaminate anything." She handed Logan one of the packages.

"Any other rules?" Logan asked, as he ripped open the package and slid the suit on over his clothes, struggling to get his shoes through the pants legs.

"Yeah. Don't touch anything."

"You already said that."

Valerie slipped on her jumpsuit, and they entered the lab through a set of steel doors, which opened automatically as they approached. Logan gazed around in amazement at the almost two-thousand-square-meter lab, which was built on a raised floor. He saw about twenty technicians similarly dressed in white suits and working busily. Even though the room had no windows, it was well lit, and the spotless white walls enhanced the room's brightness. Voice- and motion-controlled computer displays filled the forty or so investigative stations in the lab.

Charlie had already arrived and walked over to them.

"Anything new this morning?" Valerie asked him. "Have we tracked down that Sato girl, Cynthia's assistant, yet?"

Charlie shook his head. "She's disappeared. Off the grid. Wasn't at her apartment, and her PCD location beacon is not registering. Communication satellites and all the local transportation hubs have been alerted. If she tries to leave the country, we'll get her."

Charlie led Valerie and Logan through another set of doors and into one of the analytics labs.

"The guys still don't know how any of the Council members died." He turned to Logan. "You're not squeamish around dead bodies, are you?"

Logan saw the corpses of the three Council members and Claire Williams lying inside large glass incubator-like machines. Different-colored wires were connected to the machines, and a white mist filled the cases from time to time, obscuring the corpses.

"Biostasis chambers," Charlie explained.

"We call them bio-coffins," Valerie added. "Basically, a dead body doesn't decay when it's in there."

Logan watched a lab technician with short blond hair and large black-framed eyeglasses draw blood samples from the bodies. He recognized her as one of the investigators who had been gathering evidence in the basement and the secret tunnel of the Council building. Charlie led Valerie and Logan over to another forensic agent sitting in front of a large display. "All right, Goshi, tell the chief what you have."

"Not much," Goshi said. He brought up images of the four corpses on the screens. "There are no signs of trauma. No gunshot wounds or knife wounds, nothing external. We pumped their stomachs and didn't find any poisons. Based on the evidence at the crime scene, we believe they all ate takeout from the same place, a diner."

"A place across the street from the Council building called Pepper Jack's," Charlie clarified. "We sent an agent over to speak to the owner."

"We are also checking to see if there was some kind of airborne toxin, but we've got nothing yet," Goshi continued. "The traces from their lungs look fine. It's as if their bodies just stopped working for no apparent reason."

"Well, something killed them," Valerie said, clearly exasperated. "Anything more on the burn mark on the desk or the hole we found in the basement ceiling and the meeting-room floor?"

"No signs of any combustible agents and no residue traces," Goshi answered. "I have no idea what caused the burn mark, but I'd guess some kind of laser device made the hole in the ceiling and the floor."

Logan's curiosity had gotten the better of him. While Valerie and Charlie talked to Goshi, he walked around the lab, examining the white machines that beeped and hummed and purred. He had no idea what any of them did, but he was fascinated by the ones that had screens displaying colorful graphs, pulsating dots, and complex numerical equations. He stopped and watched the blond lab technician he'd seen at the Council building manipulate the projection of a DNA strand.

"This is incredible imagery," Logan said. "The detail is certainly impressive. And the colors are so vibrant."

"I can't say that I've ever heard anyone describe DNA like that," the technician said. "But I suppose that's how an artist would see it."

"You saw me on the news yesterday, didn't you?" Logan said.

"Yeah, I think everyone did. It must be pretty cool being the son of Camden Ford," she said with a smile. "My name is Sylvia, by the way."

"I'm Logan," he answered. He felt awkward being recognized as anything else. "But you obviously know that. Please, don't let me stop you. What are we looking at?"

Sylvia smiled and started to explain. "This is a sample of Cynthia Brown's DNA. Using the quantum computer at the Akasha Vault, we can map anyone's genome in an hour. But my friend Chetan, who works at the Vault, gives me priority access from time to time if I need to get things done a bit quicker."

"Nice friend," Logan said as he pulled up a chair. "That's a pretty detailed image you're analyzing."

"It's a supercoiled alpha helix, as we scientists refer to it. If we unraveled it, it would be about one meter long." Sylvia made a few motions with her hand to rotate and zoom in on parts of the projection.

Logan noticed a tall dark-haired man wearing a gray suit enter the lab and walk over to Valerie. He gave a nod in his direction. "That's Valerie's boss, isn't it?"

"Yes, that's Director Burke," Sylvia confirmed.

Logan watched as they spoke. Burke made only a few remarks and then left the lab. Valerie didn't seem happy with what he'd said. Logan turned back to Sylvia.

"I really don't see anything out of place here," she was saying. "Let me try this." She slid the image of the helix to her right and brought up another DNA segment. "This is an older sample of Ms. Brown's DNA that we had on file. The computer can perform a detailed comparison of the two and tell us if there are any differences."

As the red laser lines started to scan each strand of DNA, Sylvia turned her attention to a different screen. Logan kept watching the first one as it shifted and rotated, studying the DNA images as if he were preparing to draw them. Suddenly, a dark gray ring appeared on one of them.

"Hey, what's that? This thing right here, this gray ring." He pointed to the spot on the image.

Sylvia paused the scanning process and zoomed in. Then she turned back to Logan. "Well, look at you, Mr. Agent," she said with a smile. "I can't say I've ever seen that before. Hey, Charlie," she called across the room. "Come check this out."

"What do you have?" Charlie asked. Valerie came over with him.

"It looks like there's a DNA insert or some kind of attachment in the DNA sample we extracted from Ms. Brown postmortem." Sylvia enlarged the image, isolating the location.

"What's a DNA insert?" Valerie asked.

"It's a result of a different sequence of DNA having been inserted into an existing strand. I've never seen one like this, though. It looks like a ring has been placed around a particular sequence." Sylvia found the angle of the image she was looking for. Logan looked at it more closely. He'd said "ring" originally, but now "collar" came to mind. Like the ones he'd seen in his candle vision.

"That looks like—" Logan began, but Valerie broke him off with an intense look of warning.

"Looks like what?" Charlie asked.

Logan picked up on Valerie's cue. "Sorry, I thought it looked like something, but I was wrong."

"It looks like a dog collar around this particular part of the sequence," Sylvia said. And there was the word again. "Collar." She continued to play around with the image. "Let's see if we can find out what this sequence does."

"You can do that?" Valerie asked.

"Sort of. Close to ninety-eight percent of our DNA is classified as junk, which simply means we don't know what it does. But all of our twenty-five thousand genes are made from their own distinct DNA segments. We should be able to figure out if this particular segment does anything useful." Everyone watched as Sylvia manipulated the computer with her swift, nimble fingers. "Voilà! This DNA sequence is used to create the VMAT-2 gene."

"What's a VMAT-2 gene?" Charlie asked.

"VMAT-2 is used to deliver neurotransmitters into the synaptic cleft of the brain. It is a protein that transports monoamines, particularly neurotransmitters such as dopamine, norepinephrine, serotonin, and histamine."

"What does that mean?" Charlie asked. "Is that what killed them?"

"I don't know," Sylvia said. "These neurotransmitters enable us to think. Without them, we can't survive." Sylvia turned back to her computer. "I'm going to need to run some more tests. We need to see if the other victims have the same anomaly in their DNA."

Valerie nodded. "Charlie, clear the road for her. Anything she needs, make sure she gets it. I have to go brief the higher-ups, and then I have to brief the media. Burke wants me to say something to keep everyone happy and occupied." Valerie tightened up her ponytail. "Some days I really hate this job," she said as she walked out of the lab.

Logan took a seat at an empty desk near Sylvia. Hoping that Mr. Perrot was having more luck finding answers in New Chicago than they were having in D.C., he took his sketchpad and a pencil out of his backpack and started to draw the DNA strand from memory. He paid particular attention to the details of the collar.

After ten minutes, he stood up, stretched, and walked over to the four bio-coffins. The last time he had viewed a dead body was at his parents' funeral, the saddest day of his life. He walked slowly from corpse to corpse now and paused when he came to the young woman named Claire Williams. *Did these people die because of the books, because of my decision to sell them?* Logan asked himself. He looked at the young face of Claire Williams. She was innocent in all of this. They all were. A feeling of guilt overcame him as he looked at them. They had died for no reason . . . Unless Sebastian Quinn was correct. Unless there really was a greater purpose to the journey of the books . . .

"None of this makes any sense," he whispered.

A red light above Claire's bio-coffin started flashing. Logan looked around, but no one else in the lab seemed concerned. He turned back to the bio-coffin and noticed through the white mist that strange green lines were beginning to appear all over the body. The red light flashed faster, and indicators over the other three bio-coffins lit up. Logan jumped back as a loud alarm sounded. All of the lab personnel rushed over, with Charlie following them.

"We're losing stasis!" Sylvia shouted, manipulating the controls. "Quickly, someone get four ice boxes in here! We have to move these bodies right now!"

Two technicians ran out of the room.

"Those green lines on the body—some kind of chemical reaction is taking place in their bloodstreams," Goshi said.

"That's impossible!" Sylvia replied, still trying to adjust the controls. "These chambers are supposed to prevent that from happening."

While Sylvia and Goshi hovered over the controls and the other technicians checked the wires on the bio-coffins, Logan couldn't take his eyes off the corpses. Blood was starting to flow out of them. It was leaking out of the eyes and the ears. Then, as if the major veins and arteries had burst, blood started flowing through the skin.

"It's like their veins are disintegrating," he whispered.

Sylvia came over. "What's happening to these bodies?"

"Where are those ice boxes?" Goshi yelled.

Four technicians slammed through the lab's doors, wheeling in the ice boxes.

As the bloodied corpses were transferred from the bio-coffins to the ice boxes, Logan realized that this was another part of his candle vision: the green vines and the bloody faces he had seen in the painting . . .

He grabbed his backpack and ran out of the lab.

24

A warrior knows his time.
—THE CHRONICLES OF SATRAYA

NEW CHICAGO, ILLINOIS, 11:00 A.M. LOCAL TIME,
3 DAYS UNTIL FREEDOM DAY

Using the key that Logan had provided, Mr. Perrot entered Logan's house and hung his hat on one of the coat hooks near the front door. He was accompanied by WCF agent Jogindra "Jogi" Bassi, whom Valerie had assigned to watch over her father.

"I'll just take a look around, sir," Jogi said politely in his acute Indian accent. "Let me know if you require my assistance."

Mr. Perrot thanked him and walked into the study, a room he was most familiar with. It looked much the same as it had when Camden and Cassandra had been alive. Camden's desk stood where it always had, and the shelves behind it held the same books that Camden had read and reread, along with the origami figures he had enjoyed making. Hanging on a wall were two mosaics, which Cassandra had created. Mr. Perrot and Camden would sit in the study late into the night, drinking wine, smoking their pipes, and debating the many mysteries of the universe and the *Chronicles*. They would also reminisce about the past and the what-ifs of their lives. Cassandra would join them from time to time, but usually, she'd go to bed when the grandfather clock in the corner struck the witching hour. Those wonderful times were indelibly etched into Mr. Perrot's soul, and he could easily get lost in those happy memories.

The gentle smile on his face gave way to a more solemn expression. *Now is not the time to indulge yourself,* he reminded himself. *You have a task to perform, a duty to your old friends . . .*

There was a small closet in the study, which Logan had told him contained the boxes of his father's belongings that he had packed after his parents died. Logan recalled storing a large brown envelope stuffed with numerous folded sheets of paper he hadn't had time to look at. Having now read some of his father's journal entries, Logan suspected the papers might be the "flame notes" that his father had taken with him to Baté's old study. But when Mr. Perrot opened the closet door, he groaned. There weren't just a few boxes but at least ten, and none of them was labeled. Jogi returned to help Mr. Perrot remove all thirteen boxes and place them on the floor of the study. Then Jogi left him to his search.

"Which one to start with?" Mr. Perrot mused aloud. With nothing to guide his selection, he was forced to rely on random choice. *Maybe luck will shine on me today,* he thought. *Maybe Camden's journal will be the first thing I find . . .* Unfortunately, it wasn't.

The chiming of the grandfather clock marked the passing of time. The once neat and well-organized study was now cluttered with boxes, papers, and files that were of no use and had to be repacked. He had found old photographs and financial papers, trinkets and novelties, old government policy manuals, and other personal documents. He had even found a few childhood works of art signed "Logan Cutler." It seemed Camden had saved everything, which did not make the search easier. Mr. Perrot paused for a moment and looked at a photograph of Logan's mother who was wearing an elegant gown and holding the violin she loved to play.

"Is everything all right, sir?" Jogi asked when he returned to the study. "Looks as though you have found a great many things."

"Yes, but not the thing I am looking for, I'm afraid," Mr. Perrot said.

"Let me know if I can be of any assistance," Jogi offered. "I'll be outside if you need me."

Mr. Perrot continued his rummaging, and after digging halfway into the contents of the eleventh box, he came across a large brown envelope. He dared not hope, but when he opened it, he found numerous folded sheets of paper with notes jotted in Camden's handwriting. These were the "flame notes" that Logan had remembered seeing. Mr. Perrot quickly cleared off the long coffee table in front of him and removed the notes one at a time from the envelope, reading each one before setting it on the table. All started with the words "To my dearest friend Baté Sisán" and were signed "Your friend Camden Ford." There were a total of ten notes, one fewer than the number Logan had seen in the candle voyage. Mr. Perrot pulled from his pocket the note about the King's Gambit; it began and ended in the same manner as the other ten, which meant it had to be the eleventh. He returned his attention to the ones he had just discovered.

To my dearest friend Baté Sisán,

I am beginning to see things on the blank pages of my copy of the Chronicles. *Do you know if there are things hidden there? The harder I look, the more difficult it is to see them.*

Your friend Camden Ford

To my dearest friend Baté Sisán,

Did you write The Chronicles of Satraya? *If you didn't, then who did?*

Your friend Camden Ford

To my dearest friend Baté Sisán,

Deya is very worried and scared of Fendral. She is leaving for India today, and she gave me a strange gift and instructions that I didn't question.

Your friend Camden Ford

To my dearest friend Baté Sisán,

Who are you? Maybe a better question is, what are you?

Your friend Camden Ford

To my dearest friend Baté Sisán,

    I can see all the images now but one. I only see a small part of it on the page. Is there more to it? Am I doing something wrong?

                                           Your friend Camden Ford

To my dearest friend Baté Sisán,

    The Council is in turmoil. Perhaps if you would come and say a few words, the tension would ease. Even though I have never spoken of you, I am certain they will listen to your wisdom.

                                           Your friend Camden Ford

To my dearest friend Baté Sisán,

    Can I use the Manas Mantr candle to go to other places? What will happen when the candle melts away? Will I still be able to travel to your mysterious study?

                                           Your friend Camden Ford

To my dearest friend Baté Sisán,

    You were correct. I arrived tonight without the use of the Manas Mantr candle. It was as you described.

                                           Your friend Camden Ford

To my dearest friend Baté Sisán,

    There is more uneasiness growing in the Council. Fendral is growing more militant each day. He thinks the people of the world need more direct leadership. He is asking that we, the Council, create a governing body to guide the world. I think he really means "to rule the world."

                                           Your friend Camden Ford

To my dearest friend Baté Sisán,

    The final pages of Deya's and Madu's copies of the third book of the Chronicles *also have hidden symbols, but they are different from mine. To my astonishment, the last pages of their copies also display two additional segments of the final mark. The last segment must be in Fendral's copy. But it is not wise for me to ask to see it. I believe I understand why this symbol was divided and hidden so deeply. It is not to be taken lightly or revealed freely. I dare not draw any of the hidden symbols anywhere. None of them should be treated carelessly, but the last one most of all. For I believe that the final symbol holds the promise of immortality.*

Your friend Camden Ford

Mr. Perrot sat back on the sofa, filled with great trepidation. Now he thought he understood what Simon and Andrea were after. That promise, *immortality*. If they were to uncover and harness the power of the final symbol, humanity would confront a daunting new force of never-ending evil.

Feeling a greater sense of urgency, he leaned forward and looked at the notes lying on the table. There were no dates on them or any indication of the order in which they'd been written. He flipped them over to see if anything was written on their back sides but found nothing. Then the obvious question occurred to him: Where were the answers to these queries? If Camden had indeed placed the notes in the old study and Baté had been able to read them, surely Baté would have provided answers. Logan mentioned that he had seen two piles of notes with eleven notes in each pile. That would suggest that Baté had answered Camden's notes.

Mr. Perrot sat pensively for a moment. He knew his friend Camden would have written down the responses. He recorded everything. *Maybe he wrote the answers in his missing journal.* Mr. Perrot looked at the two remaining boxes. *Perhaps the journal and the responses are in one of those.* The clock chimed again. Time was passing far too quickly.

Feeling tired and a bit discouraged, Mr. Perrot placed the lid back on the last of the boxes. Neither of them had contained Camden's journal or Baté's responses to Camden's inquiries. After looking through the contents of all thirteen boxes, the mystery had only grown deeper and more ominous. Mr. Perrot sat still on the couch and considered his next move. *Perhaps there is another closet, other boxes that Logan did not mention,* he thought.

"You are playing games with us, Camden," he said aloud. "I fear that the King's Gambit was not your only riddle."

Mr. Perrot stood, walked behind the desk, and opened some of the drawers. Then he walked to the corner of the study and opened a small access door to the old grandfather clock that had been relentlessly ticking off the minutes of the day. He shut the door in frustration as it revealed only the intricate internal workings of the clock.

He turned and looked at the bookshelves behind Camden's desk. On the middle shelf, he saw Camden's origami figures. He walked over and picked up the figure of a dog, which was his favorite. Origami was an art that Camden had perfected but never succeeded in teaching to Mr. Perrot. More fond memories flew through his mind. As he set the figure back on the shelf, a thought suddenly struck him. *Camden, you clever, clever man!*

25

*Having great questions is not enough. You must be patient enough
to wait for their answers.
Great questions will make you a great philosopher, but having
great answers will make you a wizard.*
—THE CHRONICLES OF SATRAYA

WASHINGTON, D.C., 12:30 P.M. LOCAL TIME,
3 DAYS UNTIL FREEDOM DAY

Logan ran down the steps of the WCF building. While the fresh air provided some relief, he needed to find a peaceful place where he could pull his thoughts together. The undeniable similarity between what he had witnessed in the lab and what he'd seen in the candle vision deeply disturbed him. He noticed a colorful banner hanging from a streetlight, promoting a Renaissance art exhibit at the National Gallery. *Perfect*, he thought. That was just the kind of place he was looking for.

As he turned to walk down the street, his PCD sounded. He saw from the number that it was a call from the museum in New Chicago.

"Hello, Mr. Rampart," Logan said. "Did you get my message?"

"Yes, but you didn't provide any time frame for your return," Mr. Rampart replied.

"Yes, I know, sir. An urgent personal matter came up."

"I heard about your press conference yesterday. But that does not change the fact that we have a deadline to meet. When can I expect you to return?"

Logan paused. "I'm not sure, sir."

"You are giving me no real choice in the matter. I'm going to have to find a replacement for you. The museum can't afford to let Mr. Quinn down. I'm sorry, Logan."

"I understand." And with that, the call ended.

Logan was disappointed by Mr. Rampart's news. While his finances were now in order and there was a very large balance in his bank account, he still wanted to finish the restoration work. He wanted to finish it for Sebastian.

As he looked around for a street sign, Logan was suddenly shoved from behind. He hit the ground hard, stopping himself with his hands. He rolled over quickly and saw two burly men in black leather vests over white T-shirts looking down at him through heavily tinted sunglasses.

"You're Logan Ford," one of the men said. There was a ten-centimeter scar along the right side of his face just below his cheekbone.

Without giving him time to answer, the other man grabbed Logan's arm and pulled him to his feet.

Logan struggled to free himself. Then, when he saw the slender third man in his early sixties emerging from behind the other two, he stopped. "You're Randolph Fenquist. The leader of the Sentinel Coterie."

The older man didn't answer. He moved his long, stringy brown hair out of his face and pulled a cigarette from his shirt pocket. He eyed Logan up and down as the man with the scar flicked a lighter.

Logan looked into Fenquist's fanatical eyes, eyes he had seen before in paintings depicting zealots in times past. Mr. Perrot was correct: Fenquist looked like a frustrated man bent on causing trouble.

"So you're the son of Camden and Cassandra Ford," Fenquist said. He took a few puffs and blew the smoke into Logan's face. "I bet there are quite a few people who would like to meet you." Logan said nothing. Fenquist shook his head. "Coming forward like that was a mistake, though. I wouldn't want you to get hurt like that sweet Cynthia."

"We know you had something to do with Cynthia's murder," Logan said. "They saw you give something to that girl—" Logan stopped himself, realizing he'd said too much.

Fenquist's expression darkened. He glanced at the man with the scar before saying, "I had nothing to do with Cynthia's murder." He took a puff of his cigarette. "I see Andrea suddenly resurfaced from her prolonged hiatus. Back to her old stomping grounds—North Carolina, I think it was? Maybe she had a score to settle with Cynthia. Maybe your lady friend and her government lackeys should go check her out."

He took a step forward and got right up into Logan's face, their noses almost touching.

"And if I were you, I would return to your nice brick house on your nice quiet street. You're dealing with people and things you don't understand, son."

Logan didn't respond. But the fact that Fenquist knew something about where he lived bothered him.

"Is there a problem here?" a deep voice asked.

Logan was relieved to see two policemen walking over to them, hands resting on their holstered guns.

"No problems," Fenquist said. "Our friend here fell, and we were just helping him up. We wouldn't want him to fall again."

One of the men replaced Logan's backpack on his shoulder, and the other brushed the dirt off Logan's back.

Fenquist looked straight at Logan. "I hope your sins don't keep you from heaven's gates." He patted Logan on the shoulder and, with his two thugs in tow, he got into a shiny black SUV at the curb and sped away.

"You need any help?" an officer asked, as he handed Logan his PCD, which had fallen onto the sidewalk.

Logan wanted to say yes, but he knew the officers couldn't help him. "No, thanks," he said. "I'm fine." And quickening his pace and occasionally looking over his shoulder, he resumed his trek to the National Gallery.

Maybe Valerie was right, he thought on the way. Maybe the Coterie did have something to do with the Council murders. Although the Coterie spoke of peaceful disagreements, Logan now had firsthand proof to the contrary.

He walked along Constitution Avenue and looked through the double-layered security fence that now surrounded the entire Memorial Park grounds. On the other side lay the ruins of the once-grand monuments of the capital. Rubble, stumps of buildings. A debate still raged about whether the Lincoln Memorial and the Washington Monument should be rebuilt or remain that way as a reminder that what we assume will last forever can be destroyed in an instant by man or nature.

Logan searched through his backpack and found his membership card, which allowed him free entry to all museums in the Federation. The West Building was the only part of the National Gallery of Art to survive the Great Disruption. The Sculpture Garden and the East Building of the grounds had been destroyed by an earthquake. The West Building's glass atrium had been slightly damaged but was rebuilt during the reconstruction efforts of the Rising.

Logan displayed his pass and entered. He had no particular destination; he was simply happy to be in a familiar environment. He took a seat on a bench close to the entrance and watched the people passing by. Slowly, his stress faded away. An elderly couple walked over, obviously hoping to sit down, and he gave his place to them.

While most of the museum was crowded with summer visitors and tour groups, Logan wandered into a quieter, less busy wing where the Renaissance exhibit was located. Early Renaissance statues and paintings from Florence soon surrounded him. He looked at works by Botticelli, Uccello, and Francesca, reading the curator's notes about their significance. Logan walked up a flight of stairs and entered the enormous Reproductions Room, where copies of great paintings through the ages were kept. One particular painting there caught Logan's eye. It was a depiction of a third-century Roman soldier who was bound to a tree, his body pierced by arrows. A woman gently tended the soldier's wounds. The painting was titled *Saint Sebastian Tended by Irene*.

Just then, Logan heard the sound of approaching footsteps. Still on his guard, he looked around but didn't see anyone coming. The only other people in the room were a young couple looking at a painting by Masaccio.

Logan continued to read the description of the painting: "*Saint Sebastian was a patron to all soldiers of his time, for he helped them to keep their faith. He was declared the patron of people who suffered plagues, for it was reported he cured many who were afflicted.*"

As Logan gazed at the painting, he thought of Sebastian Quinn and wondered if he'd been named after this saint. Although he'd only had two brief encounters with Mr. Quinn, he thought Sebastian was an appropriate namesake.

"Tough way to die," a man's gruff voice remarked behind him. "He must have really pissed off the king."

Logan turned and saw a blond-haired young man, more than six feet tall, standing next to him, looking at the same painting. "Yes," Logan said, a bit startled because he hadn't noticed the man approach him.

"Those were messed-up times," the man continued. "People getting killed for what they believed in."

"Still happens," Logan said. He wasn't in a mood to talk to strangers, not after what happened with Fenquist and his goons, so he walked away to explore the rest of the large gallery.

Only a few steps away, he once again found himself standing in front of the painting that seemed to be at the center of his life. It was a large reproduction of Michelangelo's *Creation of Adam*.

Is it a coincidence that the Saint Sebastian painting is so close to this one? Logan wondered. Mr. Quinn had never told him what all the faces in the painting represented, so he studied them now. Some were depicted with shadowy lighting, while others were clearly revealed. Some of the angels seemed to be holding back God's advancement, while others seemed to be pushing him. *What was the relationship between the iron collar I saw in my vi-*

sion and the DNA insert that Sylvia discovered in the lab? Artists such as Michelangelo didn't randomly put images into their works without great thought. Everything had a purpose . . . Logan felt discouraged; he would never learn the answer to this question now that Mr. Rampart had fired him. He'd never have another opportunity to speak to Sebastian Quinn.

A large—and very loud—group of summer-school students entered the hall. Gone was the silence that had aided Logan's contemplation. A teacher was leading the exuberant group of ten- and eleven-year-olds right over to where Logan was standing. He stepped aside, allowing the fifty little souls to gather in front of the painting. Logan didn't mind; the children reminded him of Jordan and Jamie and the happy times he'd spent with them at the museum in New Chicago, showing them his favorite paintings. The teacher raised a red flag, and the children quieted down.

"How many of you remember that big statue of David we saw?" All the kids raised their hands, and there was a little bit of laughter. "Yes, the man who was naked. Well, this painting was done by the same artist. Michelangelo."

"Is that David again?" asked a young boy who was pointing at the painting.

"No," the teacher replied. "This man's name is Adam. And the old man over there is God."

"Who are all the people floating around God?" a little girl asked.

"Those are God's angels."

"Oh, so the angels are telling God what to do," the little girl said.

"I hope they tell Adam to put some clothes on," a boy in the group added, sparking another chorus of laughter. He was promptly punched in the arm by the girl who had asked the question.

As Logan listened to the children's questions, he received a call on his PCD. It was Mr. Rampart again. *Well, he can't fire me twice,* Logan thought as he picked up.

"Hello, Mr. Rampart," he said, covering his ear with one hand. He had a tough time hearing with the children nearby.

"I called Mr. Quinn to inform him that in order to meet the deadline, I was going to turn the project over to another artist," Mr. Rampart said. Again, he went straight to the point. "I informed him that you had to deal with an emergency and would not be able to finish the work by the agreed-upon deadline."

"Yes," Logan acknowledged, trying to figure out why Mr. Rampart was calling.

"It seems you made quite an impression on Mr. Quinn," Mr. Rampart continued. "He told me that he did not want anyone but you to work on his painting and that I was to resecure your services immediately, as he was pushing back the deadline indefinitely. He urged me to communicate that fact to you straightaway. It appears that I was a bit hasty in my dismissal. I hope you will finish your work upon your return, whenever that might be."

"Yes, of course," Logan said, happily surprised. He walked away from the noisy group. "Thank you, Mr. Rampart. I look forward to getting it all done when I return to New Chicago. And please give my thanks to Mr. Quinn." Logan hung up and put his PCD away. *Well, that was a twist of fate,* he thought. He looked back over at the painting of Saint Sebastian, the patron saint of suffering, and shook his head. Why had Mr. Quinn taken such an interest in him? Certainly, there were many other artists who could finish the restoration.

The teacher now raised a green flag, and the children followed her out of the hall. Logan could hear the echo of their voices as they made their way out. He walked back over to the Michelangelo. *Was the little girl correct?* Logan thought. *Are the angels really telling God what to do? Maybe. Maybe they represent the conflicting voices in our own minds. Could that be the secret Sebastian referred to?*

"Adam looks like he's living a pretty good life," a familiar gruff voice said. The same tall, blond man who had snuck up on Logan near the Saint Sebastian painting was standing next to him again.

"He looks a little lazy, if you ask me," Logan said. He was in a friendlier mood after receiving the good news from Mr. Rampart. "All those faces represent the voices in our brains, you know. Some voices urging us to move forward, others telling us to go back. It's a wonderful allegory for our lives."

"You got all that from this painting?" the man asked. "You sound like one of those Satraya supporters. The world could use fewer of them."

"And you sound like one of those Sentinel Coterie members," Logan fired back, wondering if Fenquist was having one of his men follow him. He was starting to get a bad feeling about this stranger. He looked around for a security guard, but the hall was empty. The nearest exit was behind him, on the other side of the large exhibit hall, and the last of the children in the school group were leaving. Logan looked back at the man and noticed that one of his hands was concealed inside a pocket of his black leather jacket, which seemed out of place on a hot summer day.

"You're Logan Ford," the stranger said.

Logan didn't answer. He had to figure out how to get out of there. Maybe it was time to start running. "Bit hot for a jacket, isn't it?" Logan said, stalling for time.

The man looked back at the painting and started to pull something out of his jacket pocket. Logan grew tenser. "I'm cold-blooded," he said, as he pulled out a small pill box. He took some kind of green tablet from it and put it into his mouth. "Would you like one?" He showed Logan the box filled with little green tablets. "I'm told these things can save your life."

"There you are!" a voice suddenly called out. Logan turned and saw, with great relief, that Valerie was entering the hall with two agents behind her. "You can't just leave like that and not tell us where you're going!"

Logan quickly walked over to her.

"What's wrong?" she asked. "You look like you've seen a ghost."

"It's been an interesting day," Logan answered. "How did you find me?"

"We tracked your PCD and your badge," she said. "Don't leave like that again. You had me worried."

He looked down at his shirt and noticed he was still wearing the WCF badge he had received earlier. "Look behind me," he said, lowering his voice. "I think that man is following me."

Valerie looked over Logan's shoulder. "What man?" she asked.

Logan turned around. The stranger had disappeared.

26

Everything you wish to know lies in nature. Ask the tree its
purpose, and you will realize your own.
—THE CHRONICLES OF SATRAYA

Standing in front of the bookshelf, Mr. Perrot counted the origami
figures; there were ten, one short of the number of notes Camden had
written. Mr. Perrot picked up the first figure, folded in the shape of a
dog, and, with great care, began to unfold it.

"Forgive me, my friend," he whispered. "I most certainly will not be
able to put these back as I found them."

He took a letter opener from the desk and used it delicately to
pry open the many intricate folds. Soon he began to see words and
sentences written on the paper. He tempered his excitement and didn't
rush; the paper was fragile and could easily rip. After several minutes of
careful work, the origami dog was gone, and a message was revealed on
the creased sheet of paper in its place.

*Both of your questions can be answered simultaneously by my simply saying: I
am a man just like you. Perhaps another question you might like to ask is, What
do you know that I do not yet know? If that is your next query, then my answer*

would be: I know that a greater mind lives in ALL the peoples of the world. I was taught this philosophy at a very early age and have spent every day of my life dedicated to revealing this truth. It is what you are just beginning to understand. This is your childhood, so to speak. This understanding is what The Chronicles of Satraya *wish for the world and all who live upon it.* —YM

Mr. Perrot's heart raced. He had evidently found Baté's response to one of the notes Camden had left in the old study. He carefully gathered the remaining nine origami figures and took them back to the coffee table where Camden's notes to Baté lay. There he meticulously unfolded each animal figure: a horse, a rabbit, a mouse, a lion, a panda, an owl, a rhinoceros, an elephant, and finally a giraffe. Camden had recorded all of Baté's responses.

The horse note:

Things will get worse, my friend, before the new sun rises. But do not lose hope. As it is now known, the original Council will break. But the new Council that emerges will benefit from copies of the Chronicles *having already been spread far and wide. Fendral's desire cannot take hold at the moment. But stay aware. He is a diligent man, and he is not alone in wanting to enact his plan.* —SAPS

The rabbit note:

No, I am not the author. There is no single author. The books represent the combined experiences and wisdom of many like me who through the ages attained a deeper understanding of life and are waiting for all to awaken. Throughout history, other great books have been given so that people's thoughts might evolve. The Chronicles of Satraya *were not the first, nor will they be the last. But they are to this point the greatest culmination of all prior efforts. Their moment is now, and they will occupy an important segment of human history.* —DARGEN

The mouse note:

As it has always been, men and women must find their own way. Their free will must never be impeded. To do otherwise would only prolong their journey. This, in many ways, is the greatest teaching of all. I am permitted, however, to answer your questions. I am permitted to give you knowledge that will help you to direct your own power and your gift of choice. Remember the old adage: When a pupil is ready, a teacher will appear. —I

The lion note:

Remember, any flame can be used by anyone to train the mind to travel to many places. But in order to come to my study, you must use this particular Manas Mantr candle. It has a special link to me and the study. One day, you will be able to arrive without using it. Your mind will be trained sufficiently that this place will be readily accessible to you. However, if the Manas Mantr candle were to burn down before you complete your training, then I dare say you will not be able to visit here until another blessed candle is given to you. But I am certain you will use the tool diligently and successfully as I did long ago. There are other Manas Mantr candles in the world, and none of them was forged or gifted lightly. —OPND

The panda note:

Your wisdom is evident. Symbols are very much like the flame. They are also tools. They hold keys that will help the mind evolve. The secret symbols are gateways, slipstreams, to deeper levels of consciousness. When you have mastered all of them, you, too, will join those who have already traveled to that indescribable destination. —LOUDSH

The owl note:

The ancients have hidden many things. Some are hidden in plain sight; others are rooted in deeper mysteries. There is a great saying: For those who have the eyes to see, let them see. Maybe the key is not to look harder but to look softer. —LILW

The rhinoceros note:

I never met a man or a woman with the wisdom to administer the lessons of life to everyone. Man's greatest evolution is to be guided by the precepts of his own soul. The governments of your world will be restored soon enough, but let the great Satraya Council always remind people of the lessons of the Chronicles. *For if the knowledge contained in the* Chronicles *is applied, it will keep the leaders from tainting the music of humanity. But be careful, my friend. For man's desire for power is certainly a messy business. —AWY*

The elephant note:

So be it. —TONIP

The giraffe note:

You can never "do" anything wrong. "Doing" always leads to wisdom. Riddles run deep. —HET

As Mr. Perrot read each response, he attempted to pair it with one of Camden's original questions. Soon he was able to put all twenty-one notes in the order he guessed they had been written. He sat back and looked at them spread out on the table in front of him. Eleven notes from Camden but only ten answers from Baté. The note from Camden that fell out of *The Chronicles* at the auction didn't have a corresponding answer from Baté. Mr. Perrot picked it up. It was different from the other notes in that it had a valedictory tone and a date, November 19, 2037, the day before he, Camden, and Cassandra left Washington for good.

More questions had arisen in Mr. Perrot's mind. Where was the missing response? Who was Baté, and was he still alive? What were Deya's gift and her instructions?

He sighed. "One thing is clear to me, my friend," he whispered.

"Simon and Andrea are gathering the four original copies of the *Chronicles* because they have uncovered the existence of the secret symbols. They want the symbol of immortality."

As he sat forward on the couch, he examined Baté's responses again. Each one ended in a strange, seemingly nonsensical word.

"Did you find what you were looking for?" Jogi asked, entering the study and taking a seat across from Mr. Perrot. He had brought a few snacks from the kitchen.

"Yes," Mr. Perrot replied, "and the circumstances are much more urgent than I suspected."

"Is this one of the letters you were searching for?" Jogi picked up a sheet of paper and perused it.

"Yes, and they all end with a different strange word."

"That is interesting." Jogi picked up one of the other notes, replaced it, and then picked up another. "The words you're talking about seem to have all been written with the same pen. I would guess that would mean they were probably all written at the same time." He pointed, encouraging Mr. Perrot to take a closer look. "See how the main portions of the notes are written in different shades of blue ink and how the pen strokes vary from note to note, some thicker and others thinner? But look at the shades and the strokes of these final words; they're all the same. In addition to being written with the same pen, they might have also been written at the same time."

"Jogi, you're a genius!" Mr. Perrot exclaimed, as he rose and grabbed a pencil and paper from Camden's desk. He copied down each word in order: "YM SAPS DARGEN I OPND LOUDSH LILW AWY TONIP HET."

"What language is that?" Jogi asked.

"Riddles do indeed run deep," Mr. Perrot replied, referring to one of Baté's notes. "What are you telling us, Camden?"

The clock in the corner chimed.

"How about taking a break?" Jogi suggested. He handed Mr. Perrot a box of crackers, and they both munched as they continued to ponder the strange words they had uncovered. Jogi picked up one of the childhood paintings that Mr. Perrot had taken from a box. "Looks like someone was still learning to spell," he said with a grin.

Mr. Perrot took the painting of a sailboat from Jogi. "Yes, Logan must have been very young at the time," He read the message painted in red and blue above the boat: "I loev yuo mum and dad."

Suddenly, as if he'd forgotten he was holding it, he dropped the box of crackers. "You have simply jumbled the letters, haven't you, Camden?" he blurted out. "Let the children point the way," he added, as he rearranged the letters in their proper order. He sat back after some minutes and looked at what he'd come up with: "MY PASS GARDEN I POND SHOULD WILL WAY POINT THE."

"That part is solved," he observed, showing his work to Jogi. "But the words now need to be placed in the proper order."

Jogi grabbed another piece of paper from Camden's desk and assisted Mr. Perrot in rearranging the words. They tried a multitude of sentences, all of them nonsensical. Then they found the one that read: "MY GARDEN POND WILL POINT THE WAY SHOULD I PASS."

"Point the way to what?" Jogi asked.

Mr. Perrot smiled. "To an original set of the *Chronicles*. Deya often spoke of her garden pond back home in India. I believe these are the instructions she gave Camden." He turned to Jogi. "You know how to deal with my daughter in tense situations, don't you? Because she might be a bit annoyed when she hears that you and I are going to India."

27

There is a difference between being interconnected and being interdependent. The former is based in love; the latter is based in expectations.

—THE CHRONICLES OF SATRAYA

WASHINGTON, D.C., 6:00 P.M. LOCAL TIME,
3 DAYS UNTIL FREEDOM DAY

After leaving the museum, Logan and Valerie returned to her apartment for a respite from the investigation. Logan took a nap; Valerie continued to speak on her PCD with Charlie and other forensic agents.

At dinnertime, Valerie introduced Logan to her favorite restaurant, a small family-run Italian trattoria on Wisconsin Avenue. The motherly woman who owned the place always kept a special table for her in the back, near the kitchen.

"Piera takes good care of me," Valerie explained with a smile. "I never have to wait, and even if it's late, she'll find something good for me to eat."

The quiet, friendly atmosphere was exactly what Logan needed, along with a good meal, of course. He told Valerie more about his encounter with Randolph Fenquist and gave her more details about the blond-haired stranger who'd been following him in the museum.

"My day was just as crazy," Valerie said. "The lab was still in chaos when I returned from the press conference. Then, on top of that, no one knew what happened to you."

"Sorry about that," Logan said. "It was one thing to see that DNA collar, but when the rest took place just as I'd seen in my candle vision, it was a bit much. I had to get out of there." He took a deep breath. "Were they able to preserve the corpses?"

"No. Charlie called while you were resting and said the ice boxes didn't help. The bodies continued to decompose, and we can't extract any more DNA samples. Sylvia suspects the victims were exposed to some source of radiation. Oh, and more good news," Valerie added, as she took off her suit jacket and unclipped her holster. "The security footage from the National Gallery didn't get a good angle on the blond guy who was talking to you. It's like he knew where the cameras were."

"There was something peculiar about that guy," Logan said.

"Have you gotten any more insight into the whole candle thing?" Valerie continued. "I have to admit your visions have me as stumped as everything else in this case."

Logan was about to answer when Valerie's PCD lit up.

She took the call, and an image of Mr. Perrot was projected, hovering just over the table. "Hello, dear!" he shouted. "Can you see me? Jogi, is this working?"

"Yes, Dad, we can see you. Everything is working. You don't have to shout," Valerie added, smirking at Logan.

"We have made progress," Mr. Perrot said, and he went on to recount the success of his efforts in New Chicago. He explained the garden riddle, which he and Jogi had just solved, and told them about the references to the hidden symbols. "So as you can see, even more urgent questions have arisen."

"Hidden symbols on the blank pages?" Logan said gravely. "And the last symbol grants . . . *immortality*?"

"Yes, the situation is even more perilous than we thought," Mr. Perrot said. "So, you see, I believe the next step for me is to travel to India and locate Deya's set of the *Chronicles* before Simon or Andrea does."

"I'm not sure I like that idea," Valerie said. "I could have the WCF send a few agents to look for the books just as easily. Where are they?"

"Deya's message doesn't provide a great deal to go on," Mr. Perrot said. "I knew Deya. I believe I stand a better chance of finding the books than your agents do. We cannot allow Simon and Andrea to find all of the original sets."

Valerie didn't say anything, but she didn't look happy.

"Valerie," Mr. Perrot said in a softer tone, "don't fight me on this. I know what I need to do."

She pointed her finger at the image of her father. "All right, but Jogi is going to go with you. And both of you *will* keep us informed every step of the way."

"Yes, of course, Valerie," Jogi said, as he entered the projection just behind Mr. Perrot. "Nothing will happen to your father on my watch."

"Good-bye, dear," Mr. Perrot said. "And I expect you and Logan to keep me informed, too."

Logan and Valerie nodded, and the call ended.

"Don't worry," Logan said afterward. "After observing your father the last few days, I have to say he's more capable than we give him credit for. The old guy's got some moxie."

Dinner was now arriving. Piera brought out a large family-style salad with an assortment of breads and cheese. She also set down a carafe of red wine. "Don't worry, dear," she said in a thick Italian accent. "Drink some wine. No one can see you back here. It is not all the time you bring such a handsome boy to dinner." Piera winked at Valerie and pinched Logan's cheek. "*Buon appetito!* More is coming!"

Valerie rolled her eyes as Piera headed back to the kitchen.

Logan grinned. "I guess I should be flattered you brought me here tonight," he said. "It doesn't sound like you've introduced many of your boyfriends to Piera and her cooking."

Valerie blushed as she picked up the carafe and poured each of them a glass of wine. "This is a business dinner. Let's get back to the investigation."

Logan smiled and acquiesced, taking a sip of wine. "There's something more about the Hitchlords family. Camden, I mean, my father"—Logan was still getting used to his father's real identity—"tried to work out some branches of their family tree on the back of one of his journal pages. I can't help but think it might have to do with the secret my father uncovered about Fendral. And that uncovering the secret ourselves will help us understand what's going on."

"I was thinking the same thing," Valerie said. She took a big sip of wine, enjoying it even if it was against regulations. "We could search the old document archives at the Akasha Vault to see if there's anything there."

"I thought the Vault only contained post-Disruption documents and records," Logan said.

"Mostly but not only." Valerie picked her PCD back up. "There were a great many computer systems and data centers that partially survived the Great Disruption. The WCF put a lot of effort into recovering as much information from those systems as possible. They thought it might prove useful someday. Even today, when they find an old computer system, they send it to Nepal for data retrieval and storage. There's a dedicated team who does nothing but that."

"And you think there may be information about Simon's father in there?" Logan said.

"You never know." She pushed her plate aside and brought up a WCF interface to the Akasha Vault archive.

Logan leaned forward, as Valerie navigated through many topics and subtopics until she pulled up a file on the Hitchlords family. "Not much of interest about Simon," she said as she read. "Our current records show that he was about eight at the time of the Great Disruption. His father, Fendral, was thirty-eight." She continued to navigate rapidly through the archived data.

Logan pulled out a couple of the pages from his father's journal and handed one to Valerie. "This might help," he said. "The Hitchlords family tree my father was working on. Simon's grandmother, Carmella

Snow Hitchlords, had a relationship with a man named 'Maurice Rc.' My father didn't complete Maurice's last name."

Valerie read the names on the journal page and started to type them into the Vault interface. "There's some good stuff on these people. Your father may have been on to something."

Logan tried to see what Valerie was reading, but he was distracted by the flashing indicators next to some of the files in the archive. "What are all those red marks?"

"They represent missing data," she explained. "These old archives are incomplete at best. There's a lot of information they weren't able to recover. Many times, you have to fill in the blanks. For instance, Simon's ancestry dates all the way back to 1027 and Conrad II of the Salian dynasty; it might even extend as far back as the fourth century, but there are no complete records to confirm it." She turned from the projection and looked at the journal page. "What are these names and identifiers your father wrote next to some of the names in the family tree?"

James Rc. (Knights of the Golden Circle 1854)
Maurice Rc. (Thule 1911)
Maurice Rc. (Federal Reserve 1913)
Carmella Hitchlords (Bilderberg 1954)
Edmond Hitchlords (MJ-12 1978)

"When your father and I first saw them in the family-tree diagram, he inferred that they were names of influential clandestine groups throughout history," Logan answered. "He wasn't familiar with any of them, except for the middle one, the Federal Reserve."

Valerie started to enter the names into the Vault computer.

Logan continued, "Apparently, the Federal Reserve was at the center of the financial crisis that was taking place in the United States. Your father said that most people were under the impression that the Federal Reserve was a part of the government. But actually, it was a privately held bank involved in some pretty shady financial dealings. Bank bailouts earlier this century and the incestuous relationships that Federal Reserve board members had with the very financial institutions they were helping eventually brought it down during the financial reset of 2025. Your father also mentioned its behind-the-scenes involvement in something called a credit default swap that took place in 2010. Whatever that was created financial chaos and brokered a well-orchestrated transfer of wealth from the middle class to the wealthy."

Valerie kept navigating. "A lot is missing, but all of these groups have one thing in common: they were mired in controversy and conspiracy."

"Check out this information on the Thule Society," Logan said. "It was a study group created in 1911 for the appreciation of Germanic antiquity. Adolf Hitler later turned it into the Nazi Party. The group included a man named Hess and another person named Eckart."

"The family tree suggests that Fendral's father and grandfather were members of that group," Valerie observed. "And look at this about the Knights of the Golden Circle. According to this document, the Knights reordered themselves and became the Sons of Liberty in 1865. They were bent on annexing territories in the southern part of the United States and later might have played a part in a group called the Ku Klux Klan. They don't sound like very nice people."

One by one, Valerie brought up information on every name in the family tree Camden had somehow put together.

"This is starting to make some sense," she said, deep in thought. "Prior to the Great Disruption, the Hitchlords family was associated with some of these groups. Then the Disruption hits, and the world falls into chaos. The *Chronicles* are discovered, and the Hitchlords family is unable to reclaim its power and fame. Since Fendral found a set of the books, he ends up on the Council. And after a few years, he wants to transform it into a shadow group just like these other ones."

"To what end?"

"Well, if history is any indicator, Fendral needed to restore his family's standing in the world. I wonder if this was the secret your father came across." Valerie was about to take a sip of wine, but she paused, noticing the solemn look on Logan's face. "What's wrong?"

"Nothing, really. I just don't understand why the *Chronicles* chose Fendral."

"What do you mean, they *chose* Fendral?"

"The man who owns the painting I'm restoring came to the auction and told me that the *Chronicles* chose whom they belonged to. But then, why choose Fendral? I understand Deya, Madu, and my father, but why Fendral and the Hitchlords family?" Logan shook his head.

"Put your work away," a pleasant voice called. Piera appeared, holding two large plates. Valerie shut down the PCD display. "You work too much! Tonight you eat my homemade brasato!" Within moments, a waiter cleared the table, and Piera set down the dinner plates, which were filled with her beef stew, polenta, and steamed carrots and zucchini. "*Buon appetito!* More is coming!" she said once again, before walking back into the kitchen.

"I'm not sure I believe that whole thing about the books choosing where they go," Valerie continued when Piera had gone. "But if the Hitchlords family has been associated with these groups throughout history, it would be a fair bet that they're associated with another one now. I think we have to assume that whatever is going on, Simon and Andrea are not acting alone."

It didn't take long for Valerie's detective instincts to kick into full gear again. She pushed her plate aside and reconnected her PCD to the Akasha Vault's computer system. Information concerning the Hitchlords family was once again being displayed along with flashing indicators.

After a moment, Valerie raised her eyebrows. "Check this out. It looks as though the old WCF—or FBI, as it was called then—was investigating the Hitchlords family before the Great Disruption hit.

Something about gold and precious metal trading just before the financial reset of 2025. The FBI even seized communications data from servers at one of the Hitchlords companies accused of price fixing in the diamond markets. It says here that the e-mail data were encrypted. Before the FBI was able to process the information, the U.S. and South African governments put a halt to the investigation."

"Well, judging by the family's connections, I'm not surprised," Logan said. "What's e-mail?"

Valerie rolled her eyes. "Don't you know anything about how people lived before the Great Disruption?"

He shrugged.

She thought for a moment, tapping her fingers on the table. "The FBI never decrypted the data," she said.

"Can we do it?" Logan asked.

She didn't answer; with a few quick motions of her hand, she already had the quantum computer deciphering the messages.

After a moment, appearing on the projection were the last few e-mails that Fendral sent in 2024, some forty-five years ago. One in particular caught Valerie's eye. It was dated January 23, 2024.

> *My friend Dario,*
>
> *Most everything is in place. We are just about ready to execute the removal of the United States dollar as the world's reserve currency and replace it with four others. You will have until late October of this year to divest yourself of your U.S. $ holdings. After the change, our global investments should increase in value three times over.*
>
> *Catherine's family will handle all of the money exchanges for the members. She has spoken to the chairman of the Federal Reserve. All is set.*
>
> *Give my love to Maria and the children.*
>
> *FH*
>
> *P.S. We are also monitoring the activities of this newly formed Crowd Twelve. We will handle if required.*

"I wonder who Dario and Catherine are," Logan said.

"And whether they're still around," Valerie added. She skimmed through more of the e-mails, finding nothing significant. "I have a feeling they are."

"Ready for dessert?" Piera suddenly arrived with a cart full of fruit and pastries. It was almost as if nothing was wrong.

28

Pass your values on to your children, but do not be afraid to let
your traditions go.
—THE CHRONICLES OF SATRAYA

ALEXANDRIA, VIRGINIA. 7:00 P.M. LOCAL TIME,
3 DAYS UNTIL FREEDOM DAY

Black SUVs lined the circular driveway of an old Federal-style home
on the outskirts of Washington, D.C., in the city of Alexandria, Virginia. After the Great Disruption, the National Trust had sold the
historic Woodlawn Plantation to a holding company owned by Fendral Hitchlords in order to help finance regional rebuilding efforts.
While Fendral, Andrea, and Fendral's son, Simon, had maintained official residences in the center of Washington during their time on the
Council of Satraya, the plantation always remained their secret retreat.
After the splintering of the Council and the trio's departure from the
North American Federation, the Hitchlords family retained ownership
of the plantation; but over the years, the property itself had fallen into
disrepair.

No one in the area had taken much notice when restoration work
began on the plantation's house and grounds eight years ago. The lawns
and shrubbery were remanicured, the house was repainted, and the roof
was replaced. The 126 acres of woodlands, streams, and meadows that

surrounded the house provided a certain amount of privacy. Now the plantation served as Simon and Andrea's base of operations whenever their work necessitated a visit to the NAF's east coast.

Inside the early-nineteenth-century plantation house, which was guarded by armed men wearing black pants and fitted white shirts, Andrea sat in a parlor behind a rosewood desk and spoke to Simon via her PCD. "How are your travels going?" she asked.

"I find India to be hot, overcrowded, and most uninviting," Simon said. "Deya's son was of modest help. I will be commencing my search for the books tomorrow."

"Why the urgency to collect the books now?" Andrea asked, annoyed. "Can't that wait until our plans with Era have been executed?"

"The books must be located now, I assure you," Simon said matter-of-factly. "But speaking of our plans, shouldn't you be out of the NAF by now? I am certain the authorities will want to speak to anyone related to the tragedy that befell the Council."

"Yes," Andrea said, "but we have learned that the son of Camden and Cassandra Ford has come forward. After all these years, Camden still haunts us." Andrea saw a flicker of surprise on the image of Simon's face. "Did you not see the press conference?"

"I've been occupied with more important matters. Send me the video," he ordered.

"I shall. Logan Ford has taken his father's place on the Council. They are talking about a renewed vigor and commitment to their work." Andrea paused, not exactly sure how to phrase her next question. "Did you know that Camden and Cassandra were murdered two years ago? At their home in New Chicago, where they had lived since they disappeared from Washington thirty-two years ago?"

Simon was silent for a moment, then said with obvious exasperation, "Why concern yourself with them, let alone their son? What matters is that the Council will be going into retirement soon, whether they like it or not. Freedom Day is almost upon us."

"You didn't answer my question," Andrea said pointedly.

Simon waved his hand dismissively. "I am not inclined to walk down memory lane."

Andrea knew it wasn't wise to press Simon further, so, merely taking note, she moved on to more practical matters. "At the urging of Camden's son, the Council is considering delaying—or even canceling—the Freedom Day celebration this year in support of their fallen comrades."

"Of what consequence is that?" Simon snapped impatiently. "If they decide to cancel the celebration, we will still execute our plan as scheduled."

"The doctor does not think that is advisable. He told me rather emphatically that Freedom Day celebrations must take place in order for the Purging to be most effective. When people are focused on their freedom, their brain chemistry is heightened and more receptive to our solution," Andrea explained. "We would achieve an extermination rate of only fifty percent if the celebrations are canceled. Ninety-five percent if they go on as planned."

"You mean, we'd be leaving the job half done," Simon observed. Andrea nodded. "Well, that is most disappointing. But we have too much invested to delay our plans now."

"It seems that Camden's son has more information than we would like," Andrea continued. "He reportedly helped the authorities discover the secret tunnel. And they have somehow connected our operative to the murders. The WCF is looking for her as we speak." Simon did not respond. Andrea knew what he was considering. "We can trust her," she said.

"Can we?" Simon asked doubtfully.

"Yes. And if she gives me reason to change my mind, we will deal with it at that time," Andrea said. "Remember we have quite a bit of leverage with her."

"Hmm," Simon murmured. "It may be time to call in a few political favors. And perhaps making a few large donations to the Council of Satraya during these tough times might persuade them to continue their scheduled celebrations. My understanding is that their coffers could use a bit of a boost."

"There is one more item, Simon," Andrea said. "In his interview, Camden's son spoke of the *Creation of Adam* painting."

"He did *what?*" Simon shouted. "In what *way* did he speak of it?"

"It seems that he is an artist of sorts," Andrea explained. "While he did not provide any direct insight into the painting, the mere mention of it concerned me. I fear Camden told him too much about the past."

Simon stayed silent for a moment. "That would be most unfortunate," he said. "We must find out what the Ford boy knows. It seems that Hitchlords and Ford are destined to meet again."

"Agreed," Andrea said before Simon disconnected the call.

Just then, there was a knock on the parlor door. "Ah, come in, my dear," Andrea said, as the door slowly opened. Monique Sato, Cynthia Brown's former assistant, entered. "Come, sit. I am told the authorities are looking for you."

"They have nothing concrete that ties me to the Council murders," Monique said quickly. Gone was the bubbly demeanor she had displayed when she worked for Cynthia. Now Monique spoke in a cold, hard manner. "They're grasping at straws. I'm going to be leaving the NAF anyway."

"I see. And how are you planning to travel unnoticed?"

"I have a friend in the state of Quebec who has arranged for safe transportation to Japan."

"That's good to hear, dear." Andrea wrote something on a piece of notepaper. "But before you leave the Federation, make your way to this address. Lucius is waiting for you with some instructions."

"Lucius? Why?" Monique looked alarmed.

"Please, dear, he needs your assistance with one more task."

Monique took the piece of paper from Andrea and quickly left the parlor.

29

Everyone has a story. The greatest libraries in your lands could
never compare to the library that holds the individual epics of
everyone who has ever lived.
—THE CHRONICLES OF SATRAYA

"This certainly looks like the bench my father described in his journal
entries," Logan said, as he and Valerie walked around Compass Park
after dinner. "In fact, I know it is."

"How can you be so certain?" Valerie asked.

"Because of this." Logan slid his fingers across an etching that someone had carved into the back of the bench.

"This is the same symbol that my father doodled in the upper corner
of his journal pages."

Valerie's attention was drawn to the large stone monument in the
middle of a fountain pool across from the bench. It had been erected
in honor of the twelve original Council members, whose names were

chiseled into the large rectangular block of black granite. Logan joined Valerie at the monument.

> *Camden Ford*
> *Cassandra Ford*
> *Robert Tilbo*
> *Fendral Hitchlords*
> *Andrea Montavon*
> *Simon Hitchlords*
> *Deya Sarin*
> *Babu Sarin*
> *Joyti Dehuri*
> *Madu Shata*
> *Shai Shata*
> *Nadine Shata*

"I've walked past that thing a hundred times," Valerie remarked, "but now, seeing our parents' names . . . What do you do when everything you've believed about your life is suddenly flipped on its head?"

"I don't think it takes anything away from us," Logan answered. "In fact, it adds more dimension to our existence. It's like waking up into the life of a stranger. More than a few times in the past, I wished I could have done just that."

"Spoken like a true artist." She dipped her hand into the fountain that surrounded the monument. "It still makes me wonder, though."

"Wonder about what?" he asked.

She hesitated to answer, running her hand back and forth through the water. "Just about my mother," she finally confided. "She died when I was born. I wonder if she was a part of all this."

He nodded, not knowing what to say. But it occurred to him that he couldn't recall his parents ever talking about Valerie's mother.

They strolled back to the bench and sat down. It was a warm night, and, aside from an occasional blast of loud music from cars passing along 17th Street or the sound of slamming doors as taxis picked up or dropped off passengers, all was quiet. A few people were strolling through the park and walking dogs. A young couple with their arms around each other were tossing coins into the fountain.

"It's pleasant here," Valerie said. "I can see why your father chose this place."

An arched brick entranceway and a neatly trimmed three-foot-high hedge separated the park from the four streets bordering it. Wide brick pathways connected the eight distinct sections of the park grounds. Each section was named after a distinguished person or group who had contributed to the rebuilding effort after the Great Disruption. The granite monument and the infinity pool were the centerpieces of this particular section, which was dedicated to the Council of Satraya.

Logan sat silently and looked around, trying to take in the moment, trying to see the park through his father's eyes. "Do you ever wonder what life was like back then?" he asked. "You know, the days right after the Great Disruption?"

"Those were scary, interesting times," Valerie said. "But I think we also live in interesting times. Maybe one day, our kids will wonder what life was like in 2069."

Logan laughed.

"What's so funny?" she asked.

"You don't really come across as someone who wants to have kids," he said. "Your job and all, round 'em up and bang 'em up."

She laughed, too. "Yes, my job. I suppose that's true."

"But life has a way of presenting itself," he said, attempting to soften his statement. "Change happens quickly, usually when you need it the most. You would make a great parent."

The two of them sat still, enjoying the cool evening breeze. He looked again at the couple by the fountain, who were throwing more coins, and at the names on the granite block at its center.

"Wait a minute!" he exclaimed, and he reached into his backpack and sorted through the pages of his father's journal until he found what he was looking for. "Read this section right here," he said, handing the page to Valerie.

> Sit where you may mind your enemy,
> Remember forever their names as if etched into stone.
> That which supports you in your vigilance
> Will ultimately be your savior.

There was a quizzical expression on her face as she handed the note back to him.

"Look in front of you," he said. He pointed to the monument. "Sitting here, we can see, or *mind*, the name of my father's enemy, his name etched into stone."

Valerie nodded, taking the note back from him. "So what does the last part mean? Our savior?" They were silent a moment, trying to piece the puzzle together.

"The bench!" Logan cried out. "'That which supports you'—my father is talking about this bench. Somehow this bench is our savior." He stood and walked around it, inspecting it for any additional markings or anything out of the ordinary.

"Maybe it's the symbol he carved into it?" Valerie proposed.

"There has to be something more," he answered, as he walked around the bench, looking for something that might support his claim.

"Leave it for now," she said. Then she grabbed him by the arm. There was an intense look on her face.

"What's wrong?"

"That black vehicle over there, right around the corner from the park entrance, drove up about four minutes ago and has been idling there. What's it waiting for? And you see that couple over there, near the fountain? They've been tossing coins for ten minutes now. No one makes that many wishes. We need to get out of here."

"You think we're being followed?"

She ignored his question. "When I tell you, we are going to walk casually out of the park and back across the street." She pulled her PCD out of a jacket pocket.

"What are you doing?" Logan asked. "Let's just go."

"Standard procedure," she calmly replied. "Calling for backup. They will be able to track my PCD and send help." She finished issuing the distress call and put her PCD into her pocket. Then she took her gun from its holster and placed it in the other pocket of her jacket.

Logan realized his heart was racing.

"Ready?" she whispered as she stood. "Just act as if we're enjoying the evening."

As they walked away from the bench, they heard the sound of a police siren in the distance, and Logan felt a bit of relief.

Valerie looked back over her shoulder at the fountain. "Where'd they go?" she asked.

Logan turned. The couple who had been tossing coins was gone.

Valerie and Logan walked down the brick path and made their way to the street. The arched entrance to the park was about thirty meters ahead of them. Logan noticed two men entering the park, walking toward them. Valerie grabbed his elbow with her left hand and slipped her right hand into her pocket, where her gun was concealed. "Stay calm," she whispered, gripping her gun. "If they try anything, drop to the ground."

Logan's heart raced faster. As the men passed without incident, he could hear them talking about the local baseball team. The exit was only a meter away, and the sirens were getting louder.

"Almost there," Valerie said, continuing to hold Logan's arm.

They passed under the arched entrance. A sports car sped down the street, blasting music. Then the barrels of two guns were suddenly pressed to the backs of their heads, and a large hand clamped down on Valerie's as she withdrew her gun. Instinctively, she struggled for control of her weapon.

"Let go! It would be real easy to shoot your friend," a male voice warned.

Logan shoved the man's arm, trying to help her.

"Don't, Logan!" she said, reluctantly surrendering her gun.

"She's got the right idea," the male voice said.

Plastic zip ties were slipped around their wrists, binding their hands, and black sacks were placed over their heads. Simultaneously, the black vehicle came screeching around the corner and skidded to a stop in front of them.

"Deactivate their PCDs," a female voice said. "The cops are almost here."

Logan and Valerie were shoved into the back of the vehicle, and seconds later, it sped away. The last thing they heard was: "We have them."

30

If it be a lie that all people have a holy spirit within them, and if
it be a lie that you should endeavor to honor and have compassion
for all around you, then let these be the greatest lies ever uttered.
—THE CHRONICLES OF SATRAYA

NEAR BANARAS, INDIA, 8:30 A.M. LOCAL TIME,
3 DAYS UNTIL FREEDOM DAY

Sebastian Quinn sat on a hilltop overlooking a small Indian village a
few hundred miles southwest of Banaras, India. His ever-watchful com-
panion Bukya—named after a great warrior from one of the adventure
tales recounted in *The Chronicles of Satraya*—sat next to him, listening to
the sounds coming from the forest beyond the village. Sebastian sat motionless, gazing at the eastern horizon. The glorious rays of the mighty
sun had driven the haunting light of the night's moon and stars into
faded memory. A new day had dawned.

"Greet every morning. For each rising sun represents the dawning of
your enlightenment. And perhaps one splendid morning, it will be the
sun that watches you rise." Sebastian's father had spoken those words to
him as they watched a similar sunrise together from Peel Castle. Like
the sages of old, Sebastian and Bukya, two travelers from a distant land,
now watched from on high as the day began for the villagers below.

After a day of searching, Sebastian had located the remote village
he had seen in his candle vision thirty-six hours earlier. He recalled the

main dirt road that ran through the center of the village and the many small clay hovels that stood on either side of it. There was a small creek, born of a sinkhole, just to the north, which supplied water for farmers to irrigate their crops in a field nearby. During the Great Disruption, sinkholes had formed all over northern India. While the holes that accumulated water proved useful to farmers, the ones that remained dark and empty posed problems. Barricades were constructed around them to keep careless people from discovering just how deep they were.

Sebastian watched now as the villagers awoke and tended to their many daily tasks, which generations of people before them had performed. Despite its impact on the terrain, the Great Disruption had had little effect on these people. Their needs were simple and easily met, and they depended on no one but themselves for their sustenance. The younger children took care of the chickens and milked the cows while their fathers used horses and oxen to drag plows through the fields. The women of the village walked to the creek, carrying baskets of clothes on their heads. It was washing day.

Sebastian was relieved that the scene in front of him was so vastly different from the one he'd witnessed in the candle. "Looks like fortune has blessed these people and their lands," he said to Bukya, who was now starting to pant as the heat from the sun intensified. "I am most relieved that this is not the adventure I thought it was going to be." He poured some of the water from his bottle into a small bowl so his faithful partner could slake his thirst.

Bukya suddenly stopped drinking and rose to all fours, his ears pointed straight up, his nose sniffing frantically in all directions.

"What is it, my friend?" Sebastian asked. He couldn't detect anything unusual taking place in the village below. Nevertheless, Bukya began to whine. Flocks of birds flew from the trees. The livestock of the village became agitated and began a frantic march toward the forest. Sebastian rose to his feet, knowing that the birds and animals were reacting to something that humans couldn't see or hear.

As Sebastian surveyed the valley, hoping to ascertain what was causing the disruption, a sudden flash of intense green light filled the village below. Bukya let out a series of loud barks. Sebastian watched the light form a greenish dome over the village. He stroked the fur on Bukya's forehead to calm him. After a few seconds, the green bubble faded, and the light was gone.

"I do not know. I do not know what that was," Sebastian said, as if answering Bukya's question.

The light vanished as suddenly as it had appeared. Sebastian could see the villagers lying motionless on the ground. Helicopters could be heard approaching the village from the north. Sebastian knelt and watched as two black craft hovered low, one over the farming fields and one over the village. Three people wearing white hazmat suits jumped from the latter. Each was carrying a black case to which some kind of measuring device was tethered.

Sebastian watched their activities as they moved from body to body along the main road, but from his distant vantage point, it was difficult to tell what they were looking for. After no more than three minutes, the people in the hazmat suits reboarded the helicopter, and both craft sped off to the north, the same direction from which they had come.

Sebastian rose to his feet, closed his eyes, and took a deep breath. His vision had been accurate after all. His initial relief was replaced with sadness. He gathered his belongings and walked back to the Jeep with Bukya. Then he cautiously drove down a winding trail that led to the village.

He parked the vehicle at the edge of the village and walked slowly down the center street. A strong wind from the east blew dust around. Bukya had ventured ahead, weaving his way in and out of the small hovels and sniffing the numerous bodies now lying on the road. Sebastian stopped and knelt by an elderly man who had been carrying a basket of wheat, which had spilled on the ground around him. He examined him for any signs of life, but there was no breath or pulse. He pushed open the man's eyelids to examine his pupils. *What evil is at work here?* he thought, as he left the man and walked over to a teenage girl who was still grasping the sack of dirty clothes she must have been carrying to the creek. He checked her pulse and sadly confirmed that she, too, was dead. He removed an empty syringe from his bag and extracted a sample of blood from the girl's body. Ten or more other corpses lay scattered on the main road, more could be seen in the farming fields, and yet others lay near the creek. Sebastian looked around for any sign of survivors, but he saw none. It seemed the entire village population had been killed. Sebastian watched as the birds returned to their nests in the trees and the animals settled back down.

A loud bark rang out. Sebastian looked around and saw Bukya standing in the doorway of a small clay house. A second bark rang out, indicating that the dog had found something.

An old woman was slouched in a bamboo rocking chair under the covered porch of the hovel. Sebastian pressed her eyelids closed. He could hear whining inside. Upon entering, he saw Bukya standing at the foot of a makeshift baby crib. A slight breeze entered through an open window, moving a handcrafted wind chime. From the crib, a set of tiny hands and feet motioned excitedly at the movement and the sound of the chimes. Sebastian walked over and gently took the baby into his arms.

"So you have been spared the fate of your parents," he said. He looked for any signs of distress on the infant's body. "And for what reason we cannot say at this moment."

Holding the baby, he examined the inside of the hut and realized it was the village's infirmary. Small shelves contained a variety of bandages and other rudimentary supplies. A corner cabinet held more potent medicines.

"So what is your secret, little one?" Sebastian said in a soothing voice as he walked over to examine the contents of an open box that displayed the emblem of the World Health Administration. Sebastian took one of the medicine vials from the box labeled "Tetanus Toxoid." "Looks like your village received vaccinations recently," he mused aloud. "Did they give you some of this?" He put the vial into his shoulder bag and, with the baby still in his arms, walked back outside, Bukya following closely behind him.

He activated his PCD and reported the tragedy in the village to the local authorities.

"What should be your fate, my tiny friend, now that your family is no more?" He looked into the baby's deep brown eyes. "What say you, Bukya? Do we leave this little one here for the authorities to find? Or do we set him asail on an adventure in which this intended tragedy is transformed into his unintended destiny? This little one may hold the key to what happened here."

Bukya let out another great bark and nudged Sebastian to turn around.

Sebastian turned. Walking toward them was a young girl, about ten years of age, carrying another infant in her arms and closely followed by twin boys who Sebastian guessed were about two years old. Soon there were five pairs of innocent eyes looking up at him.

"I'm not sure how I'm going to explain all of this to Lawrence. One of you was going to be hard enough, but five?"

Bukya let out another loud bark to express his approval of the decision.

31

*See life through your own eyes, not through the lens of someone
else's advice.*
—THE CHRONICLES OF SATRAYA

ALEXANDRIA, VIRGINIA, 10:15 P.M. LOCAL TIME,
3 DAYS UNTIL FREEDOM DAY

Logan didn't know where he had been taken. He surmised that they
had traveled approximately thirty minutes, and mostly on a highway,
because there had been few stops or turns. The sack was still secured
over his head, and his hands were still bound. He wondered how Valerie
was faring and hoped his backpack was somewhere in tow. When the
car had stopped and the door had opened, he'd felt a blast of warm,
humid air. As he'd been led into a building, he'd heard the sound of
crickets. They were in the country, somewhere in Virginia or Maryland,
he figured. Now he was seated in a straight-backed chair in an un-air-
conditioned room.

"You there, Val?" he asked in a whisper.

"Yes," her muffled voice responded.

"Quiet!" a male voice yelled.

As they sat in the darkness, Logan continued to think about who
would have the audacity to kidnap him and Valerie, a WCF agent, from
a public park. *Was this the Coterie finally carrying out their threat?*

The silence was broken by the sounds of footsteps and a door closing.

"Remove their hoods and bindings," a female voice ordered. "There's little need for us to treat our guests so harshly. I am certain they will be most civil."

Immediately, the restraints were removed from Logan's hands, and the sack was removed from his head. He rubbed his wrists to regain circulation and allowed his eyes to adjust to the light. He was in the parlor of a historic old house, Federalist era, he figured, judging by the furniture and the size of the windows, which were open, letting in a welcome breeze. To his relief, he saw Valerie seated to his right. They exchanged a quick glance and then both looked at the people around them. The woman he recognized; she wore the same red hood she had worn during the auction. She was flanked by a young dark-haired woman wearing a short skirt, a tank top, and high heels and a tall blond man in jeans and a black T-shirt. Logan recognized him, too; he was the strange man from the museum. Off to the side stood two more men, large and muscular, the ones who had abducted them.

"Andrea," Logan said in a low voice, as a chill ran down his spine. He was now face-to-face with the woman he believed had helped murder his parents.

"And you're Monique," Valerie said to the young woman. "We have been looking for you."

"And you—you were stalking me at the museum," Logan said, turning to the tall blond man.

"Stalking? We were only talking," the man replied. "Perhaps you're referring to your meeting with Fenquist on the street. Now, that was stalking. You should have reported that to the police."

"Be quiet, Lucius. We have business to attend to." Andrea stepped closer to Logan. "You do look like your father, but you have your mother's eyes. They disappeared so mysteriously all those years ago, I wasn't even able to say good-bye to my friends after all we had achieved together. How are they these days?"

"You know good and well how they are!" Logan shouted. He couldn't hold back. He lunged forward, only to be pulled back roughly into his chair by one of the mercenaries standing behind him. "Who murders people and calls them their friends?"

"You shouldn't throw accusations like that around," Andrea said. "We were friends once."

"Let's cut out the pleasantries," Valerie interrupted.

Andrea turned to her. "And who might you be, my dear?"

"They were together in the park," Monique answered. "We had no choice but to bring her in, too."

"You look familiar." Andrea lifted Valerie's chin with her finger.

Valerie slapped Andrea's hand away. "My name is Valerie Perrot. I work for the WCF, and it would be in your best interest to let us go."

"Ah, yes, I thought I'd seen you before," Andrea said, continuing to gaze at Valerie. "Yet there's something else about you. Lucius, do you recall seeing her before?"

"No," Lucius replied. "Only from the news broadcasts."

"It will come to me." Andrea pulled her hood back a bit and turned her attention back to Logan. "You say that your parents were murdered? A shame that they met such a fate. They were upstanding people. And what of their friend? What was his name? Robert—Robert Tilbo. What of him? I would very much like to speak with him."

Logan didn't like where the conversation was headed. Quickly he said, "He's dead. He died of a heart attack many years ago."

Andrea gave no response. Just a short, pensive nod.

"You have to let us go," Valerie warned. "This place is going to be surrounded by agents very soon."

"I doubt that." Lucius threw two disabled PCDs onto the desk next to where Logan's backpack lay. "They're probably still searching the park. They have no idea where the two of you are."

A part of Logan was relieved to see his backpack. "What do you want with us?" he asked.

Andrea took a seat behind her desk and stared at him. "I can definitely see your father in you—always direct and to the point. So let me also be direct and to the point. Do you know why your parents were murdered?" She paused, but only for a moment. "They were weak-minded people. They had a need to save everyone they met. They were probably killed by some homeless man they rescued on the street and invited into their home." She shook her head. "The *Chronicles* can't save everybody. Sometimes, well, you just have to let people die."

"Sounds like you still harbor some resentment for their derailing your plans," Logan said. The mercenary standing behind him grabbed him by the hair and tugged on it. His neck twisted back in pain.

"Resentment?" Andrea raised her hand, signaling to the mercenary to ease up. "No, I have no resentment. Your parents lacked vision, they lacked purpose, they lacked the leadership skills required to make the Council what it could have been. What it *should* have been."

"Then why did you and Fendral threaten the members of the Council?" Logan lashed out defiantly. "Is that the type of leadership you had to offer?" Andrea remained silent, but a hint of surprise flickered across her face. "My parents left because Fendral would stop at nothing to exert his control. They split up the Council because they couldn't let you and that tyrant implement your so-called vision."

"You sound just like your father!" Andrea said, raising her voice in amusement. "This is precisely what I meant when I said your parents lacked vision."

"We know what you're up to," Logan continued. "You want all the books. That is why you murdered the Council members."

"Logan!" Valerie said, trying to stop him from saying too much.

"No, please don't interrupt him," Andrea urged. "I am most amused by this story."

Logan stopped.

Andrea waited a moment for him to say more, but when he didn't, she smiled and continued. "It is true that we are passionate collectors. And when the books came up for auction, why shouldn't we have been enthusiastic about securing them? They do, after all, represent a memorable part of our lives. And clearly, you benefited from the proceeds."

"What about Cairo?" Logan demanded, refusing to back down. "What moved you to steal those books and kill three people?"

"Collateral damage," Lucius muttered.

"Silence, Lucius!"

"What difference does it make, Mother? It's over for these two anyway. They have little value to us at this point."

"So it's true, you were behind the Cairo theft and the Council murders," Valerie said contemptuously, turning her gaze to Monique. "And those were your footprints we found in the tunnel." Monique did not answer. "No need to deny it; you're still wearing the same shoes—a size six and a half pair of Pierre Masus."

Monique's eyes darted quickly to Andrea and then back down to the floor. The room remained silent for a moment.

"I fear my son is correct," Andrea said. "It is time that we are rid of the two of you."

Lucius pulled out his gun, anticipating his mother's next instructions.

"They are all yours, Lucius."

"You don't want to do that," Logan said.

"And why not, pray tell?" Andrea asked.

"If you kill us, you'll never find the fourth set of the *Chronicles*."

Andrea paused. Her eyebrows lifted slightly. "What could you possibly know about the fourth set?"

"I know where it is."

Valerie looked at Logan, surprised by what he was up to.

"I know where Deya hid them," he continued. "She told my father the secret."

"No one knows what she did with the River Set," Andrea said. "I don't believe you."

"Are you willing to take that chance?" Logan asked. "Are you going to tell Simon you killed the only person left in the world who knows Deya's secret hiding place?"

Andrea looked at Logan long and hard while Lucius kept his gun pointed at him. "Go on," she said to Logan.

"You think I'll tell you where the books are without getting something in return?"

Annoyance flashed in Andrea's eyes, but she smiled sweetly. "Very well, I'll play your game a bit longer. What do you want?"

"First, let Valerie go."

"What are you doing?" Valerie gave him a stern look.

"If I let her go, what guarantees do I have that the books are going to be where you say they are?" Andrea asked.

"What guarantees do I have that you will let her go?" Logan retorted.

"Enough of this!" Lucius said angrily. He pulled out a small pen knife from his pocket and stabbed Valerie in the thigh.

Valerie screamed. Logan jumped out of his chair to help her, but a mercenary grabbed him in a head lock and pushed him down. He saw Valerie grimacing in pain as blood flowed down her leg.

"If you don't tell us where the books are in five seconds, we're gonna slice her," Lucius said, holding the bloody penknife in front of Logan's face. Logan watched helplessly as a mercenary drew the large hunting knife that was strapped to his thigh and pressed the blade to Valerie's throat.

"Stop!" Logan shouted, still struggling to free himself.

"Don't tell them anything!" Valerie said, pain clear in her voice. "They'll kill us anyway if you do."

Logan looked at Lucius, who seemed to be enjoying this morbid game of cat and mouse. He turned then to Andrea, attempting to mask his fright with calm resolve. "Kill us both if you have to. You'll never get your hands on those books."

Andrea, who had stepped back, allowing the drama to unfold, clapped her hands loudly. "Yes, exactly like your father! He, too, would never have given up the books for anyone. Maybe that's why he's dead." She looked from Logan to Valerie, then back to Logan. "Actually, I have a much better plan for the two of you. Lucius, have our men transport them to G-LAB first thing in the morning. Dr. Malikei can extract the information we need."

A smile came to Lucius's face as he put the knife back in his pocket. "Mother, that is an excellent idea!"

As Logan looked at Valerie, who was in great pain and still holding her leg, he experienced a welter of emotions, from fury at Lucius and Andrea to concern for Valerie and himself. *What is G-LAB?* he wondered. *And who is Dr. Malikei?*

32

You are new warriors who have joined an ancient battle.
—THE CHRONICLES OF SATRAYA

SOMEWHERE OVER THE ATLANTIC OCEAN,
4:00 A.M. GMT, 3 DAYS UNTIL FREEDOM DAY

Mr. Perrot would have welcomed a few hours of sleep on the twelve-hour nonstop flight to India, but he was beset by too many concerns to rest. His eyes were closed, but his mind was racing. *First we need to go to Deya's house and search the garden. But what if the books aren't there? What if Deya moved or the garden has been dug up?* He ordered himself to stop. He knew he needed to remain calm and focused on his goal: finding Deya's books before Simon did. It was foolish to dwell on the dire consequences of Simon's getting his hands on them first.

He opened his eyes and looked over at Jogi, who was seated next to him, engrossed in a documentary about the days preceding the Great Disruption. Mr. Perrot realized how he could put this time to better use. He undocked the entertainment display from the seat in front of him. Each seat was equipped with a mini HoloPad device that allowed passengers access to just about any kind of data they wanted. Mr. Perrot used his device to navigate to the literature section. Many works, both popular and scholarly, had been written about *The Chronicles of Sa-*

traya, but he was interested in only those that dealt with the discovery of the original sets. After a little searching, he found an old article from a newspaper in Deya's hometown of Banaras that told her story.

June 21, 2034. Deya Sarin stood waist-deep in the slow-moving river. The many ancient ghats provided a colorful and mystical backdrop to her daily routine. There was a sad, empty look on her face this morning, because she knew that very soon she would be leaving her son and her husband for good.

As they had done for thousands of years, people went to the great Ganges River to pray and to greet the rising sun. This day started out no differently for Deya. Each morning, the young mother would swiftly make her way through the busy streets, walking for a half-hour from her home in Banaras to the Ganges. It is said that the meek shall inherit the earth; that statement could not have been truer than in our city of Banaras. For after the Great Disruption, when most people around the world suffered from its devastation, those who had nothing to lose lost nothing, and their lives quickly adjusted to the new reality. While electricity and other conveniences were lost, most of the rural people of our great land simply continued to do what they had always done: they lived off what the gods provided.

The water of the Ganges was warm that morning. Deya unwrapped an old scarf from around her neck and ran her fingers over the long surgical scar on her neck. It reminded her each day of her imminent death. The doctors had been unsuccessful in removing all of the cancer from her throat. Only a few more months of life, only a few more sunrises to witness. She could see the fires of the cremation ghats along the river, their smoke rising high into the sky, another reminder of what was coming for her. As the glow of morning was coming over the eastern horizon, Deya stood motionless, her eyes closed, her head slightly bowed, her hands pressed together in prayer. No sound could be heard from her lips as she recited an ancient Sanskrit mantra. Even if she'd wanted to recite the words aloud, no one would hear her, for the cancer had taken her voice, the musical voice that had once sung lullabies to her son. The sun was beginning to break over the horizon, its light illuminating the faces of all the greeters as they also stood in the river. "Please, God, take care of my son when I am gone. Please, God, take care of my husband after I pass." Deya's mantra was simple and sincere. Over and over she repeated these words, her lips forming them as tears flowed down her face, falling into the timeless flow of the river.

The heavily populated cites of Delhi, Mumbai, and Bangalore had suffered inconceivable destruction. Many had died in those cities, and the few survivors scattered to the countryside looking for food and water. Many stood in the river that day praying for salvation, praying for deliverance from the devastation and tragedy they'd endured during the last three years of their lives. What had they done to bring such karma upon them? Where were the gods of Brahma, Shiva, and Vishnu? Why had they abandoned the world?

As Deya stood in the river, something struck her right leg. She bowed slightly in response, thinking perhaps it was a passerby walking deeper into the river. But something kept nudging at her. Reluctantly, not wanting to break her concentration, she opened her eyes a bit. A small wooden box had floated up to her and was bobbing up and down against her leg. Her scarf had snagged on one of its rough edges. She opened her eyes further, letting them adjust to the light of the sun, which had now fully risen over the horizon. Deya reached down and lifted the small box from the water. There were no markings on the outside, only a simple latch that secured the lid. She carefully lifted the latch and found three leather-bound books inside.

A little homeless girl, who was standing close to Deya in the river, waded over to her, wanting to see what was in the box. Deya looked down at her with a smile and handed the little girl the box to hold as she removed the first book. The book was titled The Chronicles of Satraya. *When Deya opened it, a small blue orb of light emerged from the pages. Even amid the full glory of the sun, the blue light was startling. People began to gather around it. People standing on the shore waded into the river, and soon a great circle formed around Deya, as the orb hovered like a hummingbird in front of her face. The warmth of the blue light filled Deya with hope, something she had not felt since the cancer had been diagnosed. Holding the book in her left hand, she placed the palm of her right hand under the orb. People in the gathering crowd jostled to get a clearer view. Even those in the nearby pilgrim houses of Manikarnika Ghat crowded at the windows to witness the blue light. The little girl tried to reach up and touch the orb, but it was too high for her to reach. Something that could only be described as a thread of blue energy emerged from the orb, the tip of which penetrated Deya's throat. Deya began to cough; her right hand let go of the orb. She was grasping her neck, trying somehow to ease her discomfort. She coughed more violently, almost losing her balance in the water, but the little girl, who was still holding the box, quickly slipped an arm around Deya's waist, steadying her. All in the crowd were amazed by what they were witnessing. A moment later, the thread of light retracted from Deya's throat back into the orb. Then, just as mysteriously as the orb had appeared, it settled back into the pages of the book.*

Deya looked at the little girl by her side and the large crowd that had gathered around her. Her lips automatically formed the words, "What happened?" She was surprised when people standing close to her answered her question. Even the little girl had a few tidbits to share. "You can hear me?" Deya asked. Stunned, she rubbed her throat, but she felt no scar. The constant pain that had troubled her since the surgery was gone. She could speak! Her voice had been miraculously restored to her. Some of the people in the crowd who knew of Deya's plight shouted, "A miracle! A miracle! Deya has been cured! The gods have returned!"

Mr. Perrot docked the terminal back into the seat in front of him. The newspaper story was very close to what Deya had told him and Camden many years ago.

"What were you reading?" Jogi asked.

Mr. Perrot told him about the article. "I was hoping that learning more about Deya's discovery of the *Chronicles* would prove helpful in our quest."

"Maybe I can find some information about her in the WCF database," Jogi suggested. He took his PCD and connected it to the interface on the seat in front of him. He brought up a display and started to search for anything related to Deya Sarin. The top story, which was dated only a few days ago, captured their attention immediately.

Banaras, India, June 16, 2069. Lokesh Sarin, the son of the late Deya Sarin, who discovered an original set of The Chronicles of Satraya, *was reported missing today. Authorities are baffled by the disappearance of the forty-five-year-old father of two from his place of work in the city of Banaras. Mr. Sarin, a mechanical engineer who graduated from the University of Banaras, was last seen walking outside during his lunch break. Authorities suspect foul play.*

Mr. Perrot sat back in his seat; he didn't bother to finish the article. "I fear we are a bit behind in this game of kings and pawns," he said.

33

What makes a warrior great is not his ability to master a weapon
but his ability to know when to wield it.
—THE CHRONICLES OF SATRAYA

ALEXANDRIA, VIRGINIA, 11:10 P.M. LOCAL TIME,
3 DAYS UNTIL FREEDOM DAY

Logan assisted Valerie as they were escorted to a bedroom on the second floor of the plantation house.

"This is for your girlfriend." The guard accompanying them threw some gauze and tape on the floor. "We wouldn't want her to bleed out before you see the doctor." He slammed the door shut and locked it.

Logan helped Valerie to the bed. He looked around and grabbed a pillow. He yanked the pillowcase off and used it to wipe away the blood from Valerie's wound.

"I'll be all right," she insisted. "Stop fussing."

"Hold still." He carefully worked two of his fingers through the bloodied hole in her right trouser leg and ripped it open. He wiped away some more blood to get a better look at the wound. "It's not as bad as it looks."

"Tell that to my leg," Valerie said, as she watched him use the gauze and tape to stop the bleeding and wrap her leg.

"This should hold for a bit," he said.

"That feels better, thanks." She glanced around, examining the large bedroom: the heavy mahogany furniture, including a chiffonier, the heavy drapes on the windows, the tattered wallpaper whose pattern could barely be distinguished.

Logan used another pillowcase to wipe the blood from his hands and walked to the foot of the old-fashioned four-poster bed, looking at the large fireplace in the corner and the old chair in front of it. "There's something about this place," he murmured. "It seems familiar to me."

"Well, I don't want to get any more familiar with it than I have to," Valerie said, as she struggled to rise from the bed. Logan came over and helped her up. "Let's look for anything that can help us get out of here," she said, still grimacing in pain. "That G-LAB place doesn't sound very pleasant."

Logan walked over to the fireplace. Valerie went to the elegant dark blue brocade drapes and pulled them open, revealing two closed windows that had been fitted with iron bars. "I guess Andrea wants her guests to feel safe," she said drily. She opened the windows to let some air into the warm room, but there was no breeze to speak of.

"Wait. The iron bars!" Logan said, in sudden awe. Valerie put her finger to her lips. "I knew this place seemed familiar," he said, more softly now, as he realized a guard might be standing in the hallway. "This is the room I saw in my candle vision." He walked over to the wall adjacent to the windows. "Check out the peeling wallpaper, the huge fireplace in the corner. And look at the dark wood floor with the pale blue rug on it. That's the same bed. This is the same room. I'm certain of it."

Valerie looked around skeptically. "Assuming this is the same room, was there anything in your vision that might help us get out of here?" She looked out the window and saw people leaving the house and a guard carrying luggage over to a black SUV parked on the circular driveway. "Looks like our captors are leaving."

Logan joined her at the window and watched as Andrea spoke to one of the mercenaries, seated now behind the wheel of a black van. After a brief conversation, she joined Lucius and Monique, who had entered the black SUV parked on the other side of the driveway. After a moment, it drove away.

"So is there anything else you remember about this place?" Valerie asked again.

Logan sat on the bed and closed his eyes, trying to recall more details of his candle vision. "Not much," he said. "At the time, it just seemed like an old-fashioned bedroom. I never thought I would be trying to escape from it."

As Valerie continued her inspection of the room, she opened a tall wardrobe cabinet that yielded nothing of consequence except for a couple of folded towels, a bar of scented soap, and a brass candle holder. "Could you go back to that room you saw in your vision?" she asked, as she picked up the candleholder containing a short, stubby candle. "I know it's not the blue candle you found in the box your father hid, but it is a candle."

Logan looked at the candle for a moment. "I don't know . . . I don't see why not. If my father was right, the candle is only a tool. It all comes down to mastering your thoughts," he said, trying to sound confident. "That's the theory, anyway."

Valerie handed him the candle and a box of matches. "You get set up however you get set up, and I'll turn off the lights when you're ready."

Logan grabbed a pillow from the bed and tossed it onto the floor. He stacked a couple of books in front of it, placed the candleholder on top of them, and lit the candle.

"You ready?" Valerie asked, as she stood by the light switch.

He got into position and nodded. He took a few deep breaths and attempted to replicate what he had done in Valerie's apartment only a couple days earlier.

While he sat on the floor perfectly still, Valerie sat in a chair near the barred windows. The room was dark except for the light of the candle and a hint of hallway light coming from underneath the door. Time passed as Valerie watched the coming and going of armed guards on the driveway below. The stars were bright in the night sky, and she could see the blinking lights of an airplane flying silently by above. She thought of her father, who was on his way to India. How much time did they all have to stop Simon and Andrea? What was going to happen to her and Logan if they couldn't escape? Her anxiety was mounting as Logan focused on the flickering flame.

Suddenly, he broke his stillness. "It's not working," he said. "No ringing, no sound, nothing."

"What do you mean?"

"I mean it's not working."

"Maybe you just need to give it more time. My father told me it didn't happen instantaneously when you did it in my apartment."

Logan shook his head. "I'm doing everything the same way." He leaned back against the bed, punching the side of the mattress with his fist. "It just sort of worked last time. I don't know how, but everything just worked like it was supposed to." He shook his head again. "Maybe I need the blue candle; maybe there *is* something special about it. I don't know." He moved forward to blow out the candle.

"Wait!" Valerie said.

He stopped himself and looked up at her.

"Why is the flame flickering? There's no breeze coming through the windows, and these old homes don't have any air conditioning." Valerie closed the brocade drapes to be sure; the flame still fluttered.

"Probably from under the door," Logan suggested.

Valerie grabbed the candle and bent down as best she could, placing the candle near the door. Seeing the flame stand still, she shook her head. She stood and returned to where Logan sat. "See, there's more of a breeze over here."

"Give me the candle for a minute," he said. She handed it to him; he put it back on top of the books. After studying the flickering flame a moment, he pointed straight ahead at the chiffonier. "It's coming from over there," he said. He crawled over to the large piece of furniture, whose lowest drawer was about thirty-six centimeters above the floor. It was high enough for him to crawl underneath it. "Hey, the wallpaper down here is peeling," he said. "Turn on the lights!"

Valerie flipped the light switch on.

Logan tore off some wallpaper and tossed it behind him. "There's some kind of door back here," he said, before he crawled out from under the chest of drawers and stood back up. He grabbed hold of the chest and pulled it away from the wall, making a loud dragging sound across the floor. Behind it was a small wooden panel about half a meter wide and an almost equal distance in height.

Valerie ran her hands along it. "What could that be for?" she asked.

But Logan didn't have a chance to answer. They could hear footsteps coming down the hall.

Quickly, Logan pushed the chiffonier back against the wall, and Valerie blew out the candle. She picked up the books and put them and the candleholder on the bedside table. Then she hobbled back to the chair by the window, and Logan flew across the room and dove onto the bed. Someone was unlocking the door. They both noticed a couple of pieces of ripped wallpaper on the floor, but it was too late to pick them up.

"What's going on here?" the guard asked as he came in. "You're making a racket."

Valerie stood and walked over to the guard. He drew his gun. "You need to let us out of here," Valerie said, trying to distract him from the wallpaper on the floor.

"Little chance of that," he said. "It smells like something was burning in here." After a quick glance around the room, he noticed the candle. "How did you get that?"

"It was in the wardrobe," Valerie said.

The guard eyed her and Logan suspiciously. "Back up," he told Valerie. As soon as she moved back to the windows, the guard went over to the bedside table and grabbed the candleholder. "Don't want our guests to burn the place down," he said. "Now, rest up. We have a trip planned for you tomorrow." The guard backed into the hallway and closed the door.

The dead bolt in the lock slid into place with a click.

"That was close," Logan said, as he got off the bed and went back over to the chiffonier.

Valerie joined him, and this time, Logan was careful not to make any noise as he moved the large piece of furniture away from the wall. Valerie unlatched the little door behind the chiffonier and opened it. The breeze coming from below became more pronounced. "What is this?" she asked.

"I think it's a dumbwaiter," he said. "They were common in late-eighteenth- and nineteenth-century homes. They were little elevators used to deliver food and dishes between floors."

He grabbed the lamp from the bedside table, tossed aside the lampshade, and plugged it into an outlet near the dumbwaiter. Then he poked his head into the shaft. "Doesn't look like the dumbwaiter goes any higher than this floor—down is the only option."

"How do you know it still works?" Valerie asked.

"I don't," he answered with a slight smile. He grabbed the rope and tugged on it. "But at least we know the pulley up there is still hooked up." He backed himself out of the opening, so that she could see for herself.

She popped her head in. "What do you think is at the bottom?" she asked, her voice echoing down the shaft.

"My guess is the kitchen," he said. "Let's try it." He grabbed the rope and slowly pulled the delivery cart toward them. Even after all the years of disuse, the pulley wheel still worked and squeaked only slightly as the wheel rotated. When the cart arrived, Logan and Valerie dislodged it from the rail and brought it quietly into the room.

"Now what?"

"Now we secure the rope from the cart to something immovable." Logan unhooked it from the cart and secured it to one of the iron bars on the windows. "Then we climb down the rope. Can you manage that? How's your leg?"

Valerie didn't respond. She just grabbed the rope and gave it a couple of good tugs to make sure it could handle her weight. Then she climbed into the shaft, pressing her feet against the cart rails along the wall to steady herself as she descended. It seemed her leg was good enough.

Logan took hold of the rope to provide additional security as he tracked her progress. Soon she reached the bottom, and he heard her fiddling with the access door in the darkness below. Then he heard the squeaking of hinges as she pushed the door open.

"You're right," she called softly from below. "It's the kitchen. There's no one here."

Logan clasped the rope with both hands and swung out into the shaft. Like Valerie, he used the rails to steady himself as he climbed down. He squeezed through the access door and emerged in the corner of a large kitchen where brooms, mops, and other cleaning equipment were kept. The room was dark except for the moonlight that shone through the windows.

Valerie was crouched down by one of the windows, cautiously peering out. "Get down!" she whispered urgently.

Logan moved over and squatted beside her.

"There's one guard with a flashlight patrolling the back gardens. While you were coming down, I found a back door, but it's double-locked. Opening these old windows might make noise, but the window over the sink"—she pointed to her left—"is open. If we time it right, we could slip out without the guard noticing."

Staying low, she hurried over to the kitchen sink window. When she turned to beckon Logan over, she saw him standing by the kitchen's interior swinging door, peeking out.

She ran over to him. "What are you doing? There are guards all over the front entrance!" She looked over his shoulder into the main hallway, where a small table lamp cast a dim light, but no guards were in sight.

As Logan looked down the hall, he saw the doorway to Andrea's parlor. "I need to get something before we leave," he whispered, suddenly turning around. "I want my backpack."

34

If all of your excuses were removed, how would your life change?
—THE CHRONICLES OF SATRAYA

ALEXANDRIA, VIRGINIA, 12:42 A.M. LOCAL TIME,
3 DAYS UNTIL FREEDOM DAY

Valerie wanted to yell, "What are you doing?" She was not at all happy with Logan's hasty move, but she kept silent and quickly followed him into the hallway, which was quiet except for the muted sound of a HoloTV in one of the front rooms. She was on Logan's heels as he entered the parlor.

"Found it," he said, as he grabbed his backpack and also gathered the dismantled pieces of their PCDs and stashed them in the pack.

Valerie spotted her gun and badge and scooped them up, too. She heard footsteps and men talking in the hallway. "We have to get out of here!"

She tucked her gun into the waistband of her pants, and she and Logan ran to the open window that faced the back of the property, pushed out the screen, and climbed out.

Running silently through the gardens by the light of the moon and the stars, they made their way into the vineyard behind the house and continued down one of the long rows of grapevines. Logan could see that Valerie's leg was bothering her, wincing as she was with each step. They took cover behind a small stand of trees and bushes along the perimeter of the vineyard.

As Logan looked back at the house to see if their escape had been detected, he handed Valerie the parts of her PCD. "Dammit, they smashed the activation chip," she said. Then she took her WCF badge out of her pocket.

"What are you doing?" Logan asked, watching as she carefully pulled off the laminate coating and then used her fingernail to pierce the paper and extract a small, thin piece of glass. "Tricks of the trade," she said. "Every WCF badge has one." She inserted the glass chip into the PCD, and in moments, it sprang back to life. The same instant, a call came in from Charlie.

"Are you all right? What the hell happened?" he said. "We've been searching everywhere for you two."

Before Valerie could answer, the exterior lights of the plantation house came on. Floodlights illuminated the house and the grounds. Men brandishing guns were running out, shouting at one another. Logan and Valerie's escape had been discovered.

"Can't explain right now!" Valerie answered frantically. She heard the sound of barking dogs. "We need backup here ASAP!"

"Already en route, Chief," Charlie said. "We have your position, two teams airborne. I'll be there in two minutes."

"Come in *loud*," Valerie said with emphasis, as Charlie's projected image gave her a thumbs-up. She shut down her PCD and looked through the bushes. "Let's hope they get here before those dogs do."

Logan saw dogs prowling, searching for their scent.

"If they get too close, we need to split up," Valerie said. She readied her weapon. "You run that way toward the main road, and I'll go the other way and provide you with some cover."

One of the dogs let out a loud bark and started to lead his master into the vineyard. The other dogs followed, weaving back and forth down the aisle of grapevines.

"On the count of three, I want you to run as fast as you can down to the road," Valerie instructed. "One." Logan readied himself. "Two." She pointed her gun toward their pursuers.

Logan took a deep breath, preparing for his dash, but a roaring sound in the sky made him look up. "Do you hear that? Sounds like helicopters."

"Thank you, Charlie!" Valerie sighed. She relaxed her weapon hand and watched as the guard leading the search party looked up at the night sky, too.

"That was fast," Logan said, trying to spot the helicopters.

"They're still probably a few miles away," Valerie said. "But they have their sound-magnification devices on so they sound closer."

He looked at her. "So that's what you meant by coming in loud."

She nodded. "Looks like some of the guards are not going to wait around." She watched as the three men handling the barking dogs yanked the animals' leashes and quickly led them back to the house, while a few of Andrea's mercenaries jumped into black SUVs and sped away from the plantation. Several tense moments passed. Then, suddenly, the helicopters came into view. Just as Charlie had promised.

Gunshots rang out as the remaining mercenaries turned their weapons skyward and the arriving helicopters returned fire. As the mercenaries scattered in the face of superior WCF firepower and the gunfight wound down, Valerie and Logan emerged from behind the trees and cautiously made their way back to the plantation house. A slew of WCF ground vehicles pulled into the driveway. WCF agents started fanning out to secure the plantation.

"I can't wait to start looking around that house," Valerie said, hurrying forward. "There should be enough evidence in there for us to track all these criminals down."

Just then, her PCD rang again. It was Charlie, wearing a headset with an attached microphone. "We're over the plantation house now. Looks like everything is secured. Nice to see you two alive down there. Head to the house. I'll just—"

Valerie and Logan were thrust to the ground by a massive blast. Fiery debris rained down on them. They could feel the heat as they covered their heads and stayed close to the ground. When they looked up, they saw the plantation house had exploded and was now immersed in flames. One of the helicopters turned on its side, out of control. Another blast from the ground engulfed the falling copter. All of a sudden, the blades splintered off and smashed into parked vehicles and a nearby water tank. The helicopter disappeared into the burning building, releasing a plume of dark smoke and ash.

"Charlie! Charlie!" Valerie screamed into her PCD. But there was no answer. She made a dash toward the house, but Logan reached out and stopped her. Fiery shards were still falling to the ground. "Charlie," Valerie said softly as she fell to her knees and dropped her PCD. Logan knelt down beside her and put his arms around her shoulders.

Ten minutes later, Valerie and Logan were watching from the back of an ambulance as the local fire department dealt with the burning plantation house.

"You need to have a doctor look at this," a paramedic said, as he redressed Valerie's leg.

Valerie wasn't going anywhere to get anything checked out. She had just lost the only partner she had ever had. She looked at Logan, saying nothing.

"You all right?" he asked.

"No," she said. "But that doesn't matter." Without another word, she got up out of the ambulance and quickened her pace.

"Where are you going?" he said as he followed her across the driveway. She was heading toward the black van she had seen Andrea's mercenaries get into after speaking with her. The door was still open.

She slipped into the driver's seat and searched for the key, which she found stuffed behind the sun visor. Logan joined her on the passenger side. "I think this is the vehicle they were going to use to drive us to

G-LAB," she said as she started the van. "If it is, either the guards knew exactly where to take us because they had been there before, or Andrea left a map or directions for them."

Logan looked straight ahead at the dashboard and the other devices that had lit up. "Or she programmed the address of the lab into the GPS."

Valerie nodded. She pressed a few buttons on the GPS and brought up a list of destinations the vehicle had traveled to. "This van has been all over in the last ten days. There must be fifty addresses in here. Richmond, Philadelphia, Rockville." Logan listened as she scanned the list. "Back to Richmond, to Norfolk, then to Triangle Park—"

"Wait," Logan said. He grabbed Valerie's hand, stopping it from scrolling down the list any further. "Triangle Park. That's in North Carolina, isn't it?"

Valerie selected the address and brought it up on the van's GPS system. "Yes, it's near Durham, North Carolina. Why?"

"Randolph Fenquist," Logan said, thinking back. "When he confronted me in the street, he told me Andrea had been spending time in North Carolina. Maybe that's where they were going to take us."

He paused. Had Randolph purposely given him that information? he wondered. Why would he have done that?

Valerie, meanwhile, used the GPS controls to zoom in closer on the address. It was an abandoned Army building.

"Why would they go there?" Logan asked.

"I have no idea. But we'll soon find out, because that's our next stop," Valerie said. Then she turned to Logan. "I'm sorry I wasn't more sympathetic when you found out Andrea and Simon might have killed your parents," she said quietly.

"What do you mean?"

"I mean, I know how you felt. Charlie was the only partner I ever had. I understand why you were so focused on tracking them down. And I'm not going to stop until we get them now, either."

35

How would you teach yourself?
Could you be a prophet in your own land?
Could you be your own greatest teacher?
—THE CHRONICLES OF SATRAYA

NEAR RESEARCH TRIANGLE PARK, NORTH CAROLINA,
6:00 A.M. LOCAL TIME, 2 DAYS UNTIL FREEDOM DAY

WCF snipers had taken their places and radioed in their positions. Their advanced weaponry systems could track multiple targets and instantly communicate that information to other snipers in their network. With a single order, they could make a deadly and coordinated strike. An assault team was also ready, waiting for the go-ahead from Valerie.

"We're not sure what we are going to find in there," she announced on the secure communication link. "Be ready for anything. Alpha team, once you're in, start looking for any type of self-destruct device. I refuse to have a repeat of the plantation house."

It was just after 6:00 A.M., and a formidable group of WCF personnel had gathered at the location retrieved from the van's navigation system. The two-story brick Army research office building was located near Research Triangle Park in North Carolina. It was listed in WCF records as having been abandoned since the time of the Great Disruption. Some of the windows on the second floor were broken and abandoned, and stripped cars were scattered throughout the parking lot.

A downed electrical pole lay over a shattered blue sign from an empty tavern next to the building.

Logan stood next to Valerie, where she and the rest of the operation support team had created a small command center behind the tavern building. A clump of trees stood between them and the former research facility.

"Alpha team, you have the lead," Valerie ordered. With that, a member of the assault team blew open the lock at the back entrance and tossed a gas grenade inside the building, quickly filling the first floor with smoke. Twelve heavily armed men wearing gas masks and helmet-mounted cameras ran into the building. Logan and Valerie watched as a HoloPad projected what each team member was experiencing. While it was sometimes difficult to see through the haze of smoke, they could make out collapsed old-fashioned furniture and office machines coated in dust and cobwebs.

"They were going to bring us here?" Logan asked. "This place looks like it was abandoned after the Great Disruption."

Valerie didn't answer. She was intently watching the twelve separate images coming from the team inside. The smoke from the gas charges began to dissipate, and the images became clearer. The team broke up into four groups. One group made its way up a set of stairs to the second floor, while a second group of three went to the basement. The two other groups searched the first floor, an open-plan office with about twenty workstations and large metal filing and storage cabinets along the four walls. Several closed doors suggested access to a few private offices, supply closets, and lavatories. Two members of the assault team were prying open the door to the building's elevator.

"We are not encountering anything unusual," Luke Bradford, the team leader, announced from the first floor. "Wait, I'm picking up something on my thermal scanner, something near the southwest corner."

"Careful," Valerie said on the secure link.

Six of the twelve displays started to track toward the southwest corner of the building and approached a closed door. The thermal scanners of all six men indicated that something was moving behind the door. One of the men stepped forward and placed a small device near the handle; within moments, it blasted the door open, and the men rushed in.

"Negative! Negative!" Luke said. "We've got a momma and her kittens inside a small office that contains a desk, a chair, and some ancient computer equipment. Stand down. Stand down."

Valerie frowned. "Keep going. Check behind those other closed doors." Then she turned her focus to the videos coming from the groups on the other floors.

The second floor was another large open space with rows of laboratory tables, several of which had collapsed. Dusty microscopes, computers with old-fashioned display screens, and racks of test tubes and beakers covered the tables. One of the cameras zoomed in on a corner of the lab filled with stacks of wire cages containing small bones.

"Probably the remains of animals they used in experiments. But I'm not seeing any indications that anyone has been working here recently," Logan said, puzzled.

Valerie shook her head and pointed to the video streaming from the group in the basement. All three cameras conveyed images of large corroding oil-storage tanks, oil burners, and water heaters.

A half-hour later, the entire search team congregated on the first floor.

"Alpha Dog," Luke said, using Valerie's code name, "we've uncovered no signs of recent work or visitation on any of the structure's three levels. If anyone was in here recently, and I doubt anyone was, they have left the building."

"Dammit! You have to be kidding me!" Valerie kicked a small table that had been set up in the command center. "Fine. Clear out of there. This is a dead end." She turned to Logan; he could see the frustration and disappointment in her eyes.

"We must have gotten it wrong," he said. "The map in the van must have been referring to another place. Or maybe the explosion damaged the GPS and corrupted the location data."

"I thought for sure we had it," she said. "These people are like ghosts. You think you have them, and all of a sudden, they're gone."

Luke had come back to the command post. "Sorry, Val," he said. "We didn't see anything out of place." In a softer voice, he added, "And sorry to hear about Charlie. He was a good guy." It was clear he was not used to having to console his tough boss. She barely raised her head to thank him. He walked away, joining the other members of the unit.

Valerie and Logan stood and watched as the WCF assault and sniper teams packed up and drove away from the old Army research building. When dawn began to lighten the sky and only the unmarked WCF car Valerie had driven to the site was left among the corroding Army vehicles in the parking lot, she put her hands on her hips and said, "I'm not accepting this! I'm taking a look myself." She didn't invite Logan, but he followed her anyway.

They walked through the trees and across the parking lot and entered the building through the back door. Once inside, Valerie and Logan turned their PCDs into flashlights. They started on the second floor, walking carefully between the rickety lab tables and checking all of the offices and closets. The basement didn't yield anything of interest, either. When they returned to the main floor, they went their separate ways, frustrated that they weren't uncovering anything the WCF team had missed. There was nothing to indicate that this building had anything to do with the place called G-LAB.

Logan wandered around with his backpack on his shoulder, scavenging through the toppled furniture, kicking papers to and fro. Valerie, meanwhile, retraced the path of the assault team to the office where they had found the mother cat and her kittens. Logan was checking the drawers of a desk when Valerie ran over to him, grabbed him by the arm, and pushed him into a coat closet near the front entrance.

"Turn off your PCD," she ordered in a whisper. She pressed her finger to her lips. "I just saw a black SUV pull up in front of the building."

She left the double doors of the coat closet slightly ajar so that she could look out into the office. They heard a rattling sound as the glass entrance doors were unlocked and opened. Then a deep voice.

"Hurry up, Doctor. Go downstairs and get what you need, and don't forget to set the timer. We need to do this fast. They might come back."

"But how am I to bring all of my records? There is too much to gather. Perhaps they won't return."

"We can't take that risk. Just get down there and take what you need."

Logan and Valerie continued to listen from the closet. The larger of the two men looked like one of the thugs they'd seen at the plantation. He was dressed in black pants and a fitted white shirt, and he had a handgun strapped to his belt. The smaller man wore glasses and spoke in a thick German accent.

"That sounds like the doctor Andrea was referring to," Logan whispered.

Valerie readied her firearm. "And it also sounds like they intend to blow this place up, just like they did with the plantation."

Logan and Valerie watched as the doctor walked over to one of the large filing cabinets that lined the wall opposite the coat closet and slid open the middle drawer. He reached in and started to fiddle with something.

"Let's call the team back," Logan whispered.

"No time." Valerie had to act now. "Freeze! Don't move!" she yelled, as she crashed through the closet doors. Logan followed her, moving off to the side. "WCF. You two are under arrest."

The doctor froze, but the mercenary instantly drew his weapon and pointed it at Valerie, activating a red targeting laser that beamed onto her forehead. "For what?" he said. "Trespassing?"

"For killing my partner," she answered. "Put your weapon down. No need for anyone to get hurt."

"You're right," the gunman countered. "But you'll be the one putting the gun down."

Valerie shook her head. "This place is going to be crawling with agents in two minutes."

Logan knew that was a bluff. He was standing only a few steps to Valerie's left, and the doctor was still standing near the open file cabinet. With her weapon in her right hand, Valerie displayed her WCF credentials with her left. "My name is Valerie Perrot—"

"We know who you are," the mercenary interrupted. "We know all about you and Logan over there."

"Then you probably also know that I'm not interested in you," she said. "I want the doctor. We have a few questions about G-LAB."

"They know," the doctor said, now looking even more agitated. "Andrea—"

"Quiet, Doctor," the mercenary interrupted, suddenly pointing his gun at him. "There's no way you're taking him in." The red laser that had been fixed on Valerie was now pointing at the doctor's chest.

"Then it looks like we have a real problem," she said. "Logan, get behind me, and crouch down."

He quickly moved as instructed.

"Yes, we do," the mercenary said. Then he whipped out a second gun with his left hand, pointing it at Valerie. "I got no problem taking out the doc *and* you."

Logan watched anxiously. He knew that he and Valerie could die.

"Just me and you," Valerie said.

In a flash of movement, the mercenary pointed the laser of the gun in his right hand toward Valerie's eye, attempting to blind her. The moment the laser struck her in the eye, she dropped to the ground and fired off a round. Another was fired in the same instant. The sound was deafening.

Logan saw the mercenary spin around and fall to the floor. He couldn't see the doctor. He lunged toward Valerie. "Are you all right? I heard two shots!"

"I'm fine," she said. Her adrenaline was at full speed as she jumped to her feet. "But the doctor's not."

Logan rose, too. He saw the doctor lying still on the floor.

Valerie walked over to confirm that the mercenary was dead, and then she went to the doctor. She took his pulse, then shook her head. "He's dead. I guess the mercenary cared more about killing the doctor than killing us or saving himself. Interesting set of priorities."

Logan was still stunned by the shooting. He went over to the open file cabinet drawer where the doctor had been standing. "There's some kind of electronic pad in here. It looks like the doctor was typing in a code." He looked into the open drawer and saw an eight-digit numeric display with the numbers 0721206 shown in red. "Looks like we just need the last digit."

Valerie put her hand out. "Don't touch anything. How can we be sure it's not a detonation device?" She paused and thought for a moment. "Didn't he tell the doctor to go downstairs?"

Logan nodded. "He told him to go downstairs, gather his things, and set the timer."

"That number looks like a date. Nine. I bet the last digit is a nine. It's the date of Freedom Day."

"That seems too easy," Logan said. Apprehensively, he placed his finger just above the button.

"Do you have a better guess?"

He didn't. He pressed the number nine on the keypad, and the cabinet slid to the right, revealing something they did not expect to find. An elevator. Valerie pressed the call button.

36

A master speaks of his past in terms of the wisdom it has provided to him. He does not speak of it in terms of how he might
have changed it.

—THE CHRONICLES OF SATRAYA

BANARAS, INDIA, 6:00 P.M. LOCAL TIME, 2 DAYS UNTIL FREEDOM DAY

Mr. Perrot found Jogi to be of great assistance in tracking down Deya
Sarin's home in Banaras. He was Indian, so the locals trusted him, and
Jogi was able to navigate the many idiosyncrasies of their culture to get
directions and the latest information on Deya's husband's doings.

Two hours after their flight had landed, a state-of-the-art electric
rickshaw dropped them off in front of a modest two-story cement
house. It was separated from the street by a stone wall with a wrought-
iron gate. Similar houses lined both sides of the street in the quiet
residential neighborhood only a half-mile away from the densely populated, bustling area by the Ganges River.

Mr. Perrot pushed a call button at the entrance gate. He and Jogi
could hear the faint sound of its ringing inside the house. When no one
answered, he rang the bell again.

"The neighbors say that Babu Sarin rarely leaves the house," Jogi
said. "Ever since his wife died, he has become a recluse. His son's recent
disappearance has only added to his misfortune."

They waited patiently, ringing the bell a few more times. Finally, the front door swung open, and a rickety old man emerged. With the assistance of his cane, he slowly walked down the dirt pathway toward the gate, his long white tunic flapping in the wind. Mr. Perrot observed the sadness on the wrinkled face of this feeble gentleman. His heart sank as he recognized his former comrade and fellow Council member.

"Hello, Babu, my old friend," he said in the gentlest of voices, as Deya's husband finished his trek to the gate. There was no sign of recognition on his face.

"How may I help you?" Babu asked, his voice strained.

"They say that he has forgotten a great deal," Jogi whispered to Mr. Perrot. "The neighbors say that he has a hard time remembering people and past events."

Mr. Perrot did not give up. "You might remember me as your old friend Robert Tilbo," he said. The man just stared at him blankly. "I was a dear friend of your wife, Deya."

"Deya," Babu said. "Do you know where she is? She has not returned from her trip. Nor has my son returned from his."

"Unfortunately, my friend, we do not know," Mr. Perrot said, understanding that Babu's mind had indeed declined into the forgetfulness of old age. "However, we would very much like to see her garden, if you would permit."

"You seem somewhat familiar to me," Babu said, as he struggled to open the gate. His hands showed signs of advanced arthritis. Jogi provided assistance. "Come, come, the garden is over there. Go see, follow the path—you cannot miss it." He pointed to the side of the house, barely able to lift his arm. "I will bring some water to drink," he said. Then he turned and slowly walked back toward the house.

Mr. Perrot and Jogi continued down the weed-ridden pathway, which took them under a vine-covered stone pergola. Instead of a garden, they found themselves standing in a ten-by-ten-meter space enclosed by a two-meter-high wall that could only be described as a conservatory of weeds. Massive urns containing the ruins of once-lush trees crowded the corners

of the space, while six free-standing square pillars stood in a circular formation in the middle. An elaborate cistern system had been built there, but
the cement tank was cracked, and the irrigation system was falling apart.

"Are you sure this is a garden?" Jogi asked as they looked around.

"Deya has been gone for quite some time now," Mr. Perrot said. "It
seems that no one has tended the garden in her absence. It is a shame—
you should have heard how lovingly she spoke of the flowers and trees
that grew here . . ." His voice trailed off into a sigh.

"What are we looking for?" Jogi asked.

"We have only the clue Deya left for Camden." Mr. Perrot took the
note from his pocket and read it out loud: "'My garden pond will point
the way should I pass.'"

Jogi looked around again. "I don't see anything that looks like a
pond here."

"Pond!" another voice cried. Babu had returned, his cane in one
hand and a small jug of water in the other. Mr. Perrot moved to take
the jug and helped him sit on a stone bench. "The other man wanted
to see the pond, too. When Deya returns, she will restore the garden.
My son will also help."

"Someone else was looking for the pond?" Mr. Perrot asked. "When
was that?"

"Yes, another man came looking for Deya's pond. Just yesterday, it
was," Babu continued. "Would you like some water? When Deya returns, she will restore the garden." His mind was jumping from thought
to thought.

"What did this man look like?" Mr. Perrot asked.

Babu did not answer right away. Instead, he moved the jug of water
closer to him on the bench. "They were taller than you," Babu said.
"Would you like some water?"

"No, thank you." Mr. Perrot understood that he could not push too
hard. "Could you just show us where the pond is?"

"There, behind those pillars." Babu pointed with his cane. "When
she comes back, she can tell you all about it."

Jogi and Mr. Perrot walked over to the dry dirt area encircled by the six pillars. "He's right. Looks like someone was here already," Jogi observed. "All of the weeds and dirt have been removed from this shallow area, which must have been the pond."

"She wrote that the secret was in her pond," Mr. Perrot said, as he walked to the center of the cracked basin. "There was definitely something written here."

"Whatever it was, it looks like it was chiseled away." Jogi bent down and grabbed a handful of broken-up cement. "And recently, too."

"You found Deya's message," Babu said, his cane still in hand, as he joined them by the ravaged pond.

"We did, sir," Jogi acknowledged. "But it has been destroyed—perhaps by those men who came yesterday. Do you recall what it said?"

"Yes, yes—yes," Babu said, but he hesitated. Mr. Perrot and Jogi waited patiently for Babu to explain. But all he said was, "Perhaps Deya will tell you when she returns."

"It is really important, sir," Jogi said gently, trying to coax the words from the old man's fading memory.

"She will tell you when she returns," Babu insisted. Jogi looked at Mr. Perrot in disappointment. "She can fix the rubble there," Babu continued. "She will restamp as she did once before."

"Restamp?" Mr. Perrot said. "Was the message stamped into the concrete?"

"Yes. She did all these words that way." Babu pointed to one of the six concrete pillars surrounding the empty basin. "I was an iron smith, you know. I made the stamps for her."

Mr. Perrot saw that words had been stamped into the pillars. "Perfection is an illusion theorized by your personality," one of them read. Mr. Perrot knew the line well. "These are all quotes from the *Chronicles*," he told Jogi. "Babu, do you know where those stamps are at the moment?"

Babu nodded. Then, without a word, he turned and walked toward the house, using his cane to assist his wobbly legs. Mr. Perrot and Jogi followed.

37

You must learn to separate your emotions from your cause. Only
then will you allow the greatest possibilities to occur in your life.
—THE CHRONICLES OF SATRAYA

As the elevator arrived, the sound of its hydraulics could be heard. The doors opened, revealing a tiny, one-meter-square car. It seemed to be new, clean, unlike the rest of the building. Logan and Valerie squeezed themselves in, letting the doors close again behind them. The elevator started to descend slowly.

"How did they build this without anyone knowing?" Logan wondered out loud, standing behind Valerie. The elevator came to a stop, and the doors opened back up.

"I think we found G-LAB," she said.

Logan followed her, amazed by what he saw. They were in a hexagon-shaped room with antiseptic white walls on which video display monitors had been installed. A long stainless-steel table with twelve chairs around it occupied the center of the room. A large holographic projection pad sat in the middle of the table. The room was quiet except for a low humming noise whose origin was unclear.

"Again, I have to ask how they built this place without anyone knowing," Logan said. "And how did they get all that equipment down here?"

Valerie didn't answer. She had activated her PCD and was speaking into it. "Luke, I think you and your team missed a little something at the Army research building. Logan and I found a sparkling new elevator behind the file cabinet on the south-facing wall of the main floor. It goes way down to what appears to be a high-tech laboratory. Get back here as soon as you can." Logan heard Luke cursing as the device clicked off.

Logan and Valerie walked over to the stainless-steel table and gazed around the room. The elevator in which they had arrived occupied one of the room's six walls. Three of the other walls had fortified doors—one was marked "Library," another "Maze Room," and the third "Testing Suites." More than a dozen monitors were mounted on the two remaining walls, and all but one of them was dark.

"Look at that display," Logan said. "Is that blood it's showing on the walls?"

A caption on the display indicated the "Hall of Mazes." Valerie readied her weapon as they walked over to the door marked "Maze Room."

Logan tried the knob, but it wouldn't turn. "Looks like we need some sort of access card."

Valerie pulled a card from her pocket. "Took it off the doctor. It says his name was Serge Malikei," she said, as she slid the card through the reader and opened the door, revealing two identical narrow hallways that turned at forty-five-degree angles every four meters or so. The white walls and closed doors in the hallways were marred by reddish-brown stains.

"What is this place?" Logan asked, as he walked a little ways into one passageway and then the other, feeling disturbed by the blood-smeared walls and the hallways' odd angles. "It reminds me of the corn mazes our parents used to take us to when we were kids."

"I remember those," Valerie said. "But those mazes always had a way out. I've tried to open about five of these doors, and they're all locked. And judging by the blood here, no one escapes unless the doctor wants you to. As much as I want to, I don't think we should go any farther. Let's go see what's behind doors number two and three."

Logan followed Valerie back into the hexagon-shaped room, where they walked over to the door marked "Testing Suites." Valerie once again used the doctor's card to gain access, and they entered a medium-sized, immaculate white room with a padded armchair similar to the ones found in dentists' offices. A hydraulic foot pedal could be used to raise and lower it. On a table nearby was a set of computer monitors whose wires were connected to hundreds of small bio-sensors embedded in the chair. A tray of syringes and vials of green liquid lay next to a sink in the corner. Directly in front of the chair was a holographic projection device. Logan set his backpack down and sat in the chair, which he found surprisingly comfortable. Suddenly, the holographic projector fired up, and the computer monitors began to display a multitude of information.

"What are you doing?" Valerie set down a vial of green liquid and turned her attention to the now-active displays. "Looks like the chair tracks all of your biometric readings. Heart rate, blood pressure, even your brain activities." She pressed a button labeled "Image Cycle." Immediately, the holographic device began to project a reel of images in front of Logan. "It looks as if this device records your biometric reaction to what you're looking at." Logan's metrics suddenly spiked. "It appears you like blondes," she added with a grin.

Embarrassed, Logan hopped out of the chair, and all of the displays went dark.

"Come on, sit back down," Valerie said. "Let's see if we can figure this thing out."

"How about we see what's over here instead?" Logan walked over to a door marked "Storage." Valerie was still fiddling with the biometric machine. He pushed open the door. "You'd better come over here!" he called, moving back from the door as soon as he saw what was behind it.

Valerie drew her gun and quickly joined him in the storage room. The two of them were surrounded by twelve vertical-standing containment devices, each housing a naked body in some kind of yellow gelatinous liquid, six males and six females.

"These are some kind of advanced bio-coffins, similar to the ones we use at the WCF lab," Valerie said, analyzing the information displayed on the biometric screens attached to the containment devices. They showed temperature and viscosity readings. "This is insane," she said, visibly disturbed by the sight. "This is evil. Who do they think they are? How can they run hideous experiments on people?"

"History is filled with crimes that were committed in the name of science," Logan answered. He was also deeply disturbed by what he was seeing. He studied the placards at the top of the containment shells. "Look at this. They have a male and a female from each of the different races of humanity. Mongoloid, Caucasoid, Australoid, Negroid, Capoid, and T-noid," he read aloud. "I never heard of this last one, T-noid."

"What do you mean, the races of humanity?" Valerie asked.

"Some anthropologists theorize that you can divide the people in the world into five races based on their physical characteristics," he explained. "The theory was very controversial. It's been argued back and forth for years. Since ninety-nine point nine percent of all humans are made up of the same genetic material, there's very little that differentiates all of us. I had to study it for an art class."

Valerie gave him a skeptical look.

"My instructor said it would help when drawing the human face. He was pretty out there . . ."

Valerie nodded. "And you said you don't recognize the last one?"

He shook his head.

Valerie heard the elevator doors closing and the car ascending to the first floor. "Come on," she said. "That's Luke."

Logan followed her back out to the main lab. When the elevator descended and the doors opened, Luke and one of his team members stepped out, lowering their weapons.

"Damn, check this place out," Luke said, an amazed expression on his face. Valerie led him to a corner of the hexagonal room.

The elevator made several trips, bringing more agents to G-LAB. Among them were local WCF lab technicians, who began gathering evidence from the maze and the testing rooms. There was still one door that Logan and Valerie had not opened. While Valerie spoke to the team, Logan took the doctor's ID badge from her coat pocket and went over to the door marked "Library."

38

*The child wishes to be older, and the old man wishes again to be a
child. But wise is the one who allows himself to be both.*
—THE CHRONICLES OF SATRAYA

BANARAS, INDIA, 7:30 P.M. LOCAL TIME, 2 DAYS UNTIL FREEDOM DAY

Mr. Perrot and Jogi followed Babu to an old storage shed at the other
end of the yard. Even though evening was approaching, the sun was
still strong, and the heat was sweltering. Babu stared at the shed blankly.

"You were going to show us your iron work, Babu," Mr. Perrot reminded him, wiping the sweat from his brow with a handkerchief. "The
stamps you made for Deya."

"Yes," Babu replied, "that is why we have come here." He walked into
the shed and started to move the pieces of wood and unused building
materials. "They are here somewhere." As Mr. Perrot and Jogi helped
him move some of the heavier items, he looked concerned. "Where is
my hammer? Where are my chisels? Some of my tools are missing."

Mr. Perrot smiled, wondering how his old friend could find anything in this crowded shed. But eventually, Jogi lifted a greasy bed sheet
from the floor and discovered seven iron templates, each attached to a
two-foot-long broomlike handle.

"Yes, yes, you have found them. Those are Deya's words," Babu said.

Jogi carried out the iron stencils and laid them on the ground. Then he and Mr. Perrot inspected each one, trying to read the words. They were stenciled in reverse, and some of the letters had broken off, making the phrases difficult to read. "We need a mirror of some kind," Jogi suggested.

"Stamp them!" Babu instructed. Mr. Perrot and Jogi didn't quite understand what he was saying. "Stamp them!" he said again, as he walked over to the side of the shed and turned on a garden hose. Mr. Perrot and Jogi could only watch, wondering what the old man was up to. He walked back and dampened the ground in front of the iron stencils. The ground soon turned to mud. "Stamp them!" he said one more time, motioning for them to pick up the templates.

Jogi picked up the handle of each template and pressed its iron lettering into the wet ground. Babu put back the garden hose and sat in the shade of a large banyan tree. It did not take long for the hot sun to dry the mud. Jogi carefully removed each iron stamp to ensure that the impression it had left in the ground remained intact, and before long, all seven were imprinted on the ground.

"Six of these messages are the same as the ones on the pillars," Mr. Perrot said. "They are all from the *Chronicles*. But this one is not." He pointed to the fifth message from the left. "This must be the one that was in the pond."

> *In the once Great House*
> *Where fire is and ashes rise*
> *Where the ear stone fell*
> *Will hold your prize*

"What does that mean?" Jogi asked, looking quizzically at the message. "I suppose that we should assume 'prize' refers to the books. The first part, then, must refer to the location." Mr. Perrot nodded in agreement. "Could 'fire' and 'ash' refer to a fire pit here on the property?"

"I would doubt that," Mr. Perrot said. "If Deya feared for the safety of the books, I doubt she would have hidden them here. She would have certainly picked a more obscure place." He continued to stare at the words. "Why did she capitalize 'Great' and 'House'? That must be a proper noun, the name of a specific place."

"A *once* Great House," Jogi emphasized. "Which means that it is no longer great or no longer used."

"Yes," Mr. Perrot said. "A once Great House of fire and ash."

Mr. Perrot and Jogi stood in the hot sun trying to solve the riddle in the ground in front of them, but their efforts stalled. They went to join Babu under the shade of the tree. While they kept repeating lines of the riddle, Babu's attention wandered to a group of people walking past the house. He went over to the stone wall at the front of the property and observed a colorfully adorned body being carried ceremoniously down the street.

"What is it?" Mr. Perrot asked.

"A funeral procession," Jogi said. "They are taking the body to the Ganges, where it will be cremated."

"It seems to have caught Babu's attention," Mr. Perrot said, taking a drink of water. "It is certainly a very elaborate procession."

"Wait," Jogi suddenly burst out. "What about Manikarnika?"

"What is Mani—?"

"The Manikarnika Ghat. It used to be considered the most auspicious place to be cremated. It is just over there along the Ganges." Jogi pointed to the east. "Very close to where Deya found the original set of the books."

"What do you mean, it used to be?" Mr. Perrot asked. "Is it abandoned now?"

"No, not at all," Jogi explained. "It still remains in use. After the Great Disruption, new, more modern cremation sites were built to handle the large influx of bodies. But the faithful still use Manikarnika Ghat."

"I see. So this place was once a 'Great House'?" Mr. Perrot said with a smile.

"And it is still a place of fire and ash," Jogi added with a nod.

"That is certainly a plausible answer to Deya's riddle," Mr. Perrot said, rising to his feet. "And there is only one way to find out if it is the right answer."

39

Everyone is an actor in his own drama. And, like all great thespians, you may forget your lines from time to time. But it is at that moment that you can improvise and advance your life's epic tale in unexpected ways.

—THE CHRONICLES OF SATRAYA

"What's taking them so long?" Lucius looked through the dark-tinted windshield of their vehicle.

On being notified by one of the mercenaries who'd escaped about the WCF's assault on the plantation, Andrea had placed a call to a number that Simon told her was only to be used in an emergency. Now the targets of a WCF manhunt, she, Lucius, and Monique waited in an abandoned parking garage in a forgotten suburb of Washington, D.C., one that had sustained such extensive damage during the Great Disruption that it had never been restored. The top three floors of the garage had collapsed. Rebar and other binding material protruded from massive pieces of crumbled concrete, which lay on top of crushed vehicles. The back doors of a nearby van were open, revealing a cot and some blankets. It appeared to be a makeshift shelter that someone had used after the Disruption.

"They said they would be here, didn't they?" Lucius persisted.

"Yes, Lucius. I'm sure they are on their way." Andrea's voice was tense, though. "Don't you think that if the plan had changed, we would have been informed?" She looked at remnants of a sports car under a large piece of fallen concrete. The door to the car was missing, and a woman's shoulder bag and a jacket were on the seat, covered in forty years of dust and debris. She wondered if the owner had made it out of the garage alive or if she'd find a pile of bones inside the car if she looked more closely. She returned her attention to her own perilous situation and picked up her PCD.

"What are you doing?" Lucius grabbed the PCD and quickly turned it off. "You make a call, and we'll have the WCF all over us."

"I need to know if G-LAB has been compromised. I've been unable to reach Dr. Malikei or his handler in the last few hours."

"How could they have found out about G-LAB? I'm telling you, G-LAB is safe—and so is the doctor."

"The plantation was also supposed to be safe," she said. She gave her son a skewering look. "All we needed to do was deliver those two insolent people to the doctor, and we couldn't even do that right. Where did you find such incompetent help?"

"You're blaming me?" Lucius said incredulously. "They came highly recommended. If you have a problem, you need to take it up with Mr.—" He was cut off by another displeased look from his mother.

Monique was seated behind them, listening intently to their conversation. "Where are we going?" she asked. "What are we going to do?" She leaned forward, hoping to get a response. But they didn't seem interested in providing her with any assurances.

Lucius gestured for her to sit back. "Here they are," he said, unlocking the doors as a blue van came down the ramp and pulled up alongside them. A well-dressed middle-aged man with a small briefcase emerged from the van and got into the backseat with Monique.

"I was told there were only two of you," he said in a monotone, looking at Monique.

"No, there are three of us," Andrea responded. "Is that going to be an issue?"

The man remained silent and continued to stare at Monique.

Monique's heart started to race. If it was a problem, she knew what it would mean.

"It shouldn't be," he replied, as he opened the silver-colored briefcase he was carrying. "Hand me your identification glasses." As he placed the glass cards on a device in his briefcase, a monitor displayed each person's name, birth date, eye color, address, PCD number, and employment, credit, and medical histories. "First, we need to reprogram your glasses with new identities." One by one, each ID card was programmed with new information. "Review your cards, and memorize your new names and addresses."

"Howard? That's the best name you could come up with for me?" Lucius looked irked. He grabbed his mother's card. "Sarah—yeah, that's even worse. Now I don't feel so bad."

Monique looked at her card. "I'm Ming-Lee?"

"See, now that name makes sense," Lucius commented.

The man didn't appear to be in any mood to banter, however. "Hand me your PCDs," he said. "I need to program new identifier codes. The WCF won't know to track these new numbers." The flat-panel display lit up each time a PCD was connected. "Except for you," he said coldly, looking at Monique again. "I only have two new codes to allocate."

"Surely you can secure an additional number," Monique said in a pleading voice. "Surely you can." All she got was a disgusted look before the man turned back to the device in the briefcase. He worked on it a little while longer.

"I can program the PCD with a new number, but I won't be able to initiate the switch until I return to the office. Until then, don't turn this PCD on. It's still programmed with the old identifier." He raised his eyes at her, his look cold and threatening. "I'll notify you when the new ID is active."

"That will be just fine." Andrea smiled at Monique, who was still shaking. "See, dear, we wouldn't let any harm come to you."

Monique swallowed, forcing herself to nod.

Now another similarly dressed man exited the blue van and walked over to the vehicle. Lucius placed a hand on his gun, which was sitting on his lap.

"Relax, Howard," the man in the backseat said calmly, using Lucius's new name. "He's going to reprogram the transponder signal from your car. They may try to track that, too."

Lucius relaxed his grip on the gun and gestured to the small device inside the silver briefcase. "That's an interesting toy you have there. Any chance you have an extra one lying around?"

The man didn't respond. Working methodically, he finally finished and handed the PCDs back to them. "Remember," he said to Monique, "yours is not to be turned on until you hear from us."

Monique nodded.

The second man completed his task under the hood and returned to the blue van.

"What now?" Andrea asked, as the man shut his briefcase and stepped out of their vehicle.

He ignored her. "They have their new identification glasses, and their identifiers have been changed," he said into his PCD. He then walked back to the blue van, climbed into the front passenger seat, and sped away in the van.

"Friendly guy," Lucius said.

As soon as it was connected, Andrea's PCD rang, and Simon's image was projected. "It seems that we have underestimated Camden's son. Or that I have overestimated your ability to deal with him. Which one of these statements is true?"

"The loss of the plantation is unfortunate," Andrea admitted.

"And what of G-LAB and the good doctor?" Simon continued. "The loss of them would be even more *unfortunate*."

"Even if G-LAB is compromised, the Purging time line remains unaffected. Once the solution has been implemented, the authorities will be concerned with more pressing matters."

"You seem to be trying to convince yourself of that outcome,"

Simon said, in a tone that indicated he did not appreciate having his concerns dismissed so cavalierly. "If the lab and the doctor have been compromised, it affects you and Lucius far more than it affects me."

Andrea did not answer. She knew what Simon was referring to. He was correct; Dr. Malikei held the key to the cure that she and Lucius desperately needed.

"We've already taken our shots," Lucius interjected. "We just need to administer the pulse. The device stored at the plantation house might be buried under rubble, but we can still use the one that was deployed in India."

"The doctor already gave you the shots?" Monique said, alarmed. "What about the medicine for my parents? You promised me they would be taken care of!"

"Of course, dear," Andrea said. "We have not forgotten our commitments. When I last saw the doctor, he was working diligently on a cure for them."

"What about the frequency device?" Monique asked.

"We have that covered. Didn't you hear what I just said?" Lucius was getting impatient. "Stop your whining!"

"I have made arrangements for all of you to leave the country and fly to Château Dugan," Simon explained. "Go to the airport. One of our operatives will meet you there."

"The Château?" Monique said, surprised. "But I need to go to Japan."

"No!" Andrea snapped. Then, in a calmer tone, she added, "We need to stay together at the moment. But once we are all in Europe, we will be able to operate more freely, and you will be reunited with your parents. Perhaps we will send for them, and we can administer our frequencies together."

"Just get to the airport!" Simon ordered. "I will deal with the Ford boy myself. And I know exactly who can assist me."

40

Wake up in the morning, and do something different.
——THE CHRONICLES OF SATRAYA

G-LAB, 10:00 A.M. LOCAL TIME, 2 DAYS UNTIL FREEDOM DAY

Logan did not know what to expect when he entered the lab's so-called library. The room was spotless and well organized, with four rows of six-foot-high bookcases occupying approximately half of it. One of the bookcases contained stacks of research papers, and Logan was surprised to see an entire case dedicated to religious documents. He walked over to a tidy desk in the corner, which held a neat stack of papers, small figures made of sticks and colored wooden balls, a rainbow-colored spiral figure that he recognized as a DNA helix, and an advanced HoloPad computer with a PCD interface port on it. Judging by the diplomas and certificates hanging on the wall, he was certain that this was the desk of Dr. Serge Malikei. Next to it was a small, crisply made bed with a single pillow and a green blanket. *Looks like you spent a great deal of time here, Doctor,* Logan thought. Papers with handwritten formulas and scribbling that Logan didn't understand were pinned to the wall near the bed. The lair of a mad scientist.

The strangest and seemingly most out-of-place item in the library was the trophy head of a lion mounted on one wall. Its mane was perfectly groomed, and Logan noticed a hairbrush with a great deal of hair tangled around its bristles on a small mantel below it. Another portion of the wall displayed a series of esoteric paintings depicting the energy chakras of the human body. *Very odd*, Logan thought. *The doctor certainly was a man of eclectic interests.* The middle painting, which was slightly out of alignment with the others, caught his eye. When he tried to straighten it, it slipped farther down on the right, exposing a wall safe behind it. He'd wait for Valerie before inspecting it, not that he could open it himself.

He continued his inspection of the library. On a bookcase, he noticed a shelf labeled "Iatrogenesis and Genetic Engineering." He pulled a document from it and read an excerpt from a research paper on a virus called HIV that caused a disease called AIDS. He was startled. Iatrogenesis, he learned, meant "physician-induced." The paper made the case that many catastrophic diseases of the past, including AIDS, the swine flu, and the Black Plague, were actually man-actuated. The paper also suggested that population control had been the purpose of the conspiracy. Logan could not help but wonder why the doctor would have been reading this macabre material.

"What are you reading?" Valerie said from behind him. She had slipped into the library without his noticing.

He showed her the documents he was browsing through. "I think the doctor was trying to create a virus of some sort."

Valerie skimmed the research papers and looked up with a dark expression.

Logan turned back to the wall safe. "And check this out," he said, removing the painting that covered it. "I need you to help me get into it."

She shook her head. "Did you see that in one of your visions?"

"Nope," he said with a smile. "Just luck this time."

Valerie walked to the door and called in a WCF agent, who entered the library toting a bag of equipment. She pointed to the wall. "We need to open that safe."

The agent called in two more members of the team. It took only a few moments for them to evaluate the situation.

"This safe has a DFL device protected by a plastic guard," one of them said.

"A what?" Logan asked.

"A DNA frequency lock," Valerie explained. "Just like the ones used on Destiny Boxes, except that if you try to break into one of these without the proper DNA sample, it will self-destruct, destroying whatever's inside. What about the plastic guard?" she asked the agent.

"I can pick that lock easy," the agent said confidently. "It's the DFL you have to worry about. It's probably linked to only one person, so we'll need a sample of DNA."

Logan and Valerie looked at each other and had the same thought. Valerie used her PCD and placed a call to an agent upstairs. "We need a hair sample from the doctor. I'm in the subbasement, in the library."

"How many chances do we get with a DFL lock?" Logan asked.

"You never know," the agent said. "Each lock is different and configured by the owner. It could be three, it could be fifty. It could even be one."

"Worse yet, we don't know what kind of destruction sequence it is set to," Valerie added. "It could just take out what's in the safe. Or it could take out this whole lab."

"Like the plantation," Logan whispered to himself.

"We're not going to take any chances," Valerie asserted, as an agent handed her the hair sample she'd requested. "After you penetrate the plastic cover, we'll get everyone out of here before we try to unlock the safe."

"Then you might as well start moving people out of here now. That elevator is the only way up, and it's small. I'll have this cover off in a few seconds."

Valerie used her PCD and spoke to Luke, who had gone upstairs, while the agent began to remove the plastic containment surrounding the safe. People began to leave the lab and ride the elevator up. "Let me know when everyone is out, and we'll open the DFL. We'll give you the all-clear once we're done," Valerie said before ending her call.

Suddenly, an alarm went off. The display on the wall safe started flashing a countdown.

"We need to get everyone out of here right now!" Valerie shouted.

"What happened?" Logan asked.

"The plastic container was wired," the agent said, as the timer counted down from ninety seconds. "Try the hair sample!"

Valerie ran over and placed a strand of the doctor's hair on the sampling pad of the DFL. A series of chirping sounds commenced, activating a flashing red light. The alarm didn't cease. "This isn't the right DNA key!" Valerie yelled. "Everyone go, right now! We have to evacuate!"

Logan looked at the timer, which now read seventy-two.

Valerie led him and the other agent out of the library to the elevator, where several more agents were waiting to evacuate. The elevator was too small, and it would take a few more trips to get everyone out. The elevator doors closed, and another group of agents was on the way. Logan and Valerie were left with the last agent waiting for the elevator to return. The agent went over to the library door and looked at the safe. "Sixty and counting!" he yelled. Valerie pounded on the elevator door, trying somehow to coax it down faster.

"I thought for sure the doctor's DNA was the key," Logan murmured, as Valerie and the agent paced anxiously in front of the elevator.

The agent walked back to the library door and took another look at the safe. "Forty-five seconds!"

The elevator was on its way back down. "Get over here!" Valerie called to the agent. The elevator door opened, and the two of them rushed in. "What are you waiting for?" she yelled at Logan, who suddenly seemed lost in thought. She grabbed him by the arm and pulled him into the elevator. She pressed the only button on the panel.

"Wait! I have an idea!" Logan cried, as he rushed out of the closing elevator doors.

41

Learn to see your future without the mules of your past. Continue
to see it that way, until it arrives burden-free.
—THE CHRONICLES OF SATRAYA

DULLES INTERNATIONAL AIRPORT, 11:08 A.M. LOCAL TIME,
2 DAYS UNTIL FREEDOM DAY

The summer travel season was in full swing at Dulles International Airport. It was the only airport in the Washington, D.C. area that had been rebuilt after the Great Disruption. The control tower, which managed the ten runways, boasted a link to the newly deployed Stranton aircraft-tracking system, a system based on sonic wave displacement rather than traditional radar. The old Reagan National Airport, meanwhile, had turned into useless marshland with the rise of the Potomac River. In memory of the people who had died when more than seven thousand airplanes fell from the sky during the Great Disruption, a monument made out of recovered plane parts had been constructed in the middle of the marsh.

Lucius rejoined Andrea and Monique after abandoning their car in the remote parking lot. The three of them entered Terminal A, where security was heavy. At least, it seemed that way to the group of fugitives. Andrea had a brown scarf draped over her head, Lucius wore a baseball hat and a pair of dark sunglasses, and Monique had let down her hair, hoping it might shield her face. People of all ages were waiting impatiently in long lines at the ticket counters and the even longer queues at the security checkpoints. There would be no private plane for this trip. Andrea, Lucius, and Monique would be traveling with the masses.

Andrea looked at the departure board. "Our plane is set to leave in an hour."

"Where's the help Simon promised?" Lucius looked around the terminal. "It won't take long for one of these facial-recognition cameras to figure out who we are."

Monique took a seat in the waiting area. "How long do you think we will have to stay at the Château? I would really rather join my parents in Japan."

"Until this is over," Andrea answered sternly. "And you will have to stay there alone for a few days. Lucius and I have other business to attend to."

"You mean the final Purging?" Monique asked.

"Shut up," Lucius whispered. "Don't talk about it here."

"Yes, let us not discuss that at the moment," Andrea agreed gently, striving to hide her displeasure that Monique had been made privy to certain pieces of information because of their unusual circumstances. "Everything will be fine once we arrive at the Château," she continued, although she was beginning to question her decision not to let Lucius deal with Monique in the parking garage.

"I'd really rather be going home," Monique said, making one last effort. None of this was unfolding as she had anticipated. She was supposed to have disappeared to Japan right after the Council members were killed. Becoming a fugitive had not been part of the plan. Nor did it seem like she was part of Andrea's plan now.

"Ms. Montavon." Andrea and Lucius both turned at the sound. A woman dressed in a dark blue suit was approaching them. She was a stocky five-foot-six and had short brown hair. A security badge hung from a thin silver chain around her neck. "My name is Gretchen. Please come with me," she said, without exchanging any pleasantries.

Monique rose from her seat, and the three of them followed their escort as she circumvented the long security line and led them to a more private checkpoint near the departure gates.

"Your identification glass, please," the guard said. The group provided their IDs. The guard scanned each one and handed them back, but he paused as he processed Monique's. "What's your name, Miss?" he asked.

"Ming-Lee Takido," Monique answered.

"Do you have a PCD, Miss?" he asked.

"Is there a problem?" Gretchen inquired.

"The PCD identifier that her glass is associated with is not registered," the guard explained.

Monique was ready to make up an excuse but was interrupted. "We know that," Gretchen stated. "We deactivated her PCD as part of an agency operation. Is that going to be a problem?" She stared at the guard. "I can make a few calls, if you need me to."

The guard looked at Monique, whose nerves were fraying, and then looked back at Gretchen. "No. No need for that. You all have a nice trip." He handed the glass back to Monique, and Gretchen led them into the departure area for their flight.

The four of them waited in a corner, away from the crowd of travelers. Monique once again took a seat. She wasn't feeling well. The stress of recent events was taking its toll on her.

"Give the agency our thanks," Andrea told Gretchen, who acknowledged her with a nod and a slight smile. "Simon and I will not soon forget this."

"I need to use the restroom," Monique said, and she rose and headed directly for the ladies' room, across the hallway from where they were waiting.

Andrea signaled to Lucius. He followed Monique to the restroom and waited for her outside the entrance.

Monique entered one of the stalls and closed the door behind her. Her anxiety level had reached its tipping point. She took a couple of deep breaths and tried to regain her composure. She tied her hair into a ponytail and opened the door to the stall a few centimeters so she could peek out. The bathroom was crowded. A mother was tending to her baby while businesswomen were adjusting their makeup and hair. A group of teenagers walked in, talking loudly on their PCDs. Monique took her own PCD from her purse and placed a call. "It's me," she said softly, with desperation in her voice. "I'm in trouble, and you have to come get me." She peeked out again. "No! You come get me right now, or I'll tell them everything! Fifteen minutes, outside the international terminal." Monique disconnected the call, placed the PCD on a small shelf in the stall, and stepped out.

Lucius waited patiently by the restroom entrance. Six minutes had passed, and Monique had not come out. But suddenly, a young woman holding a baby did.

"Someone stole the stroller and all the baby's food!" she cried, catching the attention of her husband and everyone else in the area. "And she took my hat!"

Her husband rushed over to her. But Lucius got to her first. "What did she look like?" he demanded. "The girl who stole your stroller, what did she look like?"

The mother could not say. Lucius rushed into the restroom, much to the displeasure of the females inside. He looked around, inspecting the stalls, trying to locate Monique, but all he could find was a PCD. He grabbed it and left the ladies' room in a fury, almost colliding with Andrea and Gretchen, who had noticed the commotion.

"She's gone. She screwed us." Lucius held up Monique's activated PCD. "She turned it on!"

"We need to get out of here," Gretchen said. "The WCF will trace that signal and will be here at any moment. You two are not flying any-where today."

"What about Monique?" Lucius asked, as he tossed her PCD into a trashcan. The upset mother was still making a scene about the stolen stroller.

"We will have to deal with her later," Andrea said angrily. "Stupid, *stupid* girl!"

Gretchen led them to an emergency exit, where she used her security badge to open the door without activating the alarm. Soon after, the WCF arrived on the scene.

Andrea received a message on her PCD from the man they'd met at the abandoned parking garage, saying that Monique's new PCD ID had just been programmed in.

42

The mirror reflects precisely what it is shown. Turn your frown
into a smile, and see how much lighter your reflection will make
you feel.

—THE CHRONICLES OF SATRAYA

G-LAB, 11:40 A.M. LOCAL TIME, 2 DAYS UNTIL FREEDOM DAY

Logan reached up and grabbed a strand of hair from the mane of the
lion's head mounted on the wall. He knocked over a stack of books
as he scrambled to the safe and placed the lion's hair on the security
pad.

"What are you doing?" Valerie screamed, as she came rushing in
after him.

The countdown clock was now at eight seconds. Logan watched
anxiously as the light activated again, along with a series of chirping
sounds. This time, a green light flashed, and the timer deactivated. The
alarm went silent. The countdown clock stopped at three, the lock disengaged, and the door to the safe opened.

Logan turned and saw Valerie giving him an angry look. If it wasn't
for her PCD ringing at that moment, he suspected she would have hol-
lered at him like she used to do when they were kids. He grinned.

"Yeah, we're all right," she said into her PCD. "Logan deactivated
the alarm. Everyone can get back to work."

As she spoke, Logan emptied the safe, putting its contents on the doctor's desk.

"What in heaven's name were you thinking?" Valerie said, still sporting a disapproving look.

"I told you, I had an idea," he said, as if that was explanation enough.

"An idea. How in the world did you know to use the lion's hair?"

"It was the hairbrush." He picked it up off the mantel. "Look around. Everything in this room is perfect. Not a single thing out of place. Why wouldn't the doctor clean the hair off this brush?" He pulled a strand from it. "I assumed he must have used it to access the safe."

"Well, that was quite an assumption."

Logan smiled. He picked up a small matchbox-shaped item he'd taken out of the safe. "What is this thing?"

Valerie took a deep breath and walked over to the desk, still reeling from the risk Logan had taken. "Looks like you found the security dongle for the doctor's HoloPad." She took it from him and plugged it into the interface port. Within moments, the HoloPad sprang to life. "It seems we found the doctor's personal notes," said Valerie, as she sat down in a chair in front of the display. Logan found another chair and pulled up next to her. Valerie began to navigate through the many pages of notes, some of which looked similar to the handwritten papers pinned to the wall. Many of the notes and sketches were too technical for either of them to understand, but soon they came to one they both recognized.

"Hey, isn't that the painting you've been restoring?" Valerie said, as the HoloPad displayed an image of *The Creation of Adam*.

"It sure is," Logan said, perplexed. This piece of art seemed to be following him everywhere. He read the words superimposed on the painting and then the doctor's notes beneath the image.

The Chronicles of Satraya *have led me to discover some very important characteristics of the human brain. While the books don't explicitly state that it exists, I have found a quantifiable link between the human brain and God. I*

have further concluded that this secret has been known by others throughout his-
tory, one being Michelangelo. This link holds the key to our success. Simon and
Andrea will be very pleased with this discovery.

Valerie looked at Logan. "What is going on here?" she said incredulously. "Don't tell me the painting you've been working on for months
is at the center of this whole plot . . ."

Logan shook his head in disbelief. "This is not good at all," he said
in a hushed voice. He pointed out the words overlaid on the painting.
"The doctor knew exactly what this painting meant. He identified the
various parts of the brain—central sulcus, cingulate sulcus, Sylvian fis-
sure, optic chiasm, pons, pituitary stalk, vertebral, and medulla. He
knew precisely what Michelangelo was alluding to." Logan grew more
worried as they turned to the next set of notes. "And look here. The
doctor figured out that the space between God's finger and Adam's
finger represents the synaptic cleft, where all of the brain's electrical
activity takes place. That's what the lightning represented in my vision."
Logan shook his head again as he recalled his candle journey.

"What does all this mean?" Valerie asked.

"It means that he understood the interface between the brain and
the spirit, or God," Logan explained. "Do you remember my telling you
that I met the owner of the painting at the museum and then again at
the auction?"

"Yes, that Quinn fellow."

"Yes. He explained some of this to me. For centuries, science and
religion have been at odds with each other. Michelangelo painted this
image about five hundred years ago and proposed that science and religion could be unified through the understanding of how our brains
work." Logan pointed to where the fingers of Adam and God were
attempting to touch. "Mr. Quinn told me this part of the painting
contains one of its most important secrets." He pressed a button and
went to the next display. Then he read out another passage written by
the doctor.

After all these years of research and testing, we now understand the link between
God and the human brain. The Chronicles *were correct: God does hide in*
the tiniest of places and around the most obscure corners. The secret lies in the
synaptic cleft, with the VMAT-2 gene. Our tests have proven beyond doubt that
the more efficacious the VMAT-2, the more pronounced one's affinity to the
spiritual realm. We have classified those with the most active VMAT-2 gene as
Transcendental humanoids, or T-Noids.

"Now we know what *T-Noid* means," said Logan.

"The VMAT-2 gene is the gene Sylvia was talking about back at the lab," Valerie noted.

Logan nodded and continued to navigate to the next page. It was a picture of a DNA strand with a circular disk around a single point on the helix. "It's the collar we found around Cynthia Brown's DNA . . ."

Valerie nodded. She turned to the formulas and symbols written out beneath it. "We need to send this information back to the team in D.C.," she said. She pointed to a paragraph that mentioned Andrea and Lucius:

The isolation of the VMAT-2, which will lead to the Final Purging, has also
had a beneficial side effect. I have been able to isolate the gene to cure Andrea
and Lucius. I have created a custom serum for them. I am still working on their
frequency modulation, but I should be able to isolate it shortly.

"The Final Purging . . . this just keeps sounding worse and worse." Valerie turned to look at Logan. "I think whatever they have planned is bigger than we originally thought."

Logan nodded. "And what about the cure the doctor mentions for Andrea and Lucius? I didn't realize they were sick." He went on and read another passage.

Andrea has instructed me to stop working on Project Ryōshin. She told me it
will no longer be needed and my efforts in this area are no longer authorized.

"Project Ryōshin?" Valerie said.

Logan could only shake his head again. He navigated forward a few more screens. "Here's an entry from just two days ago."

To my surprise, Simon and Andrea have accelerated our plans. After Allegiance Pharmaceuticals first started delivering the serum via qMeds last December, we agreed we would wait until Freedom Day of 2070 before activating the agent. They now say that it must happen at Liberty Moment on Freedom Day of this year, 2069. I have lost control of this project.

"Valerie, we don't have much time," Logan said, doing a quick calculation in his head. "Liberty Moment is less than fifty-four hours away." Valerie remained silent as Logan continued to navigate through the doctor's notes. "Here's more."

We have learned from the experiments we have performed with the Biometric Chair that the serum is most powerful when the test subjects are focused on concepts such as liberty and freedom. If we flash before them images that correspond to these concepts, we see an increase in the potency of the serum and a reduction in VMAT-2 activity. It has been calculated that we should be able to eradicate 89.4 percent of the target T-noid population. This translates to just over 8.47 percent of the world's population.

Valerie took a deep breath. "All right. Let's get this information and a sample of that green liquid we found in the testing room back to the D.C. lab. You and I are going to pay a visit to Allegiance Pharmaceuticals. Let's find out if this serum really did get out and who authorized its distribution. You should call Mr. Kayin and confirm that the Council has delayed the Freedom Day celebration as we discussed."

Valerie's PCD rang with a call from Director Burke. Meanwhile, Logan looked back at the doctor's notes. He felt deeply disturbed— frightened, really—by what he'd just read. He took a deep breath. The scope and magnitude of Simon and Andrea's plan was beginning to sink in.

"Change of plan," Valerie said, as she ended her call. "We're going back to D.C. to deliver the serum and the doctor's notes ourselves."

"What about Allegiance Pharmaceuticals?"

"I'll deal with that later. We just apprehended Monique at Dulles Airport. Looks like she was trying to flee the country."

43

The past haunts you because you choose to remember it.
Turn around—is it really there?
—THE CHRONICLES OF SATRAYA

WASHINGTON, D.C., 6:00 P.M., 48 HOURS UNTIL LIBERTY MOMENT

After Valerie and Logan landed in Washington, D.C., Valerie went directly to the WCF building to interrogate Monique Sato. Logan had persuaded Valerie to allow him to go back to Compass Park to figure out the mystery of his father's bench. And so, after talking with Mr. Kayin about postponing the Freedom Day rallies, Logan returned to the park accompanied by two WCF agents.

It was a cloudy evening, and the park was empty. Logan walked quickly down the pathways to the bench across from the granite monument dedicated to his parents and the other members of the first Council of Satraya. The two agents patrolled the area nearby.

Shortly after he arrived, his PCD rang. It was Mr. Perrot calling from India, where it was 3:30 A.M.

"Logan!" Mr. Perrot sounded frantic. His hair was disheveled, and he looked as if he hadn't had any sleep. "Are you and Valerie all right? Jogi just told me about the kidnapping and the explosion that killed Charlie. I tried calling Valerie, but she didn't answer."

"Yes, everything is fine now," Logan said, trying to calm him down. "Valerie and I are OK. The WCF just arrested Monique Sato, and Valerie is talking with her now. How are you and Jogi progressing?"

Mr. Perrot brought Logan up to speed on his adventure with Jogi and the secret they discovered in Deya's garden.

"You have to be careful," Logan said. "If Simon really is in India searching for the books, you have to make sure you never leave Jogi's side." He went on to tell Mr. Perrot about G-LAB and the threat they'd uncovered there. "Mr. Kayin refused to postpone Freedom Day. He told me that the Council received a very large anonymous donation yesterday. One of the stipulations was that the Freedom Day celebrations go on as planned, so that the world can honor the fallen Council members. Mr. Kayin said we were fooling ourselves if we thought that the celebration could be canceled. He said it would be like calling off Christmas."

"That is disturbing news," Mr. Perrot said. "Any more signs of Andrea?"

"Nothing yet, but we hope that Monique Sato will give us something we can use to catch her."

"Logan," Mr. Perrot said with concern in his voice, "how is my daughter coping with the loss of her partner, Charlie?"

Logan looked at the fatherly worry on Mr. Perrot's face. "She's coping with it the only way she can, sir," he asserted. "She's going after the bad guys." Mr. Perrot smiled at this. "You've raised an incredible daughter," Logan continued. "You should be very proud of her."

"I am," Mr. Perrot said. "You must be careful in your search. Andrea and Simon have surrounded themselves with people who are as ruthless as they are. I don't want Valerie to suffer another loss." He gave Logan a heartfelt smile. "And I don't want to lose you, either."

Logan smiled back. "We'll be careful," he said, and he disconnected the call.

Turning his attention back to the bench, Logan couldn't find anything on or around it that seemed out of place. He dropped to his knees and slid underneath it. In one of the corners, he saw a metal cylinder secured to the bottom of the bench by two rusty bent nails. He popped his head up to see if anyone was around, but he only saw the two agents continuing their surveillance. He ducked back down and easily freed the metal cigar holder without much effort. On the holder was etched a message: "Secrets are dangerous to all who possess them."

He unscrewed the cap of the metal container and saw rolled-up sheets of paper inside. This was not the time or the place to read them, so he put the cap back on and put the silver cylinder in his backpack. He indicated to the WCF agents that he was ready to leave.

Logan poured himself a glass of wine. The agents had escorted him back to Valerie's apartment. After taking a look around inside, one guard stood outside the door, while the other kept watch at the main entrance to the building. Logan desperately needed to get some sleep, but he couldn't rest until he read the sheets his father had stuffed into the silver cigar case. Sitting at one end of Valerie's couch under the soft light of a lamp, he began to read the pages, which bore his father's symbol in the upper right-hand corner.

February 13, 2036

The strange thing about Fendral and his copy of the Chronicles, *known as the Train Set, was that they emerged a full year after Deya, Madu, and I reported our experiences. At first, I didn't think much of it, but then something else began to bother me. Fendral never described having an experience with the blue orb as the rest of us did. When any one of us discussed our experiences, he conveniently left the room or changed the subject. We initially thought he just wanted to keep his experience private. I now know that his reason for not participating in those discussions was far more dark and ominous.*

I discussed my suspicions about the matter with Cassandra, and she urged me to go to Zurich and investigate for myself. I was reluctant to do so because we had just found out that she was pregnant. She urged me to address the issues right away and not to wait, as after our baby arrived, there would be no time. I told Robert and the rest of the Council that I was going to Europe. The work that we were doing with the Council took us to many places, so no one questioned my travel plans.

It was widely reported that Fendral's copy of the Chronicles was found at the Hauptbahnhof train station in Zurich. When I arrived there, I saw that little had changed in eight years. Zurich had been hit hard and was being rebuilt slowly. I entered the station through a missing segment of the outer wall. The main hall had been turned into a homeless encampment. It was winter, and people were tending small fires to cook by and to heat their humble living spaces. Even though I was a stranger, I found this place welcoming. I immediately noticed that the work of the Council had reached this improvised community. I saw copies of the Chronicles everywhere. As I walked through the maze of hovels, many people invited me to warm up by their fires or to eat their food and drink from their bartered wine.

I was reluctant to take food away from these poor people who had so little, but I could not pass up an invitation from a man who was enjoying a pipe as he sat on his stool in front of his meager fire. He moved another stool near the fire and poured me a glass of some very expensive scotch, which I found a bit odd. We sat in silence for a moment, and I enjoyed a toke from his pipe. He asked me why I had come. He could tell from my accent and my clothes that I was not a denizen of the train station or a native of Switzerland. At first, I was going to tell him that I was a part of the rebuilding effort, but something inside me urged me to speak the truth to this man. I told him that I was Camden Ford. He knew exactly who I was and proceeded to grab his copy of the Chronicles. He called over to his neighbor, a woman by the name of Marilyn, and told her that a celebrity had arrived. It wasn't long before a few others joined us. They each brought over a log of wood for the fire, as was the tradition in their community.

They asked many questions about the Chronicles; they wanted to know what I thought of certain passages and how I interpreted certain others. I was glad to offer my perspectives. They had questions about the Satraya Flame and *the other fundamentals presented in the books. I told them a little about my flame work, but I dared not tell them everything that Baté had taught me, for I was not yet a master of it.*

Our host continued to pour his expensive scotch for everyone. How he could afford it, I didn't know. What they really wanted to hear was the story of how I found the books. I had told that story a hundred times before, and I was most happy to share it with such a congenial group. Even though these people did not have anything to their names, they had embraced the very essence of what the Chronicles *attempt to impart. They reminded me so much of the misunderstood Forgotten Ones. I recounted the story of my long drive home, my narrow escape from the marauders, and my journey into the forest. I told them of my experience with the mysterious blue orb, and how it levitated me off the ground. I told them of my encounter with the Forgotten Ones, and how I unexpectedly fell in love and eventually married one of their kind. The woman who first spoke out to me in the darkness. The one who convinced the Forgotten Ones to put down their weapons.*

My description of the orb was of great interest to them, but not for the reasons I assumed. They told me that they, too, had witnessed a blue light. It had engulfed the station, they said, and they all pointed to track number seven. They said it had happened around six years ago. I found it noteworthy that it coincided with my discovery of the books and also Deya's and Madu's discoveries. I told them that Fendral never spoke about his experience with the blue orb. They were confused by the reports that Fendral had found a copy of the Chronicles *at the train station. They told me that the blue light they had witnessed there had been directly experienced by a man named Giovanni Rast. No one by Fendral's name had ever lived at the station. When I showed them a picture of Deya, Madu, Fendral and myself, they confirmed they had never seen Fendral.*

I asked them to tell me more about Giovanni Rast. They said that he lived in the number fourteen car on track seven. Marilyn seemed to have the closest relationship with him. She said that after everyone saw the blue light coming from the car, she went to investigate its source. She found Giovanni in his car reading from some books. He told her that he had found them enclosed in a tin can on the tracks outside his car. When he opened the first book, a blue globe of light appeared. I asked if they had ever witnessed the blue light again. Everyone there said that the blue light had never returned; they had only seen it once. This was consistent with my story and those of Deya and Madu. I asked Marilyn to continue. She said that afterward, Giovanni's life began to change. He somehow came into some money but nonetheless continued to live in his train car. Our host told me that Giovanni had given him the wonderful scotch that we were enjoying right before he disappeared. The others told of similarly expensive presents that Giovanni had bought for them before he left. I asked where he had gone, but no one could answer that question. I asked Marilyn if she would take me to the train car in which he had lived, and she agreed without issue.

It had been a while since Marilyn had last visited Giovanni's car. While we were alone, Marilyn told me something that she hadn't shared with the others. She knew where Giovanni's money came from, she said, but he'd sworn her to secrecy. Marilyn told me that one hundred gold coins fell from one of the books he'd found. Giovanni explained to her that after the blue orb disappeared back into the book, gold coins magically fell from the pages. She promised never to tell anyone, but because I was Camden Ford, who had also discovered one of the original copies of The Chronicles of Satraya, *she felt compelled to break that promise. Giovanni didn't know what to make of it. He said the books were special.*

The gold coins she mentioned confirmed something that I had suspected for many years. The blue orb and the books seemed to give to the finder the very thing or ability he or she needed most at that moment. Giovanni received treasure, Deya was healed, and I received hope. I cannot write what Madu received because I promised him never to reveal it. Nonetheless, in all cases, the books somehow knew what to provide.

Logan paused for a moment. The last few lines reminded him of something that Sebastian had said to him at the auction. It was that same phrase that had haunted him ever since: "Where the books will *choose* to go." *These books seem to be governed by some mystical law and purpose,* Logan thought. He continued to read his father's account.

I asked Marilyn if she knew where Giovanni was. She didn't; she'd never heard from him after he disappeared. Marilyn did remember, though, that just before Giovanni found the books, he had taken a job as a handyman for a well-to-do family living in the city. They paid him a meager wage, but people didn't complain back then. I asked if she knew the name of the family; she did not. But she did remember that Giovanni continued to work there even after he'd found the books and had been given the gift of the gold coins. She told me he would take the books everywhere with him, even when he went to work.

I looked around the converted train car. Giovanni's bedding was in the corner; a blanket and a pillow were neatly stacked. Next to where he slept was a small nightstand with a candle on it. I wondered if he had been working on the flame technique. He had secured a short pole from the ceiling of the car where he hung some clothes. Judging by the condition of his space, Giovanni may have been homeless, but he was not destitute. He did what he could with the circumstances in which he found himself. Displayed on a shelf were some trinkets and a picture of a woman and three children. Marilyn told me the people in the picture were Giovanni's wife and children. They had been casualties of the Great Disruption.

As I continued to look around, I spotted something in the overhead baggage compartment of the car. I reached up and brought down a box. Marilyn told me it was the tin box that had contained the books. With her approval, I opened it. Inside I found a folded piece of paper, which was a help-wanted advertisement for a handyman, and, more surprisingly, many of the gold coins. Both Marilyn and I asked the same question. Why would Giovanni disappear with the books and yet not take the coins with him? They were certainly worth a great deal; they could be used to start a whole new life. I put the job posting in my pocket and gave all of the coins to Marilyn. I told her to keep what she wished and to give the rest to the others. I asked her then if I could keep the tin box, and she agreed. I left the passenger car and exited the Hauptbahnhof through a back door. Then I continued my quest in the city of Zurich.

Logan took from his backpack the tin box that he and Mr. Perrot had found under the floor in the basement of the Council of Satraya headquarters and set it on the coffee table. He wondered if this was the box that had contained the original set of the *Chronicles* that Giovanni had found on the tracks. He set it back down to finish reading his father's account.

> *The address on the job posting led me to an unoccupied private home on Bel-lerivestrasse, which I later found out at the WRF office was owned by Fendral Hitchlords. I looked through the logs for the deceased of that time, searching for any information concerning a man by the name of Giovanni Rast. I found the death notices for his wife and children but not for him.*
>
> *All four of us had found our sets of the* Chronicles *on the same day, July 21. Giovanni had disappeared four months after his discovery. I had completed my investigation and confirmed my suspicions, but I was powerless to do much about it. I now knew Fendral never spoke of his experience with the blue orb because he'd never had one. Giovanni Rast had experienced the blue orb. While I don't have any direct proof, I know in my heart that Fendral had something to do with Giovanni's disappearance. How Fendral knew the value of the books and the exact events that took place may never be known. The bigger question that haunts me is, what am I to do with this information that I was so driven to discover?*

Now Logan knew Fendral's secret.

44

Would you follow your own advice?
—THE CHRONICLES OF SATRAYA

"Do you really think that Andrea and Simon care about you?" Valerie asked Monique Sato.

The dark-haired young woman sat silently opposite Valerie at the table in the interrogation room at WCF headquarters. Alex Daniels, a ten-year veteran of the WCF who had been temporarily assigned as Valerie's new partner, stood in the corner listening to every word. Cameras mounted in the upper corners of the room recorded everything that was taking place.

"We can place you at the Council offices the night of the murders," Valerie said. "We know about G-LAB, the doctor, and the antigen that is being deployed. We even know that the attack is scheduled to take place on Freedom Day. We know that you, Andrea, Lucius, and Simon are all working together, and that somehow Randolph Fenquist is also involved."

Monique was no longer wearing the red and white baseball cap that had ultimately led to her capture. The authorities had programmed the airport security cameras to look for anyone wearing the cap she had stolen from the mother in the airport restroom. The cameras had shown someone discarding the cap and a baby stroller at a fast-food restaurant at the other end of the terminal. Authorities caught up with her trying to exit the airport near the international terminal. The hat and the stroller were in evidence now. Monique's hair was pulled up in a knot, revealing the stressed expression on her face.

"Are you going to get me a lawyer or not?" Monique asked defiantly. She'd asked that question repeatedly since she'd been arrested. "I just want a lawyer."

"I'm surprised that Andrea hasn't sent anyone over to help you," Valerie said. "Char—" She caught herself as she almost said the name of her dead partner. "Alex. Alex, don't you think that if they cared about Monique, they would have sent their attorney over right away? They're rich people; they should know a bunch of good lawyers."

"I know I certainly would have," Alex said, playing along. "If I heard you were arrested, I would do everything I could to help you out."

"They are not going to send anyone, all right?" Monique lashed out. "You don't understand."

"Then help us understand," Valerie said.

"I ran away. They were going to kill me."

"We can protect you," Valerie assured her.

"No, you can't," Monique said. "Not from them." She shook her head, whimpered softly. "I just want an attorney . . ."

Valerie stood and left the interrogation room, followed by her new partner. They walked behind a two-way mirror where they could keep an eye on Monique.

"She's not giving anything up," Alex said. They had been interrogating Monique for more than two hours, and she had said very little.

"Well, at least we know why they haven't sent a lawyer for her," Valerie said. "She ran."

"She's scared, that's for sure." Alex looked at Monique, slumped over the table, her head resting on her arms. "And I don't blame her. On the one hand, she has them after her, and on the other hand, she faces the prospect of going to prison for a very long time."

"Don't feel too sorry for her—she helped kill four people," Valerie said. "We need something to draw her out. Did we get any information about her past? Anything about the people she hangs with, family, friends, anything?"

"There's not that much." Alex pulled up a report on his PCD. "We know she's a Japanese national. She came here when she was twenty-one and landed a job working for the New Democratic Party as a media director. After a few years there, she went to work for Cynthia Brown. She's been Cynthia's assistant for almost three years. She doesn't have any priors. But there have been five large deposits that went into her bank account over the last two and a half years; we're trying to trace where they came from. She sends money to her parents in Tokyo every month. Her father has some type of chronic disease, not sure—"

"Chronic disease? I wonder . . ." Valerie's eyes lit up. "We know from Dr. Malikei's journal that he was creating a designer drug to help Andrea and her son. What if they promised Monique to do the same for her father's illness? I wonder if that was the special project he was referring to."

Valerie went back into the interrogation room and took a seat at the table. Alex sat down beside her. "When was the last time you saw Dr. Malikei?" Valerie asked.

"I don't know who you're talking about," Monique answered. She sat back in the chair and crossed her arms.

"That's too bad," Valerie said. "We were hoping someone could help us locate his family so we could tell them he was shot in the head." Valerie brought up a picture of his corpse on her PCD. Monique uncrossed her arms and sat up in the chair, obviously unsettled. She stared at it. "I thought that might get your attention. I told you Andrea and Simon don't care about you. One of their thugs shot the doctor right in front of me. And after everything he did for

Andrea and Lucius—even for you. He had a special project for you, didn't he?"

"How do you know about that?" Monique said sharply. "Tell me! How do you know about that?"

"So you do know the doctor," Valerie said. She projected a page of Dr. Malikei's notes on her PCD and pointed.

Andrea has instructed me to stop working on Project Ryōshin. She told me it will no longer be needed and my efforts in this area are no longer authorized.

"After everything I did for—" Monique stopped herself. But Valerie could see she was trembling, and tears were welling in her eyes.

Valerie knew she had broken her. She shut down the projection and spoke softly. "The doctor was also making a serum for you, wasn't he?"

"It was for my father. Andrea and Simon promised to help him." The tears now flowed freely.

Alex gave her a handkerchief from his coat pocket. "What does *ryōshin* mean?" asked Alex, struggling to say the word correctly.

"It means 'parents,'" Monique answered. "They said I only had to do a few things. If I helped them, the doctor was going to create a medicine that would cure my father of Alzheimer's." Monique paused, shaking her head in disbelief. "They lied to me. They've been lying all along."

"I'm afraid so, Monique. There is nothing honorable about these people. You are fooling yourself if you think otherwise." Valerie paused, giving her words time to sink in. Then she continued in a compassionate tone. "How long have you been working for Simon and Andrea?"

"Two years," Monique replied. "At first, they just wanted information about what the Council was up to and any information about their activities and plans. They paid for all my father's medical bills; they paid the hospital in Tokyo directly."

"Are the five large deposits to your bank account from Simon and Andrea?" Alex asked. She didn't answer. "Well, are they? Yes or no?" Alex asked. Still she didn't answer.

"Tell me about the Council murders," Valerie said. Monique continued to remain silent. "If you want our help and protection, you have to tell us everything."

"I received a call from Simon a week before the auction," Monique reluctantly explained. "He told me not to pass on to Cynthia any information about the upcoming sale of the *Chronicles*. I was to make sure she didn't know the books were being sold. The auction house tried to contact her at the office, but I didn't relay the messages. Everything was going according to plan, but then—" She stopped.

"But, then what?" Valerie urged her on.

Monique took a deep breath and continued. "Another Council member got wind of the auction and told Cynthia about it. That happened on the same night as the World Federation of Reconstruction banquet. I made Simon aware of the situation, and then he gave me instructions." Monique wiped away some more tears from her eyes. "I was to take the EMFE and activate it in the basement of the Council building. He told me about a secret tunnel that would get me into the building without anyone knowing."

"What's an EMFE?" Alex asked.

"I heard them use the name Electromagnetic Frequency Emitter, EMFE for short. I don't know much about it," Monique said. "It's some kind of advanced weapon that they kept locked up at the plantation house. One of Simon's men brought the device to me outside the office that night. I used the tunnel to enter the basement while the auction was going on."

"Why did he ask you to do that?" Alex asked. "Why didn't he have one of their men plant the device?"

"That's easy to answer," Valerie interjected. "Once Monique helped to kill the Council members, she would be in it up to her ears. There would be no way out."

Monique looked startled, as if she had never thought about it like that. "I set the device on a table, and I had to pass a small coil through a hole that I made in the basement ceiling and the meeting-room floor."

"How did you drill a hole without the Council members hearing?" Alex asked.

"They gave me a pen laser," Monique said. "It was easy to use."

"That explains the tiny hole we found in the ceiling," Valerie said to Alex. She turned back to Monique. "What'd you do next?"

"Once I passed the coil through the hole, I put on a pair of dark glasses to protect my eyes from the blast of light, and I turned on the device. I was told the device would get really hot, but once a green light flashed, I should turn it off and pack it up and leave the building. Which is what I did."

"That explains the green flash I saw on the videos and the burn mark on the table in the basement," Valerie said. "What happened after that?"

"I went back to the WFR banquet and mingled the rest of the night."

"What happened after I saw you leave the plantation house with Andrea last night?" Valerie asked.

Monique explained how their departure plans suddenly changed after the incident there. She told them about the mysterious men who forged new identification glasses for them, the woman named Gretchen who guided them through airport security, and her escape from the restroom, which led to her eventual capture.

"Let's go through the video at the airport and see if we can get an ID on this Gretchen woman," Valerie said to Alex. Then, to Monique, "What does the EMFE device look like? Where's that device now?"

"It is about the size of a small dinner plate and about four centimeters thick. It's not very heavy, about one kilogram. They keep it somewhere in the house at the plantation. You should be able to find it there."

"That's going to be tough since the house was blown up," Valerie said. "But you know that."

"We're still combing through the rubble," Alex said. "Where in the house did they keep it?"

"I want protection, and I want a deal," Monique said vehemently.

"If I tell you where the device is, you need to ensure my safety and help me get back to Japan."

The clock was ticking. Freedom Day was now less than forty-seven hours away.

"Fine," Valerie snapped. "First, you tell us where the device is and sign an agreement to testify against Simon and Andrea when we apprehend them. After that, we'll see about sending you back to Japan." When Monique remained silent, Valerie looked directly into her eyes. "Monique, this is the best deal you're gonna get."

Monique nodded. "But I want signed paperwork now."

"Signed paperwork?" Valerie said, annoyed, as she turned to Alex. He looked ready to throttle Monique. "All right, we'll take you to the plantation, and you show us exactly where the device was stored. I'll have the paperwork brought there." She stood and gave Alex instructions. "Get a team together, and take her to the car. I'll meet you outside in ten, and we'll head to the plantation. First, I need to run upstairs and clear things with Burke."

"There's one more thing," Monique said. Valerie stopped in the doorway and turned around. "Andrea and Simon gave me green pills to take before I activated the device in the basement."

Valerie exchanged a glance with Alex and left the interrogation room.

A shot rang out just as Valerie exited the WCF offices. Instinctively, she hit the ground and took cover behind one of the structural columns at the front of the building. She peered around the column and saw Alex and two agents drag Monique behind the unmarked armored WCF vehicle they were taking to the plantation, while the other agents provided cover. Valerie drew her weapon and rushed over to assist Alex, who was kneeling beside Monique, attempting to stop the blood that was flowing from her chest as she struggled to breathe.

"Stay with us," Valerie said. "Help is on the way."

Monique shook her head. "Fireplace," she said between strained breaths. "Fireplace." They were the last words she ever uttered.

Valerie's hands and shirt were covered in blood. Helmeted WCF agents with rifles and automatic weapons were fanning out around the building, cordoning off the street, and running into the surrounding buildings. The sound of an ambulance siren grew louder by the second, but it was too late.

Valerie stood up and called an agent over. "Get down to the plantation, and search all the locations where a fireplace could have been."

"What are we looking for?" he asked.

"Anything that doesn't look like it belongs in a fireplace," Valerie said in a sarcastic, frustrated voice.

A man hopped into the backseat of a black van that was parked around the corner from the WCF offices.

"Is it done?" Randolph Fenquist asked.

"Yes," the man said, running his fingers along the scar on his face. He set the high-powered rifle between them.

Fenquist lit a cigarette. "You know, Jimmy," he said, "we saved everybody from a lot of hassles today. That girl was causing nothing but problems."

"Well, she's at heaven's gate now," Jimmy said. "I hope her sins don't keep her from gettin' in."

Both he and Randolph smiled as the van screeched away.

45

Enlightenment is not what you think it is; but you have to be
enlightened to know that.
Such is the dilemma of all master teachers.
—THE CHRONICLES OF SATRAYA

WASHINGTON, D.C., 10:00 P.M. LOCAL TIME,
44 HOURS UNTIL LIBERTY MOMENT

Logan now knew the piece of information that his father had used all those years ago to force Fendral and Andrea to disassociate themselves from the Satraya movement and return to Europe. He took his father's handwritten pages and the cigar case and put them into the tin box. He wondered if Simon, who had only been thirteen at the time, knew of his own father's despicable deed and, more important, if this information could somehow help to derail the mysterious attack he and Andrea were planning to launch on Freedom Day. Perhaps, as happened years ago, if Simon were threatened with this story going public, he would be inclined to back down. But so much time had passed. Would anyone even care anymore that Fendral Hitchlords had been an impostor? That Giovanni Rast had found the set of the *Chronicles* known as the Train Set and in all likelihood had been robbed and murdered by Fendral?

Logan rose from the sofa and started pacing the room; it helped keep him from falling asleep. He wanted to stay awake until Valerie returned from her interrogation of Monique. His thoughts went to Mr. Perrot, who was halfway around the world, working to thwart Simon's quest, and to his parents, who had risked everything to confront Fendral with his lie. He continued to pace. He needed to do something, anything, that would help stop Simon and Andrea. He remembered something that his mother told him when he was young: "Evil is not stopped by good intentions; it is stopped by fearless action." He stopped pacing. It was time to be fearless. Time to take action. He knew what he should do. He took the blue candle out of the tin box and put it in the candle holder. Then he placed it on the coffee table and sat down on the floor half a meter away. He refused to think about his failed attempt at the plantation.

The room was dark except for the flame of the candle. He struggled to stay awake and focus on the flame. His eyes wanted to close, his body wanted to fall asleep, and he had to shake his head whenever he felt himself drifting off. But just as at the plantation, he still could not hear the ringing sound. His apprehension intensified, and doubt overtook him. Disappointed, he closed his eyes for a moment.

How it happened, he didn't know, but Logan found himself back in the old study. The desk stood before him, and the written notes were all stacked in neat piles as they had been during his last sojourn. *How is this possible?* He hadn't even been able to keep his eyes open, let alone focus on the flame.

"You are here because you had no expectation of arriving," an echoing male voice said.

He turned around and saw the dark silhouette of a man sitting in a chair. He was wearing a long, flowing robe and seemed to be in a faint vortex of bluish energy which distorted his face.

"Your failure at the plantation was a result of your arrogance," the man said, raising his right hand and pointing his finger at Logan. There was a golden ring on his finger. "That is the downfall of all men on this journey. You cannot come to this place or any other in this realm if you presuppose your entitlement to be here. This is a place of sincerity, of humbleness. This realm is not subject to the conditions of right and wrong or good and bad. Did not a great master once say you must humble yourself as a child?"

"I understand," Logan responded sheepishly. He took a seat in a chair that suddenly appeared, facing the shadowed figure. "Who are you? Are you my father's friend Baté?" The shadow did not answer. Logan thought for a moment about his next question. "Is everything that I see in the candle true?"

"Whatever you see here is a possibility in your reality," the shadow replied.

"So what determines if it will happen?"

"What are revealed to you are your potentials. Some are based on your desires; others are rooted in your fears. Whatever you see that frightens you is not certain to come to pass, just as it is with what you see that brings you comfort. All is subject to change. Your fears, your uncertainties, your doubts—all are intermingled with those of everyone around you. If a single person changes his or her mind, the destiny of all will change. Everyone's thoughts are like great waves upon the ocean interfering with one another. Change the waves, and you will change how they crash upon the shores of your reality."

Logan pondered the shadow's cryptic words. Even after some moments, they still didn't make sense to him. "We need your help," Logan said. "The world is facing a great threat."

"Change the waves in your life, and you can change how they crash." The shadow stood and gave Logan a bow. "It is time for you to leave this place. Your life is beckoning you. But remember this: when the finger of the unknown presents itself, be greater than Adam, and grasp its opportunity."

Logan did not want to leave. There was something eerie yet empowering about the place. With the gesture of the shadow's hand, Logan's chair suddenly disappeared. He was about to hit the floor when he suddenly found himself in a dimly lit room filled with large floral arrangements. People were talking in hushed tones, and no one seemed to notice that he had arrived. He saw Mr. Perrot, Sylvia, Luke, and many others he had recently met, sitting in rows of chairs. On a platform, he saw an open casket. Near it, he saw Charlie. He was looking down into the casket, tears running down his burned and charred face.

Logan did not have to walk over to it; just thinking about doing so teleported him there. On a shelf above the casket, he saw framed photos of a dark-haired little girl who looked familiar to him. In front of another picture of a dark-haired young woman were a badge and a gun. Logan looked down into the casket. He saw Valerie lying there. He screamed and tripped backward. But before he could hit the ground, someone slipped an arm around his shoulder and steadied him.

"Are you all right?" Valerie asked, as she helped him sit up. "I just got home and didn't want to disturb you, but then you started screaming."

Logan took a deep breath. He was still trembling from what he'd seen on his candle journey. "Just another wild trip," he said, as casually as he could. He couldn't tell her what he had seen.

"I'm glad you're OK," Valerie said. "You're not going to believe what happened to Monique."

"And you're not going to believe what I found under the park bench." Logan rubbed his eyes and gazed around the room, trying to erase the frightening images from his mind. "Oh, no!" he burst out. "The candle!" He looked at the clock; it was just past midnight. He had lost track of time, and the blue candle had completely burned down. His link to the old study and the mysterious shadow had burned away.

46

Until you look into a starry night and can see the end of forever,
assume there is more to experience, and continue to explore.
—THE CHRONICLES OF SATRAYA

WASHINGTON, D.C., 10:00 A.M. LOCAL TIME,
32 HOURS UNTIL LIBERTY MOMENT

"This technology is like nothing we've seen before," Sylvia said. "We've analyzed the information on Dr. Malikei's HoloPad computer. Let me try to explain it as best as I can."

Valerie's new partner, Alex, entered the WCF forensics lab holding a cup of coffee and took a seat at the table next to Logan and Valerie. All of them had attended the memorial service for Charlie earlier that morning. Charlie's wife, his two children, and many friends, including a large contingent from the WCF, had filled the chapel. Valerie gave a moving eulogy for her late partner and dearest friend, which she'd had difficulty delivering without choking up a few times. After the ceremony, she and her team had returned to the WCF lab. There was work to be done in his memory, she said.

Now Sylvia used the HoloPad to bring up a cross-section image of a human skull and brain. "The green serum that we recovered from G-LAB affects brain chemistry. In particular, it messes with this area of the brain, called the posterior superior parietal lobe." Sylvia pointed to the upper back of the skull. "Based on Dr. Malikei's entries, I would say they were interested in this part of the brain because it is affiliated with the orientation association area, or OAA for short. It is the part of the brain that controls your perception of time, distance, and space. It helps you judge which way is up and which way is down. The more active this region is, the more spatially aware you are. You have a handle on where you are and what you're doing. At first, we didn't understand why the doctor considered this region so vitally important, but then we read his notes, specifically his notes about when the serum was most effective."

"Yes, the doctor said the serum worked best when people were focused on something spiritual," Logan recalled.

"That's right," Sylvia said. "This part of the brain is most affected when people are focused on abstract ideas. There were some initial studies done in the 2010s that measured the OAA region when people were praying or meditating. The activity in this part of the brain slowed down drastically, and people began to lose their awareness of space and time—they reached a sort of transcendental state."

"You're going to have to connect some dots for me here," Valerie said. "I'm not entirely sure I see where this is leading."

"Imagine what would happen to people if the OAA part of the brain could not be slowed down," Sylvia said. "Think about how you and I make decisions. Or, more important, consider how we make good decisions. When we are emotional, our choices tend to be rash, more spur-of-the-moment. But when we are able to calm down and think rationally, the OAA region slows down. We can then make decisions and choices that are not unduly influenced by our emotions."

"Are you saying that people would lose their ability to think if the OAA region of the brain were unable to slow down?" Alex asked.

"No, they would still be able to think and process information," Sylvia said, "but their decisions might be drastically different from the ones they would have made when their OAA was able to slow down.

People would make more purchases on impulse; they would eat more food that tasted good without considering how it affected their health. The world would become a much more emotional place, because people wouldn't be able to calm themselves and reduce the activities going on in the OAA region."

"In other words," Valerie interjected, "people would be more likely to end up shooting their neighbors for making too much noise or putting up a fence they didn't like."

"Yes," Sylvia said. "Once the serum is activated, it will limit people's ability to think abstractly and navigate complex problems."

"This is about control," Logan said in a grave voice. "People would be more vulnerable to manipulation by those whose OAA hasn't been messed up. They could be prodded, herded like cattle. They would believe anything they were told, and humanity would become a set of automatons following a dictator's agenda. 'All persons ought to endeavor to follow what is right, and not what is established,'" he recited. Everyone's eyes were on him. "Aristotle said that."

"I couldn't have said it better," Sylvia said.

"But there is something even more dangerous here," Logan went on, shaking his head. "The people who created this serum want to separate man from God."

Everyone in the room looked puzzled.

Logan pulled his notebook out of his backpack and turned to his drawing of *The Creation of Adam*. "They want to ensure that the finger of man never touches the finger of God. They want this gap never to be closed." Everyone looked at the picture for a moment. "I couldn't imagine a world where people could not pray . . ."

"I hadn't thought about it like that," Sylvia said grimly. "All that the *Chronicles* have taught over the last forty years about stilling our minds and allowing our free will to guide our choices would be rendered moot by the serum if activated."

"Net this out for me," Alex said as he took a sip of his coffee. "Is this some kind of mind-control experiment? What's the end result?"

"It's going to depend," Sylvia continued. "Based on the doctor's notes, people who have the ability to substantially slow down their OAA regions will suffer the most drastic effects."

"How drastic?" Valerie asked.

"If the dead Council members are any indication," Sylvia speculated, "then things are not looking good."

Logan turned to Valerie. "Andrea and Simon have found a way to exterminate the free thinkers of the world. The people who pose the greatest threat to them. Just like our parents did all those years ago." He did not need to say any more.

"Hold on," Valerie said. "Sylvia, back up. You said the serum has to be activated? It's not harmful by itself?"

"Once the serum is introduced into the bloodstream, it starts to bind with the DNA." Sylvia brought up an image on the HoloPad. "This is the image of Cynthia Brown's DNA. It shows the collar that we discovered a few days ago. That collar was introduced by the serum."

"By way of the MedicalPods?" Valerie said.

"Is that the qMeds stuff?" Logan asked.

Sylvia sighed. "Those MedicalPods are all about qMeds. It's based on an emerging science referred to as DIS, DNA-induced superconductivity. It was the brainchild of Ted Wilson, the founder of Allegiance Pharmaceuticals. He and his team used animal DNA to transmit electricity over distance. They then adapted the science to humans, in medical applications at the DNA level. It led to the creation of the MedicalPod network. The pods administer a low level of electrical current that causes a person's DNA to become supercharged and superconductive. This allows the quantum medicine to be absorbed with great efficiency. Hence the medicines are called qMeds."

"If this serum was distributed via MedicalPods, how many people would have received it?" Valerie asked.

"Let me put it this way. Did you go for your mandatory MedicalPod checkup in the last six months?" Sylvia asked a bit rhetorically. All three nodded. "Then you received the serum."

"Son of a—" Alex didn't finish the phrase.

"According to the central database," Sylvia continued, "ninety-five percent of the world's population has been injected with the serum."

Logan's eyes widened in disbelief. His immediate thoughts went to his children. His ex-wife Susan was conscientious about taking them for regular checkups.

Valerie shook her head. "We're dealing with a potentially worldwide catastrophe," she said. "And we don't even understand how this catastrophic attack is going to take place!"

"What about an antidote?" Logan said. "If we had one, we could disperse it the same way the serum was, via the MedicalPods."

"That's the problem," Sylvia said. "We don't exactly know how to remove the DNA collars. Currently, this is a one-way science. Until now, I didn't know anyone had perfected it."

"Did you get anything out of the Allegiance CEO when you spoke to him?" Alex asked Valerie.

"He said that he would get us a list of all the companies that deployed their medicines via the MedicalPods. And that he'd answer any questions he can."

"Meaning the hard questions go through the attorneys," Alex said, annoyed.

No one was sure where to go next.

"We have to do something," Logan said, desperation in his voice.

"Let's say that we knew how to remove the collars," Valerie suggested, turning back to Sylvia. "How long would it take?"

"That's hard to say," Sylvia said. "But with the proper antidote, the body could clear it very quickly, probably in a matter of hours, maybe even faster. The real problem is deploying the antidote. With the number of pods we have, it would take at least three months."

"That's three months too long," Valerie said. "All the intelligence we've gathered points to an attack at Liberty Moment on Freedom Day. We have less than thirty-two hours."

Logan looked at a clock on the wall. "If we can't remove the collar in time, then how do we stop it from being activated? How is it activated in the first place?"

"By the device the agents pulled from the rubble of the plantation," Sylvia said.

"At least Monique was telling the truth about something," Valerie said. "What does the device do?"

"To answer Logan's question first," Sylvia said, "based on the doctor's notes, the collar is activated when it comes into contact with a particular UVA spectrum wave. That causes the alternation of the DNA, which messes with the VMAT-2 gene. That's when all the bad things we talked about take place." She paused a moment. "To answer Val's question, the device creates the activation wave. Goshi is running some tests with it as we speak." She got up and led the group through a set of doors into another room.

There Goshi was working on a computer alongside a bio-coffin, which contained the dead body of an elderly man. Two other coffins stood idle behind him. "It didn't work," he said with disappointment as the group gathered around him.

"What didn't work?" Valerie asked.

"We tried to isolate the proper frequency that activates the DNA collar," Goshi explained. "We believe we did everything according to the doctor's notes."

"Did you try both frequency ranges the doctor mentioned?" Sylvia asked.

"Yes, we administered the two-hundred-five-nanometer range and the three-hundred-nanometer range," Goshi answered. "We detected zero change in the collar."

"Did you see a green flash?" Logan inquired, recalling his experience at the auction and the flash of green light.

Goshi nodded. "The three-hundred-nanometer pulse produced a green light, and the two-hundred-five-nanometer produced a violet one."

"The light is a residual echo pulse that's given off in the visible-light spectrum," Sylvia explained. "It is really just a side effect of the primary wave."

Logan and Valerie looked into the bio-coffin as one of the technicians opened the lid. They saw the frequency device Sylvia had referred to at the feet of the corpse. It was the size of a dinner plate and looked like a small replica of a flying saucer with a coiled antenna.

"These are special bio-coffins we are using to run the tests," Sylvia said. "They have the characteristics of a reverse Faraday cage, which keeps the frequency generated by this device localized. Otherwise, we could expose the entire building."

"The man inside passed away of a heart attack less than two hours ago," Goshi said. "We tested his blood; he'd been infected with the serum. I don't know why the test didn't work."

"Maybe it doesn't work on dead people," Logan said, walking over to the bio-coffin. "The doctor said that the serum is most effective when people are focused on freedom. And your investigation confirms that people who are in a meditative state or praying are more susceptible to the serum and the proper wavelength frequency." He turned and looked at Sylvia. "So all of this suggests that we have to run this experiment on a live subject. Just like the doctor did at G-LAB."

That wasn't what anyone wanted to hear.

"That could be deadly," Alex pointed out.

Goshi nodded. "How can we run the test on a live subject without running the risk of killing him?"

"We can't," Sylvia answered.

"Yeah. So who's gonna volunteer for that ride?" Alex said, finishing up his coffee and tossing the cup into a nearby trashcan.

"I'll do it," Logan said.

"Like hell you will," Valerie said.

"Listen, unless we figure this out, we're all going to die or be living as slaves. One of us has to take the risk, and there's no one here better suited for it than I am. Focusing on the candle is the same as meditating or praying."

"No," Valerie said, shaking her head as she stared at Logan, not wanting to buy into his logic.

He returned her hard look, knowing the risk he'd proposed taking. "How'd your father put it the other night? *Don't fight me on this.*"

"I don't like this idea," she said.

"I don't either," he replied. "But it's the only idea we have at the moment."

There was another long silence. All eyes were on Valerie. It was her call to make.

Finally, she sighed. "Let's run the test," she said. Everyone immediately sprang into action.

"We should cycle through both the violet and the green wavelengths just to be safe," Goshi suggested. "We should also set the duration of each pulse to less than five seconds."

"When your OAA activity begins to slow down, we'll activate the frequency device," Sylvia said. "Once we detect the slightest change in the collar, that's it. The test ends." She looked around the room for any objections to this plan. None was forthcoming. Not even from Valerie.

"Then let's do it," Logan said.

After two lab attendants removed the dead body from the bio-coffin, Sylvia and Goshi prepared it and the frequency device for the live experiment. It did not take long for everything to be calibrated and configured. Logan lay down in the bio-coffin and put on a pair of protective glasses. The frequency device was placed at his feet. Valerie hovered over him. To his surprise, she leaned in and quickly kissed him before Sylvia shut the lid.

Inside the coffin, Logan could hear nothing. He could feel only a slight breeze of oxygen entering near his face. A small portal window allowed him to see the ceiling of the lab. Goshi tapped on the glass and gave him a thumbs-up, indicating that everything was ready. Logan closed his eyes. *Humble yourself as a child.* Logan remembered the words of the shadow. *Be sincere and without expectations.* Given the circumstances, sincerity was not going to be a problem. He brought to his mind the image of a burning blue candle. At first, the image was elusive, but as he relaxed, it became more vibrant, and the bright yellow flame leaped from side to side and upward as the wax by the wick began to liquefy. The blue candle lived on. Logan started to hear the ringing in his ears. He remained calm and continued to focus. And just as the first time, the ringing became louder and louder.

Suddenly, he found himself at Valerie's wake again. He stood near the open casket, looking at her dead body.

"We say good-bye to the beloved daughter of Mr. Alain Perrot." A minister standing at a podium was giving the eulogy. "In these sad times, it is hard to comprehend God's ultimate plan and his purpose for each of us."

From time to time, the lighting in the room would flicker and turn a shade of violet, but no one seemed to notice.

Logan looked out at the people seated in the funeral parlor. Many members of WCF were in attendance. Charlie was now standing alone at the back of the room, his face no longer burned. There was a subtle blue light surrounding him. Mr. Perrot sat in the front row with close friends. Logan seemed to be invisible to those gathered. He watched as people came forward to express their sorrow and offer remembrances of Valerie.

"I loved my daughter beyond words." Mr. Perrot had suddenly replaced the minister at the podium. "She meant the world to me, and I will miss her sorely every day for the rest of my life."

"I wish I could have saved her life." Sylvia appeared at the podium next, her eyes filled with tears. "We should have waited for backup. I told her not to rush in." Sylvia broke down and had to be helped back to her chair.

There was another flicker of light, and the violet turned to green.

Suddenly, the doors to the room swung open, and in walked Andrea, wearing a black dress and a crimson scarf draped over her head. She carried a black rose in her hand and was accompanied by her son, Lucius. Just as Logan moved to intercept her, someone grabbed his arm. He looked down and saw that Valerie, her eyes still closed, had grabbed hold of him and stopped him from leaving her side. Andrea and Lucius came closer and closer, making their way to the front of the room and taking a seat next to Mr. Perrot, who acknowledged them with a nod, not seeming to mind their presence. There was a great green flash of light in the room, and Logan could hear Valerie's muffled voice calling his name. The voice was growing louder and louder. Valerie still clutched his arm and was not letting go. Once again, he heard her voice calling his name, even though her mouth did not move. Her voice now screamed!

Logan opened his eyes. The lid to the bio-coffin had been lifted, and he saw Valerie's face right on top of his. She was still calling his name.

"We thought you were gone," she said. "You were out for ten minutes after we turned off the device."

He blinked rapidly a few times, focusing on Valerie's face. It was the second time he'd seen her dead in a candle vision.

"That was close," Sylvia said. "But all of his biometric readings are returning to normal."

"What happened?" he asked, as he struggled to get his bearings.

Valerie helped him sit up. "We isolated the activation frequency," she said. "Three hundred fifteen nanometers is the collar activation wavelength."

47

The emotions of a rich man who worries about losing what he
possesses are the same as the emotions of a poor man who worries
about whether his prayers will be answered.
It is like a candle burning at both ends.
—THE CHRONICLES OF SATRAYA

EN ROUTE, 4:00 P.M. GMT, 31 HOURS UNTIL LIBERTY MOMENT

Andrea Montavon looked out the window of the transport plane. Her
crimson hood helped shield her eyes from the incoming light of the sun
as they flew over the Atlantic Ocean. After Monique's betrayal and the report of her death, Gretchen had successfully orchestrated their exit from
the NAF. Lucius was sleeping, stretched out on three seats across the aisle,
and Gretchen had gone into the cockpit to speak with the pilots. The
losses they had suffered over the last twenty-four hours weighed heavily on Andrea's mind. She wondered how much Monique had told the
authorities and how much her betrayal would cost them. She wondered
who had killed Monique. It hadn't been one of their people, and even
Gretchen was surprised by the shooting. Andrea had more important
things to think about at the moment. Freedom Day was fast approaching,
and she was engaged in a full-on battle of wits with the WCF, and with
the son of an old foe who seemed to be mocking her from his grave.

Andrea's PCD rang. "G-LAB has been compromised," Simon said,
straight to the point. "The doctor is dead."

She sighed. "Were they able to destroy the lab in time?"

"No." Simon gave her a stern look.

"Do they know about the deployment site?"

"No. But they are in possession of the doctor's journals and the secondary frequency device." Andrea remained silent, her mind numb from the endless piling on of distressing news. "Your success at the activation site is now imperative," Simon stated.

"I understand," Andrea said. "We will not fail." She drew back her crimson hood and, like a wounded tigress ready to pounce, said, "And if the pulse doesn't extinguish Camden's son from this earth, I will do it myself. We will be rid of the Fords once and for all."

"Music to my ears," Simon said with a thin smile. "Are you absolutely sure you're prepared to do what needs to be done when you arrive?"

"Yes," Andrea answered. "The advance team has already landed and is waiting for Lucius and me to join them. The events of the last few days may have cost us valuable resources, but our victory is still certain."

Gretchen emerged from the cockpit and took a seat across from Andrea.

"Gretchen, I presume," Simon said, greeting the young woman, his eyes roaming over her. "You have lived up to your reputation."

"I've received orders to accompany your team and assist in any way that I can," Gretchen said. "Though I might be more useful if I knew what the mission is."

This was the first Andrea had heard about Gretchen's joining the team. She looked at Simon for confirmation.

"Yes, you certainly have proven your worth and loyalty," Simon acknowledged. "But as I'm sure you have been told, your involvement is one-way; there is no going back."

"With all due respect," Gretchen replied, "I think I've already crossed that bridge."

Simon nodded and smiled. Turning to Andrea, he said, "Looks like you have a new apprentice. Bring her up to speed."

"I will," Andrea said with a forced smile. "But there's one last thing, Simon—"

"I have not forgotten." Simon knew what Andrea was referring to. "I have secured the EMFE device that was used at the Indian village. I will bring it to the Château when I return." And with that, Simon's projection ended.

That last bit of information brought a smile to Andrea's face, at least. Once all of this was over, she and her son could use the device to administer the frequency they needed to cure their disease.

"Before we begin," she said, turning to Gretchen, "you need to take something."

Andrea looked at Lucius, who had woken and joined them. He pulled a small tin container from his pocket, took two green pills from it, and gave them to Gretchen. Andrea poured her a glass of water.

48

If eternity is the playground of all people, what matters most to
your soul?
—THE CHRONICLES OF SATRAYA

BANARAS, INDIA, 12:30 A.M. LOCAL TIME,
28 HOURS UNTIL LIBERTY MOMENT

Simon finished sketching the outline of the symbol he was beginning
to see on one of the blank pages of the *Chronicles*. He was starting
to experience what Camden had described in his journal. While the
symbol was not clearly visible yet, he was able to distinguish some odd
shapes within the classic roped border displayed by the other Satraya
symbols. Patience was not one of his strengths, but he knew that he had
to work more diligently with the Satraya Flame and hone his focus if
he wanted to see the complete symbol and gain its promised power. He
couldn't buy, bargain, or threaten his way into learning the secrets of the
Chronicles. He had to abide by the rules of the books.

Tonight, however, was not the right time for this kind of work. Simon
blew out the candle, frustrated that he was able neither to sleep nor to
concentrate on the flame. His mind raced through all the possibilities and
scenarios that could unfold over the next twenty-four hours. Andrea's recent failures had put in jeopardy all he had been preparing for. He'd spent
a fortune to accomplish the Final Purging, but it was not just his financial

investment he feared losing. His credibility with his peers in Era was also at stake. Failure, he knew, would bring an end to the Hitchlords dynasty.

Simon walked over to the display panel that was mounted on the wall of his hotel room and ordered some food. He knew now that sleep would not come easily tonight. He looked out the window and saw the endless religious activities taking place at the many ghats along the Ganges River. He went out to the balcony, sat down, and turned his attention back to Deya's riddle:

In the once Great House
Where fire is and ashes rise
Where the ear stone fell
Will hold your prize

The answer was eluding him. He was certain she was referring to one of the ghats along the river, but which one? Large and small fires were burning everywhere. *I could go back and squeeze out some last bit of knowledge from Deya's husband. Might as well relieve him of his miserable existence.* Simon picked up his PCD and searched for any references to the phrases "ear stone" and "fire" and "ashes," but he found nothing relevant. His PCD rang. It was a member of Era. Simon rose and went back into his room. "Yes, Victor, what can I do for you?"

"The WSA will soon seize control of the investigation," Victor informed him. "The WCF has been neutralized."

"What of Camden's son and the detective? Andrea has not dealt with the two of them very cleanly, I'm afraid."

"I will address that problem shortly," Victor said. "Though there is something strange about this Valerie Perrot."

"What have you found?"

"That's just it," Victor replied. "We have found almost nothing. There is very little information available about her parents and her family history. On the other hand, we've learned that Camden's son, Logan, has an ex-wife and two young children."

"A fact I hope we won't have to make use of," Simon said, smiling. "Well done, my friend. Dario was wise to bring you into our group." Simon's PCD indicated that another call was coming in. "Speak of the devil, Dario is calling. I wish you good hunting," he said to Victor, ending their conversation and taking the incoming call. "Dario, my friend." The projected image of Victor was now replaced with Dario's image. He was wearing a burgundy ascot and clutching his cane.

"Salutations, Simon," Dario replied in his hoarse voice. "Victor informs me that we have had a few setbacks."

Dario's statement gave Simon pause. He had just spoken to Victor, and he'd said nothing of the kind. Why would Victor express concern about recent events to Dario and not to him? "No, my friend, I assure you," Simon responded. "We have restored order, and we are on track for our long-awaited moment."

"Many of us have risked a great deal and expended a tremendous amount of political capital for that moment," Dario asserted. "I would hate to see it all go to waste."

"I, too, have risked a great deal," Simon said, not at all pleased by Dario's tone. "Let us not forget that it is my family's money that has brought us to this point."

"In any case, Victor has assured me he will tend to matters promptly," Dario said. "He is proving his worth, wouldn't you agree? You should consider him for your *consuasor*."

"He is an asset. I cannot argue with you there." But Simon bit his tongue concerning Victor's elevation. He was not particularly keen on broadening Victor's role within Era. Especially now that he saw he was Dario's tool for broadening his own role in the group. "Now is not the time for change, however," Simon said. "We must respect tradition and let Andrea succeed in her task. We will deal with the question of *consuasor* later."

Dario nodded. He took a stern glance around Simon's hotel room. "Speaking of your *consuasor*, I expected you to be with her now," he said. "I would have thought you would want to oversee the deployment of the Final Purging and the restoration of Reges Hominum yourself."

Simon walked across the room and closed the balcony door. The wind had shifted and was carrying an odor of burning sandalwood from the north. Setting aside his annoyance at Dario's inquisition, he responded diplomatically, "Your concern is appreciated. But everyone is keeping me informed every step along the way. It looks as if Victor is affording you the same service." Simon gave Dario a good long stare. He wanted to let him know that he was not blind to their alliance. "What of the other tasks?" Simon asked.

"Everything has been addressed," Dario responded coolly. "After I made a sizable anonymous donation, the Council of Satraya agreed to let the Freedom Day celebrations go on as planned."

"Excellent. And how has Catherine fared?"

"I am happy to report that all has been accomplished there also," Dario stated. "She has secured two prominent financial institutions that will assist us in swaying the financial markets. Century Financial and Europa Capital will be serving our purpose. The post-purged world will be just as we have envisioned it."

"Well done," Simon said. "I am hoping to leave India shortly and return to the Château. There are too many people here and as many odors to match. Please plan to join me at the Château a fortnight after Freedom Day. We will all celebrate our triumph."

"*Bueno.*" Dario ended the call.

Simon continued to gaze at the empty space where Dario's image had been projected. He was still concerned about Victor's duplicity. Was he working on another project with Dario? Was that project Era itself? Simon's eyes narrowed. Era was not formed to be led by anyone other than him. He was not about to give up his chair at the head of the table.

Simon was so close to achieving his goals. But recent events were not unfolding as smoothly as he'd hoped. Andrea seemed to be floundering, and somewhere close by were the books he so desperately wanted. At the moment, he needed the reach of Era; he needed Dario and Victor to clear the way for Andrea's success. But Deya's riddle still barred his way to claiming his greatest prize. Once he mastered the symbols and possessed their hidden powers, he wouldn't need Era or its members. His position in history would be secured, the mightiest Hitchlords of them all. In less than a day, he would be humanity's overlord, able to separate man from God once and for all. That thought put a devilish smile on his face.

Simon walked back over to the balcony doors to make sure they were completely closed. He hadn't been jesting with Dario. The odor in the air really was bothering him.

Just then, there was a knock at the door. "Room service, sir," a voice called from the corridor.

Simon went to the door and looked through the peephole. Macliv stood beside the steward and nodded. Simon opened the door.

"Good evening, sir." The steward walked in, pushing a table full of Indian snacks, desserts, and some hot spiced tea.

Simon gestured to the balcony doors. "Is that sandalwood I smell out there?" Simon asked him.

"Yes, sir," the steward responded as he arranged the silverware and poured a glass of water. "I am very sorry about that. Many cremation ceremonies are taking place farther north at Manikarnika Ghat as part of the annual two-day puja. It is the grandest ghat of all, the most auspicious along the great Ganges River. You are smelling the smoke from the fires there. If I might suggest, sir, please keep the balcony doors closed, so as to prevent the smell and ashes from entering the room." The table was now set. "Will there be anything else, sir?" the steward asked. Simon shook his head. "Very good, sir." The steward turned and left the room.

Instead of heeding the steward's suggestion, when he left, Simon went and opened the balcony doors. He stepped outside and looked north toward the burning pyres at Manikarnika Ghat, taking a deep breath, now relishing the smell of the burning sandalwood. Then he made a call on his PCD. "Ready yourselves. We are leaving."

49

You can intellectually justify anything.
But what you feel is simply what you feel.
—THE CHRONICLES OF SATRAYA

"And that's what we know so far," Valerie said, as she finished explaining
the facts of the case. She took a seat alongside her boss, Dominic Burke,
who had summoned her and her team to an emergency meeting of top
officials. The largest of the WCF meeting rooms was filled with agents
and personnel from the world's two largest crime-fighting agencies, the
WCF and the WSA—the World Security Agency—whose efforts were
focused more closely on intelligence gathering than on solving specific
crimes. Valerie found the tension in the room almost palpable. While,
in theory, the efforts of the two agencies were supposed to complement
each other, the reality of the situation was far from it. As with children
in a sandbox, ordering them to get along only added to their rivalry.
Many of Valerie's WCF colleagues even groused that the WCF solved
the crimes and the WSA took the credit.

"Are we certain that Freedom Day is the launch date?" a WSA agent
asked.

"That's what was indicated in Dr. Malikei's computer files." Valerie brought up an image of the entry for all to see. "We are working under the assumption that Liberty Moment on Freedom Day, 11:00 P.M. GMT, will be the exact time of deployment."

"That's less than twenty-seven hours from now," someone said.

"Everyone has the facts as we know them," Director Burke announced, standing and addressing the group. "We have made all the information about this case available on the central computer under the case name Vanguard. The head of joint operations has instructed that the WSA step in." He turned and signaled to another dark-haired man seated at the large conference table. "All of you know Director Ramplet of the WSA. He will be taking the lead in the investigation. The WCF will be operating in a consulting and support role from this point forward." Director Burke took his seat next to Valerie, as Director Ramplet stood to address the group.

"As all of you know, we face an urgent threat," Ramplet began. He wore a well-tailored black suit, a white shirt, and a red tie. He stood with his hands behind his back and spoke confidently. "We thank the WCF for their efforts thus far."

Logan leaned over and whispered to Valerie, "There's something I don't trust about this guy."

"None of us likes him very much, either," she said. "My boss especially. Ten years ago, Ramplet and Burke were working for the same division of the WSA. Ramplet somehow got a promotion that should have gone to Burke. Ramplet eventually pushed him out of the way, and that's when Burke came over to the WCF." She turned and leaned over to Burke himself, who was sitting on the other side of her. She whispered, "Sir, they can't just take this investigation away from us. No one knows the facts and the players better than we do."

"This is not up to me, Val," Burke answered softly. "Three dead Council members, a blown-up plantation house, and a dead scientist. Not to mention allowing yourself and a civilian to be kidnapped. The whole thing hasn't exactly instilled a load of confidence in the WCF. And on top of that, you're telling us that a substantial portion of the world's population might die in less than twenty-seven hours? The WSA is bigger than we are and has access to more resources than we do. It's tough to argue the decision."

Valerie didn't have a response. She turned her attention back to the discussion getting under way in the meeting room.

"There isn't sufficient time to create an antidote and then introduce it into the population," Sylvia was saying. "At this point, our only option is to stop these people from delivering the activation frequency. Which brings us to the delivery mechanism."

"Where is the mini-device the WCF found?" Ramplet asked.

"It is secured in our lab," Valerie said.

"It should be turned over to the WSA at once," Ramplet instructed.

Valerie and Burke exchanged frowns.

"Perhaps they have installed many of these small EFME devices around the world," one WSA scientist proposed.

"I doubt that," Goshi answered. "These mini-devices have a very limited range. Maybe about one-hundred meters. There would have to be millions of them installed to provide adequate global coverage."

"Is it true that the frequency will penetrate walls and buildings?" asked another WSA scientist, portly, bald, and with an Italian accent.

"Yes," Sylvia said. "We had to use a Faraday isolation chamber to contain the waves. So even if people stay indoors, they will not be protected from it."

"We will have to evacuate people to underground facilities," said an American WSA scientist wearing a green bow tie. "At least one hundred meters underground."

"There's no time," Ramplet interrupted impatiently. "And we don't have enough underground facilities to protect billions of people. Focus on stopping the pulse."

"The wave pulse would have to come from the sky and be capable of engulfing the entire planet," the Italian WSA scientist asserted. Murmurs of both agreement and dissent came from the others, as they began to discuss the most likely delivery system among themselves.

"The most logical place would be the GCC here in your own country!" the scientist now shouted, trying to be heard over the rising din. The conversations trailed off as people redirected their attention to the Italian scientist. "The GCC has access to every communications device in the world." Many in the group nodded in agreement.

"What's the GCC?" Logan asked Alex.

"That's the Global Communications Center located in Denver," Alex explained. "It controls all the PCDs around the world via satellites."

Meanwhile, Logan overheard Valerie, Sylvia, and Goshi intently discussing something. They had been for some time, it seemed.

"Excuse me," Valerie said then, out loud. "Excuse me!" she yelled. The room went quiet. "We think a better choice for delivering the frequency discharge would be the Akasha Vault," she said in clear and certain voice. "The Vault's satellites are newer and cover the same land area as the GCC."

All eyes in the room were now turned to Valerie. All except Ramplet's. His, Logan noticed, were fixed on him.

"But the GCC has control of many more geosynchronous orbitals than the Vault," said a gray-haired French scientist, whose wire-framed glasses were balancing on the tip of his nose. "It has more than three hundred satellites in its network and is directly linked to the Solar Aggregation Network. The Vault has less than half that amount. The GCC satellites are the only ones that can sustain a pulse of that magnitude for the necessary five seconds. Besides, the GCC is more reliable; much of the technology at the Akasha Vault is still experimental."

"Yes," the Italian scientist agreed. "The security at the Vault is also much heavier. There are more than one hundred WSA agents stationed there permanently. And no one gets by them." The sound of muffled laughter could be heard; the statement was clearly a jab at the WCF.

"The Akasha Vault satellites are just as powerful," Sylvia said. "Each of them is powered by a Tesla coil."

The French scientist interrupted. "The coils are completely untested and unproven. They have never been pushed to that threshold, and it would be folly to expect them to perform at that level."

"I disagree," Sylvia said emphatically. "The Vault satellites' photonic link to the ground station could easily flood the earth with the precise frequency. The GCC would require more programming to burst the proper wavelength frequency. In addition, it has three major locations, whereas the Vault only has one."

"All the more reason to use the GCC," a WSA agent said. "More sites, more places to deploy from."

Various side discussions had started once again; the Vault proposal, it seemed, was being dismissed. In all of it, Ramplet remained aloof. His eyes were still on Logan.

"Why does the director keep looking at me?" Logan whispered to Valerie.

Valerie snuck a quick peek and saw that Logan was correct. She shook her head, unsure. Then she returned her attention to the room, where the noise level was escalating again. She could tell the scientists were dismissing Sylvia's Vault proposal. "Wait," she said, "you're making a—"

"We're going with the GCC as the main target," Ramplet suddenly cut in, pulling rank. The room went quieter for him than it had for Valerie. "We will notify our team at the Vault to stay alert for any suspicious activity, but we will send the primary teams to the three major GCC sites. Let's get going, people; time is not our friend." With that announcement, the meeting was over.

Valerie, Logan, and the other team members stayed where they were in the corner of the meeting room. Soon they were joined by Burke, who had just finished speaking to Ramplet.

"It's the Vault," Sylvia said, clearly frustrated. "It would take too long to program the GCC, and you would have to sync all three locations."

"I agree with you," Valerie said. She turned to Burke. "Come on, boss. These guys have been on the case for only an hour. We've been there since the start."

"There's nothing I can do, Val," Burke reminded her. "They have jurisdiction; my hands are tied."

"So now we're just observers on this operation?" Valerie persisted.

"Let's send an observation team to the GCC and one to the Vault. We'll send a few small teams to the GCC sites, Alex and Goshi will stay here at the lab, and Sylvia and I will go to the Vault."

"Me, too," Logan added. "I'm going to the Vault."

Burke didn't respond. He gave Valerie a long, hard look.

"We'll just be observing," she pressed. "If we get to the Vault and nothing happens, that's great news for everyone. On the other hand, if something happens . . . Are you going to let Director Ramplet steal this from you the way he stole the top job at WSA ten years ago?"

"Cheap shot," Burke said.

"It's all I've got left, sir."

Burke looked around the conference room, where only a handful of WSA personnel remained, then turned back to Valerie. "Better safe than sorry. Take who you need; I'll get it cleared."

"Thanks, boss," Valerie said. "We won't let you down."

"Burke," a voice called out. Everyone turned to see Ramplet walking over to them. "I'd like to meet your team."

Burke obliged and introduced everyone. As Ramplet shook people's hands, Logan couldn't help but notice the large black diamond embedded in the thick gold ring he was wearing.

"On behalf of the WSA, I would like to thank each of you for your efforts," Ramplet said. "Especially you." He turned to Logan. "It is heartening to see a citizen get so passionately involved. I'm sure your parents would be happy to see that you've followed in their footsteps."

"Thank you, Director," Logan said hesitantly. He still didn't trust him.

"Please," Ramplet said, waving a hand, and flashing that black diamond ring once more. "You can call me Victor." He smiled. "The WSA has arrived, and we'll take it from here. Once again, I thank you for your work on this case." Before the director turned to leave, he addressed Valerie, "And Agent Perrot, make sure you get that frequency device to us."

50

A scientist endeavors to explain the hows of reality.
A theologian endeavors to explain the whys of reality.
A master teacher endeavors to live reality.
—THE CHRONICLES OF SATRAYA

BANARAS, INDIA, 4:30 A.M. LOCAL TIME,
24 HOURS UNTIL LIBERTY MOMENT

"What a sight!" Mr. Perrot was looking at a tall domed temple building illuminated against the night sky. Two other structures stood to its
left, and many roaring fires cast an eerie glow over the grounds below.
Mr. Perrot and Jogi had hired a boat to take them along the river to
Manikarnika Ghat. Their earlier attempts to enter the ghat had been
thwarted by the massive crowds gathered there for the almost two-day-
long puja and prayer. Now, though, the crowds had dwindled, and the
waters of the Ganges were calm. From the boat, Mr. Perrot could see
the steep stairs that led up to the three haggard old buildings, which
seemed to teeter on the banks of the river. Jogi had told him that these
ornately decorated stone structures had once been the jewel of the river.

"I had no idea of the atmosphere of this place," Mr. Perrot mused.
"I feel as if I've traveled back in time to a world long forgotten."

The light hum of the boat's motor could be heard as they glided
across the still waters of the river. It was early morning, and the sun was
about to rise. The dark of night was giving way to the dawn.

"Deya described the river to me many times," Mr. Perrot said. "I wish she was here to share my pleasure in seeing it for the first time."

Jogi nodded. "It has been this way since anyone can remember," he said. "The pyres of Manikarnika Ghat burn relentlessly day after day, night after night."

"Do they ever stop?"

"No. This is an endless place," Jogi said. "The fires have liberated countless souls over the centuries. Look at the ash that accumulates; look how it covers everything around here. Look at the boats, stacked high with wood. They deliver the fuel to keep the pyres going. Behind the temple, a long line of bodies waits to be cremated at this auspicious site."

"Amazing continuity of effort over such a long period of time," Mr. Perrot remarked.

Jogi pointed to the middle structure of the three haggard buildings near the riverbank. "See that clock high up in the tower?"

Mr. Perrot looked where Jogi pointed. It was difficult to see through all the smoke and ash that rose into the sky. "I fear the clock is incorrect," he said. "It says six o'clock."

"It is always six o'clock at Manikarnika," Jogi said. "It is said that time stands still at the moment of death."

Their boat was getting closer to the riverbank, and the smell of the burning wood was becoming stronger. Mr. Perrot sat silently and reflected on the many sights up and down the mystical river. It was as if the Great Disruption had not touched this place.

"There are more than eighty ghats on the Ganges, most with their own temples and touchstones," Jogi said. "But Manikarnika is considered the holiest of them all. At least, it used to be."

"What is the purpose of the clock tower building?" Mr. Perrot asked.

"It and the structure to its left are the two pilgrim houses." Jogi paused a moment. He was clearly moved by the sight of those three buildings. "It is a great honor to die at Manikarnika Ghat. Those who are terminally ill stay in the pilgrim houses until they pass. My father took me into one of the houses once. I don't have the words to describe how I felt. It is not a place for the faint of heart. After the Great Disruption, a very large pyre pit was built in front of the pilgrim house with the clock tower. It is called Shiva Pyre. You can see the large glow it casts over the ghat."

"I understand what Deya spoke about now," Mr. Perrot said. "She told us that on the day she found the *Chronicles*, she was going to the pilgrim house. Her miracle in the river spared her that fate. Deya never forgot that gift. She told us she would go into those buildings from time to time and read passages from the *Chronicles* to the people there. She said the words brought hope and comfort to those who waited for the passing of their lives."

"She sounds like an incredible woman," Jogi said.

Mr. Perrot simply nodded.

The boatman, meanwhile, maneuvered the craft to a small landing in front of a set of stone stairs. Bodies were being cremated on either side, and mourners watched in traditional silence as the wrapped corpses of their loved ones evaporated into fine dust and ash.

"It is strange that we do not smell the burning of flesh," Mr. Perrot said. "Even the burning of hair should emit an unbearable odor."

"It is the banyan tree logs," Jogi said. He paid the boatman as he and Mr. Perrot disembarked. "There is something about them and the sandalwood logs that negates the smell. My father used to tell me it was the blessing of the gods. See how brightly some of the fires burn? It is because of the small bags of sandalwood that are poured upon them."

Mr. Perrot was mesmerized by the sights and sounds around him and by Jogi's explanations of their significance. They climbed the many steps and soon stood in front of the domed temple.

"This temple is now abandoned," Jogi explained. "It was built in the eighteenth century by Queen Ahalya Bai Holkar of Indore."

Mr. Perrot took a moment to look across the river at the sun, which was about to break over the horizon. "How beautiful . . ."

Jogi nodded. He joined Mr. Perrot in admiring the dawn of a new day on the Ganges. The sun had now completely risen over the eastern horizon. "So what are we looking for now that we have arrived?"

"I don't know, exactly," Mr. Perrot answered. He took a note from his pocket and once again read Deya's message:

In the once Great House
Where fire is and ashes rise
Where the ear stone fell
Will hold your prize

"So let us assume now that we have solved the first two lines of the riddle," Mr. Perrot said, thinking aloud. "We certainly are where 'fire is and ashes rise.' But what is an 'ear stone'?"

He and Jogi walked around the ghat grounds, looking for something, anything, that might help them decipher the riddle. As they wandered past the pilgrim houses, they came upon a tour group standing in front of the domed temple. The group had arrived to take in the sunrise and observe a cremation ceremony.

"There are many stories concerning how this particular ghat was created," the guide explained to his group. "So I will tell you the one that I like best. Legend has it that before the Ganges River was even a river and before man walked the earth, Lord Vishnu dug a water well—or a kund—with his own discus. The well lies fifty meters away, just up the river." The guide pointed north. "It is said that the kund was initially filled by Lord Vishnu's own perspiration as he ardently performed his mystical disciplines. Lord Vishnu was so focused that he did not see that Lord Shiva had arrived or that Lord Shiva was so pleased with Lord Vishnu's deeds that he started to dance. While doing so, Lord Shiva's earring, known as the Manikarnika, fell into the well, blessing it for eternity. And that is how the ghat received its name. It is named after Lord Shiva's fallen earring."

Mr. Perrot and Jogi looked at each other. "'Where the ear stone fell,'" Jogi said.

"It means where the *earring* fell," Mr. Perrot added. "We need to find that well."

Jogi led Mr. Perrot north along the river. Within a short distance, as the guide described, they came upon the Manikarnika Kund. The well was rectangular in shape, and all four sides had about fifteen steep symmetrical steps that sloped inward and down to a smaller rectangular basin. There was only a small amount of water left in the dried pool bed.

"Do you think she hid the books under the water?" Mr. Perrot asked.

"I don't think so," Jogi said. "My father told me that this pool fills with mud during the rainy season. Each time it does so, they have to clean it out. Which means the books would have been found or, more likely, lost forever."

Mr. Perrot nodded, surveying the kund. He pointed to the north side of the pool, where a statue of Vishnu stood. "What are those large gaps on the side of the well, there near the statue?"

"Only one way to find out," Jogi said. He started down the steps toward the openings. Mr. Perrot followed close behind. One of the gaps was large enough for a person to fit through. Jogi entered what appeared to be a tunnel. He used his PCD to illuminate the dark, narrow passageway, which didn't lead very far, only about four meters.

Mr. Perrot had made his way in and began moving his hands over the walls. He noticed that some stones seemed smoother than others. "Could you shine some light over here, please?" he asked. "There's something about this section of the wall."

Jogi came over and shone his light where Mr. Perrot directed. "These stone blocks look newer than the ones around them," he said. "Please stay here. I will return promptly." Jogi left his PCD with Mr. Perrot and hurried from the tunnel.

Mr. Perrot continued to inspect the newer-looking stones. He took a seat in the tunnel on a broken slab in front of the wall he was studying, waiting and wondering what Jogi had in mind. His thoughts turned to his daughter. He wondered how Valerie and Logan were making out.

I will call them later today, he thought hopefully. It wasn't long before he heard clinking sounds outside the tunnel entrance, and Jogi returned with a couple of hammers and small iron picks.

"I purchased them from the wood cutters outside," Jogi said. Mr. Perrot smiled. Then the two of them used the tools to loosen the stones from the wall. Soon enough, the blocks began to shift. Jogi used the pick to slide one forward and directed the light from his PCD behind the dislodged stone. He could see that there was some kind of empty space behind the wall. "Looks like there is a room back there!" he announced.

Mr. Perrot helped Jogi remove all four stone blocks from the wall, and soon a half-meter-square opening was revealed.

"I'll go first," Jogi said. He drew his gun and cautiously entered the room.

Mr. Perrot immediately followed. They were inside a small three-by-three-meter-square room whose ceiling was barely high enough for them to stand upright. The air smelled musty from the dampness of the ground under their feet.

"Well, this is most unexpected," Mr. Perrot said.

Jogi squatted down and grabbed some dirt near his feet. "It must get flooded during the rainy season. Do you think Deya built this?"

"If she did, it looks like she had some help," Mr. Perrot said. A hammer and a few other tools lay in a corner. "Maybe these are the missing tools Babu referred to. Though I don't see any books or possible hiding places. Perhaps they're buried in the dirt."

"I don't think we are going to find the books here," Jogi said. He was looking at the wall opposite the opening.

Mr. Perrot walked over and joined him. "Yet another riddle." Then he began to read the message chiseled into the stone.

It will be yours
For those who follow these understandings
Cross the great river, to the fort of old

Turn and seek the canopy protecting the jewel
Along the river to Shiva's last stand
This is the path for you
If you seek what I possess

"And I thought the first riddle was difficult," Jogi said. "The only part I have an answer to is 'Shiva's last stand.' I think that is referring to Assi Ghat. The southernmost ghat along the river, where the—"

A sound coming from the opening interrupted Jogi's explanation. He and Mr. Perrot turned around. A bright light was shining into their eyes, blinding them.

"Hello, Robert!" a voice called out as the light suddenly disappeared.

Two men had entered. It took only a moment for Mr. Perrot to recognize the dark eyes and arrogant bearing of one of them. "Simon!"

Jogi drew his weapon, and two shots rang out.

51

For a master teacher, the simple choice of a student to dare to cross into the unknown is the greatest acknowledgment of what the student has been taught.

—THE CHRONICLES OF SATRAYA

OVER THE ATLANTIC OCEAN, MIDNIGHT, GMT,
23 HOURS UNTIL LIBERTY MOMENT

"Tell the teams they can't take no for an answer," Valerie instructed Alex on her PCD. "Make sure they remind the WSA that we're consultants who are supposed to support their efforts any way we can. We need to know what the WSA is doing."

"I'll relay the message," Alex said. "The trace came back on the money deposits into Monique Sato's bank account. They came from an overseas account registered to the Sentinel Coterie."

"Well, that confirms our suspicions," said Valerie. "Fenquist must have been paying her to spy on Cynthia and the Council. Was there anyone she wasn't working for?"

"We tried the last call she made from the airport," Alex added. "But it went to an untraceable PCD."

Valerie shook her head in frustration. "I'll call you again when we land in Dharan."

"Wait, there's one more thing," Alex said. "I got a message from someone at the WSA that Director Ramplet is looking for the frequency device we were supposed to send over. They can't seem to find it anywhere."

"It's probably in transit through their bureaucracy. Tell them we'll look into it when we get back." Valerie turned off her PCD and re-joined Sylvia and Logan. The three of them were flying over the Atlantic Ocean in a WCF transport plane on their way to the Akasha Vault, which was located in the foothills of the Himalayas. Sylvia was explaining the particulars of the Vault to Logan.

"The WSA asked about the frequency device," Valerie said, interrupting their conversation.

The three of them looked innocently at one another. "We'll be sure to get it to them when we get back to D.C.," Logan said as he unzipped his backpack, revealing the EMFE device. They all grinned. None of them was going to let the frequency generator out of their sight, at least not yet.

"Now, what were you saying, Sylvia?" Valerie said.

"The Vault is in the northern part of the city of Dharan." Sylvia used a HoloPad to project a map of Nepal.

"Why choose such a remote location for storing all the world's information, not to mention that quantum computer?" Logan asked.

"For that exact reason," Sylvia said. "It's a remote location, protected by the Himalayas to the north, surrounded by hills to the east and west, and the Charkose forest to the south. Dharan has a temperate climate year-round, and there are two rivers there which are used to cool the core of the computer and the Tesla coil that powers the facility."

"The WFR spent a lot of money building and securing this facility," Valerie added. "After the world lost so much technology and information during the Great Disruption, we needed a better way to protect data and information. Hence the Vault."

"It was named after the Akashic Record," Sylvia said.

Valerie looked at her blankly.

"It's an ancient Indian term," Logan explained. "It's believed that everything that has ever happened in the universe since the beginning of time is recorded in a nonphysical realm. They call that place the Akashic Record."

"A twentieth-century quantum physicist named David Bohm performed some interesting work in this field, trying to merge certain religious beliefs with science," Sylvia added. "A couple of scientists who worked on the original design of the Vault gave it that nickname, and it stuck."

She continued, zooming in on the map. "But back to the matter at hand. The newly constructed airport is to the east of the facility, on the other side of the river. We have to cross this bridge once we land." She panned to another part of the projected image. "There's an advanced transportation system, like a monorail, that connects the main facility with the airport and the town below." She zoomed the map way out so that an image of the whole world was displayed. "There are sixty-six Vault satellites in orbit around the earth at an altitude of seven hundred eighty kilometers. They cover a surface area of almost eight million square kilometers. Every sixty minutes or so, one of them passes directly over the Vault, and the quantum computer there uploads all the new data it received within the last hour." She zoomed to an image of one of the satellites. "Once a particular satellite receives the upload, it replicates that information and sends it to the other sixty-five satellites."

"So that means there are always sixty-six constant backups," Logan said. "Gives new meaning to the term *vault of heaven*."

"That's almost correct," Sylvia said. "Deep underground, below the quantum computer, there are twelve more backup centers. They were built in case something happens to the satellites."

"These satellites can deliver the frequency pulse?" Valerie asked.

"Yes, even though those WSA scientists don't think so. I've read a lot of research on the Tesla coils in each of the satellites. They can pack a punch." Sylvia rotated the satellite image. "Each of them also has a frequency modulation array, which they use to communicate with the Vault. Each one can independently change its communication frequency based on any normal atmospheric disturbance, small radiation flares, or low-disturbance solar storms. That helps to ensure that they are in constant contact with the Vault and the other satellites around them. So among all of them, they can cover the globe and not miss one inch."

"I'm impressed that you know so much about how the Vault operates," Valerie said with a raised eyebrow. "What's the first step when we get there?"

"We need to make our way to the Satellite Control Center. If Simon and Andrea are going to use the Vault to send the pulse, they will need to do it from the SCC." Sylvia zoomed to another image. "The SCC is underground, below the transmission array and above the quantum computer. The data centers and the power plant are located even farther belowground."

The projection of the SCC was disrupted by an incoming call and a projection of Alex and Goshi. "We just got the biometric report on Monique Sato, and it confirmed that she was telling the truth," Alex said. "MedicalPod records show that she received all her quarterly injections, but she didn't show any signs of having a DNA collar. Looks like her story about the green pills is true."

"So there must be some kind of antidote out there that prevents the collar from attaching itself to the DNA," Valerie said.

"Lucius offered me one of those green pills when he stalked me at the museum," Logan broke in. "I should have grabbed the whole damn container."

Alex nodded. "We looked through the security footage from the airport and found a shot of the woman called Gretchen." He brought up the image for all to see. It showed a close-up of a woman escorting Andrea and Lucius through an exit door at the airport.

"Who is she?" Valerie asked.

"We don't know," Alex said. "There's no information about her anywhere. Even the WSA database doesn't show anything."

"We also have no idea how Monique's identification glass and her PCD were reprogrammed," Goshi said. "Whoever helped them with that had some pretty fancy equipment."

"Fancy, as in WCF or WSA," Alex added with a dour look.

"Are you saying that someone at the WCF or the WSA is helping them?" Logan asked.

Everyone was silent for a moment.

"Makes me wonder," Alex said. "How did the assassin know that we had Monique in custody?"

After another moment of silence, Valerie said, "All we can do is keep putting the pieces together. Right now, our job is to stop the frequency pulse. We'll deal with the insider problem later."

"There's one more thing," Alex said before Valerie could disconnect. "Make sure you check out the Daily."

Valerie nodded and ended her call.

"What's the Daily?" Logan asked.

"It's a report we get every day that provides a brief of noteworthy criminal events from WCF and WSA offices around the world," Sylvia explained. "Keeps everyone informed."

Valerie projected the WCF Daily using the HoloPad. There was only a single item, a report from the WCF field office in Delhi, India.

Date:	*July 20, 2069*
Field Office:	*Delhi, India*
Report:	*Eighty-six bodies were found in a remote village two hundred kilometers from Banaras, India. Cause of death is unknown. Bodies disintegrated at the morgue before autopsies could be performed. No survivors have been located, and no children under the age of fifteen were found among the deceased.*
Action:	*TBD*

"Disintegrated," Sylvia repeated. "Just like at the lab."

Valerie nodded. "It appears that Simon and Andrea may have another EMFE device or some other localized way to deploy the frequency pulse."

"Children," Logan said in a low voice, as the faces of Jamie and Jordan flashed in his mind. He saw their smiles and their matching green eyes. "What do you think happened to the children?"

Neither Valerie nor Sylvia answered. But they could see the concern on Logan's face.

He used his PCD and placed a call to his ex-wife; he wanted to speak with his children. But after several rings, there was still no answer. He ended the call and sat back in his chair. They were probably on their way to the nearby campground where they enjoyed spending Freedom Day and taking part in the lakeside activities. He shook his head in fear at the irony of it all. His children and the rest of the world would be celebrating their lives, while the Final Purging tried to end them . . .

The plane would be landing at the Vault in about ten hours. Logan asked Sylvia if he could use her PCD to view some of the doctor's notes that they had confiscated from G-LAB. She handed Logan her PCD and leaned back in her seat to get some sleep, while Valerie went up front to speak with the pilots. Logan navigated to the doctor's notes on Michelangelo's *Creation of Adam* fresco. Maybe there was something in the notes that he had missed.

52

The greatest thing that you can do for another is to take away his excuses. That way, he can never say, "I did not know" or "I was never told."

—THE CHRONICLES OF SATRAYA

BANARAS, INDIA, 7:30 A.M. LOCAL TIME,
21 HOURS UNTIL LIBERTY MOMENT

"I suppose there are worse places to die," Simon said coldly.

Kneeling next to the limp body of agent Jogindra Bassi—Jogi, as he was affectionately called—Mr. Perrot surreptitiously tucked something under his deceased friend's right shoulder.

"From what I hear, it is a great honor to die in this place," Simon continued in a mocking tone. "How convenient that the cremation pyres are just over there. Come, now, stand up, Robert. There is nothing you can do for him."

"You didn't have to kill him," Mr. Perrot said as he stood. "He was a good lad." Mr. Perrot saw that Simon's thug was now pointing his gun at him.

"I will have to take your word on that," Simon said. He took off his hat and wiped his brow with a handkerchief. "It has certainly been a long time. You and Camden had us all fooled. I have to hand it to the two of you. You certainly have made things difficult for my family over the years."

"When is this trail of bodies going to end, Simon? It seems that you are to blame for the death of every person dear to me whom I've lost over the past two years. Beginning with my old friend Camden and ending with my newest colleague here." He pointed a finger at Jogi's corpse.

"Oh, I doubt it will end here," Simon retorted with a mean laugh. "I can probably come up with a few more corpses for you, Robert."

"We know about your plans," Mr. Perrot answered in a threatening voice. "We know what you and Andrea are up to."

Simon shrugged. "Well, then you should know that everything is moving forward according to schedule." He paused for a moment and took a seat on a block of stone. He looked at Mr. Perrot inquisitively. "You know, when we arrived at the ghat, I didn't recognize you at first. But there was something that looked familiar. Didn't I say he looked familiar?" Simon asked his bodyguard.

The thug nodded. Then he walked over to Jogi's body, picked up his gun, and took the PCD, which was still illuminating the small room. "Where's yours?" he coldly asked Mr. Perrot.

"I'm an old man," Mr. Perrot answered. "What would I do with one of those?"

Simon's man walked back over to the entrance and stood there.

"I kept watching you walk around," Simon continued. "The two of you looked like you were searching for something. When I saw your friend go and get some tools, I could not help but wonder if you were looking for the same thing I was looking for. And then it hit me. Your face flashed in my mind. 'Robert Tilbo,' I said to myself. Funny how the brain works, isn't it? I have to say that it was a brilliant decision on your part to look in here. I never would have figured out that 'ear stone' riddle. That was very well done."

"I know why you want the books," Mr. Perrot countered. "I know about the hidden symbols on the blank pages."

"Hidden symbols?" Simon said, feigning ignorance with a thin smile. "What kind of nonsense are you spouting? I am a collector, a modern-day treasure hunter. I only want to complete my collection."

Mr. Perrot shook his head, giving a defiant look. "The books are not here."

Simon's smug demeanor slipped. "Then where are they?" he demanded.

Mr. Perrot stepped to the side and pointed.

Simon rose from his seat and stood in front of the words chiseled into the wall. "How many damn riddles do I need to solve?" In a fury, he took out his PCD and snapped a picture of the message. After reading it, he took a deep breath and tried calming himself. "This riddle actually seems easier than the others," he said, rereading the words. "Those instructions seem simple enough. I don't think I need you any longer, Robert."

Mr. Perrot gazed at him contemptuously. "Camden and I never saw eye-to-eye with your father during our years on the Council," Mr. Perrot said. "Now I see that our suspicions were well placed. You are as evil as he was."

"Your derision is misplaced," Simon retorted. "We only wanted to use the Satraya philosophy to unite the world. Look around you, Robert. Left to their own devices, people cannot live in peace."

"There is no war in the world," Mr. Perrot said. "Bombs and missiles have been retired."

"Wake up, Robert. You and I both know that people have replaced the old armaments with new ones. Such as information and technology. Why, that was even happening when we were children. Countries flexing their political capital over other countries, corporations squeezing the last bit of money out of consumers, people coveting their neighbors' possessions. None of this has changed, and it never will. No, my friend. People need structure. They need order and laws. And they need leaders like us to provide them!"

"Leaders? You mean tyrants," Mr. Perrot fired back. "No one should have that kind of power or authority, not even the Council."

"Speaking of the Council, it is too bad that Andrea is not here. I think she would have very much liked to see you once again. As the situation stands, I don't think she'll get that chance." Simon turned to his bodyguard. "Tie him up, and leave him here. Make sure you seal that opening good and tight. And take those tools there in the corner. We wouldn't want him to dig his way out." Simon turned back to Mr. Perrot with a smile and eyed him from head to toe. "It was certainly nice to see you again, Robert. I suppose my trail of bodies may end here with you. But as I said, this is a good place to die."

"The symbols will not give you what you want!" Mr. Perrot shot back.

"Good-bye, Robert." Simon did not turn around as he left the secret room.

53

Free will can never be taken. You will always have choices.
You even have the choice to let someone else choose what is best
for you.
—THE CHRONICLES OF SATRAYA

PEEL CASTLE, ISLE OF MAN, 7:00 P.M. LOCAL TIME,
4 HOURS UNTIL LIBERTY MOMENT

The fireplace was ablaze in the grand study of Peel Castle. Anita sat on the rug helping the two-year-old twin boys build a castle with blocks, while the infants napped in their baby swings and ten-year-old Halima colored a picture of the village north of Banaras where she used to live. Bukya sat farther away from the fire, keeping a watchful eye on everyone.

"What are we going to do with all of them?" Anita said softly to Sebastian, who sat nearby in an old tufted armchair.

Halima stopped coloring and asked, "Are you going to send us away? I like it here."

Before Anita could respond, Lawrence rolled a cart containing food and drinks into the study. Halima jumped up and ran over to him. She gazed wide-eyed at the trays of cookies, cupcakes, and scones.

"Choose whatever you'd like, my dear. But may I suggest a cookie for each of the boys? And you can give this particular treat to Bukya."

Halima nodded excitedly, filling a plate with sweets, and ran back to her spot on the rug to share her bounty with Bukya and the boys.

Lawrence, meanwhile, took glasses of wine over to Sebastian and Anita, who had moved over to the crescent-shaped sofa. After he'd poured one for himself, Lawrence took a seat on a bench in front of a grand piano near the fireplace. He played a few quick notes of a melody that he was composing. "Still a little something missing," he said as he spun around on the bench and faced the sofa.

Sebastian raised his glass. Lawrence and Anita did likewise as Sebastian made a toast. "May who we are about to become, in all the coming moments, have the courage to do what we never have done before."

Sebastian, Anita, and Lawrence closed their eyes for a moment, and each took a sip of the now-blessed wine.

"The children can remain here as long as they wish," Sebastian said. "Just as you were allowed to do after Lawrence rescued you." He smiled kindly at Anita, who appeared pleased with his answer. He looked at the clock, then at the portraits of his mother and father that hung over the fireplace. His expression turned grave. "Less than four hours now," he said.

"I am sure the Ford boy will make his way through," Lawrence said.

Sebastian seemed unconvinced. He leaned forward and placed his elbows on his knees, a troubled look on his face.

"He will come through," Lawrence reassured him. "There's a good chance he might even surpass his parents' achievements." He took a sip of wine from his glass. "I remember a few troubling times when your mother and father also felt helpless."

"Are the children safe here?" Anita asked.

"They are safe," Sebastian said. "Based on the analysis of the blood sample and the vial brought back from the village, I can assure you that all the little ones in the world are safe from this threat." He smiled as he watched the children enjoying their treats, then turned back to his companions. "My thoughts are also with the River Set. Deya's books are being avidly pursued."

"By whom?" Anita asked.

"By the one who now possesses the other three sets. Should he secure the fourth, he would be closer to mighty secrets and mighty power."

"These are the same people who have brought the world to this dark moment, I fear," Lawrence said. "A son who has taken up his father's misguided pursuits. A son who disposes of anyone who dares get in his way."

"You mean the same people who turned these children into orphans?" Anita spoke softly so the children would not hear her. Clearly upset, she set down her glass of wine. "What kind of pursuits could warrant such cruelty?"

"What does a person pursue when he has great wealth and there is no more to accumulate, but he still has not found inner happiness?" Sebastian asked. "What does a person pursue to fill that empty space?"

Anita knew the answer. "Power and control."

"That desire can indeed intoxicate a man to the point of madness," Lawrence added.

"But why are the original books so important to him?" Anita asked. "The very same words are available in millions of copies of the *Chronicles* throughout the world."

Sebastian and Lawrence remained silent for a moment. Then Lawrence said, "The originals hold secrets. Secrets that some of the most noteworthy alchemists and philosophers of old pursued all their lives."

"So it's true, then," she said. "You are speaking about the secret symbols."

"You know more about this than you have let on," Sebastian said with a smile. "It appears I should have been more careful about letting you into the downstairs library."

Anita smiled back at him. "I found an old Bible in the study. Someone had circled the phrase 'For those that have the eyes to see, let them see.' There was some scribbling in the margin: 'Illic es magis ut typicus in Chronicles quam opportunus lumen.'"

"'There are more symbols in the *Chronicles* than meet the eye,'" Sebastian translated. "Very good."

"There are more symbols than the four that can be plainly seen, aren't there?"

"Yes," Sebastian acknowledged solemnly.

"How many?" She sat forward on the sofa, leaning closer to Sebastian.

"Eight. Eight more were created to assist people along their journey. Four, as you mentioned, are plainly visible. They were given to start people on their journey. The remaining eight, which are veiled, point the way to complete it. It takes passion and a great deal of perseverance to lift the veil that conceals the eight. But once a person sees all twelve symbols, a thirteenth symbol will be revealed to him. And if a person were to see the thirteenth clearly, without distortion, that person would become legend. The owner of the world but with empty hands." Before Anita could continue, Sebastian added, "And do not dismiss the great Satraya symbol that appears on the cover of each book. It too has purpose and power."

"But shouldn't the symbols be protected from the profane?" Anita asked. "Shouldn't they be kept hidden from those who would misuse them?"

"It would seem so. But it is delicate work determining what to hide from our brothers and sisters, when we ourselves are perpetually evolving and unfolding. Who are we to veil what was once given freely to us?" Sebastian paused a moment, looking inward. He waited for his thoughts to coalesce. "The symbols do not care about the morals of men. They do not judge the intent of those who gaze upon them. There was a time when people could be trusted. Fifty thousand years ago, in an era referred to among sages as the Age of Satya—or the Age of Truth—people lived without envy, without greed. They possessed incredible respect for the life journeys of all. It was in that age that these symbols were first drawn, created by those who realized the great mysteries of life. They gave the symbols to all men, so that the paths of their own journeys would not be forgotten. That age lasted almost fifteen thousand years."

"But then came the fall of the angels," Lawrence added. "Men and women began to lose their way. They became lazy and impatient, addicted to the sensuous pleasures of life. Greed and power were the new symbols that were sought after."

"War broke out," Sebastian continued. "The wise ones were driven from the lands and fled to the great mountains. They left people to their newfound desires."

"'Better to reign in hell than to serve in heaven,'" Anita said, quoting from another book she had read in Sebastian's library.

"Milton's *Paradise Lost*, yes. That epic poem provides great insight into man's separation from God," Sebastian said. "The spirit within was forgotten; the God within was banished to live in a distant land. Humanity fell into a deep sleep. Instead of using the symbols for personal growth, people used them to wage war against one another. For this reason, the symbols had to be hidden; they had to be put away."

Sebastian looked out the windows of the study at the perpetual motion of the sea—swells building in the distance, moving ever closer to shore, and crashing on the rocks, sending sea spray high into the air.

"I'm familiar with the Fundamental Four symbols," Anita said. "They concern love, peace, freedom, and joy. But what about the others? Is it true that one of them concerns learning to heal the sick? That another deals with traveling from place to place without a car or a plane? And that yet another concerns moving objects with one's mind?"

"I'd say those are accurate descriptions of the powers inherent in a few of the veiled symbols," Lawrence affirmed, the hint of a smile on his lips.

"And the others?" Anita asked in a hushed voice.

"All in due time," Sebastian said. "Do you know how Alexander the Great conquered his lands? Do you think that military skill alone produced his victories? No, Alexander was shown one of the symbols."

"Who would do such a thing?"

"His teacher, who thought his student could be trusted. His teacher was named Aristotle," Lawrence added with a wry smile.

"Yes, Aristotle showed Alexander the veiled Satraya symbol called the Mudan," Sebastian said, and took a sip of wine. "When it has been realized, the symbol allows a person to read the thoughts of others, even over long distances. Young Alexander became intoxicated with this power and used it to outwit his enemies, which is not difficult when you know their every move."

"But his advantage ended when he entered the realm of the Magi and the land of the Indus Valley," Lawrence interjected.

"What happened there?" Anita asked, enthralled by this startling insight into the actions of one of the greatest men in history.

"Alexander's men mutinied. It is said that they grew tired of battle and weary of the march. But in reality," Sebastian explained, "they were deceived by the king of Magadha, who rose to power because of another Satraya symbol, which he stole from a holy man."

"The symbol is called the Sin-Ka-Ta," Lawrence added. "The power to enter the dream world."

Sebastian nodded. "That is correct. Each night, as Alexander's army slept only miles from the border of Magadha, the king would enter their dreams and plant visions of their homelands. He would remind the soldiers of the lives they had left behind and how long they had tarried. Alexander's men thought the recurring dreams were visions given to them by the gods. It did not take long for those visions to take root, and soon Alexander was commanding a troubled army unwilling to fight any longer."

"Fascinating," Anita said. "But these facts are not found in history books."

"For a very good reason," Sebastian said. "The protection of the symbols. The great library of Alexandria was not destroyed accidentally. Caesar knew Alexander's secret and tried to obtain the same power for himself. He surmised that if Alexander had hidden the knowledge, he would have done so in the library. But when Caesar ordered his scholars to search the library, and they could not uncover the symbol, he destroyed the library so that no one else would possess it. Those who dwell in the great mountains and the enlightened ones who walk among us hold the symbols in their minds. They are passed from teachers to worthy initiates, like a great mandala, whose image is cast to the wind soon after it is completed. These symbols cannot be seen in any physical manifestation on this earth. Today *The Chronicles of Satraya* are the only books that possess these images, and there they are veiled. Other works in the past have also contained the veiled symbols, but time has seen to their destruction."

"So you see why in these times it would be dangerous if that information were to fall into the wrong hands," Lawrence said. "It would be like a child attempting to wield a sword that was too big for him."

"I understand." Anita paused to check on the children. The infants were still napping, and the twins and Halima were playing contentedly by the fire. Turning back to Sebastian and Lawrence, she said, "But I don't understand how we can sit back and let the world suffer from the actions of such evil people. How can we do nothing to stop them from obtaining all the symbols? How can we abandon the innocent?"

"Abandon?" Sebastian leaned forward in his chair with a determined look on his face. "Our force may be unseen, but our force is the one that taps man on the shoulder and whispers, 'Look over there.' No, we will never abandon people, lest we abandon ourselves."

The soft, soothing music of the Arcis Chamber was replaced by a call to battle. The sounds of the violin and the strumming harps were replaced by the thunderous beat of a thousand drums. It was like the sound heard in times of old when great warriors were summoned to take up their arms and march against a seemingly unconquerable foe. Sebastian once again sat at the center of his great tabernacle, his eyes closed and his mind enveloping the imminent battle. Anita joined him this evening, sitting to his right, while Lawrence sat to his left. They, too, sat with their eyes closed, endeavoring to whisper to the world.

The manifesto of the lineage to which Sebastian belonged prohibited him from taking direct action in the affairs of mankind. For eons, the members of his order had watched the comings and goings of the world, hoping for a day when their continued vigilance would no longer be needed. A day when an entire civilization would come forward and ask humbly for the great knowledge. The years after the Great Disruption and the era of the *Chronicles* had provided such a promise. But alas, mankind had slipped back, as it had always done. The task of the silent ones would continue until the fabled dawn of enlightenment illuminated the dark corners of the world.

The drums beat on as all of Peel Castle quaked with the sound of war. Sebastian's compassion and love for the world alone would not be enough. His oath of ascension out of the ranks of the brotherhood of humanity bound him to a simple covenant.

> *The cycles of man cannot be tampered with,*
> *What is to be and what is to come,*
> *Must be and must come*
> *For that is the free will of all.*

As it had been since the beginning, the liberation of *all* must include the liberation of *each*. Those who play the chess game of life and death are the *only* ones allowed to move the pieces. Sebastian could not fight this battle with a sword that he possessed. Someone else would have to put aside their fear, their uncertainty, and their doubts. Sebastian focused on the face of Logan Ford, the artist who would have to become a warrior.

The drums went quiet for Sebastian, and a scene at a great river unfolded before him.

54

Who ensures that the falling leaves in autumn land safely upon
the good earth? Who watches each one to ensure its seemingly
wayward path?
That "who" is the inspiration of us all.
—THE CHRONICLES OF SATRAYA

DHARAN, NEPAL, 1:45 A.M. LOCAL TIME,
3 HOURS UNTIL LIBERTY MOMENT

As planned, the WCF transport plane landed at the Akasha Vault's airport just east of the facility. Logan, Valerie, and Sylvia walked quickly
across the bridge and toward the main entrance.

"Long way down," Logan said, as he peeked over the railing at the
river flowing twenty meters below them. The images he had viewed on
the HoloPad during the flight did not prepare him for the sheer mag-
nificence of the Akasha Vault complex. Twelve massive inward-leaning
columns rose almost thirty meters into the sky, supporting a colossal
dome. About fifty acres of land beneath the canopy boasted thirteen
glass-domed buildings, the largest of which sat at the center and served
as the main entrance to the Vault. An immense translucent column connected this central building to the dome high above. "What's that colored light coming from the column?" he asked.

"That's the photon relay that connects the quantum computer
underground with the communication array contained in the dome,"

Sylvia explained. "Rumor has it that if they ever pushed the communication column to full capacity, the glare coming from the column would light up the entire mountainside and the valley below."

"That would be an impressive sight," Logan said, hurrying to keep up with Valerie, who had quickened her pace as they drew closer to the entrance. "This place is incredible. The architecture alone ought to be worshipped."

"This is only part of the Akasha Vault," Sylvia replied. "The stuff belowground—now, *that* ought to be worshipped."

Valerie pressed the intercom button and pounded on the large glass entrance doors to the central building. There was no one at the reception desk, even though the lights in the lobby were on. "Where the hell is everyone?" Valerie asked.

Logan looked at his PCD and saw that it was close to two in the morning. "It's pretty early. Or late, depending on your point of view."

"This is supposed to be a twenty-four/seven facility," Valerie said, pressing the buzzer a few more times.

Two guards emerged from a door behind the main desk. A buzzer sounded, and the lock on the doors disengaged.

Valerie rushed in and addressed the guards. "My name is Valerie Perrot, and I'm with the WCF." She displayed her credentials. Logan and Sylvia stopped short and waited in a sitting area close by. "I need to speak with the head of security immediately."

"It's one fifty-five in the morning, madame," one of the guards said. "Mr. Khan doesn't arrive for another seven hours or so, usually around shift change at eight-thirty."

"However, I suspect that he might be a bit tardy this morning," the second guard added with a smile. "He will be enjoying the Freedom Day celebrations, which are about to start down in the city. Perhaps you can come back later this morning, even partake in the celebration yourself."

"A security breach might be taking place here right now," Valerie said firmly. "There is an urgent worldwide threat. If I can't speak to Mr. Khan right away, then I need to go directly to the Satellite Control Center and speak to whoever is in charge there."

"Yes, madame," the second guard said. "We have been notified of the situation, and the facility is at SETCON Five, which is the highest level of security."

"Then you're probably also aware that the WCF is assisting with the matter. I would suggest that you either get Mr. Khan on the phone or let me go down to the SCC."

"Please have a seat, madame," the first guard said. "We will see what we can do."

Valerie clearly didn't care for the guards' casual attitude, but she had no choice; she relented and took a seat with Sylvia and Logan.

"You're WCF," Logan said, having heard the conversation. "Who are they to stop us from going down to the Satellite Control Center?"

"This is a WSA facility. We don't have any authority here." Valerie stood and started to pace. She kept one eye on the guards to ensure that they were contacting Mr. Khan. "What are you reading?" she asked, turning to Sylvia, who was surveying a list of names on her PCD.

"I just received the list of Allegiance Pharmaceuticals' customers from Alex," Sylvia said.

Valerie took a seat next to Sylvia, and the two of them reviewed the list. The number of companies that deployed qMeds through the pods was staggering.

Katron Pharma LLC
Arcimeds International
Symtec
BioCon Inc.
AB Control Systems
Wise Pharmaceuticals
Foto-Syn Corp
BSA International
MedCo

. . .

Valerie looked up and noticed one of the guards was waving at her. She got up and walked over. Logan and Sylvia followed her.

"Madame, we have spoken to Mr. Khan," the guard said. "He wishes for you to know that he was indeed informed of a possible threat and that you should rest assured that the facility is secure and safe. He said that he spoke to Director Ramplet, and only WSA-authorized personnel are allowed into the lower levels of the Vault during the lockdown."

"However," the second guard added, "Mr. Khan also said that you are permitted to walk the surface grounds of the facility."

"We need to take a look around down there, not up here," Valerie insisted. "That's where the security breach is going to take place."

While Valerie argued with the guards, Logan noticed Sylvia stealing a glance at the electronic visitors log at the corner of the reception desk.

"Madame," the second guard said to Valerie, "we are not authorized to let you do that. Mr. Khan suggested that if you return at eight-thirty, he will be more than happy to take you on a tour of the entire complex, including the lower levels."

"Eight-thirty! Do you two realize what's going on? At eight-thirty, it might be too late!"

Seemingly out of nowhere, three heavily armed guards wearing WSA uniforms came around a corner and took up positions behind the desk.

"I assure you, madame," the second guard stated, "we have everything under control here."

Valerie shook her head in disbelief. Logan adjusted the backpack on his shoulder and waited for Valerie's next move. "You tell Mr. Khan that if anything happens, it's on his head!" She turned to exit the building, Logan and Sylvia again following her.

"We're leaving?" Logan asked when they were back outside the main entrance. "Just like that?"

"Only for the moment," Valerie said.

As the three of them walked back toward the airport, Valerie made a call on her PCD to Director Burke. She pleaded for assistance in gaining entry to the Akasha Vault, but none was forthcoming. "I understand," Valerie said before she ended the call. "Dammit! Everyone thinks this place is secured." She crossed her arms, gazing around the apparently serene complex. Other than the three of them and a few workers at the airport, there was not another soul in sight. "Maybe we got it wrong," she conceded. "Maybe Andrea and Simon *aren't* going to use the satellites here to deliver the pulse."

"I don't think so." Sylvia brought up a picture that she had surreptitiously taken of the Akasha Vault's visitors log. "Look at the third name down."

"AB Control Systems," Logan read. "What about them?"

"Where did we see that name before?" Valerie asked, thinking a moment. "Wasn't that company also on the list we received from Allegiance Pharmaceuticals?"

"Yep," Sylvia confirmed. "They arrived a few hours before we did, and look—they haven't signed out yet."

"Why would a pharmaceutical company visit the Vault? And in the middle of the night?" Logan asked. The three of them looked at one another. "So how are we going to get in there?"

"I have an idea," Sylvia said. "I know someone who works in the quantum computing facility. Over the years, we've talked quite a bit, and I've gotten to know him pretty well. Maybe he can get us in."

"Try it!" Valerie said. "We have nothing to lose."

Sylvia took out her PCD and walked off to make the call.

Valerie took out her PCD, too. "Let's see if we can find out what AB Control Systems does," she said, scrolling through the information from the WCF database. "They've been around for twenty-seven years. Mainly a technology company. They supply large data systems and construct secure operation centers."

"That explains why they'd be here," Logan said. "But it doesn't explain why they're on Allegiance Pharmaceuticals' list."

Valerie nodded. Then she brought up a press announcement. "It says that AB Control Systems purchased a controlling interest in a flu vaccine company eighteen months ago."

"Why would a computer company buy a vaccine manufacturer?"

Valerie shook her head. "It says that AB Control Systems was founded by Alfred Benson twenty years ago. He died a few years back of a drug overdose."

"Alfred Benson," Logan repeated, murmuring the name to himself and thinking. Suddenly it hit him. "Alfred Benson! Your father told me Andrea married a man named Alfred Benson."

Valerie stopped searching for more information. She paused, closed her eyes, and let all the pieces fall into place.

Just then, Sylvia returned. "Good news! My friend Chetan has the graveyard shift tonight, and he can at least get us into the computer level."

"How much did you tell him?" Valerie asked.

"I didn't say much, but he knows you and I are WCF. Let's just say that he's not a big fan of Mr. Khan and WSA. He'll meet us at the north entrance in a few minutes."

"Let's go, then."

The north entrance to the complex looked close enough, but it was easy to underestimate distances under the massive dome of the Vault. As they approached their rendezvous point, they could see a pair of bright lights approaching.

"Slow down," Valerie cautioned in a low voice.

It was a transport car speeding along a monorail track. When it stopped in front of them, the doors opened, and a young Nepalese man hopped out. "Hello, Sylvia. Welcome to the Vault. It is a pleasure to meet you in person!"

"Chetan, it's nice to finally meet you face-to-face, too," Sylvia said, giving Chetan a warm handshake. "This is my boss, Valerie, and our associate, Logan."

"Yes, yes. Please step in." Chetan swiped his ID card, and the doors to the transport opened. "This is one of the benefits of working at the Vault; we get unlimited use of the Maglev cars." Chetan pressed a few buttons, and soon the car was on its way.

"Maglev cars?" asked Logan.

"It stands for 'magnetic levitation': Maglev," Chetan explained. "Basically, we are floating on air by using electromagnets."

Valerie seemed less interested. "We need to get to the SCC," she said, getting down to business.

"That will pose a problem," Chetan admitted. "We received a communication yesterday that only scheduled and mandatory personnel are allowed on the SCC level until further notice. They have revoked all other access, including mine."

"Did the communication tell you about the current situation?" Valerie asked.

"No," Chetan said with a mischievous grin. "But I knew something was happening, so I accessed the video recording of the meeting that you had in Washington—one of the privileges of controlling the quantum computer and the data array."

"I didn't know that meeting was recorded," Sylvia said.

Chetan stayed silent and just smiled.

"They're the WSA. They have eyes everywhere," Valerie said.

"*We* are *not* the WSA," Chetan respectfully corrected her. "They just provide the security. The people who work at the Vault are employees of the Nepalese government." Chetan pointed to the image of the double-pennant red and blue national flag that hung over the doorway of the Maglev car. "Somehow I wasn't surprised when Sylvia called. I agreed with your assessment at the meeting. Working here, I know that the Vault is the best place to deploy the frequency." His expression turned solemn. "Is it true that the frequency pulse could kill that many people?"

"Yes," Valerie said. "That's why we need to get into the SCC ASAP."

They stood quietly in the Maglev car as it glided around the Vault, thinking about what the deployment of the pulse would mean. When the car came to a stop at an entrance on the west side of the complex, Chetan led them out and used his security card to open a set of doors. They continued down a hallway and stepped into an elevator.

"Are you sure we can't get to the Satellite Control Center?"

Chetan swiped his card and pushed the button labeled scc, but it didn't illuminate. "See," he said, "my access has been revoked." He swiped his card again and pushed another button, and the elevator descended.

"I feel like we're moving, but I can't hear any gears or machinery," Logan observed.

"This is the first magnetic-drive elevator in the world," Chetan said proudly. "Just like the Maglev cars. There are no cables, pulleys, or motors. Everything is done with the use of sequentially placed electrical magnets."

It wasn't long before the doors opened and they arrived at the computer facility. Logan, Valerie, and Sylvia were awestruck. The room was the size of a football field, filled with rows of computer workstations. A massive column of light stood at the room's center, extending upward through an opening in the thirty-five-meter-high ceiling.

Chetan laughed. "We get that reaction a lot. Welcome to the world's only quantum supercomputer!"

55

If you learn from an idle stone, listen to the stone.
If you learn something from the slow passing of a turtle, listen to
the turtle.
If you learn from a silent night, listen to the night.
Care not where truth comes from, care only that it comes.
—THE CHRONICLES OF SATRAYA

DHARAN, NEPAL, 2:56 A.M. LOCAL TIME,
109 MINUTES UNTIL LIBERTY MOMENT

The translucent column Valerie, Logan, and Sylvia had seen on the surface of the Akasha Vault made its way all the way down to this level, four hundred meters underground. It emitted a rhythmic hum as pulses of energy and light rose upward. Chetan led them quickly up a stairway and into a control room that overlooked the facility below, which was relatively empty, with only three workers.

"During the day, this room is quite busy," Chetan said. "We usually have eighty to ninety people on the floor."

"So where's all the additional security?" Valerie asked in a worried voice. "Shouldn't there be guards at every corner?"

"Yes, I expected the same thing," Chetan agreed. "Once SETCON Five was declared last evening, I expected to see WSA guards everywhere."

Valerie's eyebrows rose.

"Now what?" Logan asked. "We have less than two hours until the attack."

"Is the SCC the only place where they can control the satellites?" Sylvia asked Chetan.

"Yes, that is correct." Chetan took a seat in front of a control console. He pointed upward. "All of the satellite control is from the floor one hundred meters above us."

"Can you access the Vault's security cameras?" Valerie asked. "In particular, the ones at the main entrance?"

"As part of the lockdown, most of the security control has been transferred to the SCC, but I should be able to get to the cameras." With a few strokes of his hand, a large glass display came to life in front of them, showing the status of the many subsystems at the Vault. Chetan brought up the video feed and started to fast-forward it. "What are you looking for?"

"I want to see who arrived from AB Control Systems a few hours ago," Valerie said.

"I can tell you that," Chetan said. "Usually, Miko and Ledan from AB Control do all the maintenance work. They are good men." Chetan slowed the video down to normal speed. "See, there they are."

"Looks like they're not alone," Valerie observed. In the image were the two men Chetan pointed out as Miko and Ledan. But three more men and two women were with them.

"Usually, it's just Miko and Ledan," Chetan said. He paused the video and zoomed in on a stocky woman with short brown hair. "I've seen this young woman before. Her name is Gretchen. She works for the WSA."

"The WSA?" Valerie repeated gravely.

"She's the one we saw from the airport security footage," Sylvia said. "You say she works for the WSA?"

"Yes," Chetan answered. "I have never seen these others before."

"We have," Logan said solemnly. "They are the ones we've been looking for." Logan pointed to Andrea in her signature crimson hood and a long black fitted raincoat. And to Lucius, clad entirely in black.

"We have to let someone know," Sylvia said.

"Let *who* know?" Valerie asked. "Whom do we trust at this point? Clearly, not the WSA. Their agents are granting them access to the facility." She shook her head and turned. "I need to call Burke." She walked away and placed the call.

"Are there any cameras on the SCC level?" Sylvia asked Chetan.

"There are." He swiped his hands over the controls and attempted to bring up video feeds from the SCC level. "Why is it asking for a security code? These cameras have never been coded before."

"Looks like someone doesn't want us to see what's going on up there," Logan said.

Chetan slid his chair over to another display and brought up a security log. "Let us see what kind of games are being played . . ."

"You have the access codes for all of the security cameras?" Logan asked, as he observed the lists Chetan was bringing up. "Why?"

"Why, because I wrote the software for them," Chetan said with satisfaction. "There," he said, eyeing the log. "Someone added a security code to the cameras three hours ago."

"That's about the time they got here," Sylvia said.

"I wonder what other access they changed," Chetan grumbled as he slid back to the camera control console and entered the new codes. Soon the images from the cameras were displaying long and empty hallways of the Satellite Control level of the complex.

"Doesn't look like too much is happening up there," Logan observed.

Valerie looked grim as she walked back over. "We may be on our own for a while," she said. "If the WSA is involved, we can't let them know we're here. Burke doesn't trust Ramplet, and he doesn't want to alert Joint Command at this point—Ramplet has their ear. He's going to dispatch a WCF team, but it may take a few hours for them to get here."

"None of us may be alive in a few hours," Logan said.

"We're authorized to use any force necessary to secure the facility," Valerie said in a steely voice.

Chetan was still focused on the video feeds from the SCC. "Where is everyone? There should be at least ten people up there. Let's see what is happening in the control room." He swiped his hand, and a new set of video images came up.

"Looks like we found them," Valerie said. The bloodied bodies of four people had been shoved into a corner. Three other people, alive, sat tied up on the floor next to them. The rest of the SCC staffers were manning their stations at gunpoint. "All right, Chetan, how do we get up there?"

He did not answer immediately. "I just spoke to a few of them earlier this evening," he mumbled. "Where are Miko and Ledan? I don't see . . ." Chetan's voice trailed off.

"You have to stay with us here," Sylvia said sternly. She grabbed Chetan's arm and shook it. "You have to help us get into the SCC."

Looking stunned, Chetan walked to the window that looked out over the computer facility and tried to regain his composure. "The cooling tubes," he whispered. "You can use the cooling tubes." He rushed back to the control panel and brought up an image of the facility. "There are pipes that deliver water from the surface all the way down to the quantum core and the Tesla coils. That is how we are able to keep the core cool. Every hour, water rushes through these shafts, and the resulting steam is then vented out of these air locks." Chetan pointed to the massive pipes on the east and west sides of the floor. "There are ladders in the tubes that allow service people to climb from level to level. In theory, you could use these ladders to access the floor above."

"There has to be an easier way," Logan said hopefully.

"What are you complaining about? You climbed down a dumbwaiter shaft," Valerie said, turning to Logan with a slight smile. "Except this time, we're going up."

Logan nodded, the vision of Valerie's funeral flashing in his mind. He couldn't return her smile.

"We will have to time it properly," Chetan said as he looked at the clock. "You don't want to be in there when the water is released. We should play it safe and wait until after the next delivery, which is going to take place at 4:00 a.m."

"That's still twelve minutes out," Valerie said. "There're only fifty-seven minutes until they activate the pulse. We have to go *now*."

The four of them raced from the operations center to the water-cooling tube at the west side of the facility.

"Chetan, once we are in, go back to the control room," Valerie instructed. "You need to be our eyes and ears."

"Certainly." Chetan opened the access door to the tube with the swipe of his security card. "You have to hurry. Once you climb up about one hundred meters, you will see another access pad like this one. Swipe my card, and the door will open." He gave his card to Valerie. "You will have thirty seconds for all of you to pass through the door before the alarm is activated. You must have the door closed prior to the water cycle, or the alarm will also sound. If the alarm goes off, they will know that you are there."

"Anything else?" Valerie said sarcastically, as she entered the dark shaft, followed by Sylvia.

"Would you like to leave your backpack here?" Chetan asked Logan.

"Nope." Logan secured it tightly over his shoulders and entered the shaft.

"Good luck, then. The water will drop in about ten minutes," Chetan said, closing the door behind them.

56

*Contrary to what you may have been told, the little things that
bother you do matter. For who has the authority to judge what is
significant or insignificant in your life?
Only you can make that declaration.*
—THE CHRONICLES OF SATRAYA

DHARAN, NEPAL, 3:51 A.M. LOCAL TIME,
54 MINUTES UNTIL LIBERTY MOMENT

Logan's heart raced, and his muscles ached, as he struggled to keep up
with Valerie and Sylvia. The tube was at most three meters in diameter,
and the rungs of the ladder were wet.

"Be careful," Valerie warned, her voice echoing down the shaft. "The
ladder's slippery." The shaft was almost pitch-black; Valerie's only reference point was a spot of light coming from above, which she presumed
was the access door to the SCC level.

It was a tough, long climb, and Logan couldn't stop thinking about the
cascade of water that was about to shoot through the tube at any minute.
Fear propelled him forward. But as he adjusted his backpack on his shoulders, his foot slipped. Logan cried out as his hands slid down the sides
of the wet ladder as he frantically tried to place his feet on a ladder rung.

"Logan!" Valerie yelled.

Regaining his grip on the ladder, he felt his heart pounding. "I'm
OK," he said.

After several more minutes of arduous climbing, his head hit the bottom of Sylvia's shoes. She had stopped.

"We're at the door," Valerie's voice echoed from above. She swiped Chetan's security card, but the door did not open. Instead, the numeric keypad lit up, requesting an access code. "We need some sort of code!"

Logan looked at his PCD. "We have exactly three minutes to get in there before the water comes down, and judging by how long it took to get up here, we don't have enough time to climb back down."

Sylvia took out her PCD and awkwardly placed a call to Chetan, while maintaining her hold on the ladder. "Chetan!" she said urgently. "We need an access code. The keypad wants a code."

"Two minutes thirty seconds," Logan announced.

"He's looking in the security logs," Sylvia said.

"Tell him to hurry up!" Valerie said frantically. The keypad dimmed and went idle again.

Logan attempted to peek past Sylvia. He saw the light coming from above the access door. He could see Valerie's shadowed face and the access card in her hand. He looked at his PCD. "Just under two," he said. He couldn't help but think about the two visions where he had seen Valerie dead. The water was about to flood the pipes.

"Try one-four-five-five!" Sylvia called.

Valerie swiped the card again, and again the keyboard lit up, asking for a code. She entered the sequence; to her relief, the red light turned to green. Then the door opened, and Valerie climbed through, followed by Sylvia and Logan. She shut the door behind them, and seconds later, they could hear the sound of water rushing by.

They had made it into the SCC level.

"We have forty-five minutes," Valerie said.

"This level looks much smaller," Logan observed from the alcove where they were standing after exiting the cooling tube. "Do we know where we are?"

Sylvia brought up an image of the floor plan on her PCD. The Satellite Control Center was laid out in three concentric circular structures.

The main control center, where they needed to go, was in the innermost ring. It was approximately fifteen meters in width, and the inner wall was made of a single piece of tempered glass, which provided a view of the translucent quantum core that extended to the surface. The middle ring consisted of a thirty-meter-wide circular hallway, where administrative and support staff stations were located. Its three doors provided access to the inner main control center. The outer ring, where Logan and the others were standing, was the largest of the three rings. It was fifty meters wide and was used mainly for maintenance and servicing. While there were twelve doors in the outer ring, which led to the middle administrative ring, none of them led directly to the main control center.

"We can use that entrance ahead of us to get to the middle ring," Sylvia said, pointing to a door marked with the number nine. "Once in the middle, we can go either right or left to reach one of the entrances to the SCC."

"What do we do then?" Logan asked.

"We'll figure that out once we get there," Valerie said. "But we have to deal with another problem first." She pointed upward to ceiling-mounted security cameras spaced every ten meters or so. "We need to get by them first."

"Let's see if we can get some help." Sylvia engaged Chetan on her PCD. "There are cameras all over this floor. Any way to disable them, even for a moment?"

"Yes, I can issue a reboot to the security subsystem from here," Chetan said. "It will be about twenty seconds before the cameras restart. That should give you enough time to go through the door. Give me a moment—it will take a little doing."

While they waited for Chetan, Valerie pulled her gun out and checked the chamber and magazine, then reholstered it. Then she took her backup piece, which was strapped to her right calf, checked it, and handed it to Logan. "Here, you take this one."

He nodded, taking the gun and placing it in the front pocket of his backpack. He looked at Sylvia.

"I'm covered," she said, pulling back her jacket and revealing her own WCF-issued firearm.

"Everything is ready," Chetan announced. "But there is another problem. They have also locked down the middle ring!"

"What does that mean?" Valerie said. "The clock's ticking here."

"It means that they have switched the cameras there to be heat-sensitive. Anything caught moving around in there that is hotter than the surrounding air will set off the alarm. No one is going to get close to the main control center without them knowing about it," Chetan said. "We can't keep rebooting the system, or someone will be alerted."

"This just gets better and better," Sylvia said, shaking her head. "We have to be able to move around the middle ring freely because we have to figure out a way to get into the main control center."

"Too bad we don't have a cloaking device," Logan said facetiously.

Valerie was silent, contemplating the situation. "Chetan, do you have access to the heating and air-conditioning systems for the middle ring?"

"Yes, everything is controlled by the computer," Chetan said.

"Well, can you turn the heat up in the middle ring?"

"And set the temperature to ninety-eight-point-six degrees. Brilliant!" Chetan finished her thought. "Yes, I can do that. It will take a few minutes to raise the temperature. Hold tight."

"Set the temperature to just above ninety-one degrees," Sylvia corrected. "That is the typical surface temperature of the human body." She turned to Logan. "How's that for cloaking?"

A few more precious minutes ticked by as they waited for Chetan.

"Everything is set," he finally announced. "The temperature in the middle is ninety-one-point-three degrees, and the security system will reboot in fifteen seconds." Valerie drew her gun and prepared to lead as Chetan counted down the time. ". . . One and zero." Sylvia cut off her call, and Chetan's image disappeared.

"Let's go!" Valerie said, leading them quickly out of the alcove and across the hallway. She swiped Chetan's card, and door number nine opened. They walked through a large, well-lit access tube until they reached the door on the other side. With another card swipe, they entered the middle ring.

A wave of heat hit them as if they were walking out into a hot summer day, but no alarm sounded as they cautiously stepped forward. The middle ring was dark except for a few lights that dimly illuminated the circular hallway. With her gun still drawn, Valerie led them to the right, looking for the entrance door to the main control center.

"We have thirty-seven minutes before they initiate the pulse," Logan said.

"Remember, we shouldn't move very fast," Sylvia warned. "We don't want to raise our body temperatures."

Valerie slowed her pace. "Get down," she suddenly said, dropping to the floor. Logan and Sylvia followed suit. They had come to a series of large windows that looked into the innermost ring, where the main control center was. "I saw them in there," she whispered.

Logan rose to his knees and took a look himself before dropping back down to the floor. "Andrea and Lucius," he said.

"Gretchen has a gun pointed at someone sitting at one of the control panels," Valerie said. "I remember seeing two more guards on the security footage, but I don't see them right now."

"The only way to secure the control center is to surprise them. We need to sneak in there somehow," Logan said. He glanced down at his PCD. "We only have twenty-eight minutes."

Sylvia called Chetan back on her PCD. "We're outside the main control center," she reported in a whisper. "Any other ways to enter besides the main doors?"

"The only openings that I can think of are the cable access panels," Chetan said. "They are used by the service technicians to pull cables in and out of the SCC. There should be one close to where you are, just under the window." Sylvia panned with her PCD so that Chetan could see what they were seeing. "There, that silver hatch," he said, referring to a square inset under and to the left of the window. "That is one of the panels."

"How do we open it?" Valerie asked. "There aren't any handles or locks."

"They're magnetically sealed for security purposes. The lock can only be released from the security office," Chetan said. "One of you will have to go back, very close to where you entered the middle ring. You need to go into office forty-six-B. On the desk is a security panel you can use to disengage the magnetic locks. I can walk you through it when you get there."

"I'll do that," Logan volunteered.

"Chetan can guide you." Sylvia gave Logan her PCD.

"Be careful," Valerie said as she gave him Chetan's security card. "And get back here as soon as you're done."

Logan squeezed Valerie's shoulder and moved away from the windows. He stood up slowly and walked back down the hallway, looking for office 46-B. He was holding Sylvia's PCD out in front of him as Chetan's image was projected. All of the offices were situated along the long circular wall to Logan's left. The doors were made of stainless steel and bore an eerie resemblance to the maze room at G-LAB.

"You just passed room forty-seven; forty-six-B is coming up," Chetan said. "There, on the left."

Logan swiped the security card, and the door to the security office opened. The lights in the room came on automatically as he entered. A very large desk with three chairs behind it occupied most of the office. The floor had a dull gray carpet, and the walls were bare except for a few blank monitors.

"What now?" Logan asked.

"Sit in the middle chair behind the desk," Chetan instructed. "You should see a security panel built into the table."

Logan walked around the desk and took a seat, setting Sylvia's PCD down on the desk. Chetan eyed the controls and walked Logan through the various options until they found the control for the magnetic locks.

"Hit that button, and the lock should disengage," Chetan said.

Logan pressed the button on the display, and a green light came on. "Looks like it worked."

He ended the call. As he exited the security office, he heard muffled voices and the sound of a struggle coming from down the hallway. He pulled out the gun that Valerie had given him and started running back to where he had left her and Sylvia. Suddenly, he stopped; the voices had gone silent. He pointed the gun straight ahead of him, his hand shaking as he walked quickly down the hallway. He remembered something his father would say to him: "If fear is the motivation that moves you forward, then I support your fear."

Within moments, he was back in front of the access door, but Valerie and Sylvia were no longer there. He knelt down and noticed a few drops of blood on the floor. Still kneeling, he moved closer to the window. He poked his head up carefully and saw the two guards they hadn't seen earlier. Their guns were pointed at the heads of Valerie and Sylvia. Valerie's forehead was bleeding. *The blood on the floor must be hers*, Logan thought as he dropped back down to the floor.

Going through the access door didn't seem to be an option any longer. He closed his eyes, leaned against the wall, and took a few deep breaths, trying to calm his racing heart. Of all the things that should have been going through his mind, he remembered the mysterious voice that had spoken to him during his last candle journey: "When the finger of the unknown presents itself, be greater than Adam, and grasp its opportunity." The sentence ran through his mind over and over again.

In a moment of inspiration, he opened his eyes and readied himself. He had an insane idea.

Twenty-three minutes left.

57

If you had everything you wanted, would you still have the desire
to discover something new?
—THE CHRONICLES OF SATRAYA

DHARAN, NEPAL, 4:22 A.M. LOCAL TIME,
23 MINUTES UNTIL LIBERTY MOMENT

"Foolish woman!" Andrea scolded Valerie. "Did you really think that
the two of you had any chance of stopping us?"

Valerie and Sylvia both remained silent.

"And where is your little friend?" Andrea walked over to Valerie
and leaned in close to her bloodied face. "Where is Camden Ford's
son?"

"What would your husband say if he were alive today and could
see what cold-blooded killers his wife and son turned out to be?" Valerie retorted. She stared at Andrea's face, which was shadowed by her
signature crimson hood. "Wouldn't he be a little concerned about how
you've sullied the Benson family name?"

Lucius turned toward Valerie, brandishing a knife in his hand, offering her a reminder of what happened at the plantation.

"Calm yourself," Andrea told him. "She's just a desperate woman
who knows her end is near." She turned to Sylvia. "Perhaps you know
where Camden Ford's son is?"

"His name is Logan," Sylvia said in a voice as defiant as Valerie's. "And I don't know where he is."

"No? Too cowardly to join you on this suicide mission? Not surprising, I suppose, that he should turn out so like his father—"

Without warning, the door to the SCC opened, and in walked Logan with his hands raised above his head, his backpack in his right hand. One of the guards moved swiftly away from Sylvia and redirected his gun at Logan.

Logan did not resist. Lucius grabbed the backpack out of Logan's hand and shoved him into a chair next to Valerie, who looked astonished.

"It seems that I was mistaken; you *are* braver than your father," Andrea said to Logan. "But I dare say just as rash and foolish."

"Playing God is a dangerous game," Logan warned. "The blood of millions will be on your hands."

"Not as many as are already on God's hands," Andrea said. "We are doing this for a greater purpose, a greater good."

"A greater good? How many tyrants and killers before you have used those words to justify their plans? Who are you to choose who will live and who will die?"

"You sound just like your pathetic father." Andrea shook her head, as if dealing with an ignorant child. "Fifty years ago, the people of the world were set free by the events of the Great Disruption. Men and women could do as they wished; there were no rules, no laws. But look how they used their newfound freedom. They fought with one another; they stole food and hoarded supplies. Do you know how many people died *after* the Disruption, how many were killed by their friends and neighbors?"

"But the *Chronicles* set people on the right path," Logan countered. "Those books changed everything. People grew out of their desperation and fear. They were able to choose their own *greater good*, not have it done for them!"

"They did, indeed," Andrea agreed. "But Fendral knew that utopia would not last for very long, which is why we wanted to take the Council to new heights. We could have ensured civility!"

"You mean you could have ensured control!" Logan fired back. "The likes of you are trying to push the world back to where it was before the Disruption. Cynthia was right; she was right about the financial institutions, about the drug companies, and about the genetically modified food supply. You wanted her out of the way so you could plunge the world into dependency again. You'll try to take out anyone who poses a threat to your rule!"

"People have made their own choices," Andrea said. "People have voted for a restored monetary system, they have voted to advance medical technologies, and they have voted for an abundance of food. They have elected the leaders who create the laws by which citizens must abide. We are the silent wind at the backs of your officials, ensuring that the world doesn't run out of control again."

"The silent wind. True power is not the silent wind at the backs of corrupt politicians, it is the wind of encouragement that kisses the cheek of every sincere man and woman. You, of all people, should know this. Do you really think that exterminating the free thinkers of the world is going to produce what you want?"

"Mother, you're not buying any of this crap, are you?" Lucius took his gun and casually pointed it at Logan. "Let me just put one between his eyes."

"Oh, dear boy," Andrea said, as she walked over to Logan, a sad smile on her face as she shook her head. "You are so much like your father, Camden. You fail to understand the same thing he did, that people are lazy. They will always need to be guided. They can barely grasp what is in front of them. We are merely giving them what they want."

Valerie and Sylvia listened to the exchange, their eyes shifting back and forth as it continued.

"*Lazy*. Like Adam in the painting," Logan whispered.

"Yes, exactly like Adam," Andrea said. "Since you've grasped Michelangelo's symbolism, you must understand on *some* level that what we are about to do is for the greater good."

"Where is your compassion?" Logan asked.

"Compassion?" she said, as if affronted by the mere idea. "Are we not more compassionate than the kings and queens of the past? Our solution requires no war, no battles, and very little suffering. It will be quick and painless."

"This isn't going to work," Logan said. "You should stop before it's too late."

"Too late?" Andrea said in a haunting voice. "It is already too late. Look around you." She pointed to the large monitors in the SCC, which were displaying broadcasts from around the world of people dancing and cheering and singing songs in happy anticipation of Liberty Moment. Andrea shook her head with something like disgust. She pointed to a screen displaying a clock: 04:25:32. "Look at them celebrating, totally unaware of their impending liberation. When that clock reaches 04:45:00, they will emerge into a more peaceful and well-ordered world. Well, most of them will."

"Liberation!" Sylvia burst out. "All those people—why do you need to kill all those people?"

"When you don't know who your enemy is," Logan said, "the swing of your sword must be very wide."

Andrea raised her eyebrows and nodded, pleased with Logan's interpretation.

"Let's just take care of them right now," Lucius snarled. "I'm sick of his philosophical babble."

"No," Andrea said. "Let them watch. Let them witness the end of the Rising and the beginning of a new world order. Then, when Camden's son has experienced the shame of his failure, we can send him to join his mother and father. I fear," she added, looking at Logan, "your passing will have been as unceremonious as that of your parents. It is a shame that you were not able to meet with Simon. He could have told you much more about the unfortunate plight of your parents."

It took Logan a few seconds to realize what Andrea had said. She'd just admitted that Simon was indeed involved in his parents' murder. "Oh, no, I plan on meeting with Simon," he said. "In fact, I look forward to it. I have a few questions about *his* father and how he really came to possess the *Chronicles*."

Lucius lunged forward and slammed the butt of his gun into Logan's head, knocking him to the floor.

Valerie attempted to jump from her seat to assist Logan, but Lucius put his gun to her chest and forced her back into the chair. Logan lay on the floor for a moment, rubbing his head. He eased back into the chair, and he could see blood on his fingers.

"Calm yourself, Lucius," Andrea commanded.

Lucius went to a nearby desk and started rummaging through Logan's backpack.

"The activation frequency has been uploaded." Gretchen walked over, holding a gun pressed against the side of an SCC staff member. "What do we do with the remaining employees? We don't need them any longer."

"We'll deal with them when we deal with these three." Andrea looked at Sylvia, Valerie, and finally, Logan. "Oh, Simon would also like for you to know that your friend Robert Tilbo does not seem to be faring too well."

"What have you done with my father?" Valerie shouted.

"Your father?" Andrea suddenly looked confused.

"Look what I found!" Lucius called out, as he pulled something out of Logan's backpack.

"Not now, Lucius!" Andrea was still staring at Valerie. "Robert Tilbo is your father?"

Valerie was silent now. Andrea's interest in her father worried her. She looked away without answering.

"Mother, I think you really need to take a look at this," Lucius insisted.

"What in the world is so important?" Andrea said, annoyed. When she turned toward her son, her eyes widened in surprise. Lucius was holding up the frequency device that Sylvia had taken from the WCF lab.

Logan watched the clock on the device. 04:29:58, 04:29:59. While Andrea was distracted by Lucius's discovery, Logan turned to Valerie and Sylvia, looked at them intently, and nodded. Then he closed his eyes; somehow, without speaking, they knew they should do the same. Another second passed, and then a blinding violet light filled the control room.

58

Find a religion about the future,
not one locked into the past.
——THE CHRONICLES OF SATRAYA

DHARAN, NEPAL, 4:30 A.M. LOCAL TIME,
15 MINUTES UNTIL LIBERTY MOMENT

Pandemonium broke out in the Satellite Control Center. Logan heard people screaming and stumbling all around him. He remembered the blinding green light he experienced at the auction and hoped the violet light would have a similar effect now. The loudest, most bloodcurdling scream came from Lucius. Logan opened his eyes just in time to see the scorching-hot frequency device fall from Lucius's burning hands. He was stunned to see the skin on both Andrea's and Lucius's faces shriveling and splitting, exposing the raw flesh underneath. Andrea pushed back her hood as she dropped to her knees. But unlike her son, she fell to the floor without uttering a sound.

During the ensuing chaos, Logan tackled one of the guards to the ground, knocking the gun from the guard's hand. The guard's head hit the floor hard, and he lay unconscious or dead, Logan wasn't sure. Sylvia also sprang into action, overtaking the other guard, who was struggling with his loss of sight. Dazed and blinded, Gretchen drew her weapon and started to fire randomly. A single shot from Sylvia took her down. Logan looked around for anyone who still posed a threat. He saw Andrea trying to crawl over to where Valerie had fallen, struggling to say something. The only words that Logan could make out were "Robert . . . Robert . . ." He ran over to her to hear what she was saying, but she collapsed before he could reach her.

While the remaining staff members slowly recovered from the blinding light, Logan and Sylvia bound the hands and feet of the two remaining guards, one still lying on the floor. Sylvia then quickly took a seat at one of the control panels. She opened a communications link to Chetan, who had witnessed the alarming events in the SCC via the security cameras. After Chetan guided Sylvia in lifting the security lockdown, he told her he was on his way up to the SCC.

"We need to disable the wavelength pulse!" Sylvia instructed the staff members. "We don't have much time left!"

Logan heard someone calling his name. "Valerie!" he shouted. He turned around to see her lying on the floor. He ran over to her.

"I can't move my legs," she said, struggling to sit up and lean against a desk. "I can't feel them."

Logan raised the legs of her trousers to see if she had been shot. "I don't see any blood," he said.

"What happened?" she asked. "What did you do?"

"I took a chance," he said. "On the plane ride over, I read more of the doctor's notes. He said that Andrea and Lucius were given the serum to cure their disease, but they had to wait seven days until the proper wavelength could be administered, or there would be side effects. I wondered if that first wavelength, the one that didn't activate the DNA collar in the lab, was actually their activation frequency. I took a chance and set the device for two hundred five nanometers and set the timer to go off after seven minutes. It was the only way I could think of to take them out."

Logan and Valerie looked at the bodies of Andrea and Lucius sprawled on the floor. Lucius was lying next to the frequency device; it was still smoldering.

"'Side effects' is an understatement. That is one painfully gruesome way to go," Valerie said. She nudged Logan on the arm. "I'm gonna make an agent out of you yet," she joked, yet Logan could see her grimacing in pain.

"I don't understand why you were affected," Logan said.

"No time to figure that out right now," she said, weakly shaking her head. "We have to figure out how to stop the pulse."

"Sylvia is on it," Logan said. He turned and looked at the fallen body of Andrea again. "Hold on just a second." He placed a comforting hand on her cheek. Then he went over and removed Andrea's PCD from her jacket pocket.

Chetan rushed into the main control room and went directly to Sylvia, who was still seated at the controls. The two remaining SCC staff members joined them. After conferring a moment, Sylvia and Chetan went over to Valerie.

"What happened to you?" Sylvia asked, as she kneeled beside her. "A medical team is on the way."

Logan was still struggling with Andrea's PCD. "There's no button on this," he said.

"It must be one of those new DNA-activated devices," Chetan said, coming over to take a look. "They send a slight electrical pulse through the body, and if you have the right DNA, it turns on."

"Well, the security seems to be working," Logan said, continuing to struggle with the PCD.

"Let me take a look," Valerie said.

Logan handed her the device. As soon as her fingers touched it, it activated.

"I don't think that should have happened," Chetan said with surprise.

Sylvia grabbed the PCD from Valerie, and it once again deactivated. When she handed it back to Valerie, the PCD turned back on. "There must be something wrong with it," Sylvia said. "The pulse must have done something to it."

Valerie looked puzzled as she held the activated PCD in her hand. She shook her head. Logan continued to look at her.

Chetan went over to Lucius, checked his pants pockets, and confiscated his PCD. "Just out of curiosity . . ." He handed it to Valerie, who took it in her other hand. It activated, too. "So," Chetan said, "I must ask the obvious question."

"Heavens, no!" Valerie exclaimed, clearly offended. "I am certainly *not* related to either of them."

"Hey, over there!" a voice shouted from the control table. "We have a problem. We can't prohibit the pulse! And we have less than seven minutes left!"

"Go help!" Valerie ordered Logan and the others. "I'll be all right— just go!"

Logan, Sylvia, and Chetan ran over to the control table.

"We have to figure out how to override the programming," Sylvia said, as she took a seat next to the staff member. Logan huddled over her anxiously.

"The satellites are controlled by a series of operating tasks," the staff member said. He brought up a list of them on the large display in front of them. "I've already filtered out the ones that run daily and any that are set to repeat. There are twenty or so left. We have to find the right task and delete it."

Beast I
Beast II
Harvey
Pathaya
Voyager X
Opus Ninety
Orion
Denique Defaeco
Simplicity
Duplicity
Jupiter Bound
. . .

"Why do techies always have to assign dramatic nicknames to every-thing?" Sylvia cried out in frustration.

Everyone scanned the list, trying to determine which was the rogue task. Sylvia was right; none of the names seemed to have any-thing to do with what the task was supposed to accomplish. Logan felt his heart sink when he saw Chetan look perplexed and shake his head.

"Denique Defaeco!" Valerie yelled. Everyone turned and looked at her. "Andrea's PCD says the task is named Denique Defaeco."

"What does that mean?" Chetan asked.

"Of course." Logan took a deep breath as he spoke. "In Latin, it means 'final purge.'" The group looked at him for only a moment before returning to the list.

With a few motions of his hand, the staff member highlighted it. He clicked to have it removed from the list; nothing happened. He clicked again. Again and again. Still, nothing happened. "They have it protected!" he cried. "Without the proper password, it can't be re-moved!"

"Chetan! We need ideas, anything!" Sylvia called.

The clock read 4:40:05.

Chetan replaced the staff member in the chair and desperately started to work with the controls. "These passwords are stored in an encrypted file," he said. "They rotate the key every hour. It would take at least thirty minutes to decrypt the one we want."

"That's too long!" Sylvia cried.

Logan fell into a chair and shook his head. He stared at the displays showing people from around the world preparing for Liberty Moment. The first one that caught his attention was a view of local people from the city of Dharan, just down the hillside from the Vault. They all held lit candles, and the children played with theirs, delighting in pouring the melting wax onto the ground. The combined phosphorescence from the flames illuminated the streets. Logan thought of Jordan and Jamie. He might never see his children's smiles again. He would have given anything to be with them. If he couldn't protect them, he would have at least wanted to be with them.

Another screen caught Logan's attention. It showed surfers on the west coast of the NAF participating in the annual Freedom Day surfing competition. They were riding huge waves and cutting away on their boards before the waves crashed onto shore. *Waves,* Logan thought. He remembered what the mysterious voice had told him in his last candle vision: "Change the waves in your life, and you change how they crash."

"Change the wave!" Logan shouted. "We need to change the wave!"

"What are you talking about?" Sylvia asked.

"It's like mixing paint," he explained. "Everyone knows that if you mix two different colors together, you'll get a third color. We know the activation frequency produces a green light. We know that if we mix blue and yellow, we get green. In theory, if we take away the yellow, the green will turn into blue. Can't you do something similar with this wavelength pulse?"

"Are you talking about a second wave?" Chetan asked.

"Yes. Yes! That might work," Sylvia said excitedly. "If we can get the satellites to deploy a secondary wave, it will interfere and alter the frequency of the primary wave!"

"Got it! We can program a second operating task to fire at the exact same moment." Chetan started to play with the controls and brought up a display where they could define a new task. "But we need to have that secondary frequency right now. Otherwise, we won't have time to program all the satellites!"

Sylvia brought up an image of the light spectrum frequencies on her PCD. "We know the primary activation frequency from our testing in the lab. Just give me a second to calculate the resonance wave . . ." The clock read 4:42:01. Most of the people in the room were looking anxiously at the clock, but a few were gazing intently at Sylvia as she did the calculations. "Two hundred forty-five nanometers!" Sylvia announced. "Set the secondary wavelength to two hundred forty-five nanometers one hundred eighty degrees out of phase!"

Chetan rapidly programmed the number into the computer and confirmed the new task. "Are we sure about this?" A large flashing green button stood ready to deploy.

Logan rose from his chair. "AzvAsana," he said, reading out loud the name that Chetan had given the task. "What's it mean?"

"Hope," Chetan said.

Without further hesitation, Logan pressed the button. "We'll know in about a minute," he said. Then he turned back to Valerie. She was no longer leaning against the desk but slumped forward, lying unconscious on the floor. "No . . ." He ran over and knelt beside her, listening to her breathing. "This can't be happening," he said, shaking her by the shoulders, trying to revive her. The image of Valerie's funeral flashed through his mind again. "It can't be true . . ."

Sylvia knelt beside them. She put one hand to Valerie's forehead, the other to her wrist. "She's getting colder, and her pulse is weak. Where are the damn medics?"

"Sylvia!" Chetan yelled. "We have a problem with satellite fourteen!"

Sylvia ran back to the controls and took a seat next to Chetan. "What's the problem?"

"S-fourteen is not acknowledging the new program!"

"Why, what's wrong with it?"

"It has entered some kind of geomagnetic storm. The link to S-fourteen is being disrupted."

"I thought the frequency-modulation technology was supposed to take care of that."

"Only for low-end disruptions. But the current storm is too intense. S-fourteen can't adjust."

"What's going on?" Logan called. He could see Sylvia and Chetan working frantically.

"S-fourteen is pointed directly at the east coast of the NAF." Chetan tried one last code, to no avail. "It's too late. It's deploying now . . ."

"Bring Washington up on the screen, and bring up the WCF lab," Sylvia ordered. "We have to find Goshi!"

Logan joined Sylvia and Chetan at the control panel.

Within moments, Goshi's image was projected on another display. "How's it going out there?" he said. Director Burke was standing next to him. Alex was off to the side.

"Not very well," Sylvia said, her voice shaking. "We can't stop one of the satellites from deploying. It's pointed right at Washington. You're going to get hit hard."

Goshi was shocked.

"Understood," Burke said grimly. "How long?"

"Less than fifty seconds," Sylvia said. "We're so sorry, sir."

Goshi dropped his head in despair, and Burke looked around at the others in the lab.

"The coffins!" Logan yelled. "Can't we use those coffins?"

"Yes, they will act as Faraday cages and disrupt the frequency," Sylvia said. "Goshi! Get everyone into the bio-coffins!"

Immediately, Burke and Alex started calling out instructions to everyone in the lab. Each of the three coffins was barely big enough for two people, and there were seven people in the lab. Burke and Goshi helped the others and secured the lids of two of the bio-coffins. Then they had to decide which of them was going to take the last spot in the third bio-coffin. There was a moment of awkward silence, as the two men looked at each other.

Sylvia and Logan were aghast as they saw Burke pull out his gun and point it at Goshi's head.

"Sorry, guys," the director said, "but I have no choice." Then he disconnected the call.

"What the hell just happened?" Sylvia cried. "He's going to kill Goshi!"

Logan was so stunned by Burke's actions he couldn't say a word.

Chetan replaced the disconnected image from the WCF lab with one from Compass Park. The park was filled with people listening to Adisa Kayin give an inspirational speech on behalf of the Council of Satraya.

"We cannot forget our fallen comrades and what they stood for. We cannot forget Cynthia Brown's tireless efforts to remind us of our right to be free and sovereign. Remember the words from the *Chronicles*, 'Should you fail to claim your freedom, rest assured that someone else will.'" The camera panned the cheering audience.

The reporter then pointed to a spot across the main courtyard of the park, where another rally was taking place. It was led by Randolph Fenquist, the leader of the Sentinel Coterie. Randolph's right-hand man, whom Logan recognized by the scar on his face and whom he had had his unpleasant encounter with a few days before, stood next to a HoloPad that projected a double-sized image of the Coterie leader. *Was Randolph not actually at the park?* Logan wondered. *Where was he?* Despite the small size of the crowd gathered around his image, they were no less boisterous.

"The time has come for change," Randolph announced. "Those books and that Council"—he pointed to where Adisa Kayin was speaking—"have plotted for many years to enslave you by the very words they say will free you! They want you to believe that *wolves* can decide what *sheep* will have for supper. Well, I say that a well-armed sheep gets to make his own choice." The Coterie crowd broke out in cheers.

Meanwhile, there was utter silence in the SCC, as Logan and the others helplessly watched the clock continue its march toward Liberty Moment. Now it read 4:44:50. People around the world started their countdown, exuberantly shouting out the numbers. Satellite fourteen was still rogue, and no one in the SCC knew for sure if the interference wave from the remaining sixty-five satellites in the sky would work.

"It's too late," Sylvia said, tears rolling down her face.

Logan went back over to Valerie and took her hand. It felt even colder now.

4:44:55.

"The Vault satellites are charging up," Chetan said, pointing to an image of the earth and the orbiting satellites.

4:44:56, 4:44:57.

Everyone watched as the photonic core became brighter and brighter.

"Have compassion for everyone you see, for their journeys are also your own," Logan said, reciting a line from the *Chronicles* as he watched the people at Compass Park.

4:44:58.

A beam of light was launched from the Vault's domed array and struck one of the orbiting satellites. Instantly, a web of white beams connected all sixty-six orbitals.

4:44:59.

59

What is the limit of your faith?
—THE CHRONICLES OF SATRAYA

AROUND THE WORLD, LIBERTY MOMENT

High atop Peel Castle, Sebastian looked into the starry sky. Next to him stood Lawrence and Anita, who was carrying a sleeping baby. Bukya had taken up a watchful position on the ledge of the tower balcony. They all watched the vault of heaven as the night sky gradually brightened. It was as if the great Northern Lights were making their way southward. Bukya let out a bark, sensing an impending event.

The crowd of people gathered around the Eiffel Tower went silent. Even the band stopped playing. People began to point up at the night sky. An eerie silence blanketed the tens of thousands of Freedom Day revelers who had enjoyed a day of celebration at the rebuilt tower. Something unusual was happening in the sky.

✻ ✻ ✻

An iridescent blue hue emerged high above the inlet where the Sydney Opera House had once stood. In all the previous years of celebrations, there had never been anything like this. A murmur spread through the crowd that had just finished the countdown to Liberty Moment. News reporters and cameramen pointed to the sky, attempting to record all that was taking place above them.

In a moment, the blue hue spread across the entire sky over Tokyo. A humming sound was heard, its origin unknown. It seemed to be coming from everywhere. People stood transfixed as the blue light drew closer and closer to the ground. Parents pulled their children close to them. The humming noise grew louder. When the blue light arrived, people closed their eyes, mesmerized by its warmth and entranced by the humming sound that accompanied it.

Sebastian kept his eyes open and looked around. The blue light engulfed the sky as far as he could see. The baby had awakened and moved excitedly in Anita's arms, gurgling in delight as if seeing angelic beings in the glow. The blue energy lingered for only a few moments, and as mysteriously as it had arrived, it disappeared, along with the entrancing hum.

"I dare say *that* has never happened before," Lawrence said.

"Was that the blue light that was rumored to have come from the *Chronicles*?" Anita asked.

"Similar in color but different in frequency and intent," Sebastian said. "This light is a sign that young Ford has altered destiny."

"So he has succeeded!" Lawrence was exhilarated. "He has foiled the plans of the dark ones!"

Sebastian turned and looked to the western horizon. "He has succeeded for most but not for all." He closed his eyes. The others waited for him to say more, but he did not speak for a long time.

Finally, Sebastian opened his eyes, and Bukya came down from the ledge and joined him. "After tonight, Freedom Day and Liberty Moment will once again be viewed as more than just a summer holiday. Many people have paid a great price for the world's renewed appreciation of this important day."

Sebastian turned to Anita and the baby. He gently stroked the baby's cheek with his fingers. Then he turned to Lawrence and said, "In the morning, I will be making my way back to India. A friend is in need of my assistance."

60

Always give what you can to those around you.
It matters not if they are poor or rich, young or old.
Let not your judgments be the criteria for your offerings.
—THE CHRONICLES OF SATRAYA

DHARAN, NEPAL, 4:50 A.M. LOCAL TIME, FREEDOM DAY

Logan gasped. "So many bodies." Seated next to Valerie, who remained unconscious, he could see the monitors displaying the scenes of carnage in Washington, D.C.

The secondary interference wave had succeeded in neutralizing the Final Purging frequency around the world, except for the former east coast of the United States. As most of the planet celebrated in the enigmatic blue light heralding the arrival of Liberty Moment, Washington, D.C. and other parts of the eastern NAF states were thrown into chaos. The deadly green pulse had hit approximately eight million square kilometers. Most of the affected area under the eye of satellite fourteen was located in the Atlantic Ocean, a fact that provided little solace to the people in the SCC as the death toll became more evident on the display screens. Frantic cameramen panned the courtyard of Compass Park, which was littered with corpses.

Sylvia tried desperately to get the WCF lab back online, but the video link to the lab was down. The monitor displayed only static.

Sylvia recalled Dr. Malikei's estimate: approximately one out of every twelve people exposed to the frequency pulse would die. She prayed that the doctor had overestimated, but the images she was seeing suggested that he had been right on target.

Logan grabbed his PCD and quickly dialed his ex-wife's home in Nevada. Even though they were a thousand miles away from the devastation, he needed to know that his children were safe. Jordan answered his mother's PCD, and Jamie jumped in shortly after.

"Did you see it? Did you see it?" Jamie said excitedly.

"Did you see the blue light everywhere, Dad?" Jordan asked.

"Yes, I did see the light," Logan said. He gave a sigh of deep relief. "I don't have much time. I just wanted to make sure you had a wonderful day. I'll call you back as soon as I can. I love you both, very, very much." He closed his eyes and gave another deep sigh as he ended his call.

The link to the WCF lab suddenly activated. Sylvia felt her body sag with relief when she saw a slightly disheveled Goshi on the monitor. "Goshi! Goshi, what happened?"

"Burke made me get in," Goshi said, still visibly shaken. "He pulled out a gun and forced me to take the last place in the bio-coffin. He didn't make it, Sylvia. The director is dead."

Sylvia, who moments before had been thinking the worst of Director Burke, started to weep. He'd sacrificed himself so Goshi could live.

She watched through tears as she saw Alex open the remaining bio-coffins, letting out the other survivors. Goshi turned on the HoloTV in the WCF lab so that they could ascertain what had taken place outside. Chetan brought up some other news feeds on the screens in the SCC. Reporters were gathering outside the Mexico City home of NAF president Enrique Salize. Word of the disaster in Washington was spreading quickly. Other monitors showed the devastation as far north as Philadelphia and as far south as Virginia Beach. The devastation reached inland to Charlottesville.

"From what we're seeing, it's chaotic all over D.C.," Goshi reported grimly. "Where's Valerie?"

"She's down . . . unconscious," Sylvia said. "We don't know what happened to her."

"Down?" Goshi didn't say anything more except, "Look, Sylvia, I'll try to find out who's in charge and what our orders are. Hold tight."

"How many do you think were killed?" Chetan asked. Goshi didn't reply.

On one of the screens, the cameras tracked Adisa Kayin trying to revive some fallen members of the Council of Satraya. Across the park, the projected image of Randolph Fenquist had disappeared. The Coterie handlers huddled around a corpse on the ground next to the HoloPad projector. Logan could see the dead man's scarred face. It was Randolph's top deputy. Logan wondered if Randolph had survived the pulse—wherever he was.

"Why did Fenquist's man die, and why did Mr. Kayin survive?" Sylvia asked, still crying. She went over to Logan, who was holding Valerie's hand. "It doesn't make sense. Wasn't this about Simon and Andrea taking out their enemies?"

"They took out more than their direct enemies," Logan replied. "The ability to think freely, unconventionally, and creatively is not limited to good people. Even the most corrupt among us can have that ability. It was not about who supported Simon and Andrea and who didn't. They wanted to take out anyone who could pose a threat to them. Anyone who could touch the finger of God. Anyone . . ." Logan went silent as the cameras panned up and down the streets of Washington. A plane had crashed just outside the National Gallery, and firefighters were attempting to battle the raging fire it had caused. A news report from Ocean City in southern New Jersey showed a sixty-meter yacht that had crashed into the harbor. The bodies of the dead lay everywhere. Husbands clutched their wives, and wives tried to revive their husbands. Others seemed disoriented and lost, showing the effects of their activated collars. Children were crying and clinging to the motionless bodies of their parents.

"It doesn't appear that any children were killed," Chetan observed.

"Looks like that's all we can be thankful for," Sylvia said. "But how and why they were spared, I don't know."

Confronted by the scenes of devastation and chaos, Logan, Sylvia, and Chetan, along with the others in the SCC, who had saved most of the world from a similar fate, felt no jubilation. They were left to ponder what they might have done differently to reprogram satellite fourteen in time.

Logan turned from the screens and looked down at Valerie's face. "Where are those medics?" he called out. Valerie was getting colder by the minute, and her breathing was weakening.

Suddenly, all three sets of doors to the SCC opened. Logan looked around anxiously for any sign of the medics, but only WSA agents filed into the room. They were led by Salid Khan, the man Chetan held in low regard. He was a short but confident-looking man with brown skin and a goatee. His shiny bald head seemed too large for his diminutive physique.

"Secure this area!" Khan shouted as he walked over to Logan and the others. "None of you is authorized to be in here. You will have a lot of explaining to do to Director Ramplet about why members of the WCF have illegally entered a WSA-secured facility."

As Agent Khan spoke with Chetan and the other two SCC staff members trying to assess the situation, Sylvia quietly picked up Andrea's and Lucius's PCDs and put them in her pocket. Taking Sylvia's cue, Logan stood and casually walked over to the frequency device, which still lay near Lucius's body. He stepped on it, breaking it into several pieces. Then he grabbed one of the fragments and put it into his backpack. Sylvia gave him an approving look. They were not about to let the device fall into the hands of the WSA intact.

Just as Logan knelt back down next to Valerie, a WSA medical team burst through the doors. Khan directed them to Valerie, and Logan moved aside as they rolled their gurney over. They took Valerie's vitals and lifted her onto the gurney. They started to roll it away.

Logan grabbed the gurney, stopping the medics. "Where are you taking her?"

Khan walked over, bristling with anger. "First she will be treated at the local hospital. Then she will go to one of our facilities. She has a great deal to explain to Mr. Ramplet."

"We'll explain our actions to the senior staff of the WCF," Sylvia said, joining the conversation. "Meanwhile, why don't you call your senior staff and explain to them how you let these terrorists walk right into your facility and deploy a weapon that has likely killed hundreds of thousands of people?" Khan's eyes narrowed. "Even after we warned you what was going on!"

Just then, Logan's PCD vibrated, indicating an incoming message. It had been sent an hour ago, but strangely, he was only receiving it now. He looked at the messenger ID. It was from Mr. Perrot. "Give us a moment," Logan said to Khan, taking Sylvia by the arm and leading her to the other side of the room. He gestured to Chetan to join them, then played the message that had come in. It was very garbled. "Tra . . . ed. Jogi de . . . d. Plea . . . H . . . p." Logan played the message a few more times. "The first word could be 'trapped,'" he said.

"The next part sounds like 'Jogi is dead,'" Sylvia said softly.

Logan nodded. "'Please help' seems to be the last part."

"Would you like us to help your lady friend or not?" Khan asked impatiently from across the room. "Make up your minds."

Logan and Sylvia turned back and looked at Khan. Logan didn't want to leave Valerie, but he knew she would want him to help her father. "Go with her," he said to Sylvia. "You need to make sure she's all right. I'll deal with things here."

With a nod, Sylvia ran after Valerie and the medical team, who were leaving the SCC.

"Is there some way we can track Mr. Perrot's PCD?" Logan asked Chetan.

"We should be able to, provided it is still active," Chetan said. "Wherever he is, there seems to be interference of some kind."

Logan followed Chetan to a control console, where he connected Logan's PCD to an interface and began analyzing the information.

"Logan!" Alex interrupted, his image suddenly appearing on one of the video monitors. "We just received word that Director Ramplet is on the run. Turns out that Gretchen woman worked directly for him."

Logan was no longer surprised. He stood silent for a moment, gathering his composure. "This isn't over yet, Alex," he said in a determined voice. "Looks like you're in charge for now, and I'm going to need a few things. Are you ready to take all of this down?"

Alex nodded.

A few minutes later, Logan ended his call and took a deep breath. Most of the world had been spared an inconceivable tragedy. Most of the world. Not everyone. Charlie, Jogi, and Burke had given their lives, along with tens of thousands of people on the east coast of the NAF. *Mr. Perrot and Valerie, what if they don't* . . . Logan did not finish his thought. He couldn't allow himself to be beset by regrets, fears, and worries. He had to push through, just as the Satraya Flame had taught him. He had to find Mr. Perrot, and if that involved confronting Simon, so be it. He welcomed the opportunity. A face-off that had begun with their fathers was now destined to end with them.

"Banaras," Chetan suddenly said. "The message came from Banaras, India."

61

Knowing how to start something must be balanced with knowing
when to stop.
Be wary of habits that can turn into addictions.
—THE CHRONICLES OF SATRAYA

BANARAS, INDIA, 10:30 A.M. LOCAL TIME, FREEDOM DAY

The WCF transport plane that Alex had arranged brought Logan to
the city of Banaras, the place from which they had received Mr. Perrot's
last transmission. Chetan had connected Logan's PCD to the Vault satellites so that he could track Mr. Perrot's faint and intermittent signals.
The signals led Logan to the Ganges, where he hired a boat to continue
his search. He sat at the front of the ten-foot-long rustic watercraft as
its helmsman, whose name was Sinjee, maneuvered through the river
traffic past the many ghats along the banks. With the wind blowing
through his hair, Logan took a drink from his water bottle and watched
the people still celebrating Freedom Day, unaware of the catastrophic
events on the other side of the world.

"Slow down!" Logan yelled over the roar of the motors. He'd just
received another trace signal. "Pull the boat into that part of the shore,
to that building over there."

He swung his backpack over his shoulder and disembarked onto the
steps of Manikarnika Ghat. He recalibrated his PCD, finding the direc-

tion in which he needed to head. After navigating through the crowds around the burning pyres, he went up the steps and past the clock tower. He paused from time to time, waiting for the random trace signal to appear again. Before long, he was standing at the Manikarnika kund. Logan looked at his PCD for more details, but none was forthcoming.

"Mr. Perrot!" he called out a few times. There was no answer.

After surveying the area, he started to climb down the steps of the kund to have a look around. At the bottom, he saw fresh footsteps that led to some kind of tunnel. He entered, holding his illuminated PCD. Almost immediately, he noticed the newly restored wall.

"Mr. Perrot!" Logan shouted, as he picked up a rock and slammed it against the wall. "Are you in there? It's me, Logan!"

"Yes," a muffled voice answered. "I've gotten into a bit of trouble, I'm afraid."

Logan took the small beveled-edge chisel from his backpack and used it to loosen the freshly grouted stone blocks in the wall. Twenty minutes later, he squeezed through an opening he'd made in the wall and saw Mr. Perrot sitting slumped over in a small tomblike room with the corpse of Agent Jogindra Bassi next to him.

"I thought that was it for me," Mr. Perrot struggled to say, his mouth parched. "The PCD I hid under Jogi's body was my only chance."

"Don't talk right now." Logan handed Mr. Perrot his water bottle and took a seat beside him.

He looked at the dead WCF agent, the sand around his head red from blood. While Mr. Perrot refreshed himself and regained some of his strength, Logan brought him up to speed on all that had occurred at the Vault, the devastation along the east coast, and the heroic actions of Director Burke. He then had to tell Mr. Perrot about what had happened to Valerie.

"My greatest fear has manifested," Mr. Perrot said, with a grave look on his face. He handed the water bottle back to Logan. "I didn't want to put my daughter in harm's way. Not only did I do that, but I might have also brought about her death."

"It's not your fault, Mr. Perrot. You know better than anyone, Valerie's not one to back down. She never did when we were young, and she never would now. Besides, she was only wounded, sir." Logan had to fight back the memory of Valerie's funeral in his candle vision. "I've left a few messages for Sylvia," he went on. "She'll let us know as soon as she hears something."

Mr. Perrot looked at Jogi's body, trying to find comfort in Logan's words. "Jogi told me that this place was a very auspicious place to die—but he need not have died now." He shook his head. "We have to find Deya's books before Simon does. Otherwise, Jogi's life, and the lives of all those others, including your parents, will have been lost in vain."

Logan nodded. "Agreed. Simon needs to pay for his actions." He slipped his hand under Mr. Perrot's elbow to help him up. "We'll have to deal with Jogi's body later. Right now, we need to focus on finding Simon. And so, sir, where to?"

"We do as the message instructs us," Mr. Perrot said, pointing to the message that was etched on the wall. "We go across the river to the old fort."

62

You cannot fake sincerity.
Is it any wonder that it is the key to prayer?
— THE CHRONICLES OF SATRAYA—

BANARAS, INDIA, 12:30 P.M. LOCAL TIME, FREEDOM DAY

Sinjee killed the engines of the watercraft as it pulled up to the bank of Ramnagar Fort, a few kilometers south along the west bank of the Ganges River. Built in the eighteenth century, it had been the home of many of the kings of Banaras. A wide set of stone stairs led up to the massive Mughal-style fortress with open balconies and hand-carved sandstone. Mr. Perrot read from the piece of paper on which he had written Deya's latest message:

> It will be yours
> For those who follow these understandings
> Cross the great river, to the fort of old
> Turn and seek the canopy protecting the jewel
> Along the river to Shiva's last stand
> This is the path for you
> If you seek what I possess

"So, based on the message," Logan postulated, "we are to turn in the direction we just came from and look for some kind of canopy."

Mr. Perrot nodded. He and Logan looked back across the river. It was hard to make anything out from such a distance.

"What does 'Shiva's last stand' mean?" Logan asked.

"I think it is referring to the last ghat along the shore," Mr. Perrot said. "At least, that is what Jogi supposed. He told me it was called Assi Ghat and was dedicated to the Hindu god Shiva."

"Why send us all the way across the river only to look backward? It doesn't make sense."

They continued to scan the distant shoreline without success. Then someone tapped Logan on the shoulder. He turned and saw Sinjee handing him a draw tube spotting scope which looked to be a hundred years old. Logan accepted it and nodded in appreciation.

"Is there anything that looks like a canopy?" Mr. Perrot asked.

Logan adjusted the focus on the scope. "What about a really big tree?" he said. "Could that be the canopy Deya was referring to?" He handed the scope to Mr. Perrot.

Mr. Perrot scanned the tree that Logan was referring to. There was some kind of shrine under it, where a great many people had gathered. "Nothing else there matches the description of a canopy. But let's take a look!"

The pilot fired up the engines and swung the boat around toward the southernmost ghat.

"It still doesn't make sense," Logan said. "Why send us to the fort in the first place? Why not send us directly to Assi Ghat?"

Mr. Perrot remained silent; he had no answer to Logan's question.

When they arrived at the banks of the ghat, Logan and Mr. Perrot rushed up a short stairway leading to Shiva's altar under the canopy of the large tree. There was no time to waste. Having heard nothing about Valerie's condition only added impetus to their efforts. They made their way through the crowd that Mr. Perrot had seen from the other side of the river. They finally emerged next to an altar, which had been smashed to pieces. While Mr. Perrot spoke to a worshipper who was standing nearby, Logan walked around the shrine and the tree to survey the extent of the damage.

"They say a group of men came to the altar last night," Mr. Perrot said, rejoining Logan. "The men started to ransack the place, smashing the two-hundred-year-old statue of Shiva, the altar it sat on, and even the holy Lingam stone. They were looking for something."

"Sounds like Simon beat us here," Logan said. "Did they say if the men found what they were looking for?"

"The person I talked to said they did not," Mr. Perrot said. "When the crowd saw what the men were doing, they ran them off. That's why so many people remained here. In case the marauders returned."

"From everything that you've told me about Deya, I can't believe that she would hide the books in such a way that you would have to destroy a holy shrine to find them."

"No, Deya would certainly not do that," Mr. Perrot agreed. They started to walk away from the tree and the crowd. Mr. Perrot once again pulled out his handwritten copy of Deya's message. "Perhaps we've missed something . . ."

Logan, standing across from Mr. Perrot, tried to read the message upside down. As soon as he did, he saw something surprising. "Wait!" he exclaimed. "The message can be read in either direction, first line to last or last line to first." He dropped his backpack to the ground and pulled out his sketchpad. He began to write furiously. When he was done, he turned the pad and showed Mr. Perrot the new message.

If you seek what I possess
This is the path for you
Along the river to Shiva's last stand
Turn and seek the canopy protecting the jewel
Cross the great river, to the fort of old
For those who follow these understandings
It will be yours

A smile came to Mr. Perrot's face as he read the newly formed message.

"We need to look from here toward the old fort," Logan said, "for something that looks like a canopy."

"Brilliant!" Mr. Perrot proclaimed.

The two of them immediately made their way back to the boat. Onboard, Sinjee moved them out into the middle of the river, where Mr. Perrot could use the scope to inspect the fort across the way.

"There it is!" he said, inviting Logan to take a look.

Once again Logan was gazing at the large Mughal-style fortress. In front of it was a small red building with a white dome. "The canopy hiding the jewel . . ."

The motor fired up, and the boat headed back to Ramnagar Fort. The small, red, square-shaped structure sat on a stone landing. Each side was approximately ten meters wide and eight meters tall. Double wooden doors occupied the center of each side, and a lattice window was above each door. The red structure supported four small watchtowers at each corner. Between these towers was the large white dome.

As soon as they disembarked, Logan and Mr. Perrot made their way up the thirty-three steps on the riverside entrance of the fort, which had been closed to the public ever since substantial damage had been caused to it by the Great Disruption. Old-style bamboo scaffolding covered the façade of the aging fortress, and the lower part had been overrun with vines and foliage, where birds and other creatures had been making their nests for many years. Logan and Mr. Perrot climbed up a short section of the scaffolding to the large landing that supported the white-domed building.

Logan looked out over the river below and at the ghats on the western shore.

"I suppose that we're going to have to figure out how to get inside," Mr. Perrot said. He pushed on a set of wooden doors, but they didn't budge.

"I can help with that." Logan handed his backpack to Mr. Perrot and started kicking the decaying doors hard. Pieces of wood scattered across the interior floor, and he tore away larger parts with his hands. Then he and Mr. Perrot entered cautiously, startling birds, mice, and other rodents, which scurried away, frightened by the noise.

The floor was dusty and spotted with crumbling pieces of painted plaster, which had fallen from the decaying dome high above. The paintings on the walls were faded, and statues of Hindu gods sat on a dilapidated free-standing altar.

"The stories this place could tell," Logan said as he took his backpack from Mr. Perrot and looked around the room. He bent down and picked up a piece of plaster from the floor.

"I fear that what it has to tell us now is another riddle." Mr. Perrot was kneeling in front of something carved into the wall directly across from the door through which they had entered. "It seems that Deya is still not ready to give up her secret."

the Conception that supports the god of men
must be Withdrawn in order to Announce
The Great Truth

Logan walked over, squatted down next to Mr. Perrot, and read the message. "Deya was just full of riddles, wasn't she?" he said. "Another one to read backward, perhaps?"

"Maybe," Mr. Perrot said, staring intently at the writing. "But there are some interesting word and grammar choices. Look at how she only capitalized certain words and didn't capitalize others that she should have. The word God, for instance."

"Then let's focus on only the capitalized words," suggested Logan as he read them out loud. "Conception, Withdrawn, Announce, and The Great Truth."

"Deya always referred to the *Chronicles* as the Great Truth. Let us suppose this is some kind of substitution puzzle. If we replace the phrase 'The Great Truth' with 'The *Chronicles*', then . . . " Logan rummaged through his backpack and handed Mr. Perrot a piece of colored sketching chalk. Mr. Perrot crossed out the last phrase and wrote "The *Chronicles*" underneath it.

"Conception means idea or understanding," Logan said.

"A prayer or a ceremony would also support God," Mr. Perrot countered.

"If we replaced the abstract idea of 'The Great Truth' with something physical, why not do the same with Conception?" suggested Logan. "What else can support 'the god of men'? A church, a temple, a pedestal, an altar?"

"An altar," Mr. Perrot repeated. He crossed out "Conception" and wrote "Altar."

"In the next line, the words 'Withdrawn' and 'Announce' could be replaced by other verbs," Mr. Perrot suggested as he underlined them.

"Two more words," Logan said. "Withdrawn suggests taken away or extracted. I suppose it could also mean removed or moved."

Mr. Perrot nodded. "Announced. This word connotes a declaration, an articulation."

"A revealing?" Logan said, following Mr. Perrot's train of thought.

Mr. Perrot smiled. "Yes, a revealing." He chalked it in the remaining two words.

He and Logan stepped back to read the new version.

the Altar that supports the god of men
must be Moved in order to Reveal
The Chronicles

"Could it be that simple?" Logan walked over and pointed to the small marble statues that sat atop the rickety altar at the northeast corner of the building. He bent down, grabbed the base of the altar, and slowly slid it away from the wall.

Mr. Perrot quickly went over and joined him. "Just a little farther," he said hopefully.

Underneath the base was a hole. Logan reached in and pulled out a metal box. It was nearly thirty centimeters long, twenty-five centimeters wide, and seventeen centimeters tall, with a handle on one side.

"It's a Destiny Box," Mr. Perrot said. "And a large one, at that."

The voice that answered him was not Logan's.

"I could not have done this without you, Robert, my old friend!" the voice called from the smashed wooden doorway. It was deep and familiar and echoed under the dome. "It was rather fortuitous that we spotted you at Assi Ghat. I would have never thought to look here. You'll have to tell me how you figured that out."

Logan rose to his feet and attempted to draw the gun Valerie had given him, but it was too late. Simon and his mercenaries had entered the building, with their weapons already pointed at Logan and Mr. Perrot. Logan set the box on the altar and helped Mr. Perrot to his feet.

"And you must be the one and only son of Camden Ford," Simon continued. "We meet at last!"

63

Miracles are called such because they are rare events in your life.
What will you call them when they happen every day?
—THE CHRONICLES OF SATRAYA

BANARAS, INDIA, 2:10 P.M. LOCAL TIME, FREEDOM DAY

Logan and Mr. Perrot sat against a wall, their hands bound behind them. Macliv and two more of Simon's thugs had their guns trained on them, awaiting any hostile moves. Another deactivated the PCDs he had just confiscated from them. There were four mercenaries inside the old domed structure, and more could be heard outside.

"What the hell is going on? Why isn't anyone answering my calls?" Simon yelled in frustration. "The shores and the river should be littered with the dead. Instead, people are worshipping some blue light they witnessed in the sky this morning!" He grabbed one of the little statues from the altar and flung it against the wall, smashing it to bits. "Andrea and Lucius had better have a good explanation for all of this!"

"Is there a problem, Simon?" Mr. Perrot asked in a matter-of-fact tone.

"None that cannot be solved," Simon replied. He grabbed a knife from the belt of one of his men.

"I would be most careful with that," Mr. Perrot suggested, as Simon attempted to pry open his newly discovered prize. "That is a Destiny Box. If you do not open it correctly, you might permanently damage the contents."

"I know what it is, Robert!" Simon yelled back. He threw the knife to the ground. "How would *you* suggest I open it?" he asked, motioning to have Mr. Perrot and Logan brought over to him.

"Judging by that metallic pad on the surface, you're going to need a DNA sample or, more likely, a fingerprint," Mr. Perrot said.

"Probably Deya's," Logan added. "Oh, that's right—you killed her. Probably not a good move in retrospect."

Simon gave a nod to one of his men, who punched Logan just below his ribs. Logan let out a grunt and slumped in pain. Mr. Perrot was helpless to assist him.

"I have no time for your childish retorts," Simon stated. "If you don't have anything constructive to say, then keep silent!" He grabbed Logan by the arms and lifted him to an upright position.

"Let him be, Simon," Mr. Perrot said. "He cannot help you with this. If, in fact, we require Deya's DNA, we might never know what is inside the box."

"We all know what's in there," Simon said. "If one of you knows how to open this damn thing, you had better speak up!"

"It's over, Simon," Logan said, trying to ignore the pain in his gut. "Your DNA collar, the frequency pulse, everything you planned—we exposed it all. Andrea and Lucius are dead!"

"Dead?" Simon looked startled. "How could you possibly know that?"

"Because I'm the one who killed them," Logan said. "I did it with the frequency device we found at the plantation, the very same device that you had Monique use to kill the Council members."

Simon glanced at Macliv, then turned his back to Logan and Mr. Perrot. "Victor was supposed to—" he started, then caught himself.

"Supposed to *what*?" Logan pressed. "Victor has also been exposed.

The top officials know how he betrayed the WSA. I wouldn't count on any assistance from him or from Gretchen, for that matter."

Simon looked at Logan with bitter contempt on his face.

"You'll never possess the hidden symbols," Logan continued, goading Simon. "Give up now. There is nothing left for you."

"No!" Simon roared defiantly. "You should keep up with your history, boy." He walked over, pointed his finger, and pressed it into Logan's chest. "The greatest conquerors may have retreated from time to time, but they never surrendered. They never gave in to the occasional luck of their feeble-minded adversaries." He turned to Mr. Perrot. "No, I am very far from being over and done. There is more than one way to get into a Destiny Box." He placed his hand on it, caressed its surface. "It is a shame that you won't be able to witness my victory. But die assured that these books, like the others, will be mine. They *will* serve my purpose."

"And what purpose is that?" Mr. Perrot asked.

"Power," Simon quickly answered. "The world has always been about power. You know that all too well, Robert. Money and fame are backup singers to the tenor who possesses the power to command the audience. Haven't you ever wondered what this was all about, why we live the lives that we live, why we play the games that we play?"

"It is about wisdom," Logan said. "It is about learning and evolving, so that the people who come after us can continue to advance from where we left off!"

"Wisdom? Learning? Evolving?" Simon repeated Logan's words with disgust. "Those are but constructs created to keep people like you occupied with a mundane life, while we others get to play."

"Give them bread and circuses, and they will never revolt," Mr. Perrot said.

Simon smiled. "Yes. Juvenal had it right, even two thousand years ago," he replied. "You see how little has changed. Just think of the *Chronicles*, how people were enthralled by the power of the words, when the greatest power was hidden from them on those blank pages, waiting for the truly passionate to discover them. Even your father"—Simon looked at Logan—"was seduced by the promise. He told the world to live by the words that they read, while he sought out the secret power of the symbols for himself. How is that different from what you accuse me of doing?"

"The difference is that people didn't have to die for my father's pursuits!" Logan answered. "'Any desire that imposes your will on another is a desire that should go unpursued.'"

"You don't need to quote from the *Chronicles* to me," Simon said, as he turned to answer a call on his PCD.

Logan exchanged a look with Mr. Perrot. They needed a miracle, and they needed it now.

After a few moments of hushed conversation, Simon turned back to them. "I have some good news for you! Look who has arrived." He gestured toward the broken door.

Logan followed Simon's gaze. In an instant, his fear was replaced by utter shock and confusion. "How can this be?" he whispered.

Andrea was standing in the doorway, wearing her signature crimson hood. Her face was partially covered by white bandages. Logan recalled how it had been ravaged by her exposure to the frequency device. She walked into the room and stood next to Simon.

"I—I saw you die," Logan stammered. "You and your son."

"It would seem that conclusion was a bit premature. He is correct, however, about Lucius," Andrea told Simon. Her voice was tired and raspy. "We underestimated Camden's son and his detective friend, who, I am happy to say, is on the verge of death. I only hope it comes swiftly for her."

"Your face is beyond recognition," Simon said, clearly disturbed by Andrea's disfigurement. He had been scrutinizing her face since her arrival. He looked into her topaz-colored eyes.

"He did this!" Andrea struggled to yell, pointing at Logan. "He did this with the frequency device they stole from the plantation. Let us kill these two and bury them, along with Fendral's secret, forever." She walked over to Simon and whispered something in his ear.

A satisfied smile broke out on his face. "Oh, yes," he said, turning to Logan and Mr. Perrot. "It would seem that Andrea is very much alive."

Andrea nodded, then turned. "Hello, Logan." She now addressed him, her eyes the only recognizable feature on her face.

"I saw you die," Logan said again. "I *saw* it . . ."

"You always were a survivor," Mr. Perrot stated. "And you always liked to make a dramatic entrance."

"Oh, Robert," Andrea said in a gentle but haunting tone. "So good to see you after all these years. I'm so sorry about your daughter, but you have only Logan to blame for that."

"While I would like to stay and exchange pleasantries, Andrea is correct," Simon interrupted. "We have more urgent matters to attend to." He placed his hand on Andrea's shoulder. "We need to go to the island. But first, I must return to the Château to retrieve the three other sets."

"You shouldn't take that risk," Andrea said. "I will secure them for you. Tell me where the books are, and I will bring them and this Destiny Box to the island."

"No. I must secure the books myself," Simon said. "I am the only one who can open the safe."

"But how will you get in?" Andrea's hoarse voiced asked. "The Château must be swarming with police."

"There are many ways to enter the dungeons of Dugan," Simon replied cryptically. "I will meet you at the island in three days. I must also parlay with Dario and the others. But first things first: we need to dispose of these two." He gestured to Macliv, who readied his weapon. "So you see, Robert, in the end, all of your efforts have been for naught."

"Please," Andrea said, raising her hand to stop him. "Let me have this pleasure. They murdered my son. And I have a few more matters to discuss with my old friend here." She pointed a trembling finger at Mr. Perrot.

Simon paused for a moment to consider her request. "Don't tarry," he said at last. He grabbed a gun from one of his hired men and handed it to her. "I never understood why you took such an interest in him. But let's be done with it once and for all."

Logan shook his head. He refused to believe it, even now. "You won't kill us like you killed my parents."

"Killed your parents?" Simon calmly repeated. "No, I was not the one who performed that necessary deed." He shook his head and gave a scornful laugh. "You, with all your Satraya philosophy and idealist views, you think love and compassion are such wonderful things. Well, love might have been what got your parents killed."

Logan remained silent now. What did he mean? How could *love* have gotten his parents killed?

Simon turned to Andrea. "I will leave a couple of men and a boat for you. Remember: the island in three days."

"I will be there."

Simon smiled one last time, took the Destiny Box, and left the room with Macliv and one other man. The other two of his men remained with Andrea. One stood next to her, and the other maintained a position in the entryway. Andrea released the safety on the handgun.

"She's our daughter, you know," Mr. Perrot suddenly said.

"Who's your daughter?" a shocked Logan asked. He looked first at Mr. Perrot and then at Andrea. "You mean *Valerie?*"

Mr. Perrot gave a short nod. He turned his eyes to Andrea. "You thought we were gone forever when we disappeared thirty-two years ago. You and Fendral were so determined to take over the Council. I just couldn't bear to let her stay with her mother. You would have been such a wicked influence on her."

"Are you saying that *she's* Valerie's mother?" Logan asked again.

"Yes," Mr. Perrot said. "She is the mother Valerie never knew. And sadly, I see that my decision all those years ago was for the best."

"How can that be possible?" Logan was reeling from the revelation.

"Go ahead, Robert," Andrea said. "Tell us. For even I am not sure I know the full story."

Mr. Perrot shook his head, looking into her eyes. He spoke in a quiet voice. "I was very much in love with you once. You were so beautiful and idealistic and passionate. The way you spoke of women's rights, independence, and freedom—you seemed to embody the very essence of the *Chronicles*. Do you remember the spring of 2036, the group you led to rebuild Quebec City? Do you remember how powerful it felt to bring the *Chronicles* to the ragged population that flocked there after the Great Disruption? Do you remember when we held hands near the statue at the center of the Joan of Arc Garden? And I know you remember the night that followed. I put aside your past, Andrea. I put aside your marriage to Alfred Benson, which you promised me was over. I put aside the life of privilege, which you said you no longer wanted. I pushed it all aside. I believed you. I was in love with you."

He paused and looked down at the ground for a moment. He turned to Logan. "We returned to Washington eight months later, and a few weeks after that, our daughter was born. We named her Tabatha." Mr. Perrot looked back to Andrea. "I took her home from the hospital, but you stayed because of some medical complications. During that time, Camden began to unravel Fendral's true plans. I felt like a fool when he told me, when I thought back on our conversations, how much I had tried to convince myself that you wanted something you didn't really desire. I realized that the *power* you told me you found in helping people was very different from the *power* I felt in doing so. While you were in the hospital, I asked you some direct questions. Do you remember?"

Andrea stood silently, the gun steadily gripped in her hand.

Mr. Perrot continued. "You refused to speak to Fendral on our behalf, to try to persuade him to change his views and plans. You not only refused, but you said you agreed with him and intended to do whatever was necessary to help him succeed. And you told me that I didn't understand you at all." He stopped and waited for some kind of response from Andrea, but she offered none. "It was then I knew Camden was right, that we needed to leave and that I couldn't let my daughter grow up in your care."

"So that's when you and my parents disappeared and moved to New

Chicago," Logan said. "I get it now. This explains what happened with Valerie at the Vault."

Mr. Perrot nodded. "And this is why I told Valerie her mother died while giving birth to her. Camden and Cassandra guarded my secret."

Andrea continued to look at Mr. Perrot. She raised her gun.

"You don't have to do this," Mr. Perrot said.

"Yes, Robert," Andrea replied slowly. "I do."

Mr. Perrot took a deep breath. "Close your eyes," he said to Logan.

Logan did so. He jerked back as a rapid series of gunshots rang out and echoed through the domed building. He heard the frantic sound of flapping winds as frightened birds exited through the upper latticed windows. Then he heard the clinking of shell casings and the sounds of bodies falling to the ground. Then only silence. He wondered if he was dead.

"You can open your eyes now," a female voice said.

Logan saw that the two mercenaries Simon had left behind were dead. One lay on the ground next to Andrea, the other near the entrance. Andrea walked over to Mr. Perrot and knelt down in front of him, removing her hood. "I still love you," she said, as she began to peel the bandages off her face. "Even though you lied to me for all these years."

Logan once again couldn't believe his eyes. When the hood came off, Logan saw who it was who had been impersonating Andrea. She looked like her mother, especially with her topaz-colored eyes.

"How did you . . . ?" Logan began in amazement, as Valerie released her father from his bonds and they embraced each other. "What did you say to Simon that convinced him you were Andrea?"

"I told him something to do with his father's secret." Valerie smiled. "I told him we would bury the both of you just like Fendral buried Giovanni Rast."

Mr. Perrot's eyebrows rose in shock.

"That would certainly convince him," Logan said, smiling back at Valerie. She moved over to him and untied his hands. The moment he stood, he planted a kiss on her lips. "Don't scare me like that again . . . Tabatha?" Logan said jokingly. "Your legs and everything."

"I'm all right," Valerie reassured him. "I regained consciousness when I got to the hospital, and everything quickly started to get better after that. Sylvia filled me in on my father's message and where you had gone. Once we arrived at the river, we tried calling your PCDs, but you didn't answer. As we approached your last-known coordinates, which Chetan provided, we saw Simon's men patrolling the fort. As it happened, I still had Andrea's PCD." She smiled again. "That's when Sylvia and I got the idea for the bandages. You know the rest." Logan gave her a firm hug. "I'm all right," she repeated. They looked into each other's eyes for a long moment. "But where's Jogi?" Valerie asked her father.

Mr. Perrot's joy at seeing Valerie was tempered by sorrow. "Jogi died at the hands of Simon and one of his men."

Valerie shook her head. "No more," she said. "No one else is going to die at their hands—" She was cut off by the sound of gunfire in the distance. "Time to go!"

Logan grabbed his backpack, and he and Mr. Perrot followed Valerie as she ran outside. They could see WCF pontoons and a helicopter racing north along the river. Valerie had brought backup.

"Sounds like they got Simon," she said. Sylvia waved from the shore below.

"Don't be so sure," Logan cautioned. "He has all four sets of books. He's not going to give up easily. We need to see this through ourselves."

64

Hearing a single word may change your destiny.
Speaking a single word may change someone else's.
—THE CHRONICLES OF SATRAYA

BANARAS, INDIA, 3:30 P.M. LOCAL TIME, FREEDOM DAY

"Don't lose him!" Valerie shouted on her PCD over the roar of the engines as they pursued Simon and his men. "Don't let him out of your sight!"

The speedy chase headed north on the crowded river. Valerie gave orders to the WCF pontoon ahead of them and to the support helicopter flying directly above it. Logan, Mr. Perrot, and Sylvia sat under the boat's canopy as two agents who had arrived with Sylvia piloted the craft.

"They're still a thousand meters ahead of you," said a voice on Valerie's PCD. "What are your orders?"

"Take them out," Valerie ordered. "This is it for Simon Hitchlords."

"You can't do that!" Mr. Perrot yelled, as he and Logan walked to the front of the boat. "He has the box—he has the *Chronicles!*"

"You take that boat out, and we could lose those books forever," Logan added, as shots rained down from the helicopter.

"I can't care about that right now," Valerie replied, grim-faced. "There are tens of thousands dead back in Washington. What am I supposed to say to their families and the survivors? 'We let this butcher get away because we were worried about some books'?"

Logan heard more gunfire in the distance.

"We hit the engine!" the helicopter pilot announced. "Affirmative. There is smoke coming from the boat. They're pulling into Manikarnika. Hurry! They're going to disappear into the crowd there."

"What is Manik—" Valerie said, struggling to repeat the name she heard on the radio.

"They just landed!" the voice from the helicopter interrupted. "There's no place for us to set down."

"Stay in the air, and track them, then," Valerie ordered. "We will be there in thirty seconds!"

The pontoon pilot opened the engines to full, with little regard for the wake affecting the other small crafts on the river.

"It's just over there," Mr. Perrot said, pointing to the smoke from the pyres. "Manikarnika Ghat. It's where Jogi was killed."

"What's all that smoke?" Valerie asked as she readied for landing.

"It's the smoke from the cremation pyres," Mr. Perrot answered, looking at the crowds lining the shore and the stairways leading up to the temple and the pilgrim houses.

"How are we going to find them in these crowds?" Logan asked, as their pontoon moved closer to shore. The other WCF team had already landed and secured Simon's getaway craft. They used a small fire extinguisher to put out the fire in its engine.

The two piloting agents disembarked first and tied off the pontoon. "Looks like they went into that first building up and to your right," an agent from the hovering helicopter reported. "The pilgrim shed, the one with the clock tower on it. We counted three people."

Mr. Perrot looked up and remembered what Jogi had told him: "It is always six o'clock at Manikarnika."

"You stay here and secure the boats," Valerie instructed the two agents who had arrived on the first WCF boat. "If anyone—and I mean anyone—tries to board, shoot them!"

"Looks like he took the Destiny Box with him," Logan said, after taking a quick look around Simon's boat.

"The rest of you," Valerie said to Sylvia, Logan, and Mr. Perrot, "come with me." She led them up the stairs, telling the remaining agents to secure the outside of the building, identifying all the exits and entrances. "Stay alert," she said. "And if you see anything, you know the orders."

Valerie and Sylvia drew their guns and maneuvered around the large Shiva Pyre pit from which enormous flames leaped into the air. Ten prepared bodies awaited their liberation.

"What is this building?" Logan asked, as he looked up at the clock tower. Bamboo scaffolding ran along one of its sides, and carpenters were working to shore up the façade of the three-story, faded yellow building. "It looks like it's going to fall apart."

"This is one of the two pilgrim houses," Mr. Perrot answered. "Not a place for the faint of heart, according to Jogi."

Valerie and Sylvia cautiously led them through the entrance and into the darkened interior.

"Jogi was right," Logan said, as they entered.

The large, open room was filled with dying people. There was little order. Cots and pallets were haphazardly placed on the floor. And lying on the cots and pallets were pilgrims who had come from near and far to finish their journeys in this holy place. Family members held the hands of loved ones, and women covered in thin veils tended to the pilgrims, bringing them water but very little hope.

An auspicious place to die, perhaps, Mr. Perrot thought, recalling Jogi's words, *but not devoid of human pain and suffering*.

It took a moment for Logan to adjust to the gagging odor that permeated the air. Strong incense was being burned to cover the smell of death, but it had little success. Stray dogs and rats ran about, nudged away by the attendants and a few brave family members who comforted their kin, paying little attention to the out-of-place visitors who had entered.

"How many floors does this place have?" Sylvia asked, as she walked among the pilgrims.

"I believe three plus the roof," Mr. Perrot guessed, as he and Logan followed close behind. They continued searching for Simon.

Valerie carefully lifted a blanket from time to time, only to reveal another suffering pilgrim. There was no sign of Simon or his men on the first two floors. Valerie led the group as they approached a stairway leading to the third level.

She peeked around the corner of the stairwell. The third floor resembled the first two floors: dying people lying next to one another, covering almost every inch of the floor. Valerie then saw the backs of Simon and two of his men, who were looking through the large windows at the opposite end of the floor. She spun back around the corner. "They're near the open terrace," she whispered. "Simon and two more." She moved aside, so Logan and Sylvia could take a look for themselves. "On the count of three," she whispered to Sylvia. "I'll take out the one on the right, and you take out the one on the left."

"What about Simon?" Logan asked, drawing his gun from his backpack.

"You be careful with that," Valerie said.

Then she started to count. On three, she and Sylvia moved forward, firearms first. Logan followed, and Mr. Perrot peeked around the wall near the stairs. When they turned the corner, Simon wasn't there.

"Where the hell are they?" Valerie shouted.

"The scaffolding!" Sylvia called. She ran to the open window of the terrace. "They're climbing down!"

Valerie and Logan ran to the window and looked out.

A moment later, shots rang out. Simon's men were engaged in a gunfight with the two agents at ground level. Valerie could see that Simon and his men were six meters below her. She took a shot and struck one of Simon's men.

"Macliv!" Simon shouted, as the bodyguard fell from his perch, landing on the stone stairs below.

The other gunman looked up and fired off a few rounds at Valerie, who ducked out of the way, pulling Logan with her. Another series of shots rang out. Valerie looked out and saw the second gunman crashing into a large woodpile below. One of the agents had been hit during the latest exchange; the other had taken out the last mercenary. Valerie spotted Simon awkwardly climbing down the scaffolding, carrying Deya's Destiny Box under his arm.

"You guys use the stairs, and go back down," Valerie said, as she started to climb onto the bamboo scaffolding.

"I'm coming with you," Logan said. He shoved his gun into the waist of his pants, swung his backpack over his shoulder, and climbed behind Valerie. Sylvia grabbed Mr. Perrot by the arm and led him back down the stairs of the pilgrim house.

"Give it up, Simon!" Valerie yelled after him, as she paused and waited for a good shot. "There's no place left to go!"

Simon didn't answer. He was busy navigating his way down the scaffolding. Valerie couldn't get a clean shot; she didn't want to risk shooting any of the innocent bystanders below. She resumed her descent and was closing in on her quarry quickly, with Logan not far behind her. In desperation, Simon jumped the remaining two meters to the ground, his momentum causing him to crash into a chanting group of mourners, who were carrying a pallet holding the adorned body of their loved one above their heads. The body tumbled to the ground, sandalwood and garlands of flowers scattering around it. Simon had disturbed the holiest of traditions.

Sylvia and Mr. Perrot emerged from the pilgrim house just in time to see the crowd angrily surrounding Simon. The mourners looked outraged, many of them yelling and shaking their fists. Simon still lay on the ground, trying to stand up. The nearest agent was powerless to get through the growing mob, and Valerie and Logan could only watch from their positions on the scaffolding. The crowd shouted furiously, as they pushed Simon closer to the Shiva Pyre.

"You must help me, Robert!" Simon screamed, rising to his feet. "I know you're here! Surely you don't want these books to be destroyed in the fire!"

Mr. Perrot didn't have a clear view of Simon, but he could hear him and see the crowd working itself into a frenzy. "Remember what you said when you killed Jogi, Simon!" Mr. Perrot shouted back. "This is a good place to die!"

"This is not over, Robert! I know the secrets of the books—I know about the last symbol!"

"We'll see," Logan said to himself. "Because it's the only thing that can save you now."

He watched as the crowd pushed Simon, who was clutching the Destiny Box to his chest, all the way to the edge of the burning pit. The people were unforgiving, continuing to shout obscenities at a feverish pitch. In a burst of anger, they pushed Simon one more time, causing him to lose his balance and teeter on the edge for a few seconds.

A surprising calm seemed to come over Simon's face. "The final symbol won't save you now," Logan murmured as he watched Simon fall backward into the roaring flames of the Shiva Pyre that rose four meters into the air. Logan heard no screams as Simon was engulfed in flames, but he could see a light, bright and seemingly blue, burst across the Destiny Box, sweeping it out of Simon's hands.

Valerie and Logan made their way down the remaining scaffolding and joined the other agents, several of whom were bleeding from shots they'd sustained. They pushed their way through the crowd and were joined by Mr. Perrot and Sylvia at the edge of the pit.

"We need to put this fire out!" Mr. Perrot shouted above the roar of the crowd. "We need to retrieve the books!"

"I don't think that is possible," Valerie said. "Judging by this crowd, they're not going to let anyone extinguish it."

"This fire is burning too hot," Sylvia said. "There's going to be nothing left of Simon or the books."

Mr. Perrot stood in mournful silence as he watched workers throw more logs into the pit.

"Well, Simon may be gone," the group suddenly heard Logan say, "but the books aren't." They all turned and looked at him. He was holding Deya's Destiny Box.

"How did you get that?!" Sylvia asked.

"We saw it fall into the fire!" Mr. Perrot said, his sadness suddenly replaced with joy.

"There was a flash of blue light," Logan answered, "just as he fell. It seemed the books chose not to follow him any further."

"The books *chose*?" Valerie repeated. "Flash of blue light? What are you talking about?"

"You didn't see it?" Logan asked. The group remained silent, looking at him in awe as the roar of the fire continued behind them.

"It would seem that was for your eyes only," Mr. Perrot said.

65

A child never makes an assumption. He will walk to the other side
of the room to discover what is over there.
——THE CHRONICLES OF SATRAYA

BANARAS, INDIA, 5:22 P.M. LOCAL TIME, FREEDOM DAY

The accompanying agents forged a path through the crowd, leading the others away from the pyre. Closer to the river, they found a small table and a few chairs under a canvas canopy. Additional WCF personnel were arriving. They began their work securing evidence and rounding up the bodies of all who had died. Mr. Perrot stood for a moment and watched the agents carry the draped body of Jogi across the grounds of the ghat and onto an awaiting pontoon. Valerie took her father's hand, wanting to comfort him.

Logan set the Destiny Box down on the table, and everyone stared at it, still trying to reconcile Logan's version of events at the pyre with what they had seen with their own eyes or, as Logan pointed out, what they hadn't seen.

"So what do we do with this thing now?" Valerie asked. "There doesn't seem to be a way to open it."

"There has to be," Logan answered. "After investing so much time and effort in constructing the trail of clues that led to the books, Deya

wouldn't just lock them inside a box with no way to open it." *Besides,*
Logan wondered to himself in silence, *why would the blue light have salvaged
the box if it couldn't be opened?* He placed his finger on the Destiny Box's
pad, hoping inexplicably that he himself might be the key. It gave no
response to his touch.

"What if the books aren't in there?" Mr. Perrot said. Logan and
Valerie both gave him disapproving looks for even suggesting such a
thing. "Everyone has assumed that the box contains the books. What if
it contains yet another riddle or nothing at all?"

"They're in there," Logan said confidently.

"We could take it back to the lab," Valerie suggested. Sylvia nodded
in agreement. "They should be able to figure out a way to get the books
out of there."

Mr. Perrot gazed at the people milling around the area between
the pyre and the river. He was startled to see an old friend walking
unsteadily among them. "My heavens, that's Babu!" he said. "That's
Deya's husband over there!"

Everyone turned and saw the old man slowly making his way toward
the pilgrim house. He used his cane to nudge aside a pesky dog that was
impeding his journey.

"Why is he here?" Valerie asked.

"I fear he has come to join the pilgrims in the house," Mr. Perrot
said sadly. "He must believe that his time has come."

It was then that Logan saw someone most unexpected approaching
Deya's husband. A graceful-looking man with a serene countenance.
"Sebastian Quinn!"

"Who?" Valerie asked.

"He's the one I told you about, the man whose artwork I'm restoring."

"Why would *he* be here?" Mr. Perrot asked. "And how does he know
Deya's husband?"

Sebastian now stood in front of Babu. The dog that had been pes-
tering Babu took a few steps and stood alongside Sebastian, who was

whispering into Babu's ear. Then he placed his hand on Babu's chest and tapped over his heart several times.

"What's he saying to him?" Valerie wondered out loud.

Although Logan wanted to walk over to Sebastian, something held him in his place.

"I'm certain that I don't know," Mr. Perrot said, not taking his eyes off his old friend. "But whatever it was, it has brought a smile to Babu's face."

Sebastian pointed to where Logan and the others were sitting. He leaned forward toward Babu and whispered something else. The old man seemed to perk up and started making his way over to them. The pace of his gait quickened, and he waved enthusiastically. "Hello, Robert! Hello, my old friend!"

Mr. Perrot could not believe the change in Babu's demeanor. This was not the same slow-moving, confused man who had guided him and Jogi in Deya's garden just a day ago. "Babu, what has happened to you?"

Distracted for a moment by the sight of the old man walking toward them and his joyful greeting, Logan turned back to the crowd to locate Sebastian. But he could no longer find him. "Excuse me, where is that man who was just with you?" Logan asked Babu.

Babu looked back from where he had come. "Ah, it seems Baté has disappeared once again. He is strange folk, to be sure."

"Did you say Baté?" Logan asked, stunned.

"Yes. His name is Baté Sisán," Babu said. "He has always had a strange way of coming and going. Deya was very fond of him."

Logan shook his head and smiled; he wasn't so stunned now. "I should have known. It is so obvious."

"Known what?" Valerie asked. "What's so obvious?"

"Baté Sisán and Sebastian are the same person," Logan said. "'Baté Sisán' is an anagram for 'Sebastian.' He has been the unseen hand in all of this since the beginning."

"Baté wanted me to tell you something," Babu said. "He wanted me to tell you that you have the key to the box. Deya had it, your father had it, and now you have it."

Logan asked, "How can I have the key?"

"Think for a moment," Valerie said, as she readjusted her ponytail. "Is there anything that your father passed along that might have been Deya's?"

Logan watched as she fiddled with her brown hair clip. "You have to be kidding me," he said. Logan unzipped this backpack and rummaged through it. Finally, he pulled out the tin box that he and Mr. Perrot had found beneath the floor of the basement of the Council of Satraya building. Logan took from it the little plastic bag that contained the lock of hair. "What are the chances that this belonged to Deya?"

"There is only one way to find out," Mr. Perrot said.

Logan placed the hair on the metal pad of the Destiny Box. As if a magical wand had been waved and a spell had been lifted, the latch on the box suddenly disengaged, and the lid popped slightly open. Logan looked at Valerie and then at Mr. Perrot, before he raised the lid and reached into the box. Each of the three volumes of the *Chronicles* was carefully wrapped in a beautiful blue silk cloth. Logan unwrapped them and placed them on the table.

"It looks as though you found my wife's missing books," Babu said.

"They're yours, sir," Logan said to Babu. "Deya's books most certainly are yours."

Babu pressed his hands together and gave Logan a bow. "No, my life with them is finished," he said kindly. "They were my wife's passion, yes, but now they appear to have chosen you."

Logan thanked him with a nod.

"Looks like there are a few other items in the box," Mr. Perrot said. He reached in and pulled out a half-burned blue candle and a small mirror.

"Is that all?" Logan asked, sounding disappointed. "I was hoping maybe my father gave Deya his journal for safekeeping."

"Sorry, my boy, the box contains nothing else. But it does look like your journey is going to continue," Mr. Perrot said, as he set the blue candle and the mirror on the table beside the books.

Logan shook his head.

"What's wrong?" Valerie asked.

"Nothing, really," Logan answered. "I was hoping that my father's journal might explain what Simon meant when he said that love might have gotten my parents killed."

After a pause, while everyone remained silent, Logan inspected the blue candle. It was similar to the one his father had possessed.

"I suppose there are a few tricks to this thing, too," he said in a lighter tone, as he picked up the mirror and gazed into it. Suddenly, he jerked back and blinked his eyes. He could have sworn he had seen someone in it. A reflection that wasn't his.

"You all right?" Valerie asked, placing her hand on Logan's shoulder.

He didn't answer right away. "Yeah," he said, with a weak shake of his head. "Yeah. Everything is fine."

Just then, Valerie's PCD rang. It was the WCF in Washington. She stepped away from the table with Sylvia to take the call.

Meanwhile, Mr. Perrot picked up the third volume of Deya's set of *The Chronicles of Satraya*. He turned to the first of the blank pages at the end and handed the open book to Logan. "See anything?" he asked.

Logan took a couple of deep breaths and focused on the blank page. He pictured a burning candle flickering on the page. The noises of the crowds visiting Manikarnika Ghat were drowned out by the ever-familiar ringing. Logan rubbed his eyes. "I'm seeing some strange grayish-blue distortion," he said. "Kind of like clouds . . ."

He continued to stare at the page, as Mr. Perrot and Babu watched patiently.

"Oh, look at that," Logan said. "It's really there."

EPILOGUE

Remember always, you are loved.

—THE CHRONICLES OF SATRAYA

NEW CHICAGO, ILLINOIS, 6:00 P.M. LOCAL TIME, AUGUST 4, 2069

Logan once again stood in front of the painting that had been both an albatross and a revelation to him. Although *The Creation of Adam* had presented many challenges, in the end, it had provided him with the key to unlock the secrets of Simon Hitchlords's plot against humanity. As promised, upon his return to New Chicago, he'd finished the restoration work, and now the painting would be unveiled tonight at the museum's gala dinner. Colors and hues that had baffled Logan prior to his worldly adventure became obvious to him during his final days of work. He understood precisely how the plaster would absorb the pigment of the paint he applied, and he understood more purely the meaning of the original fresco painted by Michelangelo.

Wearing a black suit, a crisp white shirt, and no tie, Logan stood alone backstage admiring the grand reproduction of Michelangelo's masterpiece. It was perfectly lit by clusters of lights at its corners. He could hear the sounds of guests arriving and Mr. Rampart's voice directing staff members, but he remained focused on the painting. *The*

Creation of Adam would be his last restoration assignment for the museum. He had used some of the money from the sale of his parents' set of the *Chronicles* to purchase a large art studio in the heart of New Chicago, which, in memory of his parents, he'd named the Camden and Cassandra Ford Studio of Art.

"I wonder if Adam ever figured it out," a familiar voice said behind him.

"Mr. Quinn," Logan said, turning around. "Or should I say Baté Sisán?" Sebastian gave Logan a slight smile as Logan walked over and embraced him. "Mr. Rampart said he wasn't sure if you would be able to attend."

"The moment is always filled with possibilities," Sebastian said.

"That I have come to know very well," Logan said. "The world owes you so much."

"No, *I* am the one who owes *it*," Sebastian humbly replied. He smiled and pointed to the painting. "So I ask again, do you think that Adam ever figured it out?"

Logan looked at Adam and God for a few moments, pondering Sebastian's question. He ran his hand through his hair. "I think everyone will figure it out eventually. I think that the hand of God endeavors to reach everyone, in every moment of every day of their lives."

"Yes, that is a wonderful notion," Sebastian said, as he gazed at Logan. "Most people believe that God lives outside them. They believe that they must pray with vigor to garner God's attention and favor. But that is a fallacy. God is with all, equally and constantly. The Satraya Flame illuminates this truth. It is a simple way to see and experience what has always been within you—as you have certainly now experienced for yourself."

Logan nodded. "I saw a symbol on the first blank page of Deya's books," he said after a moment, cautiously broaching the subject. Sebastian only smiled back. "Over the last couple of weeks, the symbol has become clearer. But other pages remain blank."

"It is a progression," Sebastian said. "The symbol that you see is called the A-Tee-Na. It is the first symbol that will reveal itself in the books that once belonged to Deya."

"What does it mean?"

"Seeing the symbol is only the first step," Sebastian said. "The next step is to experience it. Then you will have the wisdom of its meaning."

The conversation was interrupted by Logan's daughter, Jamie, who ran onto the stage, desperately holding on to a large dog by its collar. "Daddy! Daddy! Look what we found!" she cried. "Can we keep it?"

"No, honey," Logan replied. "That dog belongs to my friend here. But maybe we'll get one of our own." After Logan's ex-wife had received the child-support payments she was owed, she'd agreed to give Logan primary custody of the children.

Jamie let go of the collar and grabbed Logan around the waist. Bukya walked to Sebastian and took his place beside him. "He says he likes you," Sebastian told Jamie.

"You can *talk* to him?" Jamie asked, amazed.

"Yes, everyone can talk to animals," Sebastian said, as he bent down and beckoned Jamie to come over. "Just put your hand here." He took Jamie's right hand and placed it on Bukya's forehead. "Now, close your eyes, and, using your inner voice, ask him anything you want."

"What's an inner voice?" Jamie asked, keeping her eyes closed.

"It is the voice that talks to you when no one else is around," Sebastian explained. "The one that tells you to go run into a puddle. Or help a little bird back into its nest."

"Oh," the girl said, opening her eyes in excitement. "You mean the one that tells me to look through Jordan's closet when he's not home."

"Yes, that's the one." Sebastian gave a slight laugh and indicated that Jamie should close her eyes again. "And it comes from right here." He gently rubbed Jamie's forehead with the thumb of his right hand. She did as he instructed and asked her question. "Now, just wait for him to answer."

"He answered! He answered!" Jamie shouted as she opened her eyes and looked back at her father. "I asked him if he liked to swim, and he said yes!"

"That is indeed true. Bukya and I live near the ocean, and he enjoys the water very much, like his mother and father did a long time ago."

"Could they talk like Bukya?" Jamie asked.

"Yes," Sebastian answered. "Balin and Nila spoke just like him."

"Daddy, can we get a talking dog?"

Just then, Mr. Perrot, Valerie, and Logan's son, Jordan, came backstage. Jordan joined his sister, who was now asking Bukya many more questions.

Sebastian greeted Valerie with a bow. "My name is Sebastian Quinn. I am a friend of Logan Ford and, thus, your friend if you allow it."

Valerie didn't say anything. She just looked into Sebastian's dark eyes, and he gazed back at her for a few moments.

He turned to Mr. Perrot, placed his hands together, and bowed to him. "My name is Sebastian Quinn. I am a friend of Camden and Cassandra Ford and, thus, your friend if you allow it."

Mr. Perrot cordially returned the bow.

"Your dog has made quite an impression on the children," Valerie said.

"Yes, children love Bukya, and he loves them. Recently, five little ones from an Indian village near Banaras came into my care. Bukya has been quite busy these last weeks."

Logan and Valerie looked at each other.

"So it was you," Valerie said. "You rescued the children from the village."

Sebastian only smiled.

"That's one question that scientists haven't been able to answer yet," Logan said. "Why weren't any children affected by the frequency pulse?"

"Your scientists are looking for the answer in the wrong place," Sebastian answered. "It is important to note that children do not try to rationalize and make sense of the world the way adults do. The little ones use different parts of the brain to interact with the environment around them. Rationalization, self-contemplation, introspection—

they all come later, when children mature and social constructs are taught. The pulse could not take away from them what they did not yet have."

Logan nodded reflectively. "How long will you be staying?" he asked.

"Until I leave," Sebastian said with a grin.

"I feel I have to tell you something," Valerie said to Sebastian. "We never found the other three sets of the *Chronicles* that Simon possessed. We searched the dungeon at Château Dugan, where Simon said he kept them. Strangely, the door to the safe was open, and it was empty. We searched all over the Château without any success."

"I am hiding Deya's copy of the *Chronicles*," Logan said. "But we don't know how much Simon was able to unveil in the books he already possessed. Or if he deciphered the fragmented symbol of immortality."

"Immortality?" Sebastian repeated. "No, the fragmented symbol is not about immortality. It is about something far more profound and powerful. Immortality is only a side effect of the thirteenth mark." Both Logan and Mr. Perrot looked at him with new curiosity. "Still, you are wise to keep Deya's books in a secure place," he added.

"I will give them to you if you want," Logan said.

"No," Sebastian said. "I can think of no better place for the books than in the care of one who understands their presence. Remember, they chose *you*, Logan." He smiled again and turned his dark gaze to Valerie. "There is no saying where young Hitchlords's books have gone or who might possess them now. But that is all right. It simply means the books have more to do before their time here has ended."

Everyone stood in silence for a moment, taking in Sebastian's cryptic words. Valerie raised her eyebrows; the thought of more people like Simon getting their hands on the books and being able to wield a supernatural power was not exactly comforting. Mr. Perrot could only nod; he knew that there was both hope and warning in what Sebastian had just said. As for Logan, he simply smiled, for the books had indeed chosen him.

"The world should know the truth about what happened," Valerie said with a frustrated shake of her head. "Everyone thinks that the tragedy in Washington was caused by a solar disruption and the malfunction of the Akasha Vault satellites. People should know that we are still walking around with those DNA collars inside us. They should know what happened to those who were affected by the frequency pulse and that they're being sent to the Calhoun Medical Center for so-called DNA recalibration. They should know what really happened to Logan's parents, and they should know the full extent of what happened to Cynthia and the other Council members. They should know that Simon and Andrea were not working alone, that Victor Ramplet, the head of the WSA, was helping them until he was shot dead while attempting to flee the NAF. People should know that Simon and his father plotted with a man named Dario. And what role, if any, Randolph Fenquist played in all this, is anyone's guess. This conspiracy could be greater than we realize even now." Valerie had been promoted to assistant director of the WCF, which, at the newly elected president's direction, had absorbed the responsibilities of the WSA. But even so, she was dissatisfied with the government's cover-up. "It shouldn't be this way."

"It has been this way for eons," Sebastian said. "The kings of old held tightly the truth of their worldly dealings, for they believed it was best for the people to concern themselves solely with their daily toils. Today your politicians are no different. They view truth more as a guideline than as a requirement." Sebastian put his hands together. "Leave the kings and politicians to play their endless, tiring games. Let not their folly overshadow your grace."

Mr. Rampart's voice could be heard over the intercom system announcing the start of the evening.

"I take my leave of you now," Sebastian said, as he bowed to the group. Then he turned to Logan. "Many people will see the wonderful manifestation of your talents. Six months standing in the shoes of greatness is time well spent." Sebastian raised his hand and pointed toward the fresco. "This work that Michelangelo bravely brought to the world more than five hundred years ago must not be forgotten. After it fell from the vault of the chapel during one of the earthquakes of the Great Disruption, no one thought it could ever come back to life." Sebastian turned and looked at the painting for a moment. "Now we know that they were mistaken."

And with that remark, he left the backstage area, followed by his ever-faithful partner. Logan, Mr. Perrot, and Valerie watched as he walked away.

"Wait!" Logan burst out. He looked at the fresco and then at Valerie and Mr. Perrot, who were as surprised as he was. "Did he just imply that this *is* the original painting that was on the ceiling of the Sistine Chapel?"

"I think he did more than just imply that," Valerie said with an astonished smile. "I'd like to hear the story of how he came into possession of it."

Mr. Perrot shook his head in amazement. "I wonder if we will ever see him again."

Logan nodded. "I don't know for sure," he said. "But I do know where to find him. He is only a candle flame away."

"Hey, Dad, what's that near your feet?" Jordan asked, as he picked up a folded piece of paper lying on the ground. He handed it to his father. Logan unfolded it, and a smile came to his face as he read it.

"It's the answer to the question I first took into the Manas Mantr candle and left in the study," he told Mr. Perrot.

"What question was that?" Valerie asked.

"'Will you help us like you helped my father?'" Logan replied.

"Well, let's hear the answer," Valerie said.

"Yes, yes," Mr. Perrot prodded. "Let's hear how he answered, even if we already know of his involvement over the last few weeks."

The note was written with exquisite penmanship, in regal blue ink. Logan read it aloud.

"Salutations.

"The timeless and never-changing answer to your query is yes.

"No one is so special as to be alone or abandoned; that is impossible in the universe in which we exist. We are all connected in a great tapestry that was woven at the dawn of time. Pluck a string at one end of the tapestry and it will quiver at the other. A willful wave garners the attention of the many who are listening.

"All are loved without condition, and when they are ready, they will seek out truth and wisdom. And if there be only one of you left upon the earth, rest assured that there will also be one of us for you to call upon.

"We are waiting with love for a thread to be tugged, waiting for someone to reach out and ask the great questions. It is inevitable that all will come to see that day. Help is as far away as you perceive it and as close as you allow it to be. But remember that we cannot do it for you. You must be the main actor in the great epic story of your life.

"When men and women are no longer afraid to look into the mirror, they will see beyond their limits and expectations.

"You will never be alone.

"For the moment,
"Baté"

Silently appreciating Sebastian's answer, the three of them exchanged hopeful glances. The bell rang again, and they started for their seats.

"Wait for me!" Jamie said, as she grabbed Valerie's hand.

Logan took one last look at the fresco.

Logan sat between Valerie and Mr. Perrot at a table in front of the stage. The children sat next to Valerie. They were joined by Ms. Crawley, from Mason One Auction House, and her date, along with Mr. Rampart's wife and daughter. Mr. Rampart stood onstage, delivering a few opening remarks. Logan was only half-listening to him, because he was thinking about the note that Sebastian had written, particularly the phrase about the mirror.

When men and women are no longer afraid to look into the mirror, they will see beyond their limits and expectations.

Logan hadn't told anyone what had happened that day at Manikarnika Ghat, when he'd first looked into the mirror they had found in Deya's Destiny Box. But what he'd seen was a reflection of his mother's face, as clear as his own. He'd been so startled by it that he hadn't looked into Deya's mirror since.

Loud applause pulled Logan out of his contemplation. The curtain had been opened, and the painting that Logan had spent so much time restoring was now on view. He still couldn't believe he'd restored an original Michelangelo. Mr. Rampart motioned for him to stand so he could be recognized for his contribution to the art world. He obliged but only for a few seconds.

"I have one last announcement regarding this work of art," Mr. Rampart said. "While I would love to see this Michelangelo reproduction remain here as part of the museum's permanent collection, it will soon be finding a new home. Mr. Quinn, its owner, has instructed me to deliver the painting to the newly established Camden and Cassandra Ford Studio of Art here in New Chicago. The studio belongs to our very own Logan Ford."

Valerie leaned over and gave Logan a congratulatory kiss on the cheek. Mr. Perrot squeezed his shoulder. Jamie and Jordan cheered. Mr. Rampart once again asked Logan to stand and be recognized. The crowd applauded with enthusiasm. Logan stood and looked around for Sebastian. But, as usual, he was not anywhere to be seen.

Logan sat back down, and Mr. Rampart continued with the night's festivities, presenting all of the other recently restored works of art. But Logan's thoughts were still on Sebastian. *How did he know three weeks ago that I would have an art gallery? He told me that he was donating the painting to an acquaintance of his who owned an art gallery. Did he know that it was going to be* my *gallery?*

Logan turned and looked fondly at Mr. Perrot, who appeared enthralled by another painting that was being rolled onstage, then at Valerie, who was helping Jamie butter a piece of bread. He was happy that Valerie was moving back to New Chicago and was going to be a bigger part of his life. He wondered once again about the three missing sets of the *Chronicles* and what could have happened to them. He thought about his parents and how he'd seen his mother's face in Deya's mirror. Then his thoughts circled back to the mysterious Sebastian Quinn, whose life's work seemed to be to contribute to humanity the one thing that it always needed and should never be without: hope.

Compass Park appeared empty except for a single man walking with a cane. The rhythm of his walk was jagged, inconsistent, with his right leg dragging. His cane supported him as he stepped into the fountain pool and splashed his way to the monument. He stood there looking at the names carved into it. He ran his fingers slowly across the name of Fendral Hitchlords. He whispered something to himself.

The sound of a struck match caused him to turn and look at the man seated on the bench behind him. The same bench where Logan had found his father's hidden message. The man hadn't noticed the stranger sitting there before.

"Did you know that Fendral fella?" the stranger asked, before dragging on his lit cigarette.

The man splashed forward, making his way back out of the fountain. He stopped a few meters from the stranger seated on the bench. As he stood, water dripped from the bottoms of his pants legs and puddled on the ground.

"Yes, I knew Fendral. He murdered me once," the man said in a calm voice, as he adjusted the gold buttons on his coat. "There's something his son owes me."

The stranger on the bench began to nod. "The sins of the father are passed down to the son," he said as he took a puff of his cigarette. "What's your name, friend?"

"Giovanni," the man answered, water still dripping to the ground. "Giovanni Rast."

The stranger threw his cigarette to the ground and put it out by stepping on it. "Well, Giovanni," he said. "My name's Randolph Fenquist, and I suspect that you and I have something in common."